the
Par
Gi

BOOKS BY NATALIE MEG EVANS

the
Paris
Girl

NATALIE MEG EVANS

bookouture

Published by Bookouture in 2019

An imprint of Storyfire Ltd.
Carmelite House
50 Victoria Embankment
London EC4Y 0DZ

www.bookouture.com

ISBN: 978-1-83888-122-1
eBook ISBN: 978-1-83888-121-4

For my son Sam,
the best thing that ever happened to me

Part One

Chapter One

Montmartre, Paris, May 1922

'You really want to marry me?'

Tatiana Vytenis stared at the ring on her finger. An oval ruby, surrounded by seed pearls, it looked valuable. Deeply serious. As did the man who had just slipped it on her finger.

Gérard de Sainte-Vierge was rarely anything other than serious, but that was part of his allure. He was so unlike the rowdy, puppy-dog men she and her friends went dancing with. Gérard carried his good looks and ancient name with conscious dignity.

'You want me to be your wife?' Tatiana couldn't tear her eyes from the ruby. After months of dashed hopes, break-ups and misunderstandings, he was finally taking the plunge. In, of all places, a studio behind a house on Place du Tertre, on the butte de Montmartre. In front of a mob of other girls. Who, like Tatiana, were clad in knitted leotards and silk tights having just completed a strenuous, two-hour ballet class. She was slick with sweat; the wall mirrors made no bones about it. A raspberry flush crossed her nose, and her scraped-back hair was dark as rain-washed copper.

'You really, really—'

'Want to marry you. Do you imagine I would have put my grand-mother's ring on your finger otherwise? I've been pacing outside for an hour, waiting for the music to stop. I want you to set the date for our wedding, Tatiana.'

'But why now?' Gérard worked for the Ministry of Finance, where swift decisions were considered unhealthy. He was never impulsive.

A slow smile woke the latent charm of his eyes and his dark moustache curved seductively. 'It's a beautiful May morning. You are a beautiful woman. Need I say more?'

The other dancers crowded around, bringing with them the healthy smell of skin salts, and Tatiana extended her left hand and let them feast. Gérard was the marquis de Sainte-Vierge. On marriage she would become his marquise. But that wasn't why she loved him. She wanted to laugh, to cry. All around, congratulations rang out.

Two onlookers held back. One was her teacher, retired ballerina Rosa Konstantiva. Thirty-seven and childless, Rosa often treated Tatiana as a surrogate daughter and she disapproved of this love affair. Not on moral grounds – Rosa had enjoyed a catalogue of lovers in her time and had one now, an illustrator several years her junior. No, she plain disliked Gérard.

'Wonderfully well connected, *chérie*,' was her opinion, 'and provably unreliable. Stay with him, you're nailing your heart to a windmill's sails.'

Rosa was wrong and Tatiana looked forward to proving it.

The other person showing no joy sat at the piano. Unlike Rosa, who had assumed her Russian name for professional reasons, Larissa Markova was Russian by birth, as was Tatiana. Like Tatiana, she was a mannequin at the fashion house Javier, employed for her stunning looks and her ability to make clients desperate for the clothes she modelled. Larissa was also a classically trained pianist, and though being a ballet school accompanist did not dig deeply into her skills, she needed the extra income. She pursed her lips each time the word 'marquise' was mentioned. In Larissa's opinion, aristocratic titles should be extinguished. She and Tatiana had never hit it off. Larissa's family had been Muscovite tradespeople whereas Tatiana was the daughter of the late Prince Ulian Vytenis, entitled to call herself Princess Tatiana. Which she made a point of doing when Larissa was nearby.

'Madame la marquise de Sainte-Vierge,' Tatiana said with a chuckle, ensuring Larissa heard. 'Imagine embroidering that on one's pillow slips!' She flung her arms around Gérard, feeling him flinch at the contact of her rapidly cooling body. He was squeamish about the realities of being human. 'Can we go home and tell Mama?'

'Perhaps in a few days? Let us keep it to family and close friends only.'

'But Mama is family!'

'She's unable to keep a secret. "More child than parent". You said so yourself.'

True, but why should their engagement be a secret at all? 'Surely, I must call on your mother, Gérard.'

'Let's leave that a while.'

'At least let me tell Constanza. She's my best friend.'

'Constanza Darocca? Mm. I'd prefer to keep it under wraps until I have informed my wider family.'

'If you wanted to keep this engagement under wraps, Monsieur, why go down on one knee in front of twenty ballerinas?' Rosa Konstantiva tapped an impatient foot. 'We have not finished our class.' Though she was the only professional among amateurs, Rosa maintained rigid etiquette, as if this were a morning class at the Bolshoi, or the Paris Opéra Ballet where she had trained.

Gérard apologised, but with that twitch of the lips that made Tatiana ache to kiss him.

'Go and get a coffee on the square,' she suggested. 'I'll join you shortly.'

After he'd gone, class concluded, finishing on a deep curtsey. Rosa made a reverence of the arms in reply and acknowledged Larissa who played a flighty arpeggio to sign off.

'*Au revoir, mes filles*,' Rosa waved her pupils to the door. 'Go and cover up. Tatiana, a word.'

'I'm so sorry, Rosa,' Tatiana burst out when they were alone. 'I had no idea.' She gazed lovingly at her ring. 'By its very definition, this won't happen again.'

'Apologies have no value when the giver is grinning all over her face.' Rosa gave the reprimand in English. She'd been born in London and because Tatiana was determined to improve her languages, often spoke English to her. 'We have a saying where I come from: "Marry in haste, repent at leisure". I don't deny he's suave as a velvet coat but have you forgotten how he abandoned you when you were gravely ill?'

'That was three years ago, Rosa, and he had no idea I had Spanish flu. He thought I'd collapsed because I'd been under-eating and staying up too late. He's apologised since, truly he has. He can't bear illness, you see. A sister of his died of diphtheria. He's never got over it.'

'I see.' Rosa placed her hands over Tatiana's. 'Speaking of siblings, a little bird tells me that his brother is also in love with you.'

Tatiana dashed a damp strand of hair from her brow. 'Armand? He's besotted with all the Maison Javier mannequins. Ask Larissa.'

Larissa, who had followed the dancers out but was now back to collect her music, replied with a flat contradiction. 'I've never seen

Armand de Sainte-Vierge offer flowers or attentions to any other woman. If he's besotted, it's with you.'

This was not what Tatiana wanted to hear. Armand de Sainte-Vierge had pursued her relentlessly for months. The fact that she loved his brother seemed to make him all the more determined to win her heart.

Larissa went on, 'He is also a deeply troubled young man. His mind is scarred.'

'You think I don't know that?' Tatiana burst out. Nobody understood better than she that the pain Gérard's brother carried like a nail-riven cross was the consequence of surviving horror. Horror that could not be talked away or dispelled. Tatiana's response to the inrush of emotion was a characteristic one. She flounced to the door, saying, 'Thank you for spoiling my special moment, both of you.'

Leaving Rosa's house, Tatiana spotted Gérard at once, sitting at a table under freckled shade. Rosa's and Larissa's warnings faded at the sight of him. It was too lovely a day for shadows other than those cast by venerable acacia trees, artists' easels and the green metal legs of café tables. Place du Tertre lured creative people from all over the world. As Tatiana strode through patches of sunshine to where Gérard sat with a newspaper, she picked up bursts of conversation in English, Spanish, Polish and Russian. Gérard was deep into that day's edition of *Le Figaro*, an empty cup by his wrist, and she indulged a secret pleasure at the sight of his fingers wrapped around the paper's edge. Long, clever, lover's fingers. His skin was that very French olive-almond colour.

'Anybody home?' She plumped down opposite him.

He lowered the paper. 'Good. You're not as pink as you were. I always imagined ballet was ladylike, mostly consisting of floating.'

'It's very physical. More like rowing a barge than pretending to be a feather.'

'You have a furrow between your brows.' He traced it with a finger. 'You don't regret accepting me?'

'Of course not! Shall I prove it?' She peered at the newspaper, read '13 May 1922', stood up and threw her arms wide. 'I hereby rename this square "Place du Treizième Mai" in honour of the day that Gérard proposed to Tatiana.'

He smiled. 'Sit down. Coffee?'

'Citron Pressé, a large glass.'

Gérard folded his paper and clicked to a waiter. 'Darling, it might be an idea only to wear the ring when we're out together. People will talk otherwise.'

She stared at the ruby, then at Gérard. 'Engagements are public news, otherwise it's an "understanding". "Unknown to their families, they had an understanding." You surely aren't asking me to take the ring off the minute after you've put it on my finger?'

He gave her a small antique box. 'It's rather old, that's all. I wouldn't want you to wear it for... I don't know... household chores.'

She laughed. 'I don't do household chores. We pay a maid and a cook for that. My job demands I keep my hands unblemished.' The perfect excuse for avoiding all unpleasant work. 'Let me keep it on. I promise I won't go gassing and gossiping about it.'

'Very well. And may I say, you look particularly edible today.' Gérard's gaze appreciated her outfit, a blouson top and skirt of dove-grey linen, chic and simple. Tatiana's crowning glory, her auburn curls, nestled under a hat of Italian straw. She was turning heads. An artist a few paces away had begun sketching feverishly, no doubt eager to capture her so he could 'sell her on' to a tourist. Normally, the idea would make her tense, but now she was more concerned by the reticence of the man in front of her. Gérard was saying all the right things, but he wasn't bubbling over with happiness. His expressions, his words, were too orderly for her liking.

'Are you worried what your mother will say? She won't approve of me, I know. Foreign. Russian Orthodox. Your lover for the past three years, not a virgin fresh out of a convent.'

He cleared his throat, discomfort swiftly swallowed. 'I wouldn't mention that in front of Mother. She will come round. Only, we have to play it carefully.'

'You will tell Armand, though, won't you?'

He made a 'perhaps' face.

'Only, Rosa and Larissa worry he'll be distressed.'

'Rosa and Larissa are experts on my brother, are they?'

The shift of his tone jolted her and she rushed to placate him. 'No. Forgive me. They seem to imagine he's in love with me, that's all. Of course he isn't.'

'Ah, but *of course* he is. You have so little idea of your charm, my darling. Men want to take care of you and women are jealous.'

She laughed uncertainly. There'd never been a queue of men offering to take care of her. Somewhere along the way, she'd learned the trick of offending the male sex. Coldness and caprice. Men never knew where they stood with the 'prickly princess'. Part of Gérard's attraction was that he took none of her nonsense. 'When would you like the wedding to be?'

'When would you like it to be?'

It was like being shown Ali Baba's cave and told to fill her pockets. 'Um... October. I turn twenty-three on the eighteenth, so perhaps the end of that month. By then, the fittings for the midseason collection will be over.'

'Fittings? Midseason collection?' Eyes the colour of varnished teak widened in amusement. 'My wife will not need to work.'

She grasped his hands. 'I adore you, my darling. You make me feel utterly, utterly safe.'

Chapter Two

From the square, they took the metro to central Paris, then went on foot to rue Molière and the pied-à-terre flat Gérard rented in the shadow of the Louvre palace. After they'd made love, Tatiana basked in an unfamiliar sense of optimism. In just a few months, she would be a cosseted wife, protected by a powerful name. Gazing at her lover stretched out on the pearly linen, she imagined breakfasting with him every morning. Dining with him every night. She lingered on his concave stomach, the shadows of hair across his lean chest and in the creases of his limbs. Like her, Gérard ate sparingly. He was not a man of animal appetites, as his lovemaking proved. She compared him instead to a violinist, a virtuoso in stroking, plucking and teasing out cadences of erotic sensation. He had used a condom as he always did, withdrawing before climax, almost obsessive in his determination not to impregnate her. She appreciated his care but longed for the day they would no longer need to be constrained.

We're perfectly matched, she told herself. Just look at the way we've arranged our clothes. Her grey ensemble hung on the back of the bedroom door. Her hat was on a stand on the dresser while Gérard's things made a straight-edged stack on a chair.

He gave a reluctant yawn.

She smiled. 'I thought you were falling asleep.'

'No, and I ought to stir, I'm needed elsewhere.'

'You're needed here, Monsieur. Can't we spend the day together?'

He rolled towards her. 'My angel, I have a pile of papers on my desk at home that will get snow on top if I don't decrease their height.'

Tatiana laughed more heartily than the joke deserved, it so surprised her. Her sister Katya had once said, 'Your Monsieur de Sainte-Vierge has an underdeveloped sense of humour.' To which Tatiana had retorted, 'It's the only underdeveloped part of him, I can assure you.' Her smile faded as she saw he was serious about getting up.

He leaned over and kissed the end of her nose. 'How about I brew a pot of coffee? Shall I run you a bath?'

'Yes to coffee, no to a bath. I'll wash at the sink. Since I'm being kicked out, I might as well go home and be useful to my family. Darling, when we're married where will we live?'

Gérard had swung his legs off the bed and looked at her across his shoulder, his mouth turning down. Had she said something vulgar? Being Russian, she was forthright in her questions and opinions, often transgressing French subtlety. His irritation was fleeting, however.

'Summers and Christmas will be at Tournon-sur-Rhône,' he told her. 'Only fair I spend time at the family chateau, otherwise the staff lose heart and the estate workers get lazy. The rest of the time we'll be in Paris.'

'But where in Paris? What of your mother and Armand?' Gérard's family home was exactly that, in that it contained his mother and younger brother. A sprawling mansion, to be sure, on one of Paris's premier avenues, but even so, Tatiana couldn't envisage her position there with his mother in residence. She'd feel like a second cherry on the bun.

'Maman will return to her apartment on Malesherbes when I'm married,' Gérard said calmly. 'As for Armand... well, you won't notice him. He keeps to his rooms at the top of the house.'

Without waiting for her response, Gérard knotted a sheet around his loins and left the room. Tatiana reached for her robe. For all they were long-term lovers, the intimacies of the bed remained within its sturdy frame. Beyond the bedroom, modesty prevailed. Blame their formal upbringings in households with servants and, in her case at least, religious icons on every wall. She'd no more wander around a flat naked than walk down the street that way. Which was why she gasped when she strolled into the bathroom and saw Gérard's unclad buttocks as he shaved at the sink. '*Mon Dieu!* I'm sorry.'

Their eyes met, his reflected in the mirror. The lower part of his face was slathered in foam, through which a blade had made a single sweep. Black, glittering eyes offered a comical contrast to the whiteness below. Except there was nothing funny in their expression. Hate, love, lust…

She stood, transfixed. She'd heard him in the kitchen as she left the bedroom. Heard him opening a cupboard, and the 'pop' of the gas as he lit the stove. Could the cleaning woman have let herself in and be making their coffee for them? Tatiana stammered, 'I'm sorry… I didn't mean—'

'Tatiana.' He turned, naked and obviously aroused.

'Armand!' She clutched her robe in a convulsion of embarrassment. 'When did you—? No, don't!' Gérard's brother stepped towards her, eyes flicking to the engagement ring, and she let out a scream. A moment later, Gérard was behind her.

'*Putain!* Armand? What the devil? Tatiana, go to the lounge.' Gérard gave her a push, though she hardly needed it. She scurried to the kitchen, where she shut the door hard. Through the pumping of her heart, she heard muffled exchanges between the brothers. Gérard's voice remained the loudest. As the elder, the one with the influential position as well as being his mother's favourite, he easily dominated.

How could this have happened? Her cheeks scalding with mortification, Tatiana took the coffee percolator off the flame. Strong brew was pulsing under its glass dome.

Gérard joined her as she was placing cups on the kitchen stand. She muttered, 'Has he gone?'

'No, but he will the moment he's dressed. What made you scream like that, Tatiana?'

'You mean, "Haven't I seen a naked man before?" Yes. You and you alone, and I'm starting to find Armand's interest in me deeply unpleasant.'

'Then you should have walked away the moment you saw him. Loitering at the bathroom door only encouraged him.'

'I thought he was you!'

'It didn't occur to you that under such circumstances, I'd have locked the door?'

'No,' she sighed, pouring a wavering stream of coffee. 'Armand looked so shocked and angry at the sight of me, though he must know we're lovers. Or suspected it, at any rate.' The way he'd stared at the ring on her finger disturbed her. More, perhaps, than the memory of his physical response. 'What's he doing here anyway? He has a key?'

'Yes,' Gérard admitted. 'I gave him one so he could use this place after a night out if he was unfit to go home. I didn't invite him to avail himself of it during the day.'

'So… he was here all the time we…' Tatiana shuddered. Gérard shrugged uncomfortably.

The crash of the front door announced that they were alone.

As Tatiana drank coffee she no longer wanted, she wondered why every supposedly happy occasion in her life turned into heartache and conflict.

Chapter Three

Instead of going straight home, Tatiana called on her best friend. Constanza Darocca lived in Batignolles, a couple of metro stops north of the eighth *arrondissement* where Tatiana lived. She and Constanza had first met as novice mannequins at Callot Soeurs, the couture house on Avenue Matignon, and for a while had shared the Batignolles flat. The more confident of the two, Constanza had shown Tatiana what bohemian Paris offered fashionable young women. In particular, those who could dance and weren't burdened with chaperones tapping their wristwatches at midnight.

That first taste of freedom had thrown Tatiana into the path of young men released from war and there had been many flirtations, but nothing serious until she tumbled into Gérard's arms. The fun had skidded to a halt when she'd succumbed to Spanish flu in the summer of 1919. Pulled back from the brink of death, she'd taken weeks to recover and had only restarted her modelling career after her sister Katya founded Maison Javier with two colleagues. Tatiana had become their first mannequin, joined by others as the couture house roared into success.

Bumping into each other at a party, she and Constanza had slid back into their old, gossipy ways. Constanza declared herself bored with Callot. 'It's growing frumpy and smells of violets and old lace.'

'Then join me,' Tatiana had invited. 'It would be a dream to have you along. The other girls resent me for being the boss's sister and you'd frighten them into being nice to me.' Half-Argentinian with obsidian eyes, jet-black hair and creamy skin, Constanza Darocca magnetised all who met her. Cats adored her, but women and most men were afraid of her. For his part, Gerard was unenthusiastic.

'An acquired taste, but I'll work at liking her, for your sake.'

Even after Tatiana had moved back to live with her mother, the Batignolles flat was a sanctuary when she was too tipsy to go home or needed to share turbulent feelings.

But even best friends can disappoint. Shown the ring, Constanza's mouth made a sour little shape.

'Not you as well!' Tatiana wailed. Wasn't anybody she loved going to congratulate her?

Constanza collected herself. 'It's fabulous news, but Tatya, I'll lose you. Married women have no time for friends.'

'That's not true.'

'My mother didn't. And what about Katya? How many get-togethers or long lunches do you have with your sister?'

'Not many, but Katya works so hard. Being a wife, a designer and director leaves little time for anything much. But she has her circle. As will I, and you will be friend-of-honour.'

'You'll choose a wedding dress from Javier?'

'I suppose.'

'You have to, and ask Katya to design it or risk offending her.'

Tatiana groaned. 'I didn't realise before today there were so many people to offend. I've already snubbed Rosa and Larissa. As for Gérard's brother...' She sketched the hideous incident outside the bathroom.

After she'd howled with laughter, Constanza warned Tatiana to treat Armand de Sainte-Vierge with care. 'He's not a man to withstand having his heart broken in public. You had better write to him.'

'What on earth would I say? "Dear Armand, sorry I encountered your backside, oh, and by the way, I'll soon be your sister-in-law."'

'Let's throw you an engagement party and invite him. Give him a chance to get used to your new status. I'll bring some unattached girls and hope he falls in love with them instead.' Constanza showed her teeth in a smile, which implied, 'There – all arranged.'

Tatiana couldn't see how a rowdy night out would alter Armand's obsession with her. 'I'd rather not be in his company at all.'

'That won't work, not once you're married. You'll be constantly thrown together,' Constanza persisted. 'The only way to avoid him is to break off your engagement. No? Then put your head in the lion's mouth.'

Tatiana sighed. 'I suppose that in a public place, surrounded by others, he can't harm me. Fine. Organise a party but nothing showy and not too many people. Armand doesn't cope well with noise.'

'He is not made of eggshell. He needs to be treated as a grown-up. Agree?'

'If you say so. I agree.' A concession that was to rebound fatally.

Constanza threw the party the following Saturday night. The location was the Café Select, a fashionably raffish place in Montparnasse. Locals in shirt sleeves mingled with girls in evening gowns and boys in black tie, while older women entertained their gigolos at discreet tables, safe in the knowledge that their husbands were dining somewhere smarter with their mistresses. It was the Left Bank, the hub of creative Paris.

Had Constanza not called for her in a taxi, Tatiana might have cried off. It wouldn't feel such an ordeal had Gérard been one of the party, but he was dining at Les Ambassadeurs, the café-restaurant of the Hôtel de Crillon. His position as a high-ranking *fonctionnaire* often obliged him to entertain. Tonight it was visitors from a London bank, enjoying a true 'Parisian night' without straying too far into the hinterlands. It had struck Tatiana that she ought to have been asked along, but when she'd suggested it, Gérard had assured her she'd have much more fun with her own set.

'Surely, though, I ought to learn the ropes. Won't entertaining be part of my job when we're married?'

'Exactly,' he'd replied. '*When* we're married. Have a splendid time and I'll join you if I can.'

Truth was, Gérard disliked her friends. His efforts at 'acquiring a taste' for Constanza were not progressing well either. 'I daresay some men admire smouldering sexuality,' he'd said when Tatiana had pleaded with him to get to know her friend better. 'For my part, I prefer not to be scorched.' Places like the Café Select grated on him. Loud, with perspiring waiters serving hearty dinners. Artists vying to out-shout novelists while trying to out-smoke poets. All to the strains of popular music. Gérard liked opera, and would book the best seats once a month. In between, he listened to gramophone discs in his flat. So while she hoped to see him later, Tatiana wasn't counting on it.

As for Armand, he had accepted the invitation by return of post, and when Tatiana and Constanza arrived he was already at an inside table, a pastis glass and water jug in front of him. He watched their approach. Their previous meeting uncomfortably fresh in her memory, Tatiana knotted her silk stole tighter around her shoulders. Better not reveal her evening dress with its cutaway back and shoulder straps.

Not until she was safely ensconced in a crowd. Initially she'd chosen a modest tunic dress for tonight, but Constanza had shouted in protest when she saw it.

'I'm not taking you out looking like a nomad camel-driver!' She'd made Tatiana change into something 'that makes you look female'.

Shaking hands with Armand, Tatiana blushed. Armand remained unabashed.

'I'd prefer it were just the two of us,' he murmured as the rest of their party arrived.

While they ate he said nothing to cause alarm. Everyone around the table knew he'd had a bad war and made concessions. He'd hung on the margins of Constanza and Tatiana's set for months. In fact, Tatiana had known him before Gérard. Her first job in Paris, following her family's flight from Moscow, had been as a waitress in a tea parlour. Armand used to come in with his mother. His gaze would follow her as she worked her way between tables. The red star medal on his lapel had told her that he'd been invalided out of the army and was one of the legion of damaged men vying for compassion. Except she hadn't much compassion for anyone back then. Leaving the tea room to start work as a mannequin, she hadn't given him another thought. Not so for him. He'd tracked her down to Callot Soeurs.

He'd pressed hothouse flowers upon her, invited her for coffee, riverside strolls, dinner, ignoring her protestations that she was not seeking admirers.

'Thank you, but I mean to be independent. I'm not looking for love.'

Words that had slid like rain off an oilskin coat. Armand had become a fixture at the salon, watching the afternoon parades with twitchy intensity, impatient for Tatiana's appearance on the catwalk.

In the end, Callot's *directrice* had telephoned his mother, asking her to please discourage her son from being quite so... ahem... regular in his presence. That had brought Gérard to the salon to investigate the situation. A fateful visit; Tatiana, who was convinced she was too cold-hearted for love, had fallen. And yes, she could certainly pity Armand now. Imagine, if Gérard told her he was in love with her sister! But that was life, wasn't it? A relentless stream bringing joy one moment, misery the next. At least tonight Armand was behaving. She could hear his monotone drone. He was telling one of the married women in the party about his law studies, which war had cut short. He would return to university, he said, but for the intense headaches that plagued him. 'I don't sleep.'

Tatiana whispered to herself, 'Insomnia is another price of survival.'

'You said something?' Armand shot her a look she wasn't fast enough to avoid. Giving him a nervous smile, she pushed away her unfinished plate of food and leaned towards Constanza.

'Shall we skip dessert? Go straight to coffee?' She wanted the evening to end. The earlier they ordered their taxis, the better.

But Constanza only laughed. She looked magnificent in red, her caramel skin glowing in the globe lights. 'Home by ten? What are you, a baby?' She raised her hand to summon their waiter, though in the end she had to stand and wave both arms to get attention. Over in a corner, a group of intellectuals were noisily sharing their argument with everyone. Who was the greater genius, James Joyce or Marcel Proust? 'Who cares?' Constanza roared. 'Shut up so I can make my waiter hear me!'

Armand leaned forward and murmured to Tatiana, 'If we sent a taxi to rue Hamelin and fetched Monsieur Proust here, he would settle the argument at once. He would say, "The greater genius? Myself of course!" Tatiana, when I got your invitation, I was so happy.'

'It wasn't from me. Constanza sent it.'

'At your insistence. No?'

'Oh, for heaven's sake—' Tatiana tried to get Constanza's attention. It didn't matter what she said, or how she said it, Armand wilfully misread her. Just then, two waiters walked up. One carried a jeroboam of champagne, the other a tray of goblets.

Constanza laughed at Tatiana's expression. 'A certain gentleman left instructions. Gérard may not be here, but he makes up for his absence in bubbles.' Lifting the first sparkling glassful to her lips, Constanza called for a toast. 'Everyone, charge your glasses. Darling Princess, may you revel in being Madame la marquise, captor of the elusive Gérard, while bringing forth plentiful heirs to fill that vast house on Avenue du Bois de Boulogne. I promise I'm not at all jealous!'

As the company merrily repeated the toast word for word, as Tatiana's cheeks bled scarlet, Armand took out the invitation card he'd been sent and slowly tore it up.

Tatiana drained her glass and signalled for a refill. The sooner the bottle was emptied, the sooner this nightmare would be over.

'Let's see that ring. Come on, show,' coaxed Mary-Jo Winterton, another of Javier's mannequins. An English girl, Mary-Jo spoke French as if sitting an exam somewhere in the Home Counties. She liked giving orders too, in a whimsical voice that disguised her bossiness. Reluctantly, Tatiana extended her left hand.

'An antique,' Mary-Jo cooed.

'No, an heirloom,' Armand growled, not bothering to hide his opinion of the English girl. 'Gérard took it from the safe without mine or my mother's agreement. I'll tell you this…' – colour drained from his lips – 'Maman will not give her permission for Gérard to marry a foreigner.'

'Gérard does not need his mother's permission.' Tatiana was surprised by the hard ring of her voice. Champagne, drunk too fast, was giving her false courage. 'If you can't be nice, I wish you'd go.'

Armand stared and twitched and all around, throats swallowed in embarrassment. In one of the swerves that made him so hard to predict, he smiled and raised his glass. 'To the future, Tatiana. Good luck. You'll need it.'

Constanza called for gin and vermouth so she could mix up her own, special Martini cocktail. Her way of serving it was to drop in a sugar lump rather than an olive, to counter the bitterness. She poured a generous measure for everyone and asked Armand to hand the glasses round, giving Tatiana a wink as if to say, 'Keep him busy!'

Tatiana, already too full of wine and champagne, drank hers to please her friend. It really was bitter and she crunched on the sugar with some relief. Someone suggested they go on somewhere, and what about the Rose Noire, near Place de Clichy? She hadn't the strength to argue... she was beginning to feel robbed of the power to make choices. Conversation flowed around her like water; Armand making a remark about sugar lumps and horses, Constanza asking one of the men to get their bill, another voice pointing out, 'We'll need three taxis to get us all to Place de Clichy.'

'Let's go over the river on foot, it's such a delicious evening,' Mary-Jo proposed. They'd take Pont de Passy, under the viaduct so they could scream if a train went overhead. Such fun! They could decide how to continue once they reached the Right Bank.

'I can't take any more of Armand,' Tatiana muttered in Constanza's ear.

'I'll get rid of him,' Constanza whispered back. As they rose from the table, Constanza linked her arm with Armand's, drawing him out ahead of the others. On the busy boulevard, she waved down a passing taxi, urged Armand into it. Before climbing in after him, she called to the others, 'I'm taking him home. See you at the Rose Noire.'

Watching Constanza's cab pull away, Tatiana felt like a drowning mariner watching his ship sink. She knew she was on dry land, on the corner of Boulevard Montparnasse and rue Vavin but couldn't think where that was in the world. Or the universe. Car headlights burst against her eyes, making her feel dizzy. She looked for another taxi, without luck. The others in her party were already walking away.

Pont de Passy, the route chosen by Mary-Jo, was a pedestrian river crossing under a railway viaduct; halfway along, Tatiana fell further back. Everything felt like an impossible effort. Leaning on the bridge rail, she gazed into the river. Tonight it was a damask sleeve blistered with gold, a partial moon stitched on like a broken pearl button. When staring down made her gag, she dragged her gaze upstream where the Eiffel Tower threw its corkscrew reflection. Black on black, but for the winking red eye on its summit. She'd never looked at the tower from this angle before.

The third weekend of May, air soft as butter. When she'd first arrived in Paris the city had been austere as a monk, prone to power cuts, everything rationed and coloured by war. Now, it was again the City of Light. Gaslight through the embankment trees. Barge lamps spilling from wharves. Her eyes followed the beam of a motorcar crossing Pont d'Iéna, the next bridge upstream. Far ahead, she heard her companions howling the latest hit song. It was all about a giraffe. You had to pretend to be a giraffe when you sang it. Was it Gérard's influence? Because suddenly, it felt unbearably silly.

She'd promised Gérard not to get tipsy in public again. She didn't think she'd survive the Rose Noire where the heat and the beat of snare drums meant you had to dance or die. She ached for Gérard's arms. Might he be at his bachelor flat? He stayed on rue Molière two or three nights a week. His bolthole, though not quite that if Armand also had a key.

A train thundered overhead. A typhoon, driving thoughts from her mind as her skirts wrapped around her calves and her long, bead necklace rattled like dry seed heads. Her silk stole caught the slipstream and she experienced a moment of freedom.

Just as suddenly, the train was gone. She yelled into the dark, 'Mary-Jo? Isabelle, Henri, Thomas, all of you, where are you?' Nothing. Her friends and their silly song had been absorbed by the night.

Kicking off her shoes, sacrificing her stockings, she forced herself to run. On Port Debilly, on the other side of the river, she stopped, panting and gasping. Which way? Towards Pont d'Iéna and the Trocadero palace, or straight ahead to the station at Passy? Had they decided on the metro, rather than taxis? Never let others make judgements for you, Gérard constantly told her. He was right. She thought she heard her name being called from the direction of Iéna bridge.

'I'm coming!' She put her shoes back on and set off, keeping the river to her right. Running had left her legs as weak as melted cheese. She stopped a few paces from the bridge, smelling its pungent tang. Five half-moon arches funnelled the power of the Seine, straining out debris which then rotted on the piers. Close up, the river's voice was like rocks tumbling over iron.

'Tatiana? Is that you?'

She almost sobbed in relief and stumbled towards the male silhouette, into his arms and let him take her weight. 'Gérard! How did you find me?'

In answer, he kissed her. When he forced her up against the stonework and pushed up her skirt, she at first resisted. Until a rush of pleasure doused her misgivings. She gave herself up to the intense pleasure, vaguely mindful of the public location but revelling in the erotic shock of Gérard acting so out of character.

'I love you,' she whispered.

He replied, 'I love you too, Tatiana. To the end of life.'

It wasn't Gérard.

The ground tipped. Her legs went from under her and everything turned black.

Chapter Four

She came round amid familiar scents of polished floors and bookcases, the residues of coffee heated on gas. The flat on Molière. Her sense of smell was acute, the others blunted. 'I need water,' she moaned.

She was lifted into a room with a different smell. Hair oil and laundry starch. She felt mattress springs beneath her.

'Armand, no. Don't. I don't want—'

He climbed on top of her and thrust his tongue deep in her mouth. She clawed at him until he withdrew it, kissing her face instead. His breathing clogged her ears. His upper lip felt rough in an unshaven, late-night way, no clipped moustache gently chafing her. He rasped, 'I love you' as he pinioned her, and she was completely immobilised.

'Look at you, a drunken sailor tipped into his berth.' The judgement boomed over her head. A female voice. 'I will not let your niece come upon you like this. Nor, I think, will you like your mother to see the state of you.'

'No, keep them away.' Tatiana briefly opened her eyes, shutting them again to block out the pugnacious scowl that told her exactly where she was. Home. Yana Borisovna Egorieva, their family maid for twenty-five years, stood over her, fists on hips. Tatiana slowly worked out that she was on the sofa in the drawing room, still wearing evening dress. Someone had brought her home, taken the key from her purse to let her in. That someone had laid her out and removed her shoes.

Armand. Everything came back, an ulcer bursting in her head. He'd used her, usurped his brother, and she had pleaded with him afterwards, 'Don't tell Gérard. If you care for either of us, don't ever speak of this.'

She sat up, screwing up her eyes. Her brain felt dried, her lips parched. 'Yana, would you bring me a cup of strong tea?'

'I am nursemaid, not kitchen maid.'

'Oh God.' The ceiling light was spinning. Tatiana put out a hand. 'Help me to the bathroom, please.'

'Yes, for you smell like a goose girl on market day.' Yana hauled Tatiana to her feet. 'Wash yourself, then I will boil eggs for you.'

'God, no. Not eggs.' Tatiana remembered leaving the Café Select. She recalled a train clattering overhead and a moon reflected in the river. Constanza, Mary-Jo, Isabelle. Men too. They always had escorts, but she couldn't bring any to mind. Only Armand, emerging from the darkness under Pont d'Iéna, allowing her to mistake him for Gérard.

I love you to the end of life.

And I detest you, to hell and back.

Later, lying in warm water, having lost the soap over the side of the bath, she brought her attention to the soreness between her legs. What of the insult to her soul? Could she cure that? At this moment, it felt unlikely, but she could hide it. Armand would never divulge his guilt – of that she was as certain as she could be. As for her, she'd cut out her tongue before she told a living being. She must bury the memory so deep it never resurfaced.

A pattering of feet in the corridor outside roused her. Before she could reach for a towel or get out of the bath, a child's voice was calling her.

'Tatie-Tatya, are you there?'

It was Anoushka, her niece, the daughter of Tatiana's eldest sister whom they'd been forced to leave in a Russian jail and whose fate was unknown. Not yet four, Anoushka was far too young to see her aunt in this condition. 'I'm having a bath, precious. I'll be out in a minute.' There, see? She could sound perfectly normal if she tried.

Tatiana cried off church and, when everyone had left, she telephoned Constanza. Not to bare her soul, but to test the ground. Constanza reached the telephone ahead of the maid she now employed and got the first question in.

'What happened to you? We thought you must have ended up at the wrong club.'

'I… I went home. I felt ill. Conny, what did you do with Armand? I thought you were escorting him home.'

From the other end came a gasp of annoyance. 'What a pill that man is! Last time I try to help him, I assure you. The cab had to slow down on Pont d'Iéna and he jumped out. Last I saw of him, he was hurtling along the embankment, looking for a way down to the river. Frankly, I don't care if he threw himself in. Has he?'

'No.'

'Hmm. You do sound dreadful. Shall I bring chicken broth over?'

'No. I need sleep, or I'll be unfit for work tomorrow.' After she'd hung up, Tatiana toyed with calling Gérard at home. But she couldn't muster the courage. His mother or, worst of all, Armand, might be brought to the phone. Nor did Gérard call her, and she spent the rest of the day and most of the night imagining a series of dreadful, damning conversations taking place inside the Sainte-Vierge home.

It wasn't until Monday lunchtime, and starved of sleep, that Tatiana telephoned Gérard's office. An assistant put her through. No time for small talk, she had to know.

'Did Armand say anything about our night out on Saturday?'

'A little. I believe you added to the racket at the Café Select, but the two of you decided to give the Rose Noire a miss. Very wise, in my view.'

'That's all? Did he say anything about me?'

'Aha! Caught you.'

Sweat sprang under her arms. She stammered, 'C-Caught?'

'Didn't I warn you to never get tipsy in public and not mix your alcohol?'

'Constanza whisked up a last cocktail and I didn't like to say no.'

'And you wonder why I don't admire the girl. Armand had to take you home, he said. You don't remember?'

'I do. He was… there. When I got lost.'

'He mentioned finding you alone by the river. I'll give him some credit. Armand is a cracked vessel, no getting away from it, but he'd never see you in trouble and not step in. Tatiana, can you hear me?'

'Yes. Sorry.' To her consternation, Gérard then invited Tatiana, her mother and sister Katya and Katya's husband Harry to be his mother's guests for dinner the following week.

'Best we make things formal to our nearest and dearest.'

'Please say Armand won't be there.'

'I can't speak for him, but Armand is too honourable to mention any little foibles of yours in front of our mother. Speaking of foibles, this nonsense about him being in love with you will blow over, but only if you behave sensibly and let it. You'll be sure to invite your sister and brother-in-law? I shall enjoy engaging Monsieur Harry Morten on the state of the textile industry.'

Tatiana couldn't hold back a dig: 'You can ask Katya about it. She knows almost as much about cloth manufacture as her husband.'

'Yes, patterns and colours, no doubt. But not profit and loss, which is what interests me, *ma chérie.*'

Chapter Five

'You're sure you want to marry into that family?'

Tatiana ignored her sister's question. She'd got through the day in a state of numb detachment. She could have described the clothes she'd worn on the catwalk in minute detail, but only because she'd shown them countless times already. She recalled not a single face from the audience, nor could she have repeated anything said in the *cabine*, the upstairs room where the mannequins gathered to put on make-up and get dressed.

It was now half past five and she and Katya were travelling home together from rue Duphot where Maison Javier operated out of sprawling premises. The sisters lived a short distance from each other, Tatiana on rue Rembrandt, Katya in a flat her husband had bought some years before, on rue Goya. Both streets radiated off the green oasis that was Parc Monceau, and on the rare occasions Katya left at the same time she did, they'd share a cab home. As they crossed Place Vendôme where the first and eighth *arrondissements* shook elegantly gloved hands, Katya struck again.

'You mean to marry the first man who has ever asked you?'

'You did. Harry was your first love. Your first lover.'

'True, but he was also my dearest friend by the time he proposed. I don't think Gérard de Sainte-Vierge knows how to be anybody's friend. I haven't forgiven the way he abandoned you in the summer of 1919, and if you have, it's because you were dying. Or don't want to see the truth.'

Tatiana flourished her ring. 'This belonged to his grandmother. It proves he loves me.'

'Have you told Mama?'

'Not yet. But I will, because we're all invited to dinner to meet the marquise.'

'Ugh. Mama won't have forgotten Gérard's treatment of you. As for his mother, she was appallingly rude when we worked in that tea room, and if she's as insolent to Mama as she was to us, I won't keep my mouth shut. I'm not a humble waitress now.'

'For goodness' sake, I'm marrying the man, not his mother.'

'*Au contraire*, my love. Marry into an aristocratic French family, that's exactly what you'll do.'

Tatiana pointed out that the marquise had only been positively rude to her the day she poured scalding tea over her skirt. 'Mostly, she ignored me.'

'Exactly,' Katya hit back. 'She's the worst snob in Paris. I was serving her once, and Armand was staring at you. She immediately began a diatribe on the danger of foreigners tainting French bloodlines. It was all I could do not to lump her with a cake stand. How does she stand on Russian Orthodoxy?'

'I haven't the faintest idea.' Tatiana yawned indulgently. 'If necessary, I'll convert. So, will you come to dinner, you and Harry? Gérard has booked the Aigle d'Or on Quai d'Auteuil.'

'Oh, very smart and a short drive from the Sainte-Vierge mansion. Heaven forfend that Madame should put herself out.'

'You're determined to hate her.'

'Believe me, it takes no effort at all.'

'Well, make an effort. I need to show that I have respectable relations.'

'I won't bring Harry,' Katya declared. 'I won't do it to my darling man.'

All at once, Tatiana crumpled. For all her show of indifference, she was dreading the dinner. Every time she rested or sank into reflection, Armand's lust-soaked face manifested in front of her. 'Please, Katya. If we don't include Harry, Gérard will be offended. Tell Harry my future happiness depends on it.'

In their apartment, Harry Morten listened as his wife related that conversation.

'… and we're all bidden to dinner at the Aigle d'Or.'

'Well, well,' Harry said flatly. 'Has your sister abandoned every shred of sense?'

'Stop it. Tatiana's intelligent!'

'So intelligent she's entrusting her future to a man who hadn't the guts to stay with her when she was at her most vulnerable?'

'She's conveniently erased his cowardice,' Katya admitted. They were in the back room Harry used as an at-home office, where every surface was strewn with samples of wool cloth sent from his English mills. Harry was alarmed by the strain around his wife's eyes. With Maison Javier rising up the ranks of couture houses, Katya was becoming an influential figure in Parisian fashion. One day, perhaps, she'd be a very powerful woman. For now, she was simply overworked, and tragic evidence of the toll this was taking came with the two miscarriages she'd suffered the previous year. Her corn-blond chignon was slipping from its pins and Harry knew she was longing to kick off her shoes, plump up the sofa cushions and have him brew her a cup of her favourite liquorice tea.

As he would, once he'd shared with her a letter that had arrived with the mid-morning post. A letter that would change their lives. He was in no mood to let Tatiana's latest melodrama add to the stress. 'Darling?'

'She needs to believe in Gérard,' Katya was saying, 'because she cannot square his callous neglect with the ideal she's in love with.'

'Forget Tatiana. I have something serious to show you.'

'She wants to share his title. That and living at the gates of the Bois de Boulogne means everything to her, but don't judge her! Our life has been so treacherous. Running from Moscow with only what we could carry, bloodstains wet on our shoes—'

'I know,' he interrupted gently. 'And if we must talk of Tatiana, allow me to say that every privation she suffered, you suffered doubly. While you scrubbed your hands raw to take care of your mother and niece, Tatiana sat back and watched. She's got it into her head that being a French noblewoman will absolve her of the responsibility to make something of her life. Like sweeping a dud hand of cards off the table and breaking open a new deck.'

'She has a fractured soul, Harry.'

'Will marriage to a poker-faced bore mend it?'

'Gérard *is* humourless, but even I have to admit he curtails her wildness. He discourages Constanza Darocca, which I applaud. He doesn't like fashionable young things, modern music, cocktails—'

'Or short hair on women, let me guess?' Harry put in drily. 'A true progressive. I won't be paraded for inspection in front of his mother, though I'm curious to know one thing. Gérard has slept with Tatiana for nigh on three years, without any hint of wanting to marry her. You know better than I – what's he up to?'

'I believe he hopes to be finance minister one day so it could be that he wants to be seen as a family man… Harry? You brought a letter out of your pocket a moment ago, then put it back again.'

'I did indeed.' Harry presented it, turning it so she could read the Swedish postmark. 'From my father in Gothenburg. He's had a reply from the contact Larissa Markova gave us.'

'The man at Bolshevik committee headquarters?'

'Abel Yenukidze is the name.'

'Her father's old friend, the one she said might have news of— '

Harry interrupted, deliberately. 'I'm not sure "old friend" quite describes him. After all, he allowed Larissa's family to be hounded out of Russia at bayonet-point. Let's call him "an influential 'yes-man' with an eye to his own advantage". My father wrote in the New Year and it's taken this long for Yenukidze to respond. Katya, don't read too much into this.' In the space of moments, she'd turned white as a Pierrot doll. From the envelope, Harry removed a square of the low-grade paper common in Russia. 'Shall I read it, or would you like to? It's in Cyrillic.'

She was shaking. 'You do it.'

'All right. It's a prisoner list, from a forced labour colony near Moscow. Not the whole damn thing – I expect that runs to a hundred pages or more. Just the names of those ranked under the letter "S".'

'Oh God. Tell me, Harry.'

'Prisoner number 293, Starova.'

'My sister Vera, she's alive!'

'She was when the list was compiled but my father thinks it's a good sign that his request for information has been acknowledged.'

'They trust him, don't they, in Moscow? Your father has friends at the Kremlin?'

'They do business with him and he's a valuable source of foreign currency. Father expects they'll want payment to let Vera go.'

'A ransom?'

'Vera won't be allowed simply to leave the country.'

'Will your father act for us? Russia is only five days' journey from Gothenburg.'

Harry shook his head. His father was far too brusque and impatient for a task needing careful diplomacy. And a little too old for the rigours of a winter journey. Moreover, as Harry said, 'This man Yenukidze could present any woman as Vera, and my father wouldn't know they'd tricked him.'

'Then who should go?'

'Me, obviously. You tell me Vera looks like a younger version of your mother, so I'd know if they were showing me the right woman.'

'You would go so far for us?'

'I'd be prepared to risk it. I promised your mother before I married you that if the political situation ever allowed it, I'd try to find Vera. I know how much it cost you to leave her behind when you fled Russia. And I hate political bullying as much as anybody. So long as you accept that she might be dead, might have been for months...' He wiped a tear tumbling down Katya's cheek. 'It's worth a shot.'

He folded the letter. 'We won't speak of this to anyone. You've confided in Larissa Markova, a good decision since she has better contacts in Moscow even than my father, but leave it there. If your mother were to find out, she'd lose...' He'd been about to say, 'what few wits she has', but checked himself, saying instead, 'much sleep. And if we fail, it will crush her.'

Katya nodded. 'Not a word. Not even to Tatiana.'

'God help us, certainly not to Tatiana. I'll write and ask my father to negotiate with Comrade Yenukidze's people and find out what they want.'

'And when we know, Harry, we go to Russia.'

A chill ran through him. His cherished wife, returning to the country that had nearly destroyed her? 'No. *I* go to Russia.'

'No, *we* go.'

He tried a different tack. 'Who would take care of your mother and niece if we both left? It won't be a quick business.'

'Yana looks after Anoushka most of the time. And Tatiana can step in. If she's old enough to marry, she's old enough to assume some responsibility.'

'Hmm.' He led the way to the kitchen where their maid had laid out a salad supper. They would eat, then spend the remainder of the evening listening to the gramophone. Perhaps talking, perhaps not. 'Does this at least get me out of dinner with Tatiana's awful fiancé?'

Chapter Six

Harry was allowed to claim a business meeting and avoid the event. Tatiana's mother, Princess Irina Vytenis, cried off too with a migraine. Since the death of her husband at the hands of the Russian secret police and the incarceration of her eldest daughter, Irina had become nervous of company. And so, the party at the Aigle d'Or consisted of Tatiana and Katya, Gérard, his mother and Gérard's cousin, Agnès, the duchesse de Brioude. Armand was dining elsewhere, Gérard explained. Tatiana released a breath she'd been holding for hours and was able to greet his mother, and then his cousin, with a show of composure.

Agnès de Brioude was a friend of Katya's, a widow of around thirty whose husband had been one of tens of thousands killed at the battle of Verdun. Katya dressed her, with the result that Agnès had metamorphosed from a black-draped ghost into a stylish woman-about-town. Tonight, violet silk with a yellow orchid corsage made a dramatic statement, matching the amethyst-and-topaz clips in her dark hair.

Gérard's mother also liked high fashion, which she wore without regard to its suitability. She suffered curvature of the spine and, as it affected her height, was rarely seen in public without some flourishing headwear to add inches. Tonight it was a black dress by Patou with a puffball skirt, teetering shoes and a satin turban with a red-dyed goose feather. Tatiana had dressed down in midnight-blue silk. Katya wore one of her own creations of brown and gold organza.

Gérard, immaculate in a starched collar and a tie of watered silk, ordered champagne. He proposed a toast, saying how honoured he was that Tatiana had accepted him, that October was the month chosen for their union. She was invited to show off the engagement ring and his mother scowled.

'You did not ask permission.'

Gérard replied coldly, 'I am not required to, Madame.'

'It matches the tiepin I gave him.' Desperate to lighten the mood, Tatiana thrust her ring finger close to Gérard's shirt collar, to illustrate her point. He pulled back and she added frantically, 'Not a ruby, I'm afraid, only red jasper. The tiepin, I mean. Tell your mother, Gérard, how I bought it for you on the first anniversary of our meeting. Don't you love red, Madame? Well, obviously.' Tatiana blinked at the marquise's feather. 'Red suits dark people. Like you.'

'I am not dark,' the marquise snapped.

Things went further awry as their hors d'oeuvres arrived. Gérard had ordered oysters, which Tatiana couldn't abide. Gamely swallowing one, she almost retched.

'Leave them,' Katya hissed, then said to their hosts, 'I'm afraid my sister had a bad oyster the day we arrived in France and it's scarred her.'

For her main course Tatiana chose duck, assuming she would get a few slivers. It came very pink and there was enough for a hearty trencherman. Her desire for food had vanished some years ago, shrunk further by her illness. And, of course, her profession discouraged a good appetite.

Gérard noticed her picking. 'Tuck in,' he told her. 'We can't have you withering to nothing. You fashion girls, you're all skin and bone.'

'Don't you eat?' The marquise had also ordered the duck and had summoned a waiter back for extra sauce and more pureed spinach. Where she put it in that question-mark body, Tatiana couldn't imagine. Being singled out was making her throat tight, and in the marquise's features she saw strong reminders of Armand. She reached for her champagne, to give her something to do with her hands.

'There's no excuse in this sorry world for girls to starve themselves.' The marquise poured red wine sauce onto Tatiana's plate. 'Let me see you eat that up.'

'Tante Clothilde,' Duchesse Agnès remonstrated, 'don't badger your guest.'

'I'm not badgering. How will she bear sons with hips like coat hangers? She has no bosom to speak of! I don't understand modern figures. I've seen girls dancing and they rattle as though somebody's upset the cutlery drawer. Do you have children, Madame Morten?'

Katya, lost in her own thoughts, looked startled by the question. When the marquise repeated herself, she gave a clear, sharp reply. 'No. None.'

'But why not? You don't have the look of a new bride.'

Agnès, who knew how dearly Katya longed to be a mother, redirected the conversation by asking Gérard how his car was running. 'Such an indulgence, keeping a private motor in Paris, but have you seen the Quadrilette, Tatiana? Such a pretty blue colour.'

Gérard took the bait. His car was his one concession to modernity. 'It's going sweetly, thank you,' he replied to his cousin. 'I plan to motor to Saint-Vincent at the weekend, if it doesn't rain.'

'You could go with him, Agnès,' the marquise suggested.

'No, thank you. Gérard must take his fiancée.'

'I understand you are one of three sisters.' The marquise put it to Tatiana almost as an accusation.

'That's right, Madame. Katya is four years older than me and we had – have – another sister, Vera. She was – is – the eldest.'

'Have or had? How can you not know?'

Gérard finally intervened. 'I explained, Maman. Tatiana's family were victims of the Red Terror after the revolution. Their father was murdered by the Russian police and her sister Vera was imprisoned.'

'Why, what did she do?'

Katya and Tatiana locked eyes. It was Tatiana who answered. 'She wrote letters to her husband while he was fighting at the front. She railed against the Bolsheviks and the letters were betrayed.'

'How unfortunate.' Madame de Sainte-Vierge looked about the table, spied sautéed potatoes on her niece Agnès's plate and demanded they be put on hers. 'I hate waste. You young ones should have lived through the siege of Paris, when the Prussians blocked our supplies and people were reduced to eating rats.'

'We have known hunger, Madame,' Katya said softly.

'So, no children.' The marquise gave a grunt. 'How long have you been married?'

'Almost two years. My career takes the place of a family, for now.' Katya was refusing to be baited.

'Rubbish. Leave careers to the ugly bitches who can't find husbands.' The gasps that greeted this daunted the marquise not a jot. 'Does your jailed sister have children?'

'A girl, Anoushka, who we managed to bring out of Russia. She is—'

'So, three sisters and one female child to show for it?' The marquise turned to her son. 'Our family needs heirs, Gérard.' People at a nearby table turned to listen. 'You must marry a well-born, fertile girl with a family history of boy children. Not this emaciated *amuse-bouche*, no more bite to her than a candied cherry.' The beaky glare headed back to Tatiana. 'You're very lovely but you won't do.'

'Tante Clothilde, I'm ashamed,' Agnès breathed.

The marquise speared a carrot. 'Tell me this, Agnès. If in twenty years' time your son Philippe brings home a pretty bit of chiffon with no name and no family, and says he means to marry her, what will you say?'

'I would refuse my consent,' her niece answered. 'The duc de Brioude could not make such a marriage.'

'There you are, then.'

Katya pushed back her chair, anger burning her cheeks. 'Tatiana, I shall call a taxi and will give you a lift home.' To the marquise, she said, 'Good breeding is more than a pair of fertile ovaries, Madame. Sows in a sty birth twelve offspring at a time. Good night.'

Watching her go, Gérard looked as if he'd been slapped. 'This was meant to be dinner with your family, Tatiana. And now there's only you.'

Tatiana would have liked to follow her sister. Not even her love for Gérard would let her sit mute while her family was insulted. But a greater threat loomed. Armand had come into the restaurant. He must have passed Katya on the way out. His arms were full of red roses which he dropped in front of Tatiana.

'A token of my great regard.' Like his brother, Armand was olive skinned and dark but without much flesh to soften his looks. He too found eating difficult. Gérard had told Tatiana that during the war, in the trenches, he'd been forced to consume his food in company with decomposing bodies, and the smell lived inside him. Tatiana stared at the roses, anger and shame battling to possess her. Why had she agreed to this ordeal?

Armand reached out to touch her, oblivious of the way she shrank from him. 'They're hideous, aren't they, my brother and mother? Come away with me and we'll find a cave, live in it and be happy. You know I'm ready to die for you. Hello, cousin Agnès,' he said, bowing. 'Has mother dropped any more embarrassing hints about it being time you remarried?'

Agnès de Brioude got up from her chair. She held out her hand to Tatiana. 'My car is waiting a little distance away. My dear, let me put it at your service. You look quite fatigued.'

Tatiana grasped the offered arm.

The journey home allowed time for awkwardness to retreat and for the duchesse to say, 'I don't know you well, Tatiana, but I hope my affection for Katya allows me the privilege of speaking bluntly.' She paused until Tatiana gave a brusque nod. 'The man you wish to marry is the most driven human being I know. He wants what he wants and will do what it takes to get it. Ambition courses through the family.'

'Perhaps I'm ambitious too, Madame.'

Agnès acknowledged the possibility. 'But are you ruthless? Not if you're anything like darling Katya. Sainte-Vierge men come into this world ridden by demons, and both Gérard and Armand have that affliction. Have you ever watched a boy pull the wings off a butterfly? It's vile, disturbing.'

'Armand did that?'

'No. Not Armand.'

Nothing more was said and Tatiana spent the rest of the journey repeating to herself, 'Everybody's wrong about my love. Even those who should know him best.'

Chapter Seven

Late August, three months later

The world of couture referred to girls like Tatiana as 'mannequins', as if she and her colleagues were animated versions of wax figurines. It was a job a million girls would die for – showing high-priced clothes to the crème de la crème – but a mannequin's pay was pitiful. Most of Tatiana's colleagues lived at home or in flats paid for by lovers, but even in their little *cabine*, there was disparity in circumstances. One of Javier's mannequins, Marianne du Gard, lived in a garden apartment in the home of her diplomat father. Larissa Markova, by contrast, rented two rooms in a house on the Left Bank. As rent day approached, Larissa's trademark serenity frayed whereas Marianne sailed through life with unquestioning contentment. Dressing like queens while earning poverty wages. It was no surprise that many of Tatiana's colleagues regarded their beauty as their passport to a good marriage and security.

Tatiana, who lived rent-free in a gracious flat paid for out of the dividends her mother received from Maison Javier, saw her job as simply that. A job. She was not fond of early mornings, and as the daily parade started at 3 p.m., she could rise at midday. Only when a collection was being created did the job bite back and a twenty-hour working week swelled to sixty or seventy. But there were perks. With

Katya being both a director of the house and a designer, Tatiana could take her pick of each season's clothes. Shoe, hat and handbag makers pressed gifts on the girls, and Tatiana could not remember the last time she was charged entrance to a nightclub. Her biggest outgoings were stockings, hairdressing and make-up.

Gérard had been smitten by her bright hair the first time he saw her at Callot Soeurs and she often teased him that *he* was the best perk she'd ever received. *Used* to tease him. Since that hideous dinner, a coolness had entered their relationship which Tatiana dared not examine.

Thank God Armand had retired to the family estates for the summer. Gérard remained at the finance ministry, apparently consumed by his duties. They hadn't slept together for weeks. Summer's humid heat offered an excuse, discouraging close contact and relieving her of the need to keep him at arm's length. She couldn't rid her mind of Armand, nor the touch of his hot, damp hands on her skin. What would her wedding night be like if she couldn't overcome her revulsion?

Anger festered, growing a rind that hid the pain but made her more volatile than ever. She'd ruffled feathers in the *cabine*. On this particular afternoon, the last Wednesday of August, she stood waiting to be dressed, and heard other girls whispering as they got themselves ready for the parade.

'Must we have "princess-and-future-marquise" pushed down our throats every minute?' That was brunette Françoise, rolling on her stockings. Despite her irritation, she took extreme care not to tear the delicate threads.

'She's on the last lap to the marriage bed,' a girl called Suzy hissed back, 'entitled to do whatever she likes.'

'Well, I still don't see why she should be given all the best ensembles *and* the wedding gown.'

Tatiana smiled thinly. She hadn't commissioned Katya to design a new dress for her, she'd asked to keep the one she was modelling for this season's collection. It was to be her parting gift from Maison Javier. An honour which set her apart.

'What persuaded Gérard de Sainte-Vierge to declare himself, after all this time?' Françoise was still riled, and her voice was rising.

'Patience is its own reward,' countered Mary-Jo, who embroidered tray cloths between appearances downstairs and wound high-minded proverbs in among the flowers and leaves. 'Only right he should make an honest woman of her.'

'Why shouldn't she become a marquise?' Marianne du Gard asked, smiling openly at Tatiana. Marianne received five eligible proposals per month and could afford to be generous. 'She's a princess, after all.'

'Oh really? I didn't know,' Françoise burst out. 'Let me tell you, before the revolution, Russian princes and princesses were ten to the rouble.'

'Hold your tongue, Françoise.' Constanza swept in. Late, but in time to catch the tail end of the nastiness. 'Remember who pays your wages – Madame Katya Morten, another ten-to-the-rouble princess. You tell me if there's anybody in this room who could bear to have her family background looked at too closely.'

Constanza had spent her childhood with her French-born mother in Marseilles, living over a shop. On her mother's remarriage, she'd fled to Buenos Aires to join her Argentinian father. He was rich, having made his money supplying beef to the allied armies, but he hadn't always been so. Constanza spoke with a Spanish accent but, unlike Mary-Jo who left a space between words, French poured from her lips at Gatling gun speed. Always the first to say she wasn't beautiful – her nose had a bump and her black hair rejected all attempts at curling – Constanza had made a career from her mixed heritage and indefinable 'attitude'. She moved with the replete grace of a panther, and it was whispered she'd once killed a lover. Whatever the truth, as she sat down at her dressing table, Tatiana felt the atmosphere shift.

The parade got underway. Two hours later, Tatiana's dresser helped her into the wedding gown for the finale. Constanza was still downstairs in the salon, and Françoise couldn't resist a final, sly dig. As the veil flowed over Tatiana's shoulders, she sighed, 'So brave.'

'Why?' the dresser asked as she smoothed invisible wrinkles from chiffon velvet.

Françoise looked surprised. 'It's an ill omen, isn't it, to appear in the dress she's chosen for her own wedding?'

'Why so, Mademoiselle?' the dresser persisted.

Tatiana knew exactly what Françoise was getting at and explained. 'Were my husband-to-be to see it, I'd be in for bad luck.'

'Abominable luck,' Françoise corrected.

'But he won't. He hardly leaves his office. Gérard has a proper job.'

'Unlike us, you mean?' Françoise smiled. 'Mere walking coat hangers, so they say. He can't be all that busy. I saw him only this morning, strolling down rue Molière.'

'So? He owns an apartment there, five minutes from his office.' And ten from rue Duphot. Before their engagement, Tatiana and Gérard had enjoyed lunchtime trysts at the flat. She wondered fleetingly what had taken him to rue Molière today. So early, and without her.

Constanza came in, the scarlet train of her evening dress looped over her wrist. 'Tatiana, they're all holding their breath for you. No, not so fast.' Constanza held her palm out. 'Your ring. No personal jewellery. Anyway, I thought you agreed never to wear it in public.'

'I never promised that. Who said so?'

'You did, my darling. You are growing forgetful. Come on, give.'

Tatiana gave the engagement ring to Constanza for safe keeping. 'I've grown too used to having it on.'

'There's a surprise waiting in the salon.' Constanza's voice pursued her to the door.

Tatiana hesitated. 'What surprise?'

The reply was lost as Larissa Markova followed Tatiana to the door, urging her to get a move on. Larissa was showing the penultimate gown, a silver beaded evening dress. As they picked their way carefully down the stairs, Larissa seized the opportunity for a private word. 'Rosa wants to know why you've missed her last ten classes. She's worried about you.'

'No need,' Tatiana replied curtly.

'She's auditioning for a ballet, her own creation. It's a modern, expressionist work and I'm helping her orchestrate the music. You could be in it, Tatiana. You're good enough.'

'I'm too busy.' Tatiana's dancing had become a casualty of this tarnished summer. The thought of being in a crowd, wearing only a leotard, pushing her body into shapes, scared her. Rosa had written, asking why she'd become a stranger but she hadn't answered. She cut the conversation and hurried down to the antechamber next to the main salon. At a given signal she would step out in front of the gilt chairs. If today was like every other day, it would be to a delighted intake of breath and applause. The bride of the hour. Feeling light-headed because she'd skipped lunch, she poured herself a glass of iced lemon water and perched on a satin chair.

A dresser offered Tatiana a long-stemmed calla lily, the one accessory allowed with the dress. Whispering, as everyone did this side of the salon door, the dresser added, 'There's no pollen on the rude bit. I blew it all off with a paper straw.'

Tatiana stifled a giggle. 'The rude bit' jutted up inside the flower. Waxen white callas were everywhere at the moment. Sent up by train from the Côte d'Azure, shockingly expensive, their hooded cups chimed with this season's slender silhouette. Tatiana touched the yellow spike. Not a speck of pollen attached to her finger. If only every threat could be blown away.

Larissa came to sit beside her, but it was Françoise's malice that intruded. At Vera's wedding in 1914, a few weeks before the world tumbled into war, the household mirrors had been shrouded. Even the silverware in the dining room had been draped so Vera might not catch so much as a glimpse of her reflected self until after the ceremony.

'The bride who sees herself in the glass on her wedding day is cursed.'

Fifteen years old, miffed because all the attention was on her eldest sister, Tatiana had taken that as a challenge.

Larissa's cue came and she went out into the salon.

'Any moment, Princess,' the dresser advised Tatiana. 'As soon as Suzy and Mary-Jo come back in—'

'I go out. Yes. I've done this a thousand times.' Tatiana handed the dresser her water glass, stood up and readied herself.

On the other side of the baize-covered door, 'Sparkle Shoe Rag' was being played. Maison Javier had its own jazz pianist, setting it apart from every other couture house. Jazz and ragtime were the rage, and even ladies who never danced loved to see clothes move to the new rhythms.

The baize door opened. Twin wraiths in silver-grey, Suzy and Mary-Jo glided past in a miasma of flower essence.

'Keeping the best till last, Princess darling,' Mary-Jo tittered. 'Your beau is waiting.'

'Who? Who is waiting?' Tatiana demanded, but she had no choice but to move forward. She couldn't make out much as the salon lights were always turned off for her final appearance. It was part of the stage setting. The pianist had begun a new tune, a dragging melody by Scott Joplin. Tatiana adjusted her face to noble serenity. Larissa was also on her way back to the antechamber and stole a second to murmur, 'Third row back, behind the lady in blond mink.'

'Who, Gérard?' But she didn't catch Larissa's reply.

Lilliane Germond, the salon's *directrice*, announced, 'Mesdames et Monsieur, we present the elegant "full stop" to our season's offering, a bridal gown for autumn's cooler days.'

So what if Gérard had dropped in to watch her? Tatiana told herself. Let him see the dress. Tatiana believed in bad luck, but not the sort delivered by curses.

'Light-as-mist chiffon velvet, with an underskirt of layered tulle. A fairy tale for today's bride.' Lilliane's voice had a swooning quality. 'Modernity meets myth in this lovely gown.'

As Tatiana progressed along the catwalk, staff dressed in black lit banks of church candles. The effect was to reveal the dress by degrees, and the audience to Tatiana, row by row. Smart town dresses. Hat brims tilted forward. Of course, Mary-Jo could have been referring mischievously to Roland Javier, the male director of the fashion house and its principal designer. He often watched the collection parade. There was nobody as safe as Roland. She wondered if her sister was here, or shut away in her office.

She fixed her eyes on an arrangement of calla lilies at the end of the catwalk, then turned to display every aspect of her dress. She raised the overskirt, coaxing the sumptuous fabric to catch the air. Making her way back between the gilt chairs, she bit back her dismay. There was the woman in blond mink and sitting behind her, Armand. When had he got back from Tournon-sur-Rhône? He leaned forward and flung a bouquet of pink roses at her feet.

'My love! Meet me tonight by the Pont d'Iéna.'

Tatiana raced out of the salon, not stopping until she reached the floor above, tripping on her train and tearing the velvet chiffon. A capital offence, but all she could think of was getting to Constanza. Her friend would know what to do.

Madame Anna Markova, the *chef de cabine* and Larissa's aunt, gazed in consternation as Tatiana stumbled past. Constanza's dressing table was tidy, the chair pushed up tight to it.

'Has she gone?'

'Constanza? Just this moment.'

'Fetch her back, please.'

Madame Markova clicked her fingers at a dresser, who instantly set off.

Somebody had pulled a huge cheval mirror into the centre of the room. Tatiana was confronted by her full-length reflection. An ivory column, a broken calla lily in her hand. A victim inviting a curse. Suzy, Mary-Jo and Françoise giggled. Tatiana spread her arms to fill the entire glass.

'Damn the lot of you,' she flung. 'A few weeks from now I'll be downstairs seated on my gilded chair, watching you three hobble by in clothes you don't own. A trio of witless coat hangers.'

Constanza took her to the Tuileries gardens, the closest green space to rue Duphot. Ushering her to a bench, where none but pigeons would overhear, she let Tatiana tell her story.

It didn't take long. Tatiana kept her descriptions spare. Constanza made a guttural noise of pity.

'So that's why the cad leapt out of the taxi and scampered down to the river. To intercept you. Why, *why* did you let the others get ahead of you that night?'

'I suppose I was drunk... it felt as though oil had been poured into my brain. Armand meant it to happen. He's a predator.'

'Have you confronted him?' When Tatiana shook her head, Constanza let several seconds pass. 'You've kept this secret all summer?'

'Yes. Gérard must never know. Promise you'll say nothing.'

Constanza took Tatiana's hands between hers. 'Poor, poor girl, but it could have been any of us. Armand is not right... shell shock, isn't that what Gérard says? Sometimes they have to have the doctor sedate him.'

'When did Gérard say that?'

'When you first introduced us and I made that gaff, remember? Asking Gérard why his brother stared so piercingly.' Constanza made a rueful face. 'Armand has nightmares, he told me. Sometimes he spends days staring at the wall. Are you sure you want to marry into the family?'

'That's what Katya asks.' Tatiana stared at their entwined hands, Constanza's the colour of caramel, hers pale because she protected them with gloves summer and winter. 'I'll die before I give up Gérard. I can't live without him.'

'Then tell him what Armand did. He needs to know so he can protect you.'

But all Tatiana could do was cry. Between sobs, she told Constanza what Gérard's mother had implied about her fertility. 'Apparently, I don't have the haunches for childbearing.'

'Neither does she, but she managed! If you're worried, you could always consult a specialist.'

'Do you know one? I think Gérard's mother has got him worried. He's been rather distant with me lately.'

'I can find someone – one of my married friends will know a discreet doctor.' Constanza put an arm around her. 'Katya is having trouble conceiving, isn't she? But it doesn't follow that you will. Her problem is that she works such long hours. Does her lovely husband ever get to see her?'

'She and Harry make time for each other. It isn't children I need to produce, it's sons. Girls are irrelevant to Madame la marquise.' Tatiana wiped her tears away. 'What will I do if Gérard ever looks at me through his mother's eyes? She hates that he's given me the family engagement ring.' She gasped, splaying out her fingers. 'Where is it?' She felt her reason unravel. 'It's gone!'

'I have it, don't panic.' Constanza had put it on her own finger, and because her hands were a size larger than Tatiana's, it took a bit of twisting and wiggling to remove it. Giving it back, she said, 'You know, if you were to break off with Gérard, you'd soon find somebody else.'

Tatiana hit back with, 'How many more times must I say it? There is nobody else.'

Chapter Eight

September arrived. August humidity was replaced by teeming rain. On Saturday, 2 September, Tatiana tapped her umbrella dry at the top of an imposing set of steps. She had come to an address on Quai de l'Horloge on the Île de la Cité, the ancient heart of Paris.

Constanza had been as good as her word, finding her a private doctor, even making the appointment for her. To judge by the sweeping staircase, this building – colonised by offshoots of the medical profession – had once been a grand, riverside home. Its upper storeys would give a fine view of the Seine, though perhaps not today. Still, Tatiana was thankful to be out of the rain. Taking off her raincoat and headscarf, she shook them out and laid them on a cold radiator to claim later.

Her appointment was with a Dr Jolivet, whose surgery was one floor up according to an engraved board. 'Discretion guaranteed and open Saturday morning,' Constanza had assured her, 'so you can pretend to be shopping with me.' She'd booked Tatiana in under a false name. 'The fewer people who know you're being inspected like a brood mare, the better.'

After a brief sit-down in a waiting room where, in a fashion magazine, she came across a year-old picture of herself, Tatiana followed a nurse into a consulting room. It was brightly lit by angled lamps, which showed that the walls needed repainting, that the cork tile floor was scuffed in front of a curtain drawn across one corner. Tatiana imagined unwilling feet being dragged… It was a worn surgical couch which held her horrified gaze the longest. What were those stirrup-things hanging from the bar above it?

'Go behind the drape and remove your lower garments,' the nurse said.

'Must I?'

'Indeed, to allow for a proper examination. Take off your dress but keep your slip on.' When Tatiana made no move, the nurse raked the curtain back. 'Let's not keep doctor waiting.'

Behind the none-too-clean chintz, Tatiana unbuttoned, unlaced, unclipped. She was looking down at her legs, which were shaking, when she heard a man's voice. Dr Jolivet, presumably.

She emerged to find the nurse arranging a fresh sheet on the couch. A middle-aged man in a white coat was sitting at a desk, his back to them. He seemed to be consulting notes. The nurse took in Tatiana's slipper-satin camisole and waist slip, the scared eyes. 'Jump up, please, Madame Valois.'

Valois. Constanza's humour could be a touch insensitive. The royal house of Valois had ruled France for roughly two hundred and fifty years before coming to a violent end, and many of its members had been mad. Tatiana eased herself into a lying position, teeth clenched. Dr Jolivet had yet to utter a word.

Chapter Nine

An American in Paris

A stone's throw from Tatiana's purgatory, on the wharf below Quai de l'Horloge, Regan Dortmeyer wiped moisture off his binoculars. Rain blurred the line between sky and river and bounced off the cobbles, making his hoped-for shot of Pont Neuf near impossible. The rapids sluicing between the bridge arches would make a powerful photograph when – if – the sun came out again. He was setting up the shot, using binoculars so his camera could stay dry in its case.

So much for the City of Light. Barges slumbering at their moorings heaving out the stink of wet coal. Sky the colour of old wash rags. The Seine resembled the bathwater his grandma used to throw out after all eight of them had used it. The Worldwide Picture Agency had signed him up to produce a montage they could syndicate across America as 'The Eternal Romance of Paris'. Two days into the job, the results were truly romantic. If you happened to be a duck.

Last time he'd been in Paris, on leave from the front, the skies had been unblemished blue. What a paradox. To get decent weather, start a war. When he raised his binoculars again, the rain found the gap under the cuffs of his trench coat and trickled all the way to his elbows.

It was during a gloomy reflection on his chances of getting paid for this trip that he sensed a softening of the wind. Pushing up his sodden hat, he peered into the sky. All at once, like a tarpaulin whipped off a baseball pitch, the clouds parted. A daub of blue appeared. The Seine burst into diamonds. Regan Dortmeyer shot the clasps of his camera case and whistled a few bars of the 'Hallelujah Chorus'.

He took out his Speed Graphic, slid a preloaded film into the back and positioned his fingers under the side straps, adding another infinitesimal scuff mark to the camera's cheeks. His finger hovered over the shutter release… damn. A man wearing a Homburg hat and a coat with the collar turned up had wandered into shot.

'Scoot,' Regan muttered. He would defend to the death any man's right to march back and forth along a bridge, but precious seconds were wasting.

When the man took up a stance against the rail, Regan lowered his camera in defeat. The sun dipped behind the clouds.

'Endurance, Madame.' Dr Jolivet must have offered this advice many times to women protesting at the freezing implement being ratcheted into place inside them. His voice had a mechanical flatness.

Tatiana's fingers curled against the sides of the couch, and when the implement was withdrawn, she cried out.

The doctor then gave her a manual examination. 'Hmm' he muttered. Then, 'Aha' and finally, 'Nurse, you may assist Madame now.'

Freed from the stirrups, Tatiana had to be helped off the couch. It took her ages to dress, everything shaking, her insides cramping. Blood on her inner thigh. Stumbling out from behind the screen, she saw that a fresh white sheet had been laid over the couch, but the nurse was gone. Without turning from his desk where he sat writing, Dr Jolivet gestured to a stool. 'Sit there.'

She spent the next minute listening to his scraping pen, taking a thorough dislike to his long skull, side whiskers and droopy moustache. She expected the pain in her abdomen would have eased off, but the cramping went on, blood trickling into the handkerchief she'd used as an emergency pad.

At last, the pen was laid down. 'So, Madame Valois, I can tell you that inwardly, all seems well.'

'I can bear sons?'

'Or daughters. If God chooses daughters for you, there is nothing to be done.'

'But I can bear children?'

His lengthy contemplation of her bare second finger reminded Tatiana that Constanza had advised her to borrow a gold band for the day. 'I'm getting married very soon,' she burbled.

'Quite so.' Eventually, he asked, 'Have you reason to believe you may have difficulty in giving birth? A history of miscarriage or prolonged labour in the family?'

She could have told him Katya's heartbreaking story, but nothing about Dr Jolivet encouraged confidence. So she muttered, 'I don't think so. I haven't had, you know, the curse for a while. I get the pains every twenty-eight days but no… um…'

'No bleed?' Jolivet asked her to come nearer. When she was close enough to smell the scurfy odour of his moustache, he pulled down her bottom eyelids and made a sound of disapproval. 'Pale as a magnolia petal. Put out your tongue.' After that, he examined her fingernails and tutted. 'Have you experienced breathlessness?'

'Only when I dance too fast.'

'Tiredness?'

'I never sleep well.'

'Restless legs?'

'I'm not sure. I've been fidgety all my life.'

He asked her to open her dress and examined her breasts as she sat rigid and mortified. When he'd finished, she buttoned herself up with unsteady fingers.

Jolivet wrote a few lines, then sat back. 'Madame Valois, had I not examined you earlier, I would have suspected that without a monthly bleed, taking into consideration your low weight and the pale nature of your conjunctiva—'

'Con-what, please?'

'Eyelid tissue. Under normal circumstances, I would have diagnosed severe anaemia and given your chances of conceiving as adjacent to zero.' He tore out the page he'd been writing on. 'Consume the foods I've written down for you and come back in three months. Meanwhile, I most strongly advise you to bring forward your wedding.'

A blush claimed her. 'We have a date for the end of next month.'

He flicked that away. 'France needs sons, strong specimens to repopulate our nation after the terrible toll of war. You, young woman, are in no fit state to bear them.'

'Don't say that.'

'For all that, God has given you the blessing you seek. You are at least twelve weeks pregnant.' As she stared at him, her eyes glazing with denial, he rang a bell for the nurse. 'Go home,' he told her, 'and put yourself on a rational diet, so you may bear a healthy child and do your duty to your future spouse and your country.'

Chapter Ten

'Honey, don't move.' Regan refocused the Speed Graphic. A girl had come onto the bridge from Quai de l'Horloge.

She couldn't be more Parisienne if she tried, with her headscarf and raincoat collar pulled up to her cheekbones. Those bones and a pointed chin gave her a feline character. When he saw she was clutching a bunch of yellow sunflowers, Regan smiled.

'Got you too, did she?'

A flower seller on Quai de l'Horloge had looked so pitiful, trying to sell a cartload of damp wares, he'd paid for a bunch and then handed them back, sufficiently laden already with photo paraphernalia. In return, he'd taken her picture. Not that she quite fitted the brief of the Eternal Romance of Paris, being matronly and toothless. Unlike this girl. Her eyes caressed the horizon as if a lover waited upstream… Regan's skin rippled with a vibration like bees' wings. A feeling that overtook him when the perfect image was a blink away. She was tall for a dame, he thought as he depressed the shutter release, forcing a three-tone sound from the Speed Graphic. Now she was leaning right over the water. She wasn't going to jump, he told himself. Jumpers don't bring flowers. To get her perfectly in frame, he needed to be further to the right. Without stopping to think, he leapt a metre-wide span of water, landing on the deck of a coal barge. Taller than average, with a boxer's physique, he did not make a balletic landing. If anybody was sleeping below, well, they wouldn't be now. Regan listened for the roar of the disturbed but none came. The bargee must have tied up and gone somewhere drier.

The girl still hadn't seen him. Regan edged round the wheelhouse, the Speed Graphic cradled against his middle. The boat was dipping up and down from the force of the water.

He removed the film pack from the camera, turned it over and reinserted it for a second shot. Clouds split, releasing sunlight sharp as lemon juice. Bracing himself against the wheelhouse, Regan adjusted focus then hovered his finger over the shutter release. His instinct was correct because the next moment, she pulled off her headscarf and let her coat fall open.

As the light caught hair the colour of a polished penny, Regan Dortmeyer, the least romantic photojournalist ever employed by the Worldwide Agency, fired off a picture that changed his ideas about light, life and Paris for ever.

This time, she saw him. A fat sunflower got Regan in the face. Another almost took his hat off. The rest of her flowers hit the barge deck like suicidal flying fish.

'*Quel culot!*'

'Thank you, ma'am.' He used English because his French accent was bad enough to cause a diplomatic incident. He understood he'd just been informed that he had a mighty nerve. Well, so had she. Those sunflowers could have wrecked a fifty-dollar lens.

He called up, 'Hey, Mam'zelle, how about I take one of you walking along the bridge?'

'*Va te faire voir! Dégage!*'

That was 'Get lost' in frank terms. He grinned, saluting her with a broken sunflower. 'Like to drop in on my studio, see the proofs?'

Throwing him a look that would sauté a kidney, she was out of sight by the time Regan had leapt clear of the barge, gathered up his equipment and made it up the embankment steps.

The man in the Homburg had not left the bridge at all. He was staring after the girl, like a starving dog watching a hot-sausage cart.

Chapter Eleven

Vera

When Russia's revolutionary rulers turned a monastery north of Moscow into a women's prison, it was for the incarceration of 'Enemies of the People'. Ordinary working women for the most part, convicted of 'capitalism', which often amounted to selling vegetables or furniture to buy food, or for muttering too loudly against Comrade Lenin's utopia. A men's wing had since been added and a new kind of trouble had been born.

Though there were strict rules against fraternisation, the one place of contact was the prison laundry. Male prisoners brought in baskets of soiled linen, the women worked the tubs. When the guards' eyes were elsewhere, brisk sexual transactions occasionally took place. No money passed hands, for there was no money. A nugget of stale cheese, a page of poetry. Small treasures, worth risking everything for.

Vera Starova, who had worked in the laundry since receiving her ten-year sentence for subversion in 1919, saw it all through lowered eyes. She held her tongue. Laundry duty was the only benefit to be scraped from this appalling place. Though the steam made her cough and the caustic peeled her hands, she was warm during the day and laundresses got extra rations. Potato broth at midday, a chunk of rye bread in the afternoon. The difference between life and death. Let her but survive another seven-and-a-bit years, she might see her family again. Kiss her mother and laugh with her sisters, Katya and Tatiana. She might learn where her baby Anoushka was buried.

She might again hold her husband, Mikhail.

Mikhail, so fair and handsome. Katya, bold and true. Tatiana, wild but fragile. Vera held hard to her dream of freedom until the day she saw auburn-haired Polina exchange a wink with one of the basket-lumpers. Saw the girl slip out with him through a side door, under the bored eyes of the female guard. Something about Polina's flirtation with doom brought Tatiana to mind and overrode Vera's caution.

She caught up with the pair in a corridor. The man was hiding something in his hand. 'Polina Nikolaievna,' Vera hissed, 'your absence will be noted. You, comrade,' she urged the man, 'go about your work. You bring danger to us.'

'What's this, a meeting of minds?' Behind them, the guard – not so bored now – drove her baton against the wall. Her uniformed frame blocked their escape. 'Starova and you, whoever you are,' – Polina was new to the laundry crew – 'are you being dirty bitches?'

'We were urging this man to work faster, Comrade Guard.' Vera's voice cracked. Why had she interfered?

'Urging – yes, I bet! *Blyad!*' Whore. 'You,' the guard commanded the male prisoner, 'open your hand.'

Reluctantly, he did so, revealing a corner of wheaten bread, the kind reserved for staff.

They were marched into a yard and in front of their fellows were doused in cold, caustic water and tied to posts. Two days they would stay there. As it was the first week of September they wouldn't freeze as some poor souls had last winter, but the ropes bit into their flesh and as afternoon turned to evening, clouds of midges feasted on them, invading their eyes, nostrils, mouths. Princess Vera Starova survived by retreating into the past. She mentally re-enacted her wedding day, July 1914, and summoned the faces of her loved ones. She even imagined Anoushka, who would have celebrated her fourth birthday... had she lived. Vera knew her child was dead. She'd held the tiny, ice-cold body in her arms.

Katya couldn't sleep. Getting out of bed, she threw a wrap around her shoulders. In the lounge, she opened the window shutters and stared out into the dark, listening to the rain bouncing off the balcony rail. She was still watching as dawn rose, pallid but imbued with the scents of late-summer trees and half-drowned roses. It made her think of Vera who had loved walking on wet grass. So clear was her sister's face, Katya wasn't all that surprised when, a couple of hours later, as she and Harry ate breakfast, the mail brought a new letter from Harry's father. Harald Morten wrote: 'Comrade Yenukidze's office has put before the ruling commissariat the viability of a pardon for the prisoner, Starova.'

Katya put down a corner of toast. 'Why don't they just say "Yes" or "No"?'

Harry looked surprised. 'They're saying "Yes", Katya. The rest of it sets out their terms.'

'This is it, then. We go to Russia.'

He sighed. 'I wish you'd let me do it. If they delay – as they're bound to – we could be stranded as winter sets in.'

'And I have never known a Russian winter? I said before, Harry, it is not "I" but "we".' Katya glanced around her dining room with its bright paintings and modern furniture. 'We'd better start planning for a lengthy absence.'

'In secret,' Harry warned. 'We'll announce our going at the last minute. It makes the goodbyes easier.'

Part Two

Chapter Twelve

Friday, 8 September

There was a myth among Americans that Paris was cheap. Sure, the dollar bought a lot of francs and daily living was inexpensive, but landlords made you pay six months down even if you were only keeping an apartment for three weeks. Regan's miniscule Left Bank flat had cost him most of his available funds.

Thanks to nine days' straight rain, he had nothing like enough material to fulfil his contract. He'd had to cash in his liner ticket and reset his departure date. Today, though, the sun had stayed out for an entire eight hours. Regan had whistled all the way across the river. On the Right Bank, in the Tuileries, he'd run into a pod of nuns who had cheerfully posed for him. Two strolling lovers had agreed to embrace on the Pont des Arts. So enthusiastically that Regan had begun to feel both voyeuristic and not a little envious. The romance of Paris might just be unfurling, like a sweet rose...

The day was now sliding into dusk, café interiors beckoning, but dinner had to wait. Having criss-crossed the Seine all day, Regan was back on the Left Bank, striding past the locked booksellers' chests of Quai de Montebello on his way to the offices of a daily newspaper, *Paris-Jour*, where he had been granted a week's rental of a darkroom.

This was the moment he'd discover if leaving New York to try his luck in Paris had been worth it.

The first proof he developed was the shot of Pont Neuf. It looked sharp under the enlarger, the sky as temperamental as a film star. The girl leaning over the rail added a note of drama. The shot taken from the deck of the barge captured her an eye blink before she'd hurled flowers at him. She was holding them above her shoulder, like Liberty with her torch. 'Liberty with her Missiles'. He had a perverse desire to see her again – though, recalling the man staring after her like a hungry dog, she probably got enough of that kind of attention.

He made proofs then enquired at the newspaper's picture desk where he might buy supplies of developing formula and 'hypo', which was fixing solution. He hadn't brought much in the way of darkroom chemicals from New York in case they leaked on the voyage.

He was told that since the war you needed a permit to buy darkroom fluids. To get a permit, you needed to be an accredited photographer. Getting accreditation took weeks. Or months. Course it did. *Vive la France.*

He strolled back along Quai de Montebello, irritated by this latest setback. Photography was life and death, and that wasn't him being theatrical. As a child of Hell's Kitchen, just about New York's toughest neighbourhood, he'd literally swept his way into his career. Starting out as head broom-handler and errand boy in a small-time photographic studio, he'd graduated to snapping people in the streets. Eventually, he'd got into news journalism, risking his limbs chasing police wagons, snatching scene-of-crime pictures of mobster murders, robberies and suicides. Hardly a day in twenty years when he hadn't taken a picture. In 1917, aged twenty-six, he'd answered the call-up, sailing to France with the American Expeditionary Force. He'd ended the war as a military photographer, which had been his passport when he got home to a staff job on a top newspaper. Finally, a post as editor on a monthly journal, *Era* magazine.

Marrying Janet-Marie Slinfield, whose father owned *Era*, should have set the seal on his achievements. Instead, it had been like being taken into a hall of mirrors where every glass is tilted to capture your shortcomings in enlarged detail. He wished Janet-Marie no ill, but after their divorce her father had sacked him. Regan was climbing back up from the bottom. This Paris junket was supposed to be a new start.

He leaned against the embankment wall to watch the sun sinking into the water. Orange streaks palette-knifed onto a shining canvas. One benefit of Paris was that nobody knew him. A problem with Paris was… ditto. But wait…

A flock of starlings jolted a memory by swooping into a tree below and putting pigeons to flight. He had a friend here. Matthias Boccard, known to all as 'Pigeon' lived on the butte de Montmartre.

'Call any time you're in my city,' Pigeon had insisted. 'You'll find me in my studio or at Mère Richelieu's on Place du Tertre, which some call an artists' café but I call "my dining room".'

Regan had nothing to do tonight, so why not?

Chapter Thirteen

He'd long meant to make this trip up the great Montmartre hill. His landlord had laughed when he'd said so.

'Take a bus or a cab if you do.'

Regan now knew why. The butte was ten hills in one, and Place du Tertre was almost at the top. Still, it was worth heaving lungs and aching calves. Gaslight globes and coloured bulbs strung through acacia boughs made him feel he'd walked in on a gala night. The artists who set up each day under the trees had gone, leaving the square to late diners at outdoor tables. Regan loaded his camera as he spotted a brightly illuminated tree with an iron seat beneath, occupied by a young woman who, curiously, looked to be stuffing hundred-franc notes into an envelope. A pert profile, open coat and cloche hat added piquancy. Cloches were unforgiving to broad faces and double chins, but she had neither. The three-tone click as he took his picture brought her head up. Their eyes met and he braced himself for fury.

'*Hé*, a gentleman asks permission!' As she got to her feet, he saw she was above middle height and had bow-shaped lips. Smiling lips.

From habit, he replied in English. 'When I ask permission, people get self-conscious.'

'And that ruins a good picture? Course it does. The unobserved form speaks clearest.'

She'd answered in English too, and her accent made him feel homesick. 'You sound like a refugee from Queens,' he told her.

'Maybe.'

'You wouldn't know a place called "Mother Richelieu's"?'

She pointed across the square. 'I'm headed there myself. You look just about presentable enough to accompany me, but take off your tie or the clientele will think you've come to inspect the kitchen.'

He did so, rolling the silk tie – a sardonic parting gift from Janet-Marie – into a ball and shoving it in his jacket pocket.

'Am I right, you're from Queens?' he asked as they walked together.

'Hoboken, New Jersey originally, but my family moved to Forest Hills some years back. So yes, I'm a Queens girl.' That put her many rungs above him. Liking well-shod women was a dangerous pastime.

'You?' she asked.

'Most recently? Hudson Street, the meatpacking end.'

She asked his name. 'Dortmeyer...' she echoed. 'I knew people of that name. Leather-goods manufacturers in Elmhurst.'

'No relation I know of.'

'I expect you all came from the same hamlet long, long ago. I'm Una McBride.' She pointed at a rickety building with a hanging sign depicting a wine pitcher. 'There it is, the watering hole of holy Mother Richelieu. Hide your camera, I would.'

'Rough company?'

'Artistic. If they see a lens, they pose like children at a beauty pageant.'

Ducking to avoid cracking his head on the stone lintel, Regan entered a roaring morass. Bearded men in paint-smeared overalls,

women in fur collars and extravagant hats. The air sang with garlic
and herbs. Pipe and cigarette smoke wreathed around the beams. Una
McBride stewarded him towards a group of people clustered next to
a piano. '*Salut, mes braves!*' she shouted. 'Let me introduce a fellow
American, so go gently.'

Ultra-fast French broke over Regan's head. Though he pretty much
got what they were asking him, they weren't listening to the answers.
A wine jug was being passed around. Not the first jug, if he was any
judge. 'Anyone here know Matthias "Pigeon" Boccard?' he asked.

They all knew Pigeon! Was Regan a friend of his?

'We met during the war, when he was sent to photograph us firing
our first shells at the German lines.'

'You were a Sammy?'

'We called ourselves "doughboys". Is Pigeon—'

'You came here to fight, call yourself what you like.' A burly man
threw an arm around him and kissed him on the cheek.

A tumbler of rough, red *pinard* wine was thrust at him. They
wanted to laugh. Shout. Drink. The end of a long day. Same the
world over. Except in America, of course, where Prohibition made
after-hours conviviality an offence. A reason many of his compatriots
fled here. Regan gathered that Pigeon would be in later. Or not. One
took one's chance.

Una steered him to a corner table, retiring briefly to 'powder her
nose'. She returned without her hat, revealing dark blond hair oiled
close to her head with a side parting. From the shoulders up, she could
have passed for a boy. She most definitely was not, proved by a slim
jumper and a knee-length pleated skirt. She had shapely legs.

'More wine?' she asked.

'No thanks.' *Pinard* had been issued to the troops with a generosity Regan's stomach and head still remembered. 'Any hope of a beer? Or coffee?'

She waved to a man collecting glasses and asked for coffee, adding in her fluent French, 'Put in a drop of medicine, will you, Gaston?' She showed her dimples to Regan. 'You'll like it, trust me.'

'I hope so. Tell me about the Hoboken McBrides.'

'"McBride" is my married name. Divorced,' she added quickly. 'I was born Eunice Bigelow, British on my father's side with roots in County Donegal on my mother's. You? "Dortmeyer" is German?'

'My father's name was Ludvic and he liked putting mustard on his fish, so I guess so. He was cagey about his origins. Mom's side, the O'Regans, are third-generation Irish, from County Meath.'

'Big family?' Her mouth turned up mischievously.

'Seven surviving, four girls, three boys. Grandma brought us up after Mom got ill.' If he kept his attention on her lips, he could imagine himself with a movie star. If he glanced at her ultra-short hair, he was suddenly seeing his brother Eric, a Catholic priest in New York. It was disconcerting and Regan changed the subject. 'On holiday or resident?'

Resident since the end of the war, she told him, when her nursing service had ended. 'I sail home now and then, but I always come back. Most Americans stay home and dream of Paris. I do it the other way around. You?' She leaned her chin on the back of her hand. Her irises were honey brown, her lashes carried a lick of mascara. He was aware he was being seduced, at a café table on a black velvet evening. Circumstances so loaded against him, not even his brother Eric would blame him. 'I'm here for a job,' he said, as a reminder to himself. 'I'm a photo-journalist.'

'You don't say.' She looked at the camera hanging over the side of his chair. He'd laid his hat on the table and she turned it over and read the maker's label. 'Bollman. Trade must be good.'

Let her think it. The fedora had been a present from Janet-Marie.

'A good-make hat like that deserves more love than you show it,' she said. 'I know someone who will re-block it and take the dents out. Entrust it to me.'

'No time. I sail home on September 17.'

Their coffee came with bread and a dish of black olives. Regan stirred in sugar, took a mouthful and nearly choked. The brew was fifty per cent bourbon. 'Lady, if that's your medicine, you must have been one hell of a nurse. If you didn't look so innocent, I'd be thinking you were trying to get me drunk.'

Lashes beat over honey. 'Would that be a bad thing?'

'I'm too busy for hangovers.' *Or for affairs.* 'What do you do for a living?' The severe hair hinted 'authoress'. Of oblique novellas with tragic endings. Or perhaps poetry.

'I work in fashion.'

Yeah. He could see that neat little head under a workbench light. 'You got a shop?'

'We call them boutiques here. Guess again.'

'You make clothes.'

'Not if I can help it. I used to put dressmakers and clients together, a sort of fashion midwife. But I've taken a new job, writing a weekly column for a New York syndicate. "Fashion notes from Paris. The freshest news from one who knows." Five hundred words a week, printed in six regional newspapers back home. Impressed?'

'In awe. You live here, on the butte?' She couldn't be much older than his sister Gracie, the youngest of the family.

'I lodge with a friend across the square. A former ballerina. It's an artistic set-up.'

'That so? When I saw you first, you were bundling currency into an envelope. Was that your rent?'

She treated him to a rye-dark study before offering an opinion on his jacket. 'Your sleeves are *that much* too short. I know someone who could let them down for you.'

'Like I said, I'm leaving in just over a week. I'll take it to my tailor in Manhattan.'

She turned away and he jumped as she gave a station porter's whistle to get the attention of a man who had just walked in.

'Pigeon! Over here. I've saved you a chair.'

A figure in a crumpled suit and mashed-down hat of no discernible make was picking his way between tables. A cigarette drooped between unsymmetrical lips. A canvas bag hung across his barrel chest. When seen in profile, Matthias Boccard's nickname made perfect sense.

'*Moment, chérie.*' Pigeon headed for the bar but the tail of his eye caught Regan, and he performed a double take a cabaret comic would have been proud of. He threw his cigarette aside and laughed. 'When did you creep into the country, *mon pot*, and why did they let you?'

'You know what they say: when good Americans die, we come to Paris.'

'Ah, but you assuredly are not good.' A robust embrace followed and Regan was reminded that when Pigeon had visited him in New York, they'd walked eight blocks to find the brand of tarry cigarette he liked. His watch strap dug into Regan's neck, reviving a jarring memory. How Pigeon had acquired that watch was an unresolved episode that revealed another side to the Frenchman's character.

'Not so hungry now, *hé*?' Pigeon looked Regan over. 'The money flows from the news desks, into your pocket?'

'Not really. Change of circumstance. You?'

'These days, I forage in richer soil. I have my little muse to thank for that.' Pigeon sat down beside Una, frowning at her head. 'Ah, *m'amie*, where are your pretty curls?'

'I'm a lady journalist now, so I reached for the pretty scissors.' Una called their waiter. 'Gaston – Pigeon's usual and a carafe of red. You?' she asked Regan.

'Straight bourbon on ice – a double,' he told the waiter, then explained to Pigeon what had brought him to Paris.

'"Eternal Romance"?' Pigeon curled his lip. 'Why do your countrymen imagine we are always falling in love?'

'We don't. We project our yearnings onto you.'

'What is here that you can't get at home?' Pigeon demanded. 'In New York, when was it, two years ago? You and your wife were about to move into an apartment by the park.'

'I don't live there now.' Regan was glad to see the waiter approaching with their drinks, including pastis and water for Pigeon. The pouring of liquor and the clinking of glasses killed the subject.

Una put the last olive in her mouth, delicately extracting the stone. 'Pigeon, darling,' she purred, 'anything for me in your bag?'

'Anything for me in your pocket?'

Una placed an envelope on the table, the one Regan had seen her stuffing earlier.

In turn, Pigeon laid down a shallow box, saying, 'This will be the last for some time.'

As Una opened it, Regan went to stand at her shoulder. What he saw made him reel.

Fashion shots. 'Pigeon?'

Pigeon grunted. 'I told you, I have moved to better pastures. Following the money.'

The prints were of aloof-looking girls. The racehorse type that graced Janet-Marie's couture journals, and what they wore, even Regan could see, was no five-and-dime schmutter. 'Let me guess,' he said as Una's banknotes disappeared into Pigeon's pocket. 'A fashion palace commissions you to photograph the new season's line. You give this lady a preview, for a small consideration.'

Pigeon did not deny it.

'Monsieur Dortmeyer,' Una said, fluttering her lashes, 'I daresay you were not averse to a tip-off in your time? You'd take a phone call from a friendly police lieutenant, giving you first dibs on a fight? Letting you know that some low-down dive was to be raided. And you happened to turn up with your camera, by magic, so to speak.'

'I guess.' She'd made her point.

She suggested they order dinner. 'It's only ever a one-pot meal, but good.'

'Fine,' he said. And it was delicious, casseroled hare and an enormous pot of steamed potatoes. Over a dessert of plum tart, Regan got his first sight of a woman smoking a cheroot. A Creole singer who accompanied herself on a piano covered in wine-glass rings, her voice like melon juice over gravel. Her rendition of 'Margie' sent Regan straight home to the 142nd Street club where he'd lived for a while after Janet-Marie threw him out. She delivered 'Oh, Daddy' a cappella directly to him, then came to drape her arms around Pigeon and Una, and blew smoke rings. Regan took a picture that would feature in a book he didn't yet know he was going to write. The next hour changed his life.

*

Over the cheese course, Regan asked Pigeon where to buy supplies.
'Developer and hypo is harder to get here than liquid gold.'

Pigeon nodded. 'For most, but I'm swimming in it. Manufacturers
send it for free so they can put my name in their sales brochures.
Where are you working?' When Regan answered that he was renting
a darkroom by the hour, Pigeon looked appalled. 'What happens if
you run out of time while your prints are still in their bath?'

'I make sure I don't.'

'Photography cannot be done by the clock.' Pigeon cut a wide
triangle of camembert. His appetite was prodigious. 'Use my studio,
mon pot. It's right next door. There's running water and a couch.' He
winked. 'Keep it warm while I'm away.'

'You're leaving?'

'Hell, when?' Una, cutting grapes off a bunch, looked as though
she'd been slapped.

'Tomorrow,' Pigeon told her, unconcerned. 'I am invited to
Havana. That's in Cuba.'

'I know where it is. How long for?'

Pigeon shrugged. 'Until I am bored and decide to come home.'

'What about that commission for *Ravissante* with Javier? You can't
miss that!'

'*Tant pis.*' Too bad. 'I leave at first light.'

Una looked shaken. 'You can't do this to me. Oh, you'll be fine,
they'll just say it's Pigeon being capricious.' She turned to Regan.
'*Ravissante* is a top fashion journal, using photography in a really
interesting way. None of the usual simpering editorial mush either,

and I *so* want to write for it. I set up this shoot at Maison Javier and if Pigeon doesn't deliver, the editor will never take my calls again.'

Pigeon complained that Una had pressed the job on him. 'My travel plans are a perfect excuse not to be in the same room as that so-called princess.'

'You mean Katya Morten? She's lovely and she *is* a princess!'

'Her sister, Tatiana. A self-important minx who gives minxes a bad name.' Pigeon swallowed his drink and shouted to Gaston for another. 'Two weeks ago, I was booked to cover a *vernissage*. A private view at a gallery,' he explained to Regan. 'It was the place to be seen. Everyone wanted to be in my pictures. Except *la princesse* Tatiana who turned her back. "Your camera strips a little more from me each time," she wailed. "What are you?" I asked. "A primitive tribeswoman who believes her soul is captured on the negative?" Though I told her that she was right. "One day you will be nothing and nobody will want to photograph you."'

'Promise me you didn't!' Una looked aghast.

Pigeon watched his pastis turn cloudy as he diluted it, as if seeing the miracle for the first time. 'You should not have given my name to *Ravissante*.'

'Who owns "Ravishing"?' Regan was not enjoying being middleman.

'Slinfield & Gish.' Una sounded breathless with vexation. 'Big dollars behind it.'

Regan smiled coldly. 'That's my ex-wife's father's publishing company.'

Una's eyes grew round. 'Lemuel Slinfield is your—'

'*Was* my father-in-law, so don't get hopeful. Seriously though… Lemuel, getting into fashion?'

'I told you, it's where the money is now.' Pigeon turned his glass in his fingers, an idea visibly taking root in his eyes. 'Why not take the job, Regan? Go to Maison Javier and photograph beauty.'

'I don't fit in fancy places,' Regan answered. 'I can't tiptoe nicely.'

Pigeon knocked back his drink. 'Una can fix it for you.'

'Oh, can she?' Una was still fuming.

'I don't do fashion,' Regan hung on stubbornly. 'And what about Princess Thingummy, sounds like she'd make sparks.'

'Sparks are good,' Pigeon insisted. 'The angrier you make Tatiana Vytenis, the better the picture. Call it a favour to me, in exchange for using my premises. You could employ my assistant while I'm away. I don't pay him much, a little teaching and his lunch. Say yes.'

Maybe it was the bourbon, but the idea suddenly appealed to Regan. A visit to a classy salon surely fitted the banner of 'The Eternal Romance of Paris'.

'What's the fee?'

Pigeon named it, Regan mentally converted it to dollars. Not bad. It would make up for the time he'd spent splashing through puddles. 'How about it, Mam'zelle McBride?'

Una threw up her hands. 'All right. But you'd better be good. And please, don't ever say "Mam'zelle" here. You're not a doughboy now.'

The following day, Una made the necessary phone calls and Regan had his first commission as a fashion photographer. 'Tuesday, 12 September,' she told him. She was the first visitor to call on him in Pigeon's studio. 'Set up in time for the afternoon parade.'

'Horses and a brass band?'

'Fashion parade. Girls in frocks.'

Chapter Fourteen

On the day of the shoot, Tatiana lounged at her dressing table, listening to fugitive piano phrases from the salon below. Her dresser was waiting to help her into her first outfit. Constanza, seated beside her brushing on mascara, threw a searching glance. 'Are you all right?'

'Fine,' Tatiana answered.

'Only, you've been touchy since you visited that doctor.'

It was true. Tatiana had withdrawn into herself since her visit to Quai de l'Horloge. Polite but distant, always too busy to join Constanza for an after-work glass of champagne at the Ritz Bar on Place Vendôme. The shock of Dr Jolivet's examination and diagnosis still vibrated through her. Pregnant. It had to be Armand's. The dates matched and Gérard had always been so scrupulously careful. Pregnant by her fiancé's brother. Her sole focus was to prevent anyone guessing while she figured out what to do. She wasn't showing yet, but then, she wasn't eating enough to keep a sparrow alive. She'd dropped Jolivet's list of 'healthy' foods into the river. Liver. Rare beef. Milk and goat's cheese. The mere thought… She spent whole days battling nausea.

And thinking of her feet clamped in those stirrups still gave her cramp. Constanza began a question but Tatiana picked up a hairbrush, using it to flatten her curls so she could fit a tight velvet cap on her head. The cap matched the cocktail dress she was wearing for her first appearance, and made her look like a novice nun, all eyes. Cheekbones sharp as fish fins. Thirty-eight days to her wedding. Until Jolivet, she'd been longing for that day with spiritual ardour. Now she simply needed it to come. She didn't remember leaving his consulting room. She must have walked downstairs and put on her coat and scarf in the lobby. She'd left her umbrella behind. She didn't remember going out into the rain, though she did recall a flower seller stepping in front of her.

'Madame, *s'il vous plaît*? Beautiful blooms, half price.'

She must have opened her bag, taken out money. Had to have done in order to have hurled the flowers off Pont Neuf at that scabrous, laughing photographer.

Horrible man. Horrible day. Thirty-eight to go until her wedding. An age in which to hold on to a secret.

'Princess?' Her dresser was at her shoulder.

'Give me a second.' Tatiana reached for a glass of water, spilling some on her robe because her hands were shaking. If Gérard found out, she'd be on her own. He'd not touch her with another man's child inside her, brother or not.

'Princess Tatiana! Suzy and Françoise will be through the door in two ticks.'

On cue, they came in and eased off their high T-bar shoes to give their toes a moment's freedom. Tatiana stood and raised her hands and her dresser dropped a knee-length dress of velvet-flocked taffeta over her head. She went downstairs to the antechamber where she paced, her heart matching the syncopated beat of 'Sparkle Shoe Rag'.

Larissa joined her, and moving close so an assistant standing by with sewing kit and clothes brushes would not hear, asked if Tatiana had spoken with Katya today.

'No. Should I have done?'

Larissa looked grave. 'Your brother-in-law, Monsieur Morten, has been to her office twice. I overheard him mentioning train tickets and passports. Is it happening? The trip, I mean?'

'Trip?' Tatiana dragged her attention away from her troubles. 'What are you saying?'

'Perhaps I shouldn't have spoken.'

'Wait.'

Larissa's words touched on an incident a couple of nights ago when Katya's housekeeper, Madame Roche, had called at rue Rembrandt, asking to see the travelling trunks the family had brought with them from Moscow. Katya needed one, she explained. After Yana had lugged the trunks down from the top floor, grumbling loudly, the housekeeper had selected the most battered of them and a pair of dusty carpet bags. Her explanation: 'Madame says one cannot get quality luggage like this any longer.'

Quality? Perhaps they had been, back in the last century. Katya and Harry could easily afford monogrammed luggage from Hermès. There was something fishy going on, and Tatiana's voice was sharp as she asked Larissa, 'Are you telling me they're leaving Paris?'

'I have no reason to think so.' The guilty look on Larissa's face gainsaid it.

An assistant came up just then to whisper, 'You know there's a photographer in the salon today, Princess Tatiana?'

'No! Oh God, why did nobody warn me? Who is it?'

'I think it's Pigeon Boccard. I recognised the lad, his assistant, carrying equipment in.'

'It can't be Pigeon,' Tatiana declared. 'He doesn't do fashion.'

'I heard he did work for Molyneux recently,' Larissa commented. 'You don't like him?'

'He hates me, that's the point.' Tatiana wanted to throw herself to the floor. Let Pigeon but catch a hint of her pregnancy, he'd train his lens on her out of malice. They said the camera never lied. On impulse, she took the tray and water glasses from a side table. It was an ultra-modern Bakelite set, tall glasses and a jug painted to look like tortoiseshell. A perfect accessory for disguising a waistline. She tipped the water into a vase of flowers.

By the time she stepped into the candlelit salon, the pianist was playing her signature tune, Scott Joplin's 'A Real Slow Drag'. Tatiana felt a breeze against her face as she sashayed to the music, trying to locate Pigeon. It was vital she avoided giving him a sideways view. When a flash exploded in front of her, she dropped her tray. Laughter spurted from the audience. She scrabbled to retrieve the glasses, which, thanks to the miracle of Bakelite, were unbreakable. Spots danced before her eyes.

What the devil? To get that intense brightness, magnesium powder had to be ignited. The vapours got in your throat. Now she understood why the windows were open.

The *directrice* coughed and began her commentary on Tatiana's outfit: 'A smart little dress for the newly fashionable cocktail hour…'

'Or the fashionable cocktail waitress,' said somebody in the audience.

Where was Pigeon? Tatiana could see Benjy Crouch, the pianist, his starched cuffs chalk-white in the gloom. And there was Pigeon's assistant, the taciturn adolescent they'd christened 'Petit-Pigeon'. The lad was pouring flash chemicals into a jar. At the end of the catwalk, Tatiana posed briefly, then turned. Pigeon couldn't train his lens on a moving subject. Last time they'd met, she'd tried to make him understand her growing discomfort at being photographed, only she'd sounded pretentious. A mannequin who hated to have eyes on her? Absurd. *Look at me, don't look at me.* No excuse for his retort, though. 'You'll end up a failure. Nobody will want to photograph you…'

Good God. Was that him, lying on his belly *on* the grand piano? Actually lying on the spruce-wood apron, his camera obscuring his face? How had he got up there? With his drinker's girth, he'd probably have to be lifted off again. The boy, Petit-Pigeon, had his fresh jar of magnesium powder ready. Any second now.

The flash didn't come. Waiting for her to come closer? All right. She ran lightly forward. A couple of paces from the piano she balanced on her right foot, her left leg raised to spread the kite-shaped panels of her skirt. Lifting her arms, she crossed her wrists to create the sylph outline Rosa had taught her. The pose flattened her stomach completely.

The three-tone click wasn't Pigeon's usual shutter signature. The intense flash left spider legs on Tatiana's retinas. As she blinked away the after-glare, the *directrice* declaimed, 'See the long, slender bodice, designed as a foil to a deceptively full skirt. A dress stolen from fairyland, bestowed upon Princess Tatiana.'

'Princess Tatiana? Well I'll be,' came from behind the camera. 'New film, please, kid.'

This wasn't Pigeon, who chewed out his French and never said please. Tatiana ordered the lights to be turned on.

'Keep 'em off,' responded a masculine voice.

She'd heard that voice before.

Petit-Pigeon was preparing another flash. 'No more, I've had enough.' Expecting the lights to come on instantly, Tatiana was perturbed when her command was ignored.

'Will someone bring me a pair of candles?' came that deep, staccato voice. 'Yup, you honey, in the black. Fetch them over and stand behind the fairy princess.' It was said in French, but in such inventive idiom Tatiana's mouth dropped. She regained her poise.

'Monsieur, didn't you hear? I said, no more pictures.'

'I heard you, doll.' He was more interested in the saleswoman, the *vendeuse*, approaching with candles. 'That's it, bring them closer, Mademoiselle.'

'She is "Mademoiselle" and I am "doll"? Where did you learn your French?' Tatiana demanded.

'You don't want to know. Closer with the candles,' he told the *vendeuse*. 'I want this lady lit up, like she's wearing a halo.'

'You want me to catch fire?' Tatiana was aware of breaking the sacred rule of *hush* in the salon. Mannequins were the sleek conveyors of desires and, as with any expensive transport, the wheels were not expected to squeak. 'Whoever you are, I won't go up in flames for your benefit. Where's Pigeon?'

'On his way to Cuba. Why are you holding a tray of drinks?'

Behind her, the *directrice* murmured, 'Tatiana. Princess, if you please? The clients… the parade… the reputation of the house.'

The photographer climbed off the piano, his camera lodged against his ribs. 'You look familiar.'

'And you look like the stuffed bear outside the curiosity shop on rue Jacob. Except he speaks better French. Take another picture and I will have you barred from every couture house, every magazine in Paris.' When a throaty chuckle came back, Tatiana hurled the contents of her tray at the man's head.

He dodged.

The English pianist took the full force and stopped playing in disgust. The photographer gave a signal, the magnesium lamp flashed, the camera clicked. Finally, someone turned on the house lights.

Tatiana reached for the edge of the piano and found the photographer's arm instead. 'I thought so! You're the *voyou* on the boat!'

He said in English, 'I should have guessed you'd work somewhere like this.' *Shoulda guessed.*

'How did you get past the doorkeeper?'

'On my two legs. It's all legit.'

'I don't believe that, any more than I believe Pigeon has gone abroad. He'll be at his cottage by the river at Barbizon, getting drunk.'

'Is there a problem?' Katya came from the far end of the salon. She must have slipped in through a staff door, and gave the impression of being summoned from something important.

'A little misunderstanding,' the *directrice* insisted. 'A creative difference between Princess Vytenis and this… this new, er—'

'"Man" will do,' the photographer cut in. 'You French don't really have a word for "gentleman". I'm not one, anyway. And our disagreement sure is creative.'

'Monsieur Dortmeyer?' Katya Morten put out her hand. She was wearing one of the jacket-blouses and draped skirts she'd made prominent this season, reflecting her passion for spice colours, gold and topaz. Owing to Harry's ability to ship in fabrics from India and Indo-China, Katya had stolen a march on rival houses still struggling with post-war shortages of textiles and dye. A string of unpolished amber beads tumbled to her waist, linking the colours to her corn-blond, upswept hair. 'Una McBride spoke highly of you and I'm so pleased you could fit us in.'

'Never trust a photographer with space in his diary,' Tatiana sniffed.

Katya ignored her. 'I apologise for not being on hand to greet you, but… Ah, here's Monsieur Roland Javier. May I introduce you to each other? Roland…' Katya turned to the dark-complexioned man in his middle thirties who had come from the back row to join them. 'This is Regan Dortmeyer, who has stepped in for Pigeon after he was called away.'

'To his country wine store,' Tatiana said with authority.

Roland added his thanks to Katya's and said in his Spanish-accented French, 'I trust you were given every help, Monsieur Dortmeyer?'

'Sure, but call me Regan. "Monsieur Dortmeyer" sounds like a dollar-a-cut barber shop trying for better clientele.'

'You are American, yes?' Roland inclined his sleekly pomaded head. 'It is the thing in artistic circles to reduce oneself to a single name: "Mistinguette", "Colette", "Tatiana".' He slanted a mischievous smile. 'Perhaps one day, I will declare I am to be only "Javier". But we are keeping our audience waiting.'

The parade continued. Tatiana showed dresses, suits and autumn coats, and no more pictures were taken of her. When, at the end of the show, she came out in the bridal gown, the air was tangy with magnesium particles. She coughed pointedly, though there was an upside. Lilliane couldn't orate with a handkerchief pressed to her mouth. Tatiana turned and preened, velvet and silk chiffon flowing around her until it hit her that she'd forgotten her condition. Thinking about it instantly brought the misery back.

'How about one last frame with the lights fully on?' Katya asked when their clients had left. 'It's not every day we have a photographer in, and I'd like a picture to show—' she broke off.

'Who?' Tatiana swung her gaze on Katya. Arrows shot between green eyes and blue. When Katya shook her head, Tatiana dug in. 'Larissa let slip that you're going away.'

Katya said quietly, 'I'll explain later.'

So it was true. Her sister was abandoning her. Feelings welled up. Tatiana's habitual release valve for pressure was to yell or throw something – though she'd done that already with little result. She felt so weak. Her stomach was cramping. So painful, it ravelled up her breath. She did the only safe thing: lay down on the catwalk and let tears pool from the sides of her eyes. Nothing to blot them with but her veil, and she wouldn't risk damaging the fragile fabric. This, after all, was to be her wedding gown. In thirty-eight days. She shut her eyes and listened to Katya hastily explaining to the staff, 'Tatiana is feeling faint, please carry on,' and opened them only when she heard the scrape of a chair.

Regan Dortmeyer was bringing her a seat. Her loathing lost a little of its intensity. Until she saw him climb on it.

'Are there any barrels you will not scrape?' Rosa had taught her some pithy English idioms.

'Drama lies in the unexpected, don't you think?' Only he said *doncha*. 'You put me in mind of the bartered bride who throws herself in front of the marriage broker.'

'Or a dead body.'

'Trust me, for a time, bodies were my speciality and you're prettier than most.'

The click of the shutter release covered her response which was not one the salon often heard. She tried to get up but hadn't the strength.

A hand closed over hers, hauling her up. Tatiana detected a waft of Hungary water. He was anything but smart and she'd expected stale sweat. A good smell didn't mean he could keep his hand over hers, however. She shook loose. Knifing pain – she doubled over. Would have fallen but was scooped up and carried out of the salon. She didn't struggle. So much in her life was beyond repair, she decided not to humour the gasping, tittering salesgirls.

She was set down on a sofa in the antechamber. Someone gave a little shriek – a young, inexperienced dresser by the sound of it. Had the girl never seen a man before?

'He isn't staying,' Tatiana groaned. 'Will you fetch me a glass of very cold water?'

'With lemon, Princess?'

'No, nothing sharp.' She drew up her legs like a colicky infant. Where had this pain come from?

Hunkering in front of her, Regan tilted her chin to inspect her. He had eyes as dark as Roland's, with a chip of denser black at their heart. Deep-set, and with such thick lashes he might have been accused of employing mascara had he been less male. His hair was an untamed mass of blue-black curls, no trace of oil for the popular drawing-room style of the day. The sort of hair combs got stuck in. He'd joked about a dollar-a-cut barber shop earlier, but it must have been a while since he'd entered one.

'Been fainting like this a lot?'

'I'm tired. You may not believe it, but this job is hard.'

'On the feet, sure.'

'It was my feet that gave way.'

'And that's all?' He was absorbing every inch of her face. 'You went pale then crossed your hands over your stomach. I got four sisters. I'll tell you their names some other time.'

'There won't be another time.'

'The younger two made it through school, but Vicky and Elsie…'
He shook his head. 'They found trouble like ducks find water and that
was when they came looking for their bossy brother. So if you need a
shoulder any time…' He patted his. 'It's kinda solid.'

Tatiana thought how good it would feel to crumble against it. But
it was the wrong shoulder. She reached for the water the girl brought
her, turning her face away. As clear a dismissal as anything.

She heard him say, 'Message understood.'

And then he was gone, leaving nothing but the memory of Hungary
water and a card which she hadn't seen him take out. It read 'Regan
Dortmeyer Photographic' followed by a New York address. That part
had been crossed through and '*Place du Tertre, 18ième*. À côté de la
Mère Richelieu' written to the side. Tatiana drank her water, her face
contorting because the girl had put lemon juice in it after all. It hardly
mattered. Her world had shrunk to a single, all-encompassing question:
If a total stranger was close to guessing her secret, what would Gérard
see next time he looked?

'Tatiana?' It was the *directrice*. 'Your sister asks, could you please
go to her office?'

Chapter Fifteen

As Katya shut her office door, her amber beads looped around the handle, giving her a few seconds' grace while she disentangled them. Having sent for Tatiana, she had crossed the courtyard to the single-storey building which housed the company's design ateliers and offices. This building occupied one side of Cour du Comte, a historic courtyard off rue Duphot. The salon, reception desk and *cabine* had recently relocated to the other side of the yard, to a building that had been the headquarters of Harry's firm until he moved to bigger premises south of the river.

Freeing her beads, she turned to the two people already seated. Roland was fiddling with his cuffs. Their director of manufacturing, Pauline Frankel, sat with her knees pressed together, clearing her throat to keep in questions that clearly wanted to jump out.

Katya pre-empted them both. 'I too am apprehensive about Tatiana. Actually, I'm downright worried.'

Roland let his cufflinks alone. 'Madame Markova says she never eats any of the snacks prepared for the mannequins, but drinks only water or herbal teas.'

'She's always been a picky eater.'

'She isn't eating anything, Katya.' Roland gave a growl. 'This mania of today, to be thin as knitting needles!'

Pauline Frankel nodded. 'I see it all the time, ladies whose measurements used to be ample are starving themselves to skin and bone.'

'Then perhaps we should stop designing clothes for figures without hips or bosoms,' Katya said dryly. But she hadn't called this meeting to discuss the modern malaise of dieting. This was about her sister and the immediate future. She weighed her words, unsure if she had the right to say them at all. 'To understand Tatiana, you need to know something about her.'

Outside the door, Tatiana listened tensely.

She heard her sister say, 'You know that I and my family were forced to flee Moscow in November of 1918. We came to Paris by train and ship, with only what we could carry, trusting we'd find safety. What I have never told you is that days before we left Moscow, the police stormed our home.' Katya explained that the counter-revolutionary police, known in Russia as the Cheka, were nothing like French *gendarmes*, who were by and large reasonable. The Cheka recruited zealots, often violent thugs, who took pleasure in brutalising and murdering suspected enemies of the state. 'They burst in on us. It was breakfast time, but they were already drunk.'

Tatiana swallowed. She knew what was coming.

Katya found her voice again. 'They murdered our father as he tried to defend us. Bludgeoned and stabbed him with bayonets. It was senseless and inhuman. My mother was forced to watch, as was I and my eldest sister Vera who was clutching her baby, Anoushka, who was then a newborn.'

'What of Tatiana?' That was Roland, speaking with intense pity.

'She darted into the window bay as the police came into the breakfast parlour, behind the curtains, shaking in terror.'

'Paralysed in terror' was a truer description, Tatiana silently corrected. She'd stood motionless, as though liquid gum had set inside her.

Katya continued, 'After they'd killed Papa, they dragged Vera away. I can never shut out her screams, nor those of her baby. I think it was worse for Tatiana because she heard all but saw nothing. Her mind recreates the scene in nightmares. She's still trapped.'

'Or still hiding?' Tatiana heard Roland sigh. 'My dear Katya, how will it help your sister for you to go away at this time?'

So, it was true and they'd been told already. Tatiana hardly heard Pauline's observation. 'You and your husband have had no honeymoon since you married, and you've hardly stopped working since, so we understand your desire to get away. But to turn to us as you did this lunchtime and say, "I'm off next week"—'

Tatiana stumbled into the room. 'Katya? You and Harry will be back in time for my wedding?' When her sister replied with an awkward grimace, her anguish flared. 'Say you will!'

'I don't think we can be.'

'You have to!' Tatiana had only four people to call 'family'. Her mother, Anoushka, Katya and Harry. She needed them on that day, buffering her against myriad Sainte-Vierges. Pauline spoke again, airing very different objections.

'The midseason collection has yet to be pulled together and next year's spring–summer needs to be started or we'll lag behind schedule. Roland cannot do it all alone. And what about our publicity campaigns, and the retail buyers? You deal with them so well, Katya. All that will fall on us and it isn't our métier.'

Roland agreed. 'We would need a replacement "you". But can we afford it?'

'Somebody else should take over from me temporarily.' Katya's eye moved cautiously. Her colleagues followed its direction.

'Tatiana?' Incredulity reduced Roland's voice to a croak.

'Why not?' Katya replied, though a blush hit her cheeks. 'My family owns a third of Maison Javier's shares, after all.'

Pauline's manner became crisp. 'The same Tatiana who lay down on the catwalk in the bridal gown? The Tatiana who comes late to work having been delayed by a lunchtime tryst with her lover?'

'Husband-to-be,' Tatiana corrected fiercely. 'But I take your point and I don't know whether to have hysterics or to laugh. I'm a mannequin, not a manager.'

But Katya wasn't giving up. 'Why shouldn't you take a bigger role, Tatiana? When I pick up the telephone to the store buyers, they always ask after you. Everyone knows you.'

'They adore Tatiana as a mannequin,' Roland pitched in. 'We adore her too until she loses her temper and throws things.'

'I am told she hurled a laden tea tray at Monsieur Dortmeyer,' Pauline said severely, 'and it hit our pianist.'

'A very small tray,' Tatiana amended. 'And there was no liquid involved.'

'Had it been glass, I shudder to think what the result would have been.'

Katya soldiered on. 'Give my sister a serious job and you'll see a different person. And really, what damage can she do with you two alongside?'

Stern silence was the clear reply. A member of staff bringing in canapés and a carafe of wine was Pauline and Roland's chance to politely excuse themselves.

Katya slumped on a vacated chair. 'I handled that badly.'

'Where are you going? And why now?'

'To England first, because Harry needs to meet his factory managers over there.'

'Let him go on his own. If you leave, things will fall apart. Pauline runs the sewing ateliers brilliantly, but she is no businesswoman. As for Roland, he lives and breathes couture, but he'll forget to pay the suppliers, or put in the fabric orders and then, the night before the collection show, he'll have a spectacular breakdown and declare they're the wrong colour, weight and texture.'

Katya pulled a painful frown. 'From England, we're going to Sweden to stay with Harry's father and stepmother. Their little boy is growing up. Harry has never seen his half-brother.'

'Little prince Morten takes precedence over this business and our livelihoods?'

'Don't be bitchy. Oh, please eat something, Tatiana. Your hands are shaking.' Katya pushed a tray of canapés at Tatiana who gave them a famished glance. Biscuits dressed with smoked fish and dots of caviar, frilled with salad leaves and matchstick vegetables, the kind of light snack she loved. Except that her gorge rose at the fishy smell. She lurched from her chair, groping for the doorknob. In Cour du Comte, one hand against the wall of the building, she filled her lungs with evening air, driving down the desire to retch. Hearing Katya calling, full of concern, she hurried out into rue Duphot and kept going.

She bumped into Constanza. A soft collision, as Constanza was swathed in a coat of ivory cashmere, its collar touching the brim of her cloche hat. The bump to her nose seemed larger without the thick frame of her hair.

She gaped at Tatiana. 'Darling? I was at the Ritz Bar, only I left my door keys on my dressing table. You didn't fancy it?'

'I wasn't—' Tatiana tried to say 'asked' but out came a gagging sound. She pressed her hand to her mouth. 'Oh God, Conny, I'm in a terrible fix.'

Constanza found a clean handkerchief and, as Tatiana clamped it to her mouth, signalled to a taxi driver who was setting down a fare at a restaurant opposite. 'Drive around for half an hour,' Constanza instructed, ushering Tatiana into the rear seat. Once they were in motion, tucked behind motorbuses on rue Saint-Honoré, she squeezed Tatiana's fingers and the ruby ring dug in. 'You're with child. Shall we cut through the nonsense?'

Tatiana nodded. 'How did you know?'

'Call it female intuition. How many weeks?'

'Fifteen, sixteen.'

Constanza sucked a whistle through her teeth. 'Whose? Gérard's of course.'

'No – Armand's. I'm pretty certain.'

'The beast. He deserves… I won't say what I think he deserves. You have told Gérard, naturally?'

'Are you mad?' Tatiana snatched her hand back. 'What are you doing? Oh – don't!' Constanza was counting on her fingers.

'Say you're at fifteen weeks now, you'll be in your fifth month by your wedding. A visibly pregnant bride. You have to tell Gérard or the next time you take your clothes off in front of him, he'll see for himself.'

'I'm not taking my clothes off,' Tatiana hissed. 'I won't share his bed before the wedding.'

'Bit late for that. Virginity doesn't grow back, you know. And say you manage to fool him, what about the wedding night itself? Or do you intend to keep your figure by starving? That's a death knell for you and the baby. Even if Gérard is too spectacularly short-sighted to guess, his mother will and I wouldn't put it past the old crow to stand up in front of the wedding guests and denounce you.'

Their driver turned into Place Vendôme, where patrician terraces matched the grandeur of the principal building, the Ritz. The first time Tatiana, her mother and sister had been inside that hotel, they'd been in no position to pay the bill. She hadn't known at the time. Katya had spared her the worry. How would she fare without her sister over the coming weeks?

'I don't know what else to do, except pretend it's all a dreadful dream.'

'Confess to Gérard, marry quickly or call it all off.'

'It isn't my choice, Constanza. None of this was my choice.'

'Tell him that! It isn't as though you knowingly went with a stranger, it was his brother's heinous conduct that landed you in this fix. Likely, the baby will look like Gérard anyway, so who else need know?'

Tatiana shook her head violently. 'You don't know him, Constanza. When Gérard's set his mind to something, he does not deviate. Honour and respectability are his gods, and I will be damaged goods. He'll turn me away.' She couldn't stem her misery, and wept into her hands. Marriage to Gérard was the only light in her life. Once she was his wife, her nightmares would stop.

'In that case...' Constanza tapped on the screen behind the driver's head. She gestured for the man to make another circuit of Place Vendôme. 'Desperate measures are needed.'

Chapter Sixteen

Stepping over the threshold of home, Tatiana paused as she always did. Should she brace herself for an onslaught, a scolding or both? Anoushka lived for the moment her 'Tatie-Tatya' came home, racing up for cuddles. Yana would follow as escort vessel, rarely failing to criticise Tatiana's appearance, or complain about the cook, or the latest domestic ruction.

Tatiana's mother, Irina, would also vie for Tatiana's attention, eager to offload the minutiae of her day. Anoushka's babble, Irina's weary monotone and Yana's pronouncements sometimes reached the pitch of a modern, polyphonic symphony.

But as she stood in the hallway, silence. Mama and Anoushka might be strolling in Parc Monceau, forty steps from the front door of their building. Yana would doubtless be with them, driving away strangers and acquaintances alike.

Their daily cook had likely slipped home for a rest before returning to prepare the evening meal. Tatiana swept her eye across the hall table. Two letters, one from Gérard which she opened feverishly. A couple of lines, letting her know that he was off to a conference in Bordeaux. Regional trade. Sadly, he must suspend their dinner date the following night. Tatiana felt a guilty relief. Kissing the letter, she caught a drift of his cologne. Thirty-eight days.

The second was from Katya, which her sister must have hand-delivered on her way home.

'If I upset you earlier, I ask pardon. We must talk tomorrow.' *Must* was underlined.

The kitchen was empty, a covered pan on the stove containing soup. There was a cold joint of meat on a slate under a muslin tent. Tatiana turned her back on the meat and stood at the sink, downing tumblers of cold water until the nausea subsided.

Constanza had prescribed three ingredients that would encourage her womb to contract and eject her baby. That was what desperate measures meant.

Tatiana went into the lavatory, locked the door and clenched her fists. Over the last few weeks, releasing urine had been painful. She blamed Dr Jolivet's awful contraption. She hadn't been right since lying on his couch. Whenever she got over-anxious, the burning redoubled. And tonight it was excruciating.

Afterwards, she ran a bath. Warm water eased the soreness. Opening the medicine cabinet, she located the Sirop Roze which her mother took for pollen allergy, insomnia, headaches... everything, really. Tatiana swallowed straight from the bottle. Its light-pink colour belied its potency. By the time she'd bathed, let out the water and retired to lie on her bed, sedation was washing through her. In her bedroom with its cream carpet and honey-blond curtains, she reread what Constanza had scribbled down before the taxi dropped her off.

Ruta graveolens.

The herb rue was familiar to Tatiana as a bitter tea. A long-ago governess had brewed it as a treatment for mouth ulcers and dandruff. It could be bought from the apothecary on nearby Boulevard Malesherbes where Tatiana went to buy razors for hair removal, as well as her mother's Sirop Roze. Rue was the herbal expellant, to be taken with the second ingredient. Gin. The third ingredient…

She fell asleep, dreaming she was on a river bridge. Armand de Sainte-Vierge was below her on a barge, cradling a baby in his arms. He wanted to hurl the infant into the Seine and she was pleading with him, except her voice was reduced to a tiny rasp. He was laughing, mocking her. A knock saved her from knowing the ending. She sat up to see Yana peering in.

'You are here,' the maid informed her. A white 'babushka' scarf framed Yana's face, making her full cheeks collide with her turned-down smile. 'You have used all the hot water. I know because *this* is expert.' Yana tapped the broad tip of her nose. A nose capable of sonorous snores, as Tatiana knew having shared train compartments and hotel rooms with her during their escape from Moscow. 'Always, I know if you have been in a room, your perfume is so strong.' Yana made her accusations in Russian. She had enough French to navigate her way round Paris's markets and shops, but any more smacked to her of surrender, and she always spoke Russian at home. 'Why are you sleeping?'

'I wish you'd wait to be invited in before opening my door. Did you go to the park?' Tatiana longed to flop back down. Weak, muddled, hungry.

Yana answered with another question. 'Why is the medicine cabinet open in the bathroom? I went to fetch Anoushka's cod liver oil. Inside are many things dangerous to a child.'

'Anoushka's far too small to reach to that cupboard,' Tatiana replied. 'But you're right. I should have been more careful.'

'You are ill?' Yana pulled off her headscarf, uncovering a braid of greying hair. She approached the bed. She wore a red, ankle-length pinafore dress over a gathered blouse. Despising French fashion as much as the language, she had adapted the clothes she'd travelled in from Moscow. During the day, a voluminous apron protected her dress and its absence was a sure sign that she'd been taking the air, or had been to the Orthodox cathedral, a twenty-minute walk across the park. A three-bar crucifix around her neck suggested that had been her mission.

'What is this?' Yana picked up Constanza's note. '"Ru-ta",' she read. Yana had learned the Roman alphabet at the insistence of the cook following some spectacular mistakes with shopping lists. 'For what is Ruta?'

'It's a salve. My hands are dry.'

Yana inspected Tatiana's hands, sniffing, 'Soft as milk.' She displayed her own square ones. The nail beds were ragged because she bit them. 'In Moscow, your sister swore I would never have to skivvy again.'

'You don't skivvy. You're a nursery maid with one, small child to care for.'

'Katya promised, "In Paris you will have a bedroom overlooking a park." It was a solemn vow.'

'Given before you abandoned us, taking all our money and papers. Have you forgotten?'

Yana gave a sneer, as if only she really knew the truth. 'You look feverish. Too much heat in you.'

Jolted into a confession, Tatiana admitted, 'When I pass water it… it hurts.'

'Acid on raw flesh?' Yana placed a hand on Tatiana's brow. 'Perhaps you have what is called "bride's disease", from enjoying the pleasures of marriage before the ring is on the finger. You must visit the family doctor.'

At Tatiana's brusque, 'No,' Yana nodded. 'I will bring you something after I have put Anoushka to bed. Cook is back and will serve dinner soon.'

After lying for a while curled like a shrimp, Tatiana got up and chose a suitable dress for an evening at home – dark-blue satin lined with brushed cotton, loose-fitting and comforting. On her way to the drawing room, she heard splashing from the bathroom and put her head around the door. Anoushka sat amid bubbles, all pink skin and steamy curls the same flaxen silver as her mother's. She was running a tin train around the bath rim under Yana's watchful gaze. The third item on Constanza's list was a scalding hot bath.

Seeing her aunt, Anoushka squealed, 'Tatie-Tatya, the runaway train is going to crash.'

'Good heavens, the poor passengers.' Tatiana knelt by the bath and dropped a kiss on the damp head. 'What have you done today, *pchelka*?'

'Reading. Some drawing. I had egg custard for lunch. Piano practice, not very good. I wore my yellow coat to the park and frightened the ducks.'

'Because you were naughty and ran on the grass,' Yana put in.

'Did you go anywhere else?' Tatiana probed.

'Church. We lit candles for Papa Mikhail and Mama Vera.'

'For your Mama and Papa. And for grandpapa Ulian?'

'For him too. Choo-choo-choo-choo-splash!' Anoushka's train dived into the bathwater.

Tatiana got up as water splashed the floor. 'Shall I read some more of *Dans le Forêt* when you're in bed?'

'Yes please.'

'That book scares the child.' Yana leaned over the bath, giving Tatiana little choice but to retreat. 'She is tired. Too long in the cathedral. Too many candles, too many tears.'

'My mother was upset, I suppose?' The question was redundant. Irina always cried in the cathedral. 'She misses Vera so much.'

Yana said flatly, 'Your mother forgets Anoushka never knew her parents. She forces her to pray for ghosts.'

Tatiana had no answer because at some level, she agreed with Yana. 'Don't forget to bring me something for my, um, fever. I'll go and tell Mama that dinner's ready.'

Their first course was clear chicken broth served in tiny bowls. Cook had long ago learned to rein in her talents for Princess Irina Vytenis's table. Tatiana consumed her portion slowly, but her self-denial passed unremarked. Irina looked but did not see. Conversation was placid, predictable. By the time they had retired to the drawing room for coffee, Tatiana couldn't have repeated any of it. Constanza's advice marched in circles through her brain. *Ruta Graveolens* taken as an oil. 'A strong infusion brings a miscarriage so you must be in absolutely no doubt it's what you want. Run the hottest bath you can bear, and drink gin while you sit there.'

When Yana took away the coffee things, Tatiana followed her out. She needed the closet and knew it was going to hurt. 'Will you give me that remedy?' If the pain would only subside, she'd be able to think more clearly.

Yana looked her up and down. 'I will bring it to your bedroom.'

Expecting a steaming tisane – camomile or fennel perhaps to sooth the internal tissues – she was perplexed when Yana dropped something black and bruising on her bed. A bible.

Yana thrust the book into Tatiana's unwilling hand. 'Read it, then go to the cathedral to ask remission of sin. Your carnal ways bring shame on your mother, on your father's memory.'

Tatiana lay awake all night, reliving Yana's brutal words. That's what I can expect if I continue with this pregnancy, she told herself. Blame, rejection, exile. Only one way out of that fate.

Chapter Seventeen

The apothecary on Boulevard Malesherbes refused Tatiana's request.

'*Pardon*, Madame,' the owner, Monsieur Léonce, informed her politely, 'the law is strict on what we can and cannot sell these days. Oil of rue can be bought only with a doctor's permission.'

'I need to treat a scalp condition. It's the only thing that works.' Tatiana had got up especially early that morning, to visit the shop before it became busy with customers.

The apothecary sucked his lips into a tight plug. 'I can sell dried leaves. Steeped in boiling water, the bitter ingredients make an effective scalp wash to alleviate...' He twitched as he met Tatiana's granite gaze, daring him to say 'flaking' or 'dandruff'. 'Perhaps I misjudge in assuming it is for your own use.'

Tatiana said, 'It's for my maid, Yana Egorieva, whom you know.' Revenge for the bible and the harsh words. 'She is thirty-seven, unmarried and a good Christian. Whatever harm you might be imagining, I assure you it hasn't entered her mind. D'you imagine I'd be running this errand otherwise?'

'Indeed no, Madame la Princesse, but parliament has decreed that preparations such as oil of rue can be put to... shall we say, injurious uses. *Their* wishes I dare not disobey. If I may suggest my own preparation of rosemary water and rose essence?'

Tatiana bid him an abrupt good day, and part of her was glad to have been thwarted. But as she stepped out onto the pavement, a taxi cruised past, Gérard's mother in the back. The marquise saw her and threw her a look of implacable loathing. Tatiana returned to the counter. 'Is Madame Léonce available?'

'My mother cannot overrule my decisions.'

'I wouldn't ask it. I want to speak with her on women's matters.'

The apothecary made a fast exit. A minute later, an old lady with ice-white hair gave Tatiana a conspiratorial smile.

'Gone upstairs, urgent business in the stockroom, so it's just us. What can I help you with?'

Feeling suddenly tearful, Tatiana explained the pain she was experiencing in passing water. 'My maid calls it bride's disease but I had an examination a while ago. A routine procedure to prepare me for my marriage and ever since I've been, um—'

'Pissing petrol.' Madame Léonce pushed a stool up to a shelf and stepped up with admirable agility. She brought down a glass jar containing what looked like dried straw. 'How I wish those infernal medics would sterilise their instruments.' She put the jar on the counter. 'Ever thought of consulting a female physician, Madame?'

'I didn't know there were any.'

'Indeed there are. Any time you want a name… Meanwhile, this is mallow root.' She poured a quantity of the dried particles onto the scales. 'It's a demulcent. That means it will form a velvet glove within the sensitive parts. Make a tea from it and drink several cups a day. Take warm baths and rest. No close-fitting underwear, go as nature intended, and do not give way to fretfulness. Anxiety is the enemy of good health.'

Madame Léonce's eyes, within their folds of flesh, were compassionate. 'My son muttered something about oil of rue?'

'For my——. For my maid's itchy scalp.'

'It is banned, I'm sure he told you. If, Madame, you ever wish to talk, I am to be found here, an hour before we open in the morning. Rap upon the door and I will spare you a few minutes. Resist being pressed into doing what you do not wish to do. Yes?'

Instead of replying, Tatiana asked for a bottle of Sirop Roze. She paid for it and the mallow and left.

As she walked the last metres to home, a high-pitched cry of 'Tatie-Tatya!' made her look up. Anoushka was jumping up and down on the balcony. As Tatiana waved, Yana appeared and, with cries of alarm, pulled Anoushka inside. Yana spared Tatiana a crushing glance, as though she had enticed the child into danger.

In the drawing room, she found her mother propped up on sofa cushions, sipping tea. Anoushka, none the worse, was sprawled on the floor, playing with a spinning top. A new toy. Yana was watching resentfully and visibly curbing her tongue. Tatiana saw why.

Katya stood by the piano, leafing through musical manuscripts. She looked up. 'Tatya, are you playing again? These are scores I brought from Moscow. They were Vera's and far too complex for Anoushka, unless she's a child prodigy.'

Tatiana confessed she hadn't played a note in months. 'I expect someone's been tidying up.'

They both looked at Yana. Katya said quietly, 'You won't let her throw them away?'

'I'll try.' Tatiana was anxious to brew her first cup of mallow tea. It was approaching lunchtime and getting in cook's way caused disproportionate offence.

Belatedly, the sisters kissed cheeks and Katya sniffed. 'What's in your handbag?'

'Um, medicines for Mama.' Tatiana glanced at their mother who was gazing at the spinning top, half hypnotised. 'Sinuses. Corns. Nerves. Take your pick.'

'I want to talk, in private,' Katya said. 'Shall we go into your bedroom?'

'It's a bit of a mess.'

'I doubt it, you're the tidiest of us all. We could use the dining room. It won't take a minute.'

Tatiana gestured towards the folding doors that separated the two rooms. After closing them behind her, Katya pulled out chairs. 'I'm sorry so much falls on you these days.'

'It doesn't, really,' Tatiana replied. 'Yana does most of the caring, cook gets on with her job and our cleaning woman comes and goes like an efficient ghost. Of course, Yana extracts her pound of flesh in sighs and reproach.'

Katya cradled her chin. 'Imagine if she quit, though.'

'We'd get another nursemaid. One who doesn't control Anoushka's soul or throw bibles at me.'

Katya laughed a little nervously. 'You're quite capable of throwing them back. Not, of course, that one should ever throw a bible. Yesterday you hurtled from my office, white to the gills, Tatiana.'

'I'm absolutely A1.'

'Hmm. "A1" is stretching things, I suggest. Would it help if I took Yana aside? It's obvious Mama's letting her rule the roost.'

'Yes, talk to her.' Being mistress of her own home and lynchpin of a successful business had imbued Katya with a confidence Tatiana envied. Authority with tact, along with the skill of making her point without causing a quarrel. A talent she, Tatiana, singularly lacked. Gérard had said once during a row, 'You would lock horns with a person giving you roses if he'd brought you less than the full dozen.' The comment had hurt, implying a sense of entitlement that Tatiana felt was a misinterpretation of her character. Actually, she found extravagant attentions embarrassing which was why she so often appeared ungracious. Gérard had again misjudged her. Why did she love him so incurably?

A form of possession. Tatiana longed for a mouthful of Sirop Roze. 'If you've come to pressure me into taking over your job, you're wasting your time.'

'I know better than to try, but please know that on Sunday, after morning worship, Harry will pick me up from the Orthodox cathedral. We'll go to Gare du Nord, and from there take the train to Calais. Our first stop is London.'

'Lucky you.'

'We have no choice, Tatiana.'

'I think you're doing it on purpose. Gérard's clan already thinks I'm a well-dressed interloper, shorn of family. The moment they learn that my sister and her husband have left on business because they care so little about me—'

'We do care.'

'Whose arm will I take when I walk into the civil ceremony and into the church afterwards, if not Harry's?'

'You could ask Roland.'

Tatiana shook her head. 'Gérard won't have it.' As a Spaniard and a Jew, Roland Javier would meet with the kind of disdain from the Sainte-Vierges that disguises itself as ultra-politeness. She glanced at the watered silk curtains, the walls of robin's-egg blue hung with

heavy-framed portraits. Katya had bought the pictures as a job lot
when they'd moved in, and who they portrayed, nobody knew. A girl
in rose satin, whose farouche expression had led to her being christened
'Great-Aunt Tatiana', seemed to be laughing at her. A young man
in brown velvet gained a sinister leer; for a second or two, he was
Armand. Tatiana reached for a glass preserve pot, left from breakfast,
and spooned raspberry jam into her mouth. 'I smell a rat. Whenever
Harry has to parley with his factory managers, he goes alone and he's
away a week. Or you join him for a couple of nights in London. Why
so sudden and why for so long?'

When Katya shook her head, Tatiana felt the prick of a new fear.
'Is it about money? Is Harry's business in trouble?'

'No, and don't bandy that around. You know how news spreads.'

'Is one of you ill?'

'We're fine.'

'Then what?' Tatiana loaded another spoonful of sweet preserve.
She stared at her sister. 'Is it to do with Harry and the *Syndicale*?' She
was referring to the official body governing haute couture in France,
which Harry had recently been invited to join. 'A secret mission to
promote our fashion industry?'

'I wish I could tell you. Believe me, I would if I could.'

'If you could trust me, you mean?'

Katya's eyes swam with emotion. 'You're right. I cannot trust you
with the information I hold. Nor Mama. It's not personal, Tatiana.'

'No, of course not. You wreck my wedding, refuse to say why.
Naturally, it isn't in the least personal.'

'There's an alternative possibility. Postpone your wedding. Wait
till spring when we'll be— Oh, good God!' Katya jumped up as the
preserve pot shattered against the face of the young man in brown

velvet. Where his smile had been was a jagged grin. The impact had split the canvas.

Tatiana screamed, 'If anyone else tells me to postpone or cancel my wedding, I'll hang myself!'

Chapter Eighteen

That night, when the soft clicking of doors told her that everyone had retired, Tatiana pushed back her bed covers and went to her dressing table. She took Constanza's written advice from a locked box.

Reading it for the tenth time, Tatiana locked it away again then crept barefoot to the hall and picked up the telephone. In a whisper, she asked the operator to connect her to a Boulevard de Clichy number. 'The Rose Noire cabaret.'

Her call was answered, probably from an office behind the bar. Whoever was on the other end had to shout over the snarl of trumpet and saxophone playing mile-a-minute blues. The resident band must be performing. It was after midnight, though that was early by the gauge of a Clichy nightclub. 'Is Benjamin Crouch in?' she asked. Maison Javier's pianist had a regular slot at the club.

Yes, Monsieur Crouch was relaxing in the green room. Did she want him fetched?

'Yes. Tell him it's…' she hesitated. 'It's his wife, and it's urgent.'

'He has a wife?' came the reply and a low whistle. 'That cat never fails to surprise.'

When Benjy came to the telephone, he sounded as bewildered as any unmarried man might be at being summoned by a wife. When Tatiana identified herself, he was unimpressed.

'I nearly broke my ankle getting downstairs. And if you think I'm taking shellfire for the way you behaved yesterday... I've had to cover up a black eye with greasepaint to be allowed to play tonight. Pianos are not set dressing, you can tell that to your photographer friend.'

'He's not my friend and I'm asking a favour.'

Silence met this comment.

'You owe me. I got you your job at Javier.' Hearing Benjy performing at the Rose Noire some months back, Tatiana had been impressed by his skill. She'd then learned on the grapevine that he was struggling to support himself on club wages, and had persuaded Katya to employ him during the day. 'It's down to me that you get ten hours' easy work a week.'

'Not easy when you throw things at me.'

'Sorry. But can you procure a bottle of gin for me? I'll pay you back.'

'I've never seen you drink gin. What do you want it for?'

'To make martini cocktails. Bring it to the salon tomorrow, but don't tell anyone.'

'How mysterious. I'll see what I can do. I must fly. I have to go calm down the girl I brought with me tonight. Couldn't you have called yourself my aunt?'

Friday, 15 September

Regan Dortmeyer came back to Maison Javier at Katya's invitation to photograph the mannequins informally. It was after hours and a small cocktail party had been arranged, in part as a farewell do for Katya. Squeezed on the piano stool next to Benjy, wearing a day dress of blond lace, Tatiana watched her colleagues striking poses for the camera.

Breaking off an arpeggio, Benjy asked, 'Don't those antics ever grow tiresome?'

'What antics?' She was snappish as Benjy was refusing to confirm he'd carried out her commission regarding the gin. Moreover, she'd not heard from Gérard who had been back from Bordeaux for a provable thirty hours. She'd called his office and been told that he had returned yesterday morning. Half of her was relieved that Gérard wasn't demanding to see her. The other half was piqued and insecure. She'd left a message with his assistant, insisting he join her here later. It was like inviting a fox into the chicken coop. Was she mad? Answer: she had thrown jam at her dining-room wall, so yes, probably.

'What antics?' she asked again.

'Sulking. Tutting loudly,' Benjy said, as he began playing a lazily slow version of 'Maple Leaf Rag'. 'Staring up at the ceiling. Tossing your mane.'

'Being a mannequin, you mean? So, come on. Have you brought what I asked for?'

'It's in my music case. Gilbey's finest.' Benjy narrowed his eyes. 'Cleaning your tsarist diamonds tonight? I've heard gin's the best way of bringing back the sparkle.'

'I'm having a select party,' she said. 'Just me and Constanza.'

'Where is the diva, by the way?'

Constanza had rushed off straight after the parade that afternoon. A tooth was coming loose and only her own dentist could be trusted, so she claimed. Tatiana would have valued her support right now. Having dosed herself with Sirop Roze to get through today, she was feeling weirdly as if there were two Tatianas. One bantering with Benjy, the other intent on damning her immortal soul. Earlier, when Regan had moved her arm before taking a picture of her, she'd been seized with the desire to throw herself against him. To cry on that broad shoulder, or maybe to rake his face with her nails. She edged closer to Benjy. 'Large bottle or half-size?' She'd brought her make-up bag down with her, to hide it in.

He returned a look. 'As a point of interest, why can't you buy your own?'

'Princesses don't go liquor shopping.'

'Wear your title lightly, sweetie, or you'll catch it on the light fittings.' Benjy's fingers leapfrogged to a different key, frothing up 'Maple Leaf Rag' to its correct time signature. 'Our American photographer can't get enough of Marianne and Larissa. Handsome, isn't he?'

She turned in Regan's direction. 'I see nothing attractive in a man who is unable to find his way to a barber's. Shirtsleeves are inappropriate.'

'You're sticking daggers in his back because you don't like his shirt?'

'His attitude. His effrontery.'

'"Brash" is the word we use in England. "Brash" well describes a certain kind of American.'

She tried it. '"Qu'il est *brash*!"'

'Yet see how the girls flock.'

There came a flash as Regan captured Larissa, Mary-Jo and Marianne in a tableau of friendship. Tatiana called out, 'Someone open a window so we don't all choke.'

'Looks as though he's finished,' Benjy observed. 'Lordy, lordy, Mary-Jo's tussling with his tripod. Wars have started with less, though doubtless so have affairs. Go upstairs and change, Tatya – stop scowling at their innocent joy.'

'I'm not scowling. And I'm waiting for Gérard.'

'No, you're waiting for your gin. Take it. I'm not going to be seen giving it to you. What's the matter? You keep screwing up your forehead.'

'I'm perfectly fine,' she lied. Madame Léonce's mallow root tea had yet to start working. She felt hungry and sick. Wiping jam off expensive wallpaper had brought home to her how out of control her reactions had become. The paper would have to be replaced, the picture sent to a restorer. Katya had repeated, 'Harry and I have no choice but I hate leaving you like this,' as if she dreaded her trip. As if she doubted Tatiana's ability to survive alone.

Wait a minute… There'd been the awful matter of Katya's double miscarriage last year. A pregnancy at two months in January, the same again four months later. Could they perhaps be consulting some obstetric miracle-worker in London or Sweden?

Tatiana stared at Larissa Markova, who was chatting to Marianne. Larissa had known of Katya's travel plans though they'd never appeared particularly close. Certainly, their political views were radically at odds. Una McBride and Agnès de Brioude were Katya's closest friends. And there was Una herself, relieving a cocktail tray of a glass. I'll talk to her, Tatiana decided. When I've got the gin in my bag.

Benjy abandoned his ragtime and struck up a popular romantic ballad, one Armand was particularly fond of. She said sharply, 'Play something American.'

He grinned. 'Why, has he still not looked round?'

'Get it out of your head that I care about Regan Dortmeyer.'

Benjy settled into 'Down by the Old Mill Stream'. He squeezed the life out of every phrase until Regan fixed him with a puzzled frown. Katya came over, put a hand on Benjy's shoulder.

'This is not a cabaret, *mon ami.*'

Chastened, Benjy segued into a classical piece.

Katya gave Tatiana a nervy smile. 'Monsieur Dortmeyer has asked if he might photograph you and the other girls in the changing room. Not in your underclothes, I hasten to add. Decently dressed and properly chaperoned, but he'd like to get some behind-the-scenes pictures. Will that be acceptable?'

'Tell him to give me a few minutes. I want to change – lace is so itchy. Whoever designed this afternoon frock ought to be made to wear the thing all day.'

'I designed it.'

Somehow, they'd returned to the embattled relationship of their first months in Paris. Both grieving, minds perforated by the horror of what they'd left behind, they'd reacted as drowning people do – pushing the other away, lest they get pulled down. Katya had been the rail to which Tatiana and their mother had clung, the rope that had pulled them from the vortex. Here was a new, vulnerable Katya. And I don't have a rope to throw, Tatiana admitted wretchedly.

Upstairs, she let the dresser take away the chafing dress and changed into one of black knitted cotton, a favourite daytime textile these days. It had a drop waist, a skirt at mid-knee and a black-and-white bow at the hip. She put on black silk stockings and mid-height crocodile shoes. Colour came from a hat of green, knitted silk which she pulled down so that it covered all but the flick ends of her hair. A final touch – green malachite beads wound around her left wrist. As a very young woman, she'd worn nothing but greens and green-blues, because they intensified her eyes and the golden skein of her hair. These days, she tolerated certain shades, but green brocade, which had hung at the windows of the Moscow breakfast parlour, put her in a cold sweat. She retrieved the Sirop Roze from her dressing-table drawer, concerned to see it was already half gone. Tomorrow, she'd buy two bottles. She finished what was left.

A touch of her favourite perfume behind her ears and she was ready. The mannequins, Marianne, Suzy, Françoise, Larissa, Isabelle and Mary-Jo trooped in, escorted by Madame Markova. Regan knocked a few moments later and inspected the room while Petit-Pigeon set up a tripod and camera.

Regan suggested a single picture, as magnesium smoke would be unbearable in such a small space. He created a stage set, two dressing tables pushed close together. Marianne and Isabelle were seated, one touching up her make-up and the other adjusting her headband in the glass. Mary-Jo and Larissa were placed at their tables, their reflections in shot.

'Mind if I open a window, ladies? There's a corn-syrup sunset.'

Tatiana noticed how every sentence of Regan's was pared down. Phrases like, 'If you lovely ladies would please oblige…' or references to 'hosts of angels' or 'bevies of celestial beauty' had not, so far, dropped from his lips. He hadn't read the French handbook of gallantry.

Perhaps Americans didn't go in for it. The look he served her seemed to confirm this. 'Where shall I put you, doll, in all that black?' He consulted his light meter, stepped back until he was at the furthest end of the room. 'I'll take the shot from here, with the sunset and the romantic chimneys of rue Duphot. Folk need to know we're in Paris. Princess Tatiana, could you stand at the window, gazing out?'

'I could climb in from outside,' she suggested. It came out slurred. The others stared at her.

'You could do that?' Regan looked unconvinced. 'We're pretty high off the ground.'

'Are you daring me?'

Marianne laughed. 'Don't, Regan. Our darling princess is crazy enough to take you up on it.'

'Well, I'm not crazy enough to let her. Princess, go behind Mademoiselle du Gard's dressing table, as if you'd stopped to chat with her.'

Fine, Tatiana thought. Put me behind the furniture. I'll behave. And she meant to until Marianne whispered, 'He told me it's more fun to photograph a butterfly in flight than one sitting on a petal.'

No sooner was it said than Tatiana was astride the windowsill, an uncomfortable pose that for some reason made her laugh hysterically. 'Take your picture before I fall out, Monsieur,' she invited, shifting her weight to give the impression she was tumbling into the room, having scaled the wall outside.

Regan squeezed the button and flash filled her vision. She overbalanced and thrust her arms down to save herself, putting herself into a bent-legged headstand. She heard shrieks, and Madame Markova's '*Oh, mon Dieu!*'

Her skirt was over her head. She was just about level-headed enough, and certainly vain enough, to ask herself what underwear she'd put on this afternoon. Chantelle brand. A silk corselet with suspenders and knickers of... oh God, no knickers, because Madame Léonce had advised her to 'go as nature intended'.

She crashed down onto Isabelle's dressing table, shattering pots and dishes, perfume bottles and a crystal ring-tree. Alarm switched to fury.

'Now look what you've done!'

'Idiot!'

'Show-off!'

Madame Markova, who had urgently instructed Regan to turn his back, and was usually so motherly and patient, ordered her out of the room. 'If you cannot behave with dignity.'

'That ring-tree was my mother's,' Isabelle cried.

'I'm sorry, I'll buy another.'

'How can you? You are an utter silly ass,' was Mary-Jo's stinging verdict.

'She didn't mean to fall the way she did,' said Larissa.

'No indeed,' agreed Constanza, back from the dentist looking flushed but with no swelling to mar her exquisite jawline. 'Tatya, I promise on my honour never to say a word of this. None of us will. Agreed, not a word?' Nobody answered. They were comforting Isabelle.

A chastened Tatiana picked up her bag, the gold-hinged make-up case that accompanied her from home to work and back each day. Regan was still tactfully inspecting the back wall of the room.

Chapter Nineteen

At least I fell forwards and not backwards, she told herself as she went down to the salon.

'I'm intrigued to know how that will turn out.'

Tatiana paused at the foot of the stairs, allowing Regan to catch up. 'Rushing off to your darkroom or staying for a cocktail?' she asked.

'If you saw my pad, you'd realise that's a redundant question.'

'Your *pad*?'

'Home, residence. My bohemian artist's garret.'

'Are you Left Bank?'

'Sort of. I have rooms in the fifth, but I've temporarily moved over the river, to butte de Montmartre. Pigeon's place. One room, no carpets, no heating.'

'Winter should be fun.'

'I'll be long gone by winter but I'm no stranger to roughing it.'

'It gets tiresome.' Tatiana and her family had lived in one room when they first came to Paris, and she would take their étage noble apartment on rue Rembrandt any day. Yet Paris teemed with émigré artists, Americans, Russians, British, chasing the dream of a slant-ceiling room in a tatty Left Bank eyrie. Regan's expression had turned sardonic. She guessed what he was thinking. 'I will pay Isabelle back for everything I broke, you know.'

'Sure. It didn't occur to me that you wouldn't.'

She looked at him, unusually tongue-tied. Had he truly averted his eyes the moment Madame Markova ordered him to? Nothing in his face, beyond a twitch of an upper lip, suggested that he had seen more than he ought.

It had been Katya's idea to invite guests to the photo session. A select gathering of fashion insiders – perfectly groomed men and women who could be relied on to gossip in all the best places. Seeing Lilliane Germond and two saleswomen greet Regan as though he were a lost explorer safely returned, Tatiana shook her head. Oh, the intolerable excitement of a photographer who was thirtyish and passably attractive. She'd like to know how Regan had managed to exchange the wet wharf of Quai de l'Horloge for Maison Javier in under a week. The answer, it seemed, was Una McBride.

The American girl was looking chic in matelot white-and-blue. Tatiana watched her hail Regan like an old friend. They did not kiss in the French way, but shook hands. Which Tatiana approved of for reasons she didn't want to admit to. Was Una meaning to keep that hideous male undergraduate hairstyle forever? Tatiana suspected that Una longed for a faithful relationship but no man would fall for her while she kept her hair cropped and oiled. It would be like being seduced by Gertrude Stein.

Tatiana would always love Una who, using nursing skills she'd acquired as a military nurse, had pulled her back from near-extinction by Spanish flu. Una had been there the day Tatiana was brought home from Callot Soeurs with a burning fever, and had taken control. Calm and assured. But at this moment, love was a little bit clouded. Una was laughing and Tatiana was convinced Regan was describing her disastrous headstand.

Constanza came up and in an undertone, asked, 'Did you visit the apothecary?'

'Yes, and was shown the door. I've done something awful.' Tatiana told Constanza about asking Benjy to buy gin. 'Made him guilty of assisting. It's illegal. It's wrong, Constanza.'

'Buying gin isn't illegal. You haven't done anything wrong yet.'

Yet. The moment the gin was in her bag, she would have taken the damning step. Noticing Constanza running her tongue against her teeth, she asked, 'How was the dentist?'

'Oh, the tooth is fine but another is erupting beneath it. Outcome – it will hurt and be expensive. Can I ask, will Gérard mind about your floor show upstairs? I mean,' Constanza glanced to where Regan now held court at the centre of a group of women, 'with him in the room.'

'He didn't see anything.'

'And the other day? Lying down on the carpet...'

A saleswoman came by with a tray of dainty cakes. Tatiana popped a miniature madeleine straight into her mouth, sweetness rocketing into her system. When the cocktails passed by, she reached for one.

'Steady,' warned Constanza.

The Javier cocktail was a concoction of strong sweet coffee folded with cream, a dash of cognac strained over shaved ice. Tatiana downed hers and, goaded by Constanza's cool smile, took another. She sauntered over to the piano, where Benjy was deep in the 'Moonlight Sonata', and put her bag down in its shadow. Constanza followed her.

Benjy had reached the middle movement and Constanza clinked her fingernail against her glass rim, deliberately interrupting him as he raced over a difficult run of notes.

'Glad to be alive, piano-player?'

'Strange question.' Benjy spoke without missing a note. 'I go to bed, I get up. I live in hope that somebody will save me.'

'A good Samaritan?' Constanza asked.

'Ideally, a bad one. There are more wicked people in the world than good.' His smile challenged Constanza, who showed by her ice-sculpture glare that he was overstepping a line.

Murmuring, 'Careful, Tatya, mm?' Constanza walked away.

Petit-Pigeon sidled up. He'd come for the camera case beside Tatiana's feet. 'Monsieur Dortmeyer n-needs it—' he stammered to a stop. 'Have I your permission to reach for it?'

'That's my make-up case,' she informed him. 'Unless Monsieur Dortmeyer has a pressing need for face powder and eyebrow pencil, I suggest you take *that* one.' She pointed to the more battered article by the leg of the piano.

'*Pardon*, Madame, my mistake.'

She stopped him going. 'Has Pigeon loaned you to Regan?'

'While he's away, Madame.'

'He really has left for Havana?'

'Er…' the boy didn't seem sure.

'How do they know each other, Regan and Pigeon?'

'The w-war, Madame. They were in the army, taking pictures of the action.'

On a different day, in different circumstances, that would have interested her. 'Have a cake,' Tatiana invited. A tray of chestnut-cream macarons was passing by. A speciality of the English Tea Parlour in nearby rue Cambon where, seemingly a lifetime ago, she and Katya had worked their first paid jobs. Tatiana reckoned she'd been indisputably the worst tea-room waitress in history. The proprietor, genial Monsieur

Aristide, had not sacked her, but only because she had flounced out before he got the chance.

The boy took a cake and retreated. Tatiana took one for herself.

'The power of a beautiful woman. To reduce men to quivering jelly with a single look,' Benjy teased.

'My fiancé doesn't quiver,' she replied.

'Indeed. Gérard de Sainte-Vierge speaks to you as if he's dictating a departmental memo. "Situation intolerable, Tatiana to remain silent on all subjects until further instructions".'

'He says nothing of the sort!'

'He reprimands you, I've heard him.'

'Because I need it.'

'Why do you love him?' When she gave no answer, Benjy supplied his own. 'He's hypnotised you with his own sense of self-worth. The answer, of course, is that you don't love him. Not truly. You *need* him.'

'You have no right to an opinion.' She crammed the rest of the macaron into her mouth. Cocktails were passing again and she drank her third as quickly as the first two, then leaned across the piano. Matching her voice to the low black notes Benjy was playing, she asked, 'Now?'

Playing fill-in chords one handed, Benjy bent sideways. 'Grab your bag,' he hissed. A moment later, he was passing her a sloping-shouldered bottle.

A voice beside her shocked her into dropping the bag. 'You wear simple clothes well, Princess Tatiana.' Regan's eyes outlined her dress, the tapering sleeves, the beads at her wrist. 'There's an affinity between good clothes and good photography. I never saw it before.'

He was looking straight at the bottle.

'Thank you,' she flustered. 'A beautifully cut dress will always be...'

'Beautiful?'

Somehow, her bag had refastened itself and she couldn't get it open. Couldn't rid herself of the gin. 'I'm merely the frame for what others create.'

'Without which, all they've got is an expensive heap of cloth. I'll praise them when I'm done complementing you.' He looked into her face. 'Will you allow me one more photo? With that hat and those beads.'

'I'm spent! Posing is harder— Oh.' Holy mother of God, she'd just seen Gérard walk in. He was coming towards her. Tall and debonair, his hardly-there moustache outlining a faint sulk, he dragged attention from every corner of the room.

Gérard must have called at his flat since leaving work. Instead of the ultra-conservative jacket, waistcoat and trousers required by his office, he'd changed into a suit of light-grey Prince of Wales check with a nipped-in jacket and wide-leg trousers.

Constanza peeled away from the group she was centre of to intercept him. She leaned in to kiss him on the cheek, but Gérard politely evaded her. Tatiana, meanwhile, was sandwiched between Benjy and Regan, her bag in one hand, the bottle in the other. She whispered desperately to Benjy, 'He calls gin the drink of whores.'

Regan took the bottle. A moment later, Gérard put an arm possessively around her, and dropped a kiss on her cheek. Seeing the gin in the American's hand, he gave his fastidious smile.

'Not interrupting the fun, I hope?'

'Nope, this is for later.' The question had been put in French. Regan had answered, as he usually did, in English.

Tatiana hastily explained Regan's presence. 'A picture spread in *Ravissante*. A day in the life of a couture house. You haven't a clue what

I'm talking about, how could you? And I shan't tell you, my darling, because it is entirely irrelevant.' She needed to prise Gérard away. Benjy was hammering out a jazz piece. Deliberately, she suspected. Gérard loathed American music. 'Shall we go and talk to Katya?' she suggested.

But Regan had other ideas. 'You owe me a picture.' When she shook her head, he held the gin to the light, saying, 'Gilbey's of London. Looks like quality hooch.'

'Really? I wouldn't know. Sorry, I'm terribly, terribly tired.'

'One more shot, then I'll have eleven. That's my lucky number.'

'I believe Princess Vytenis explained that she was tired.' Gérard used the voice he employed with waiters and taxi drivers.

Regan shrugged and said, 'Shame. Enjoy your evening, both of you.'

'Why does he speak to me in English, when I speak to him in French?' Gérard asked as she steered him to the other side of the room. 'Is drinking hard liquor a professional requirement, or does he have an addiction?'

'I've no answer to any of those. Why have you neglected me, Gérard?' She expressed it as, '*Pourquoi vous m'avez abandonné?*' using the polite form of 'you'. Having witnessed Gérard's mother addressing her son this way, she'd always assumed he preferred it.

Gérard replied in the same vein: 'Because – *vous êtes tellement, tellement, fatiguée.*' Poking fun at her claims of exhaustion. He believed that being a mannequin was marginally less demanding than lying on a couch being fed grapes, even when she pointed out that couture brought millions of francs into the French economy.

Roland Javier came up to shake hands with Gérard and while they talked, Tatiana checked that Regan was keeping his distance. Good. He was putting away his camera. She'd seen mothers place infants into perambulators with less care. The one thing she liked about him was that he took his job deadly seriously. To him, she wasn't an object in eye-wateringly expensive drapery, but a partner in his art. And he'd helped her, condemning himself as a boozer in Gérard' eyes. She shouldn't have denied him his request.

Gérard tapped her wrist. He looked most put out. 'Monsieur Javier says your sister and her husband are about to leave Paris on an extended trip. You said nothing about it.'

'Because I haven't seen you since I learned about it.'

He grunted. 'I'd say she owes us both an explanation. After that, we'll go out to eat.'

'I'm not sure – as you say, I'm very tired.'

'But we have things to catch up on. Besides, I've invited Armand to join us.'

That clinched it. Tatiana waved frantically at Regan. 'Monsieur Dortmeyer? You may take one last photograph.'

This time Regan set up a tripod. When he'd fixed his camera to it, he bent to adjust focus and shutter speed. Petit-Pigeon unpacked a tungsten light which Regan had acquired since his previous visit. He'd set fire to enough magnesium for one evening.

Regan asked Tatiana to stand behind a silver cauldron of calla lilies. 'Imagine you've done the arrangement yourself,' he said. 'You're kinda pleased with it. Someone you love sent them.'

Tatiana instinctively searched for Gérard in case he'd overheard, but he'd winkled Katya from a conversation with Una and had his back to her.

Regan shifted the calla stems so their waxen heads made a foil for Tatiana's black-clad upper body.

'Jeez, relax. You look like you're about to receive your diploma. Move a little way back. Not that far... Yes, there.'

Always inclined to embellish the moment, Tatiana took her weight on one foot, her other pointing outwards to open the pleats of her dress like a concertina. She raised her arms *en couronne*, in a rounded attitude over her head. She missed her ballet classes. A few days ago another note had come from Rosa, reminding her that a new term had started. 'All well, my little star?' Rosa had written. 'Don't be a stranger.'

Too late. Wearing a leotard would broadcast her condition more clearly than her naked body.

'Princess? Please unclench. Stand on both feet if it's easier.'

Tatiana stayed as she was.

Regan spent the next three or four minutes refocusing his camera with such minute precision she knew he was doing it to see if she'd fall over. Nothing short of a typhoon would make her relinquish her pose, but by the time he took his shot, the tungsten light was singeing holes in her eyes and her supporting ankle was protesting. Dropping the pose with a grimace, she said, 'And that concludes our session.'

'Almost.' He came over and fished a lily from the vase. 'OK, so you're putting the last flower into the arrangement. Turn so you're partly in profile and look down. Where this flower goes is important, right? The finishing touch. I mean, you wouldn't dream of chucking it in with the rest. Or, indeed, at someone.'

His eyes were not black, she discovered, but whisky brown. It was the large pupils that made them seem so deep and intense. 'I would certainly throw it if some *balourd* had the gall to photograph me in my off-time. I might throw a whole armful. I agreed to one picture, and you have taken it.'

'For a lady who gets snapped for a living you're mighty shy of the lens,' Regan observed. 'Shoot, what about that gin? Shall I slip it discreetly into your bag?'

'Oh… yes. Please,' she conceded. 'And I'm not shy, simply protective of my privacy. I display clothes for a living, and photography is an occupational hazard, like pin-pricks and unwanted marriage proposals – what are you doing?'

He'd gone back to his tripod. 'Might as well make it a round twelve, ha?' he grinned.

She noted how fast Regan turned his film pack around and re-inserted it. Pigeon often fumbled between shots, displaying stubby fingers yellow from nicotine. And family portraits had always taken an age when she was a child. She'd never been able to sit still, always ended up being told off. On one occasion, her mother had sent her from the room and she hadn't been in that year's picture. This American was good. Professional.

'Photography is the future because we live in the age of truth,' he observed, raising his hand to warn her that he was about to squeeze the trigger. 'No, don't look at me, magnetic though I am. Eyes down.'

Caught out, because she had been admiring the line of his shoulders, Tatiana bent her knees, parted the lilies and stuck her chin between them, pulling a face at the camera lens. Regan took the picture.

'Damn, damn and damn,' she muttered.

'That's the lot, lady. I'm clean out of film.'

An abdominal pang made her gasp and brought Regan over.

'Pain and gin,' he muttered. 'You're in a fix, I'd say.'

Their eyes locked. But what could he do? What could anyone do? 'I'm fine.'

'You are the opposite. You should have said.'

'I believe I told you, "No more pictures".'

He nodded. 'Sometimes I need a kick. I'm sorry.'

Gérard was coming back, his face so tight it puckered his moustache. The conversation with Katya couldn't have gone well.

Regan trailed her gaze, observing, 'You're more than friends with that man.'

'He's my fiancé.'

'I see.'

Gérard didn't put a frill around his words. 'I've this moment learned from your sister that she and her husband cannot possibly be at home in time for our wedding. We have to postpone.'

'No, Gérard, no! There's no reason.'

'Really? You think I want a wedding where the bride can muster only enough family members to fit around a small café table?'

She heard Regan breathe, 'Jeez.'

'I have hundreds of friends!' she insisted.

'A wedding is not about friends, Tatiana. It is about family. Ties of blood. Katya's presence is important, but more particularly, I was counting on Harry Morten bringing his extended family.'

'If you mean his father, he's in Sweden and can hardly be expected to make such a long trip for his son's sister-in-law. Please don't be angry with me.' Tears leapt to her eyes.

Gérard visibly checked himself. 'I am thinking about you. How will you feel, seeing my family filling the banqueting hall, and nobody from your side?'

'Mine was almost wiped out. Do I have to keep saying it?'

He steered her away and her bracelet caught a calla lily, wrenching it out. She saw Regan move to stop the silver bowl from falling. His expression was of utter scorn. I deserve it, she thought. I don't stand up to Gérard but I'm so afraid…

Gérard stopped at a sideboard where fresh cocktails had been set out. He took one, staying her hand as she reached for a glass.

'My mother stopped drinking wine on marriage and did not start again until she had finished childbearing.' He kissed her briskly on the lips. 'I am only thinking of you. A spring wedding next year, when your sister and brother-in-law are home, and he can invite his relations so your side is properly represented.'

'Your mother hates this marriage, doesn't she?'

'She needs time to get used to the idea.'

'She hates me. Why don't you say it? Please, let's run away together.'

'All will be well, my love. Now tell me, what did Dr Jolivet report?'

She gazed at him in horror. 'How… how did you know about that?'

'Ah, yes, you have a right to ask.' He cleared his throat. 'Armand happened to have business on the Île de la Cité that morning and saw you on Quai de l'Horloge, entering a building. I won't defend his curiosity, but he went in and discovered its purpose.'

'He did that, then told you?'

'Our motto is "Family first". Yes, he told me and I've been waiting for you to confide. You are well, I hope?'

'Fine. Wonderful. A1.'

'And…' a delicate clearing of the throat, 'internally?'

'All shipshape. You can expect sons.'

He touched his forehead against hers. 'Sweet, secretive Tatiana. After dinner with Armand, shall we go to rue Molière and practise making the first of these sons?'

'What, with him looking on?' She pulled away, coshed by confusion and panic. 'No – no to both. I don't want dinner.'

'But I've asked Constanza to round up the numbers. Though I can't quite like her – where is that highly vaunted beauty? I don't see it. She can entertain Armand.'

She tried to refuse, but in the end, she gave in. While Gérard summoned someone to fetch her coat and get a taxi to the door, she retrieved her make-up bag. It was heavy; she heard the clink of a bottle against her gold powder compact.

As she left with Gérard and Constanza, Tatiana felt that Regan watched her.

Chapter Twenty

Pink shaded table lamps were designed to flatter female complexions. The soft light and a string quartet erased all the sharp edges. Gérard was well known in the dining room of the Ritz Hotel. As Tatiana took her seat, her mind formed a single purpose: to endure Armand's proximity without giving way to hysteria. To appear to enjoy course after course without consuming more than a few mouthfuls. As they sipped their aperitifs, Constanza kept the conversation moving, preventing Armand from singling out Tatiana. She engaged Gérard on the subject of tax, a sure-fire way of piquing his interest. Armand added a few, disjointed comments. Tatiana tried to join in but her remarks fell on barren ground.

'Stick to novels and fashion,' Gérard said crisply. He was taking his annoyance out on her, but Tatiana suspected that he wasn't so much angered by the delay to their wedding as by having the decision taken out of his hands.

As they waited for their hors d'oeuvres, Armand fussed with his cutlery, lining up his wine glass to imaginary coordinates. He summoned their waiter back, insisting he had been given the incorrect fork for his oysters, when it was in plain sight. The well-schooled waiter apologised and fetched another. No sooner had he walked away than Armand clicked his fingers, summoning him back to move his water glass.

Gérard's patience fractured. 'Your hands work, don't they?'

Armand froze into his blink-less state. 'It was too near the edge of the table.'

Constanza averted a quarrel, agreeing with Armand that waiters liked to feel useful, and then complimented Gérard's choice of wine. 'What made you select this one? I know about Argentinian wines, but not enough about French.'

It foxed Tatiana that Gérard should fail to admire Constanza, though to be sure he preferred softly feminine women. When their hors d'oeuvres arrived, oysters opened in star formation and dressed with shallot cream and caviar, she stared. She'd asked for tomato salad.

'What's the matter now?' Gérard asked crossly.

'Nothing.' Plenty. You could not pick at an oyster, it was all-in-the-mouth or nothing. She ate the sauce and left the body, aware of Armand's eyes following her hand movements and her engagement ring, like a kitten enthralled by a spot of light on the wall.

Seizing a moment when Gerard and Constanza were discussing grape varieties, he rasped, 'I need to talk to you, Tatiana. Time is running out.'

'Another word and I'll leave,' she warned.

When their main course came – Gérard had ordered fish for her and its smell hit the nausea spot in her stomach – Tatiana hurried to the ladies' room. Constanza joined her.

'Darling, you're doing superbly.'

'Gérard wants us to go to his place on rue Molière after this. Conny, I can't face it. As for getting into a taxi with Armand, even if you're with me…' She shook her head. 'I've got the gin, so tonight I'm going to… you know. I'm so frightened. Armand followed me into Dr Jolivet's. He told Gérard I'd been there.'

'Shush.' Constanza pinched her shoulder painfully and beckoned the female attendant. 'My friend is unwell, please look after her.' She'd have Tatiana's coat and bag brought to the lobby, she said, and a taxi called. 'Wait five minutes, then go to the main door. Go on home. I'll smooth things over with the gentlemen.'

'What will you tell Gérard?'

'That we've spent the whole afternoon being assailed by blinding lights, and you have a raging headache.'

'Tell me I'm doing the right thing, Conny!'

'You're doing the only thing.' Constanza kissed the top of Tatiana's head. 'I will pray for you.'

Within twenty minutes, Tatiana was home. By midnight, she was in her own bed. She lay with open eyes until an atmosphere of deep sleep possessed the flat. The moment had come.

Across town, from a stool at the bar of the Rose Noire, Regan watched Benjamin Crouch playing his set. He was here at Benjy's invitation. The man had an amazing repertoire, ragtime and jazz spinning out of his fingers. A brandy glass on the piano kept being filled up, which made Benjy play faster. Would it loosen his lips to the point that he'd answer a question?

Why had he supplied a shaky and patently unwell woman with gin? And why had that woman been so desperate to have it?

Chapter Twenty-One

She put in the bath plug and ran the hot tap. Scalding steam billowed as the water struck cast iron. When it was knee deep she let the cold tap run for a short while, testing the temperature every minute or so. As hot as she could bear... No oil of rue, but with the bath and the gin, she had two ingredients of Constanza's remedy.

Locking the bathroom door, she poured a dose of Sirop Roze into a tooth mug and downed it. For courage. The gin she put on the floor by the bath.

Stepping into the hot water, she gasped. Her lower legs instantly looked to be wearing deep-pink stockings. When eventually she lay back, the stinging didn't fade and, perversely, she began to shiver. She reached for the gin, broke the seal and pulled out the stopper. Put it to her nose and flinched at the astringent smell.

Are you sure you want to do this?

She was attempting to rid her body of a living child. Her child. If only she could persuade Gérard that the baby was his, but his tone with her tonight left no room for self-delusion. His time in Bordeaux had altered him; he'd come home acutely aware of her failings. Anyway, Constanza had worked out the mathematics. This baby was due at the end of February or by early March at the latest. Soon, her belly would be protruding. The axe had fallen on hope when Gérard had decided their marriage must be put off. When Gérard gave his opinion, he didn't expect to be questioned.

Her choice, then, was between marriage to the one she loved, or unmarried motherhood. Yet try as she might, she could not force her hand to tip the gin bottle, until she rammed it against her lips. Harsh liquor coursed down her throat. She retched and slid under the water, gasping and swallowing. When she finally got her head above the surface, the Gilbey's bottle was bobbing at her elbow, thoroughly diluted.

She lay back in water that was now a comfortable temperature and half sobbed, half laughed. That was that, then. She finished every drop of Sirop Roze, then closed her eyes. Pain dissolved, a heavy fatalism taking over her mind. When a rhythmic pounding penetrated her brain, she mixed it into the dream she was having. A dream of herself shut inside Benjy Crouch's piano, her ears vibrating as he thumped out a jazzed-up 'Moonlight Sonata'.

Only when the hammering transferred to the bathroom door did she partially wake.

'Tatiana Ulianova! Are you in there?' It was Yana, shouting in Russian.

A man's voice. 'Hey, Princess – you all right?'

Him? Here? She attempted to get out of the water, but she tumbled back, her head going under again. This time, she felt panic, but it was only a bath! Gripping the sides, she got her head up.

She heard: 'Stand back. I'll ram it.' Before she could protest, the door flew open, slamming against the wall with enough force to crack the porcelain tiles. In plunged Regan, who ended up with one arm in the water. His knee banged against the side. In her shock, Tatiana slipped back under again. She'd run her bath so deep, it had a tide.

A hand clamped the back of her head. Regan heaved her out. Like a calf being birthed, she flopped wetly onto the lino floor.

'Mad, mad girl!' Yana, in her nightdress, radiated incredulous fury. 'How could you behave so? In the bath, drinking!'

From terrifying dream to shameful reality. Tatiana did the only thing she could. She closed her eyes and pretended to be dead.

Chapter Twenty-Two

'Nounou? Nounou?' Anoushka, woken by the clamour and in search of the cause, was calling for Yana, who scooped her up.

'Nounou has you, precious.'

Anoushka cried, 'Why is Tatie-Tatya on the floor, all naked? Why is Tatie-Tatya all pink?'

Tatiana got to her knees. Regan, one coat sleeve dripping, held up the gin bottle. Tatiana did not like his expression and certainly, he proved a bewildering apparition to a small child: Anoushka turned into a screaming ball of pink gums, small white teeth and staring eyes.

'Give me the towel,' Tatiana hissed. Regan dropped it on her, leaving her to wrap it round herself.

'I guessed as much,' he ground out. 'Benjy Crouch spilled the beans.'

She had no idea what he was saying and neither did Yana, but the maid had every intention of making herself mistress of the situation.

'Who is this man? Why is he rampaging into our bathroom, Tatiana Ulianova? And why are you in a bath at this time of night? Is that gin you have been drinking, like a street whore?' Yana's interrogation was in Russian, but her meaning could not have escaped Regan. Meanwhile, Anoushka sank her face into the ample shoulder, her screams reduced to grizzling cries.

'You gonna tell her?' Regan crouched to put himself at Tatiana's level. He turned her chin so she couldn't evade him. 'I guess she's wondering if she ought to call the police.'

'Let her call them,' Tatiana muttered. 'I've done nothing wrong.'

'You reckon?' he said in her ear. 'Forcing a miscarriage is a felony. Least, it is where I come from.'

'I haven't done anything wrong,' she repeated.

'No? You like to sit in a scalding bath, downing neat gin? I don't see any ice or lemon, lady.'

'What is he saying?' Yana demanded, as Regan was using English.

Tatiana tried to assert control. 'Yana, take Anoushka away. She might scream again and wake Mama.' Irina rarely retired without first taking a few grains of the barbiturate, veronal, and generally slept through any disturbance. Something Tatiana had often been glad of, stumbling home in the early hours.

But not this time. The click of a door further down the corridor and a wavering voice calling, 'Who was rapping on the door, the police?' warned Tatiana that her wretched situation was about to become worse.

Fear of a lifetime's shame drove her to beg Yana. 'Tell Mama I was drunk if you wish, but don't let her see me like this.'

'Your mother has every right—'

'To be shocked to the core? Deprived of peace of mind? Yes, all right, I'm a lousy daughter, but if you tell her, you won't get a moment's peace either.'

'Who is shouting?' Irina Vytenis seemed to be feeling her way towards the bathroom.

'Yana? *Please*. This man,' – still speaking Russian, Tatiana met Regan's eyes, which shimmered with loathing – 'he meant to barge into the house next door.' Shift the blame, deal with the consequences later. 'His wife is having an affair with our neighbour.'

Yana gaped. 'With nice Monsieur Strauss?'

'He meant to catch them together.'

'Jacob Strauss who runs a hospital charity? But he is so genteel and always raises his hat to me.' Yana's mouth rejected the idea.

'Being courteous in the street is not the same as living decently behind four walls. This man intended to punish him. In France, it's called a *crime passionnel*.'

Regan's gaze narrowed. He'd understood the last two words. Yana was sufficiently convinced to intercept Princess Vytenis. Tatiana heard her stemming anxious enquiries and a minute later, doors clicked shut. Her mother was returning to her veronal slumbers. Yana would be putting Anoushka to bed and wouldn't leave the child until she was asleep.

'So – do I get an explanation?' Regan put down the gin bottle and pulled out the bath plug. Water gurgled away.

'No.'

'Guess I'll wait, then.'

He meant it, that much was obvious, so she went to her bedroom, thrust open her door and gestured him inside. She didn't turn on the light. 'Sit down, say nothing and don't look.'

Closing the door, letting the damp towel drop, she pulled a long, medieval-style tunic off its hanger. It was a Paul Poiret, something she'd bought without telling Katya, who liked her to wear only Javier. She struggled into it, saying, 'You can switch on the lamp next to you.'

He did so. 'Classy,' he said, giving her boudoir a glance, which moved to the bed, with the imprint of her restless body on the satin spread. From his pocket, he took a bottle which he tossed to her. She fumbled but caught it.

Sirop Roze, empty.

'There was another empty one on your lowboy. Your table in the dressing room at Javier? I saw it when I was pulling the furniture about. There was pink liquor on your lips too. You've been knocking it back like cream soda all day. Not to mention cocktails.'

'Then don't mention them.'

'And now gin.'

'I hardly had a mouthful. It tastes vile without vermouth.'

'Lady, if I hadn't rammed your door down, you'd have been under the water like Ophelia, all seaweed hair, "Till your garments, heavy with their drink pulled you to a… a bath-y death", or something like that.'

'You're making no sense.' She sat down on the bed.

'You'd have drowned.'

'You don't know that.' She used a cotton pillow slip to dry her hair.

'Yeah, I do. You were under the water, your feet squeaking the base of the tub. They're not pretty, you know, bathtub corpses. What if the little girl had found you?'

Tatiana stared angrily at the empty syrup bottle. 'It's only cough medicine. Sugar and rosehip. Maybe a dash of aspirin powder.'

'Yeah, right. Codeine,' he told her, 'which is mostly morphine and opium. It also contains chloroform, which is anaesthetic, and datura which soothes pain but gives you hallucinations if you take too much.'

That explained a few things.

'Straight talking, Princess – are you in the family way?'

'It's not that simple.'

He gave a snort. 'Pardon me, it really is. You are. I guessed already. Were you hoping to lose it?'

'You make it sound like a broken umbrella on the metro.'

'It's way more important than that. Is it his… your fiancé's?'

She tried to dismiss the question. But her bottom lip would not stay still. 'Of course it is,' she lied.

'Then what's your problem?' Regan came to stand by the bed. He seemed to overfill the room and she longed for Gérard whose body and face had a tidy elegance. Gérard frequently found fault with her, but in their ten-week engagement, he hadn't asked as many questions as this man had in the last five minutes. Regan said, 'He'll marry you, you'll start a family. Why the drama?'

She answered, but in so small a voice he sat down beside her.

'Say again?'

'He won't.'

'Then he's a jackass.'

'No, he's clever, sophisticated, amusing. He could have anyone. Now he wants to delay the marriage.'

'Tell him he's going to be a father. Get him to book the church, town hall, whatever it is you do over here.' Regan took her hand in his. 'My sister Vicky, she's the eldest of us, she got into trouble and didn't tell no one. Result? She's bringing up her son on her own. Then Elsie, she got in the family way with a fellow she met at a street market. Love. Ha. I had to pay him a visit. Upshot? They were married within the month. Can be done.'

'Was it "happy ever after" for Elsie?'

'No.' He sighed. 'They split up after the baby got the measles and died, but they did the right thing in the beginning.'

'I'm not asking you to pay Gérard a visit. That approach might work where you come from—'

'New York. Don't make it sound like a squatter camp. It has charm.'

It would be no use, she insisted. Gérard wasn't a man to be pressured. 'A hasty marriage would look as if he'd been careless.'

'I'd say he has been.'

She chucked the syrup bottle at the wastepaper basket. Was going to tell him to show himself out, quietly, when it occurred to her that he hadn't explained his timely arrival. 'Benjy Crouch knew what I was intending – *thinking* of doing – tonight?'

'He guessed. Told me where you live.'

It made sense. Benjy had been here. She'd invited him over to tune the drawing-room piano.

'One of my talents is being in the right place at the right time.' Regan got to his feet.

She stalled him. 'What are you, a guardian angel? Everybody's conscience?'

'What I am,' he said, striding to the door, 'is brother to six siblings who don't need me so much now, so I'm out of a job.' He gave her stomach a considering look, more pity than dislike. 'You've proved you can't drink this baby into oblivion. You better decide who its parents are going to be. 'Fess up to your fiancé.'

She hadn't the strength to argue. 'Are you heading home?'

'Yup, a nice stroll to the butte. I told you, didn't I? I'm using Pigeon's studio, sleeping there. I got work to do.'

'It must be the early hours.'

'I like the still of the night. Besides, I'm sailing home pretty soon and need to get my pictures to *Ravissante*. All those shots of you and your friends.'

'Why must you walk? The metro won't be running but there's usually a taxi or two waiting near the Opéra.'

'I like walking,' he said. Then: 'What are you doing?'

She was pulling a velvet coat out of the cupboard, thrusting her feet into fur-lined boots, cramming a fur *ushanka* over her moist curls. 'Coming with you.'

'Uh-uh.'

'I won't sleep.' Her eyes felt like bullets, and there was a savage pain in the pit of her groin. 'I can watch you develop your pictures. I can veto any of me I don't like.'

'Can't work with anyone breathing over my shoulder. Not even a princess.' He walked to her, kissed her cheek and said, 'Go to bed. You've a lot to think about.'

Exactly. Her bed held no allure. Knowing better than to trigger an argument, she said she'd escort him down. Once they were there, she stepped out after him, pulling the door shut behind her. 'Now I'm locked out.'

'You're trouble, lady.'

'Leave me here and I'll wander down to the river and, who knows, I may throw myself in. Then it would be your fault.'

Chapter Twenty-Three

'Up to the butte' was a vigorous walk through a cloudless night, the air chilly in spite of the season. For a less-than-fit Tatiana, it recalled the exodus from Moscow, those interminable trudges along station platforms and pavements in quest of shelter, lugging one end of a trunk, dragging the other end through the snow.

They heard a clock chime two a.m. as they crossed Place du Tertre, both breathing hard from their ascent up vertiginous rue du Calvaire. At first she thought he was taking her to Rosa's favourite haunt, Mère Richelieu's. Light behind its rustic shutters and the damp 'plink' of a piano suggested a gathering still in progress. At the last moment, Regan veered towards a different door. 'Here it is, *chez* Pigeon.'

She followed him in. A whiff of kerosene heaters and wormy timbers filled her nose. 'You don't lock up?'

'Generally, but I gave Benjy my key tonight so he could bring my camera equipment back here. Hope I was right to trust him.' Regan found the light switch and then Tatiana was feasting her eyes on cracked floor tiles and bilious green walls.

'I'd have thought Pigeon could afford better than this.'

'Maybe he's saving up to buy a country chateau. Or just doesn't care.' Regan thrust his hand inside a dusty flower vase and, a moment later, jangled keys at her. 'I'm guilty of prejudice. Why shouldn't an inebriated musician be as reliable as a scout leader?' He took her up two flights, stopping at a door off a dim corridor. 'I'll go in first, just in case.'

'In case of what?'

'Mice. Spiders. This place sure is picturesque.'

Pigeon's studio was a sizeable room, with bare light bulbs strung between beams. One wall was lined with shelves holding tins and canisters. Another showed monochrome prints, pinned in no particular pattern. An area was partitioned off, with its own black-painted door and 'DARKROOM, NO ENTRY' painted in unmissable capitals.

Regan headed straight there, checked inside. 'It's all here,' he reported a moment later. 'Camera, film, everything right where I asked.'

'Benjy's a good friend.'

'Ain't he though. Coffee? Can't work till I'm fuelled.' Regan lit a spirit stove and brewed up, tar-black and strong. Sugar into both cups, and she accepted gratefully. He looked doubtfully at her velvet coat. 'Hang that on the stand.'

'I'll be cold.'

'Not with this on.' He gave her his trench coat then carried a stool into the darkroom, putting it against the far wall. He fetched a cushion, then finally switched on a red light and turned off the main one. 'Ma'am? If you're gonna watch, make yourself comfortable.'

It felt good, knowing that nothing else was required of her. Drowned by the coat, which went twice round her, she allowed her mind to shut down. The darkroom had a masculine starkness with its plank shelves and deep stone sink. Brass taps were furred with chalky deposit. Plain board walls held another gallery of monochrome prints, and among them she recognised the grand salon of Maison Molyneux on rue Royale. Pictures of mannequins posing languidly in winter-season gowns. There was feted Sumurun, with her aquiline profile and whip-like figure. And another of Molyneux's beauties, Hébé. The photographer had placed them in front of a heavily panelled door. It flattened the light. The dresses were sharply focused, though, which was doubtless what he'd striven for.

'You took these?'

'My stuff's out there. This is Pigeon's work.'

'So it's true he went into fashion.'

'Taken the shilling. Maybe we all do, in the end.'

Tatiana's eyes went back to Molyneux's dresses. Low backs, long trains, fine lace. There was a noticeable kinship to Katya's work this season. Couture fed off itself, ideas drifting through the ether. Trains were 'in' because legs were 'in'. Lace was 'the thing' because a tail of expensive gossamer signalled 'high price tag'. Tatiana wondered which magazine had commissioned these pictures. 'I haven't seen these in any fashion journals,' she observed. 'Pigeon shouldn't have them on display, even in his own studio.'

Regan drawled, 'Una McBride got first glimpse over dinner next door.' He stopped what he was doing. 'Is that normal?'

'Showing pictures to an unaccredited journalist? Never! I adore Una and I'd never report her, but I wish she wouldn't cheat.'

'It's a good sign,' he said after a silence, 'that you can like people despite their flaws. I take comfort from that.'

She made no enquiry into that comment. Silence was fine by her. In shirt sleeves, apparently immune to the chill, Regan cut a shape that stirred something inside her. She'd always admired the male physique. Gérard had shown her how carnality could be taken to breathless heights. What kind of lover would Regan be? Bathed in red light, he looked a little more than human, and less than angelic. Loving him would not be ordinary.

Then Regan spoiled it. 'Twenty dollars says the baby you're carrying isn't your fiancé's.'

'You are insolent.'

'But right, ha?' He was wiping dust from shallow Bakelite trays set out along the workbench, while checking labelled bottles on the shelf above. She heard him murmur, 'Well done, Isidore.'

'Who's Isidore?'

'Pigeon's assistant, the shy kid. I sent him ahead this evening to set up the bench for me. He knows his job.' Regan filled the trays one after the other, pouring from different bottles. A stench hit the back of her nose, so evil she almost gagged.

'Ugh. Rotting onions or bad eggs?'

'Hypo.' Regan took a black cloth bag from his carry case. 'Hyposulphite of soda. It's not Chanel No. 5, I grant you.' He eased his hand through the bag's drawstring neck and she got the idea he was counting the contents. He explained, 'I shot two film-packs at Javier over two days, six exposures each. Want a job?' He passed her a timer with minutes notched around its edge. 'Set it to two minutes, or ten, whichever I ask. You'll be doing it in the dark, so use your finger to count the notches.'

He turned off the red light, putting them in absolute darkness. She heard the scrape of hard, small objects and the brush of his hand, his hips, against the bench. Otherwise he was invisible. She asked him, 'How did you learn all this?'

'Offering myself up as an errand boy to a photographer in return for tuition. Pretty much how I've learned everything. Set the timer for two minutes.'

'Two minutes.' It suddenly mattered to find the notches and line up the dial precisely. 'Done.' Two minutes to pre-soak the first 4- by 5-inch films. Never had time felt so loaded. At the 'ding' of the timer, she yelled, 'Stop!'

'You're a natural,' Regan's disembodied voice informed her. 'Set it for another two. When it rings, set it for another eight. Developing takes ten minutes, but I'm putting the next two films in to pre-rinse, so—'

'They mustn't be in too long. It's like baking soufflés.'

'Just like baking soufflés.'

'Why the pre-rinse?' She moved the timer dial to the second notch.

'So I don't get streaks on the negative. Every frame I take costs money. It's why I treat every exposure like I'm hatching the world's last remaining dodo egg. If I've taken a bad shot, my fault. But it breaks my heart to ruin a good one.'

'Do you often get your heart broken?'

'Once was enough. Pardon me, I need to concentrate.'

Rinse, develop, fix. Twenty-two minutes later, the first of Regan's exposed shots were stacked in the sink, like wet toast in a rack, a hose head gently dousing them with water. Tatiana continually reset the alarm. As the final wash must be no more than twenty-four minutes, start to finish, she had to keep a mental note every time she primed the alarm.

'That's it, twelve times,' she said as the timer went. She was enjoying the test. Her brain didn't often get such exercise. Her eyes had become accustomed to the dark. The trickle of water, like a rill through a meadow, accompanied by the glugging of the plug hole, created a soothing ambience.

She couldn't say at what point she fell asleep, only that a touch brought her out of it. She blinked and said, '*Amène-moi* à *la maison.*' Take me home.

'Sure. Let me tidy up first.'

The safety light came back on and she flinched. Sleep had made a stranger of the man moving about in the red glow: unshaven cheeks, unruly hair, foreign cologne. What had she been thinking, leaving home with a man she knew nothing about?

'Now, if you don't mind.'

He was wiping out the Bakelite trays and said wryly, 'I notice you use the informal *tu* when talking to me. But not with your fiancé. Even in the throes of passion, I bet it's, *Je vous aime.*'

'You don't speak French well enough to judge.'

'I speak it better than you suppose. I just can't nail the accent. Am I allowed to grab some coffee before we leave?'

'I suppose so. Are you done in here?'

'All done, ma'am.'

The sudden transition from darkroom to the lit studio was disorientating, though Regan was obviously used to it. He put water on to boil then looked at his watch. 'Four-thirty, the time of day most people die.' He went to the window, manipulating the espagnolette and heaving back the shutters to expose an inky rectangle of dawn sky. Cool air rushed in, bringing birdsong.

He was pouring coffee beans into the hand grinder when there came the sound of feet on the stairs. They looked at each other.

'Pigeon, come home?' she suggested.

'Your Russian maid, with a horsewhip?' Regan went to the door.

'Wait!' she hissed, meaning, *I mustn't be seen!*

Regan gripped the knob to stop anyone forcing their way in and called, 'Who is it?'

A female voice with an American accent answered, 'We saw lights, we're in search of coffee!'

Regan glanced at Tatiana and she nodded. Una McBride skipped over the threshold and Tatiana didn't have to wonder what she was doing up at so early an hour. A bias-cut evening dress of sparkling kingfisher-blue shouted 'nightclub'. Heady perfume, overlaid with other people's cigarette smoke, confirmed it. Una stood on tiptoe to kiss Regan, then saw Tatiana.

'Saints alive!' She looked at him, then back at Tatiana. 'It's over with Gérard de Sainte-Vierge?'

'Absolutely not,' Tatiana said frostily.

'And it isn't "on" with me, either.' Regan went back to grinding coffee beans. 'Princess Tatiana doesn't trust my talents as a photographer, so I invited her to see me at work.'

Una looked archly at them. 'Fine. I believe you.' Tonight, the boys' academy hair had been abandoned for finger waves, cinched under a headband that matched her dress. Una was a year younger than Tatiana, but right now, heavy-lidded from a night's dancing, she seemed the older. Confident and unapologetic. She doesn't skulk or make excuses, Tatiana thought enviously.

As Regan relit the sputtering spirit stove, a resonant voice called up the stairs, 'You up there, sugar?'

Una called back, 'Come right up, Griff-my-heart. You don't mind, Regan? I told him to finish smoking outside, in case he set fire to whatever is in your darkroom.'

'And I told her, darkroom chemicals ain't flammable.' The voice rising up the stairs had a deep American drawl.

Astonishment crossed Regan's face. 'Is that who I think it is?'

'Depends who you think I am, brother.' An apparition filled the doorway.

Tatiana gaped. Until she'd arrived on the west coast of France, she'd never seen a black person. There had been none in Russia. Not in

Moscow, nor in the countryside. The ship that brought her to France had boasted a mixed crew: Indian, Ceylonese and Chinese sailors, but not until she walked around the port of Brest and saw platoons of American soldiers lounging around in the squares, waiting to embark for home, had she seen men of African descent. That had been 1918. Three years later, as a habitué of cabarets and nightclubs, black musicians and performers had become part of her after-dark landscape. But she had never been introduced, never shaken hands.

Una laughed at her expression. 'Tatiana, let me present Griff Roy-Thomas, best sax player in town and the best dancer too. We have had the most wonderful night. Griff, I'd like you to meet Princess Tatiana Vytenis. Regan's friend and mine.'

'Princess Tatiana,' Griff whistled. 'Ain't you moving up in the world, Regan? Man, you're so high, you're doing handstands on the steeple.'

And you're high too, Tatiana thought privately. Griff's eyes had the limpid focus of a pot smoker. Una's too, now she looked closer. 'Do you all know each other?' she asked.

'Sure we do. Jointly and severally.' As Griff's hand closed around hers, Tatiana saw a gold-and-diamond cufflink, a white cuff and musician's fingers with prominent joints. Griff Roy-Thomas wore a pinstripe suit, fine as anything from Roland Javier's wardrobe, though more exaggerated with its nipped waist and wide lapels. A coat of some kind of animal hair hung over his wide shoulders. His moustache had to have been professionally barbered. No amateur hand could achieve that perfect, pencil-stroke arc. A Homburg hat on his oiled hair carried a nap so smooth, it must have been brushed minutes before. Two-tone Oxfords gleamed under his turn-ups. For some reason, she started laughing and the others joined in.

'Coffee, both of you?' Regan offered.

'Sure, brother. Good and strong.'

Regan turned up the flame on the stove, and found two more cups. 'Griff was a big noise in the Harlem clubs,' he explained to Tatiana. 'I liked to photograph the clientele so our worlds overlapped.'

'This renegade was known as "Ouija Man".' Griff laughed. 'Cos he always knew when a fight was going down, or some moll was ready to bump her lover, or the bean squad – the cops, ma'am – was gonna clean a place out—'

'You're losing Tatiana,' Regan told him.

'This cat always knew. Always got the best pictures.'

'What brings you here?' Tatiana asked. 'Apart from, er, sax playing.'

'What brings me, ma'am? The eighteenth amendment.'

'He means prohibition,' Regan explained. 'Every US state is now dry.'

'The French will ban water before they ban alcohol.' Griff lifted the coffee Regan handed him in a toast. 'So where do we get breakfast?'

'Downstairs,' Una assured him. 'Mère Richelieu opens shortly. She only shut two hours ago. Sh! Don't tell anyone. She employs a morning cook.'

'Stay here till then,' Regan offered. 'I need to get Tatiana home.'

'I want breakfast too.' It came out without thought. More than just needing to eat, Tatiana was enjoying the companionship, and if they made a lengthy breakfast, she might call on Rosa on the other side of the square. Sipping coffee, she reflected that her earlier desire to leave had been to avoid being alone with Regan. Why, though? She wasn't afraid of him, as she was of Armand. Or anxious to please, as she was with Gérard. Was she being a snob, she wondered?

Regan raised an eyebrow to ask, 'You OK?'

She nodded, and went to the window. Saturday had crept up on them, dew on the cobbles, pearls in the cobwebs stitched into the trees.

Below, she heard a door bang and the grind of shutters being thrown back. 'The chef has arrived.'

Regan ushered them out, closing the door behind him, not bothering to lock up. Tatiana saw him dig out a wad of notes, tallying the value. She'd never been out to eat with a man who counted his money before he sat down. But comparing him with Gérard felt wrong. Unworthy, somehow.

Chapter Twenty-Four

Griff complained the French couldn't do a proper breakfast. 'No pancakes, no eggs.'

'Five days from now you'll be in your favourite diner, staring into a plate of grease,' Una comforted. 'The first thing I order when I get on the boat is fresh orange juice.'

'You're leaving Paris?' Tatiana was drinking coffee from a bowl, mixed with hot milk to mask its bitterness. Good arabica was available again, having been impossible in the post-war months, but here it was still cut with roast chicory root.

'Uh-huh,' Una said. 'Today. Griff and I are going to our respective homes to change, then it's off to Le Havre to board the SS *Lafayette*.'

'You are… travelling together?' Tatiana didn't intend to fumble the question. Yet fumble she did.

'Not entirely,' said Griff, lavishly buttering a chunk of bread. 'The shipping company don't exactly have a racial segregation policy, but they sure make it hard for some of us to go first class.' He poured honey on his bread having seen Tatiana do the same, then laid grilled bacon on top. The café was busy with night workers on their way home and others stopping by on their way to their jobs. Tatiana in her velvet coat, Una in her iridescent beads and fur tippet, were winning plenty of attention. As for Griff, he drew eyes like a giant poppy in a field of green. 'It don't bother me,' he said. 'I find more friends the deeper I go into a ship.'

'I'll be one of them,' Regan told him. 'I'm taking the same vessel.'

Una grinned in pleasure at the news. 'Let's travel to Le Havre together.'

'Sorry.' Regan shook his head. 'After I've seen Tatiana home and settled up with the *patronne* here, I still have prints to make. I need to call on *Ravissante*, get paid. Say, where's their office?'

'Rue Cambon,' Una told him. 'Next door to a *chocolatier*, just up from the tea parlour. I've written pieces for the editor,' she said by way of explanation. '"Why the American Female Will Always Love Paris Style". That paid July's rent, though I had to pull the money out of the accounts department with a fish hook.'

'I thought your lovers paid your rent,' Tatiana said and immediately regretted it. Regan's imminent departure had rocked her. Somehow, she'd imagined he'd always be here, though he'd promised nothing of the sort. Taking it out on Una, who was so open about her frailties, so ready to poke fun at herself – that was cheap. Regan clearly thought so. Tatiana felt him withdrawing.

Griff gazed mistily across the table, before saying in a reproachful vibrato: 'You got lovers, sugar?'

Una creased with laughter. 'Yes, Griff. Some girls have parents and the lucky ones get left fortunes. Me, I do the best I can, balancing a limited income with a love of luxury. If nice men take pity on me, who am I to say no?'

'You *do* have parents.' Regan frowned. 'You told me your family live in Forest Hills.'

'"Lived", darling. I'm a poor l'il orphan child.' Una broke that line of conversation by turning to Tatiana. 'What's with your sister, upping and leaving? I hope there's nothing amiss with Harry's business?'

Tatiana sighed. 'I was hoping you would know. Her story is that they need to visit the English side of Harry's business. To oil the machinery and go through the books, I suppose. I have my own theory, though.'

'Go on.'

Tatiana shook her head. 'I'm not sure I ought to say.'

'Listen, if we trade hunches, we might eventually get at the truth.' Una asked Regan to pass her the brioche.

Finding the basket almost empty, Regan asked the waitress to please refill it. Tatiana challenged him. 'You spoke just now in fluent French.' Fast as any she'd ever heard. 'Why pretend ignorance? Why use English at every opportunity?'

'Because my accent is off, and I'm worried I'll say the wrong thing,' he answered. 'I employ idioms that aren't, shall we say, in the Bible.'

'What he's saying,' Griff filled in, 'is that he learned French in a Bowery brothel.'

'It that true?' Tatiana looked from one man to the other.

'I was a lodger at the house. All above board and innocent.' Regan made the sign of the cross. 'The Madame was French, as were most of her girls. They had fun teaching me.'

'Gorgeous, isn't he, Tatiana?' Una made no effort to whisper. 'I sense you've given up on He Who Must Be Obeyed.'

Tatiana's response was to observe pithily, 'I thought *you'd* given up copying couture for a living. I have one word: Molyneux.'

Una shooed the subject away, returning to Katya. 'I don't think she'll be back even for Christmas. She's going on a long haul. North. I happen to know she's had a *kubanka* made.'

Tatiana's brow furrowed at the mention of a fur hat with a dome top, traditionally worn in her homeland. Unthinkable that her sister would be going as far north as Russia. It would be suicide. 'They're travelling on to Gothenburg,' she said, 'to stay with Harry's father. Sweden can get bitterly cold too.'

'Sure, but why choose this time of year at all? And that's not all,' Una burst out with what must have been repressed jealousy, 'she's in cahoots with that yellow-haired colleague of yours. Larissa Markova. They were all cryptic whispers at Javier's cocktail party. I overheard Larissa mentioning some contact she's put Harry and Katya's way.'

'What contact?'

'I didn't catch the name, but apparently he's the only person guaranteed to deliver the outcome they want. What outcome? I detest being kept in the dark.'

'I think it may have to do with a baby,' Tatiana said quietly.

'Katya's having one? But that's—'

'No, trying to have one.'

'Adopting? Would she?' Una blinked hazily. 'Now what have I said?'

Tatiana gazed wonderingly at Una. Salvation bloomed, like a shaft of sunlight. Why hadn't she thought of asking Katya to take her child? Be its mother. 'Regan,' she gripped his arm. 'I need to go. Please? Now.'

Regan offered to ride with her but she knew she couldn't sit next to him in a taxi, in morning traffic, without divulging this radiant new hope. He would pour scorn on it. He'd ask, 'What if your sister doesn't want your baby?' And, 'How would she pass it off as her own, when she wasn't pregnant?' Or, 'What about her husband, who may well have an opinion of his own?' She wasn't going to let male logic get in her way.

So she wished Regan a preoccupied '*bon voyage*' and told the driver to get going.

On rue Goya, she dismissed the cab. As she approached Katya's apartment building, her sister's housekeeper came out. A belted gabardine coat and a shopping basket advertised Madame Roche's likely errand, a trip to the baker's.

'I'll go straight up,' Tatiana gabbled over the woman's greeting. 'I must speak with my sister urgently.'

'I'm afraid she's left, Princess Vytenis.'

'For the office?' Damn. Tatiana wished she'd kept the taxi.

'For London, Madame. She and Monsieur Morten took a cab to Gare du Nord while it was still dark. They're catching the first train to Calais.'

'They've started their journey... their trip north?'

Madame Roche confirmed it. 'A second cab took their bags and a trunk.'

A blow, but not a disaster. 'Where are they staying in London?'

'I have no idea. Madame says she will send me a poste restante address, so I can redirect their mail. To be honest,' Madame Roche admitted as Tatiana struggled to absorb this latest blow, 'they haven't seen fit to tell me a thing. Nor you, I suppose.'

Tatiana arrived home to find Yana and Anoushka preparing breakfast in the kitchen. Instead of the usual 'Tatie-Tatya!' Anoushka regarded Tatiana through wary blue eyes.

'There was a man in the bath with you.'

Tatiana crouched to be on the same level as her niece. 'Your silly Aunt Tatya slipped over and was so lucky that the brave gentleman ran in to save her.'

Yana snorted. Anoushka seemed reassured however, and went back to measuring cocoa powder into a jug.

'This man who breaks down the door,' Yana said, setting milk and water to boil on the stove, 'he went next door to punch Monsieur Strauss?'

'What?'

'For ravishing his wife.'

'Oh, yes.' Tatiana belatedly remembered how she'd explained Regan's presence. 'I mean, no. He, um, decided he'd got the wrong idea. Overreacted.'

'Pah!' Yana left the room, returning a short while later with two empty bottles. Gin and Sirop Roze. 'You cannot rob me of what I know,' she said before dropping both into the kitchen bin. 'You are in trouble, Tatiana Ulianova.'

'Why is Tatie-Tatya in trouble?' Anoushka demanded.

Yana thought long before saying, 'For not wiping out the bathtub after she used it.'

'That's naughty. I have to wipe it, even if my arms are too short. Nounou, the milk is boiling.'

'Let me.' Tatiana poured hot liquid into a cup and let her niece stir it to dissolve the cocoa.

'You have to bash the lumps or they go on your teeth,' the child told her.

'I know. I hate muddy goo at the bottom of my cup.'

Anoushka giggled. 'I eat it with a spoon.'

Yana put a stop to the harmless fun, saying sharply to Tatiana, 'Your sister and her husband called here at a godless hour, with a message for your mother. They hoped to see you but I could not tell them where you were.'

'I went for a walk, then breakfast. I'm sorry I missed them. They'll be at the coast by now.'

'What's "the coast"?' Anoushka demanded.

'It's the sea. A long way away, but they'll be home soon. My wedding is to be postponed, *pchelka*. That means you have to wait a few months to be my little attendant.' Tatiana looked past the questions in Yana's face. 'I'm going to bed. I've had a very long night.'

She lay under her covers, cold and restless. The wild notion of Katya adopting the child in her womb had briefly recharged her, and though her spirits had sunk again, she had a sharper perspective as a result. Ever since Dr Jolivet had pronounced sentence, she'd careered from disaster to disaster as if she had no say in the matter. But she did. Once, long ago in Russia, she had gone riding with her father and sisters on their country estate. Her horse, a sprightly Polish Arab mare, had raced off with her.

'Sit back!' her father had yelled, as he spurred his horse alongside. 'Take control, Tatya.'

She'd brought the horse to a jolting trot, saving herself from a nasty fall and her father had praised her courage and determination. She *could* be decisive when she put her mind to it. And she would, when she'd had some sleep.

Chapter Twenty-Five

As Tatiana slept, the rain returned. Walking across Place du Tertre, Regan resigned himself to the fact that his last hours here would be spent under a pall. Had it been worth crossing six thousand kilometres of ocean? Yes, if his agency liked his slant on 'The Eternal Romance of Paris'. He had maybe forty useable images, enough eventually for a book or – hell, why not? – an exhibition. Certainly enough for Worldwide to syndicate. The rivals who'd gloated when he'd been sacked by his own father-in-law could go find some other target. If Janet-Marie's family would stop blaming him for the divorce, he might even get work on a newspaper picture desk.

Princess Tatiana Vytenis.

'You'll never know,' he said in answer to the question that wouldn't leave him alone. Her future was not his. He had packed up his Left Bank flat, and had a couple more hours' work ahead in the darkroom, printing 8 x 10s from the Javier negatives. Petit-Pigeon would deliver one set to Maison Javier in the morning. The other set he'd take to *Ravissante* himself this afternoon and wait there until he was paid. Unlike Una, who'd mentioned she'd had to resort to a 'fish hook' to get her money, he hadn't the luxury of time. When a business owed him, Regan always let it be known that he would happily stand in reception, reading out loud from a Gideon Bible for as long as it took accounts payable to see the light. He intended to have payment in his pocket when he left, never mind that it was Saturday.

First, however, he was on his way back to Pigeon's. As he homed in on the peeling front door he'd grown unexpectedly fond of, he whistled an old marching song, 'I Love the Place I'm Leaving'. He'd miss Paris. The place and the people. In the studio, he inhaled the lingering aroma of coffee. Ghostly perfume brought him Tatiana in a velvet coat, and Una in sizzling blue.

Tatiana's plight dragged on him. She was pregnant and her fiancé couldn't be the father, because if he was, he'd marry her, right? Where Regan came from, sixteen-year-old lads with holes in their boots were marched to the altar when they got their girls in trouble. Fathers, parish priests, finger-wagging aunts all saw to it. But who would see that Tatiana was properly looked after? Not the fiancé who sounded as slippery as he was arrogant. Regan smothered an emotion he recognised as jealousy and returned to his darkroom. Switching on the light, his first glance was towards the sink where he'd hung his negatives a few hours ago. They weren't there. He stared at the empty rack, his mind trying to reverse reality. They couldn't *not* be there.

He hadn't packed them in their binders because they'd still been damp when he left with Griff, Una and Tatiana to have breakfast. From breakfast, he'd gone directly to his flat in the fifth. Could Isidore have been in and tidied? Don't say the kid had packed damp negatives. His pulse less steady than he liked, Regan lifted boxes off the bench, the ones he stored finished prints in. They felt lighter than they should. Because they were empty.

He searched the studio like a mother duck whose nest has been robbed, but in the end he had to confront reality. 'The Eternal Romance' and all his fashion shots – gone. Prints, contact sheets, negatives. Everything. Taken. Isidore lived close by on rue Gabrielle, over a shop selling household wares. Regan sprinted there and found the lad wielding a broom in a back corridor.

'What the holy fuck are you up to, kid?'

Isidore gaped when Regan repeated it in French. His mother arrived. '*Qu'est-ce qui se passe ici?*'

'Someone has ransacked my studio, Madame. Your son knows better than anyone what I keep there.'

'I haven't been to your studio, M-Monsieur Regan,' Isidore stuttered when his mother turned grimly on him. 'I took your things there yesterday, as you asked, but I haven't been back since. Tell him, Maman. I've been here.'

'It's true, Monsieur. He has been working in the shop, with his father.'

Isidore's cheeks flushed deeply, but it was an honest shade of flamingo. Regan believed him. So who had asset-stripped him?

Una? Pigeon's partner-in-crime, last seen outside Mère Richelieu's, blowing goodbye kisses and high as a cloud. He had time to catch her at Le Havre before she boarded the boat. A blonde with a hangover, travelling with a black musician in an Alpaca-hair coat and two-tone Oxfords would not melt into the crowd.

He'd find them.

No doubt he would have done, but he'd missed a whole night's sleep and he mistakenly boarded a train to Lille on the Belgian border. The SS *Lafayette* sailed on time from Le Havre on Sunday, 17 September. Regan, meanwhile, was fined for travelling beyond the value of his ticket. Being a Sunday, he was stranded in Lille. He arrived back in Paris on Monday with just enough in his pocket for dinner.

Chapter Twenty-Six

Tuesday, 19 September

Tatiana had the cab drop her at one end of rue Molière. Fastening a waxed cotton hood over her hat, to keep off the rain, she watched the cab drive away before walking the length of the street, then back in the opposite direction. The toes of her shoes turned a darker shade of tan, even though she stepped around the puddles.

Each time she passed Gérard's flat, she glanced up to check for hints of occupation. She had to talk to him. Just as importantly, she must avoid Armand. It was lunchtime, so it wasn't impossible that Gérard would be there, even though their passionate midday meetings were a thing of the past. The worst possible scenario was that both brothers were there…

The flat gave nothing away. Grey-beige shutters, a cuff of balcony with no view but the walls opposite, Gérard had chosen this building for its profound ordinariness. In rue Molière, his coming and going attracted no attention.

Tatiana used her key to get in. Letting herself into the flat itself, she closed her eyes, the better to pick up any sound. Only after several minutes' silence did she walk through to the lounge. It was the first time she'd been here alone, and she felt like a trespasser. This was

Gérard's private domain, where he displayed a collection of antique fountain pens, as well as art nouveau bronzes too risqué for the house on Avenue du Bois de Boulogne.

His classical records were stacked next to the gramophone, in alphabetical order of composers. She'd slipped up once, putting Debussy underneath Delibes. The room offered a few more clues to the man. Newspapers and books in ruler-straight piles, chair and sofa cushions placed at an identical slant. She couldn't help feeling that a bit of clutter would make her task easier. She made herself a cup of mallow tea: she kept a twist of the herb in her handbag. As she sipped it, she confirmed a decision she'd made earlier. 'I will. Today.'

Was the tea a sedative? Her eyes felt suddenly heavy. Bed? She wasn't due at work for two hours.

Gérard would hardly object. Jamming her key in the lock to stop anyone coming in while she slept, she went into the bedroom. The eiderdown was glacé smooth. As she sat on the edge of the bed she noticed a yellow button on one of the pillows. A pearl button covered in ochre-yellow silk, the stitches small as sugar grains. She had a dress that colour; *used* to have. She hadn't seen it for a while. Slipping the button into her pocket, she kicked off her shoes and lay down.

She woke, convinced a man was leaning over her. A Russian Cheka policeman, wearing a leather coat, the stink of poorly cured hide flooding her nose. Murder in his eyes. She croaked out a scream and swiped at the air. At once, the vision retreated. Rattled, she went to the bathroom to wash. What a diabolical choice, insomnia or nightmares. 'Please, God,' she prayed, 'make Gérard want to marry me so I don't have to go through life alone anymore.'

She looked in the mirror. *You'll do it, you'll tell Gérard the truth?*

A glance at her watch warned her that, if she dawdled, she'd be late for work.

Yes, but it will have to be tonight.

The first person she met at Maison Javier was Roland, who greeted her with a grim smile. 'Did you know she meant to leave quite so soon?'

'Katya?' It felt like old news to Tatiana now, but she supposed that the staff here were still coming to terms with her sister's flit. 'I don't even know where she's staying. Do you?'

Roland gave a one-note laugh. 'I hoped you might tell me.' He was heading back to the admin building to acquaint himself with the order book, he said, but paused to add, 'A message came for you from Monsieur de Sainte-Vierge.'

'He knew I was at the flat?'

Roland blinked, startled by the nervous note in Tatiana's voice. 'I have no idea. He didn't mention any flat. His message was, "Please call at Avenue du Bois de Boulogne. Six thirty will be convenient for him and Madame la marquise".'

'Oh God, a summons! I mean, thank you, Monsieur.'

Following the awful dinner, she'd sent Gérard's mother a note of thanks but the marquise hadn't contacted her in return. What a twist of fate, a meeting today of all days. But after she'd paced circles and gnawed a sore spot in her lip, Tatiana concluded that, actually, this made things simpler. Telling Gérard her secret in the same house as his mother would give him less chance to rage and rail at her. He might then tell his mother they were bringing the wedding forward. Or that it was off. One or the other.

The parade went smoothly, with few clients in. It was, after all, a drizzly Tuesday. Afterwards, Tatiana removed her make-up, replacing it with a slick of lipstick and mascara. She put on her favourite black day dress, her green hat and matching gloves. She packed her carry bag and waved a general goodbye, putting on her coat as she went downstairs. It had stopped raining, but she asked the receptionist to call her a cab anyway.

Avenue du Bois de Boulogne, jewel of the sixteenth, was a ray emanating from Place de l'Etoile. From Gérard's house the Arc de Triomphe could be seen against the twilight. Broad verges flanked the front gardens of the Haussmann mansions. Without doubt, one of the best addresses in France. Ancient woodland swallowed its western end and in days gone by, it had been a popular route for carriages and horse riders. Gérard had promised that when they were married, he would keep livery horses so they could ride together every Sunday. It hit her that her riding days might be over. She was going to be a mother.

She asked her driver to come back in one hour, and glanced at her watch. Six twenty-five. That should satisfy Gérard's timekeeping. The first leaves had fallen, making the pavement slippery and she approached the house with care. During the war, Paris's street trees had been hacked down for firewood, but here the majestic chestnuts had been spared and later in the month, they would turn gloriously bronze.

She rang the bell, which seemed to be attached by wires to her stomach. Shown upstairs by the butler, it struck her that Madame Léonce's mallow tea was finally starting to take effect. Her abdominal pains had reduced to the occasional twinge. The old lady's parting remark came back unbidden: 'Resist being pressed into doing what you do not wish to do.' She was paying for Armand's assault in misery and shame, but she had not invited it. Not 'asked for it'. Tonight, she'd reveal not only her pregnancy, she would tell Gérard how his brother had tricked and violated her.

Only when the butler threw open the doors of the drawing room and she saw who was sitting in front of the cold fireplace did it dawn on Tatiana that in taking the message, Roland Javier had failed to discriminate between the brothers. It wasn't Gérard who was waiting, but Armand.

Chapter Twenty-Seven

The butler closed the doors and retreated. Armand got to his feet and Tatiana saw then that the marquise was present. The bent figure was half-swallowed by a high-backed damask chair.

Tatiana was glad she'd worn her black, stylish and forgiving in its shape. Madame de Sainte-Vierge would not guess Tatiana's condition tonight.

Her coat had been taken from her downstairs, but she'd retained her hat and gloves. 'How do you do, Madame.' Ignoring Armand, she walked up to the seated figure, hand outstretched.

Clothilde de Sainte-Vierge's grip was momentary. A brisk wave directed Tatiana to a sofa. Tatiana sat facing the woman she had, until these last few days, truly believed would become her mother-in-law.

Armand sat beside her and tried to take her hand. She ripped hers away. *Stay in control*, she commanded herself. You can do it. Tatiana had learned her social skills at her mother's knee. Before her world crashed and she became a stateless refugee, Irina Vytenis had been every inch the aristocrat who could out-glacier a glacier. Tatiana assumed that same poise as she waited for the marquise to explain what this meeting was for. When Armand's hectic breathing became the loudest sound, however, her nerve broke. 'Why was I asked here? Not, I suspect, to discuss wedding plans.'

'On the contrary, I do wish to discuss a wedding,' answered the marquise. 'The one Gérard should have made. Before you popped onto the scene, he was about to commit himself to a lady of my choosing. A lady of birth.'

'She means my cousin Agnès,' Armand crowed, pushing closer to Tatiana. She went to a different chair, one narrow enough to only accommodate her. He followed and stood behind her. 'Our dear, drab duchesse of perpetual mourning. Maman's determined, Tatya, so you can't win.'

'There is no more suitable spouse for Gérard,' his mother agreed. 'Agnès, burdened with her late husband's property and a son years away from his majority, needs a strong and steady husband. Gérard is that man.'

'Only she won't have him.' Armand cupped his hands around his mouth, shouting the news to an imaginary audience. The butler came in with a decanter on a tray which he set down. At the marquise's command, he took up an expressionless stance at the door.

The marquise, who had been glowering at her younger son, turned her vexation on Tatiana. 'What have you to say?'

Taking off her gloves, Tatiana placed her left hand uppermost to display the ruby ring. Let that speak for her.

The marquise flushed. 'You mean to be stubborn, I comprehend. How do you react to this? You were seen on Quai de l'Horloge earlier this month.'

Tatiana went to the window. Stared out, unseeing. Where the hell was Gérard?

'Entering the premises of an obstetrician.' The marquise didn't lower her voice. In fact, she seemed to intend the butler to hear.

Tatiana blinked into the amber light piercing the trees. How much had Armand found out that day? More to the point, how much had he revealed? Don't be tricked into lying, she told herself. Truth is the sharpest blade.

She said, 'I don't deny I consulted a specialist.' Armand was moving nearer. She could smell his hair oil. Her gorge rose.

'I have enquired as to the nature of Dr Jolivet's practice,' the marquise informed her. 'Why should an unmarried woman visit a doctor who specialises in pregnancy and childbirth unless she's in that condition herself?'

Tatiana sensed the woman's eye on her waistline. Fight, or run? Fight. Take control. She turned. 'I visited Dr Jolivet because you asked it of me.'

'I?'

'You were afraid I might be incapable of bearing sons. Jolivet assured me that there was no reason I should not. Whatever your many objections might be towards me, Madame, barrenness cannot be one of them.'

'But there are many objections, Princess Vytenis.' The marquise rapped on her chair arm. 'Not least your religion.'

The setting sun was burning through the glass, changing the colour of the curtains from grey to leaden green. A memory crawled from their folds. Herself, hiding in the window bay of the Moscow breakfast parlour...

Madame de Sainte-Vierge's voice vibrated with frustration. 'Young woman, are you listening? You are not of our faith.'

'And you are not of mine, but I won't make a fuss about it. Where is Gérard?'

Her hostess snorted. 'At his office, I expect. I had Armand make the call to get you here.'

Tatiana granted Armand a direct glance. He was staring as if he didn't know whether to kiss her hem or maul her. She couldn't bear it.

The marquise was speaking again. And now her tone was conciliatory, as if their brief clash had been an aberration. 'I have a proposition I hope you will heed. Please sit down.'

'I will remain standing, thank you.'

Clothilde de Sainte-Vierge sighed. 'You wish to marry into my family, Princess Vytenis, and Armand seems to be in love with you. True, *mon fils*?'

'I adore her.'

'Marry him, Tatiana. You will gain the rank you wish for and my gratitude. Even in time, my friendship. As wife to Armand, you will never again want for money or the luxuries of life.'

Armand began laughing. When Tatiana moved, wanting only to get out of this stifling, hateful room, he moved too, a sinister game of *Jacques* à *dit*. His laughter shifted into a higher key and she thought of him following her to the Île de la Cité, watching her enter Jolivet's building. Throwing roses during the parade. Slinking into the rue Molière flat while she tangled with his brother in the bedroom.

'I love you, Tatiana, to the end of life. Say you'll be my wife.'

The dark hood of panic fell over her eyes. She was breathing from the top of her chest. Short, shallow pulls.

'Tatiana? What on earth? You look as though you're having a fit.'

She lashed out and found she'd hit Gérard. He must have come in during the last few moments.

'Armand is overwrought.' Madame de Sainte-Vierge got up urgently from her chair. 'You,' she snapped at the butler, 'take him to his room. Make sure he takes his drops.'

The butler cleared his throat and called to Armand in the voice reserved for wayward children.

But Armand came right up to Tatiana, pushing between her and Gérard. 'Maman will let me have you because I'm not the firstborn. Gérard is to marry cousin Agnès and her estates, and I get you.'

'Leave me alone!' She was right up against the window. She'd have thrown herself out had they not been on an upper floor.

'He's not good enough for you, Tatiana,' Armand persisted. 'You love him, but ask him how much he feels in return. Make him tell you.'

Gérard cut in. 'That's enough. Go to your room.'

Armand looked past him. 'Not until Tatiana has given her answer. She knows I will die if I can't have her.'

Gérard shoved him aside. 'Mother? You weren't really suggesting Tatiana marry Armand?'

The marquise had walked a few steps towards them, her bent posture giving her an attitude of supplication. 'A game, that's all. I was testing Tatiana but it seems that she is not to be bought off. She still means to have you, Gérard my love. Of course she does. She's ambitious. A second son won't do.'

'No sane woman would take Armand. Face it, Maman.'

Armand's roar almost drowned out Gérard's response. The next few minutes were chaotic as the butler, aided by Gérard, took Armand out of the room. From their efficient handling of him – Armand made it as difficult as possible by dragging his feet – Tatiana guessed this was a well-rehearsed procedure. She was now alone with the marquise, who stared bitterly into the space between them. Tatiana moved towards the door.

'He went through so much in the war – we try to forgive him, but it isn't easy.'

That demanded a response and Tatiana paused on her way out. 'I know, Madame. You love him.' But I will never forgive him, she added silently. As she went downstairs, her legs began violently shaking. She sat down on a stair, looking up at a portrait of a young woman on the wall. Dark complexioned, in satin with a cinched waist, obeying every rule of beauty laid down by the previous age. The marquise as a girl?

'Cousin Agnès, before her marriage.' Gérard was a few stairs above her. He must have seen her leaving as he returned from manhandling Armand.

'She lost her husband at Verdun,' Tatiana said, getting to her feet by gripping the rail. 'A true love-match, I believe?'

Gérard nodded, his eyes on the portrait. 'He fell in 1916.'

'Your mother wants you to marry her.'

'My mother enjoys pulling strings but, unfortunately for her, they're not attached to anything. It wouldn't be a comfortable union. Agnès outranks me.'

A little silence grew as Tatiana gathered herself to fulfil the mission she had come to accomplish. She touched her stomach. 'Gérard, I—'

'Please, no explanations. No questions. Being kicked and spat at by my brother is not a pleasurable end to a long day. Nor is it something I wished to share with anyone outside my own circle.' *Outside my own circle.* How cold that sounded. Tatiana remembered the duchesse's words: '*Have you ever watched a boy pull the wings off a butterfly?*'

Was she the butterfly?

Her cab must have come and gone. Gérard insisted on ordering the family car for her. As they waited in the downstairs hall for the chauffeur to bring it to the door, she inwardly rehearsed her next words. *Gérard, I'm carrying your disturbed brother's baby.* She rehearsed over and over but could not utter anything.

The car arrived. Gérard opened the rear door. 'Good night. Sleep well.'

Flowers came for her at work the following day, mop-headed hydrangeas with sprigs of fern tied in a taffeta bow, along with a card. A short message: 'Dearest, I hope you are recovered from yesterday's unfortunate display. I won't have the pleasure of seeing you for a while.' Gérard was being sent to Vienna for two weeks on ministry business. He would contact her on his return, on 3 October. As she blindly handed the flowers to a dresser, she felt the baby kick inside her. It was far too soon for that to be happening, wasn't it? Too soon. Far too soon.

When a note came from Rosa, inviting Tatiana 'plus friend' to the opening night of her new ballet on 5 October at the Théâtre du Tertre, she wrote back at once, saying she'd be there, and she'd bring Gérard. He'd have had a couple of days to recover from his working trip. He detested ballet, but they could have a quiet dinner afterwards, and then she would speak. She read in the newspaper that on the night of 5 October there would be a full lunar eclipse and the moon would be blood red. An appropriate backdrop to a meeting that would change her life irreversibly, one way or another.

Chapter Twenty-Eight

Arriving late to work towards the end of the week, Tatiana saw that Constanza's dressing table was as she'd left it the previous evening. She screwed up her eyes. Her head ached because, to combat insomnia, she'd stolen one of her mother's veronal tablets. Very effective. Too much so.

'Where's Conny?' she asked.

Larissa looked up from plucking her eyebrows. 'Hurried home.'

'To Batignolles? Is she unwell?'

'To Argentina for her grandmother's funeral.'

'She can't be. That's where her father lives and his mother died three years ago, when she and I were sharing a flat. It's why she couldn't be with me at a difficult time.' When she was nearly dying of flu, Tatiana meant.

'Everybody has two grandmothers,' Larissa pointed out.

'Yes, but her maternal grandmother lives in France. In Marseilles.'

'Well, then.' Larissa blew a tiny hair off the end of her tweezers. 'Won't Consty get a shock when she gets off the boat at Buenos Aires and realises she's on the wrong continent. You look awful. Can I get you some Pepto-Bismol?'

'No.' Tatiana slumped in front of her mirror, tugged open a drawer, looked down at the trays of cosmetics. 'Everyone's leaving me. Tell me something. Why did Una McBride overhear you discussing itineraries with my sister? At the party, when the photographer was here.'

The question hit Larissa like a morsel of grit, fractionally delaying her answer. 'Katya wants to look up a friend of mine. I provided a letter of introduction and the address.'

'Which friend?'

'Just someone.'

'Living in London?'

Larissa shook her head.

'Sweden?'

'Hardly.' Embarrassed but implacable.

Tatiana tried a shock tactic. 'Is it something to do with my sister wanting a baby?'

Larissa's expression gained an unsettling measure of contempt. 'You have not earned the right to know, Tatiana Ulianova.'

Chapter Twenty-Nine

Sunday, 1 October

Five days after Regan's grandmother Molly O'Regan suffered a stroke in 1903, his father had moved back into the Hell's Kitchen tenement.

'Heard the vinegary bitch was dying.' Catching twelve-year-old Regan by the collar, Ludvic Dortmeyer had forced his son to look into his pockmarked face. 'You old enough to fetch me a beer, bub?'

Regan had nodded, whereupon his father knocked him to the floor with a hambone fist. 'So you know who's boss here now. When's your birthday?'

Regan had mumbled, 'Next week, not that you care.'

'Here's an early present.' Ludvic knocked his son down a second time while Regan's mother cowered at the side of the room.

The choice had been 'get out' or get banjaxed every time he said a word out of turn. Regan had run south to the Bowery where rooms went for five cents a night. Only he didn't have five cents. Hadn't had time even to grab his coat.

He kept moving till a streetwalker took pity on him, bought him coffee from a stand and let him sleep on her floor. The second night, he hunkered in a doorway. Instinct told him he needed to change his situation before winter fell hard. One night in the open, you look abject. Two nights, you look unwashed. Three nights, you smell like a fish cart. The street digests you so gradually, you don't feel it till half of you is gone.

At St Teresa's church on the Lower East Side, he'd offered to sweep out the nave for five dollars. Instinct again: never ask for charity. The priest in charge counter-offered two dollars; they'd closed the deal at three. He'd swept every speck from St Teresa's and, after collecting his wages, he hid in a robe cupboard, scoring a free night's sleep, which put him ahead of the game. The curate who discovered him in the morning told him he could get free dinners at the local synagogue. The name 'Dortmeyer' helped, and he had become Jewish till a bigger boy found him out and suggested he find a Lutheran church to eat at.

As the New York winter sought ways to kill him, he touted himself around as a sweeper-stroke-pavement-cleaner. He got a room and free meals in Madame Angelique's whorehouse in return for running errands for the girls.

He kept at that until his grandma Molly recovered enough to threaten Ludvic Dortmeyer that 'if he wasn't after making himself vanish', she'd report him for wife-beating and child cruelty. Regan returned home in time for his fourteenth birthday, to learn that the six siblings he'd left behind were now five. A sister, Philomena, had died. His mother, pregnant with the last of her children, was a bed-ridden invalid. In two years, his voice had broken and he'd grown five inches. He'd also got his first big break, as a desk clerk in a hostel for hobos. It was during this time the owner offered him a camera left behind by a guest who had passed away in his bed. The price of that Box Brownie was one thousand hours of unpaid work.

Regan had marked off each hour spent cleaning floors and emptying buckets. His photography career began with him walking up to people in the street: 'Sir, lady, want your likeness taken? A face like yours oughta be recorded for *prosterity*.' Men in suits going to work, ladies going to church, families strolling in Central Park – for every thirty approaches, he got one commission. He learned how to process film by assisting, for peanuts, an old photographer.

Life, to Regan's way of thinking, was a blank notepad with the opening chapter already written. You filled in the rest. Which was why being stranded in Paris with ten dollars' worth of francs and a useless liner ticket did not scare him as it might some.

He could have gone to his country's embassy and begged assistance, but being sent home as a destitute alien would definitely feel like a retrograde step. His next step was clear. Move into Pigeon's full time and sublet the flat in the fifth. Mère Richelieu would give him the use of her bathroom and laundry in return for some pot washing. They had the conversation, and she brought him dinner and wine, refusing payment. 'Every former soldier gets one meal on the house.'

He topped up his glass – he was getting to like *pinard* – and a posse of interconnected thoughts rushed at him. Why had Una turned grifter? Would he ever see Tatiana again? Did it matter? She'd seen him counting his money on that last morning when he'd been checking he had enough to take his friends for breakfast. He hadn't enjoyed the look on her face.

A crowd at the piano roared a popular song, '*Madelon, Madelon, Madelon!*' A woman danced among them, swathed in robes that left her midriff bare. There was something round her neck he assumed was a snakeskin draught excluder until it flickered its tongue at him. Unobtrusively, Regan levelled the Speed Graphic. A customer here had introduced him to a man who sold cheap army-surplus film, which meant he'd survive if he could sell enough pictures. The snake flicked its tongue and its scales glowed like the river at dawn. Its owner was singing to it. Regan squeezed the shutter release. The snake lady heard and came over. He admired her pet and, *kaboom*! One picture sold.

Rosa Konstantiva came in with her ballet company. She was edgy, following a less than slick rehearsal, putting it down to lunar influences. 'I chose this coming Thursday as opening night, for the eclipse. Such a creative time. Regan, since you seem to have become a staunch resident of the square, will you be our official photographer? Name your price.'

'So long as it's low,' someone else shouted.

Nobody heard his answer, as the pianist thumped out *Madelon* again.

Harry and Katya

In the Euston Hotel where a pianist played liquid arpeggios on a baby grand, Harry Morten raised a hand to catch the waiter's eye. 'I think we deserve a bottle of the best Bordeaux,' he said to Katya. 'The further north we go, the less likely we are to get any.' They were booked in at this London station hotel for one night. In the morning they'd take the train to Manchester for a working visit to Harry's textile mills where they'd wait until his father relayed further instructions. Harald Morten Senior had promised to maintain contact with Moscow.

'How did Roland sound?' Harry asked when the waiter had taken the order. 'Over his shock yet?'

The London-to-Paris telephone call Katya had booked that lunchtime had been connected as they sat down for dinner, and she'd rushed out to take it. 'He's nowhere near over it,' she admitted. 'I had to remind him that every second on the line costs a small fortune and to *please* let me speak.' She gave a wan smile, tipping her head, and a diamond drop earring caught the candlelight. 'I wish I'd had time to appoint a deputy. If Maison Javier collapses, it's my fault.'

'You could still go back.'

Her diamonds flashed her answer. She lifted her husband's hand, kissing the tops of his fingers. 'If I'm going to be made unhappy, at least I'm with you.'

Harry answered in stiff, theatrical English, 'How frightfully reassuring, Mrs Morten.'

A second waiter arrived, asking if 'Sah and Moddom' were ready to order. When the man had noted down 'Two lobster hors d'oeuvres, one lamb cutlet, one beef *Rossini*' and departed, Harry murmured, 'We've had false hopes before.'

'They weren't false,' Katya answered staunchly. 'Just premature. Vera is alive. And don't ask me how I know.'

As they ate, Harry asked if Roland had mentioned Tatiana.

Katya put down a forkful of lobster. 'Apparently, Constanza left Paris without warning and Tatya's been racing around like an overwound clockwork toy, banging into the furniture. Roland asked me if she takes cocaine.'

'Does she?'

'I'd be the last to know. I graduated from being the spoilsport elder sister to a staid matron. I don't like her friends, though. That Armand.' She shuddered. 'Poor fellow, but I wouldn't like to be stuck in a lift with him. Constanza Darocca has always been a negative influence.' Katya picked up her fork. The lobster was delicious, not to be wasted. 'I asked Roland again to offer Tatiana a proper job and he said he might as well give a cat a pot of ink and ask it to complete the Mozart *Requiem*.'

Chapter Thirty

Thursday, 5 October,
night of the lunar eclipse

Rosa's ballet was called *Le Père Négligent* (*The Careless Father*), and was a reinvention of a popular eighteenth-century work about a wayward girl though in this case, it was the father's failings being examined. Rosa had written on her invitations: 'Bring friends, family, colleagues, enemies, bring *everyone*.' If she got her wish, the modest Théâtre du Tertre would split like an overripe melon.

Tatiana had received an assent from Gérard on his return from Vienna. He would come, and had booked a table for them at Les Ambassadeurs at the Hôtel Crillon for afterwards. A table for two. They had much to discuss, he had written in his short message.

How he'd sit through two hours of Rosa's expressionism Tatiana couldn't imagine, since he considered Tchaikovsky to be unpalatably modern; he must want to see her badly. For her part, she felt like a woman on her way to execution. Constanza's departure had deprived her of her only human outlet and, after a run of sleepless nights, worries swarmed like locusts in her head. She'd had to build her courage all over again.

She arrived early at the theatre to be sure of getting her 'good luck' card and bouquet backstage while Rosa was calm enough to appreciate it. Not only had Rosa choreographed *The Careless Father*, she was performing in it too. As I might have been, Tatiana reminded herself. Had life been simpler, had Gérard never had a brother.

The theatre was in the heart of Montmartre, hogging a steep corner of rue Lepic and rue Girardon. Rosa's first night had drawn an arty-looking crowd, trailing downhill and transforming the junction into a piazza. The night was clear, a majestic full moon not yet wearing its red veil. Auspicious for Rosa? Hopefully.

The first person she recognised was Larissa Markova, hurrying towards a side door with a music case under her arm. Larissa nodded but didn't stop. The second person Tatiana saw was Regan Dortmeyer.

She pushed towards him. 'Do you have a double? I thought you were long gone.'

He explained about his stolen material, and needing to re-shoot the lot.

'But that's awful! Who took it, do you suppose?'

'I don't know. Una, maybe, as a joke. Or a passing burglar, who for reasons unknown took my work and left my cameras alone. You OK?'

Detecting restraint in his manner, she wondered what she'd done to offend him. Their last meeting was a blur. Perhaps she'd piqued his male pride. She was good at that. 'Are you a ballet connoisseur?' she asked, to break the ice.

'Totally. My ex, Janet-Marie, liked dragging me to the Met for cultural injections.' The Metropolitan Opera House in New York, he explained. He was here to record Rosa's debut for the press and for the archive. 'You?'

'For pleasure. I'm one of Rosa's pupils. I'm…' she cleared her throat, 'meeting my fiancé.'

'Yeah? Well, all the best.'

They shook hands. She'd thought him passably handsome the first time they met properly, but since then his dishevelled charm had grown on her. Put him in the hands of Gérard's tailor on rue Auber... Ah, there was Gérard, on the edge of the crowd, looking for her. She waved. Her arm dropped as she saw a thin figure step out of a taxi and glance furtively around.

Chapter Thirty-One

So this was modern ballet.

Regan had expected white legs and gossamer fabrics, swan necks and *pointe* shoes. Male dancers like well-honed meat porters hefting nymphs over their heads. *The Careless Father* hadn't delivered. The performers – five boys, four girls and Rosa – had remained on stage throughout, clumped together in a single block. When one moved, they all moved, like a machine with interdependent parts; as they all wore identical striped leotards it had been impossible to see whose legs were whose. The music had been equally strange, piano and strings playing different melodies. Still, Rosa was getting a standing ovation. He was pleased for her. They'd struck up a rapport and he'd told her about his stolen work, venturing to ask, 'Could Una have played a trick on me?'

'Not a trick like that,' Rosa had insisted. 'Una is fay and fickle in some ways, but intensely loyal to her friends.' Which left Griff Roy-Thomas as the probable joker, which Regan didn't want to believe either.

After the applause diminished and the last carnations and roses landed on the stage, Regan saw Tatiana leaving her seat. It said something about a woman that you noticed her in the middle row of a crowded theatre. Her evening dress was the colour of olives, green and black and sleeveless but worn with long gloves, which stirred fire in Regan's belly. He'd already noted the jade circlet that pulled her hair in at the sides. She was heading backstage, the fiancé following. Carrying his sneer on a cushion. From his position in the wings, Regan decided to get to the green room ahead of them. He'd line up a picture of Tatiana as she greeted Rosa.

As he reached the backstage corridor he stopped, perturbed. Gérard was ahead of him. Then he realised it was not Gérard, but a relation, for sure. Younger, twenty pounds lighter and minus the air of entitlement.

Rosa had danced the role of the Careless Father's hectoring wife and the flush of exertion lay in her cheeks. The pink candlewick robe she'd thrown on was a little casual for the green-room bar, but it would stop her catching cold. A bandeau kept her coils of black hair off her shoulders. She was sipping a colourless drink from a tumbler while a young man with pad and charcoal sketched her. Regan knew him to be her lover.

Her free hand twirled a rose thrown during the curtain call. Regan raised his camera, but Tatiana pushed through, blocking him.

'Rosa, that was magical! Please, can I dance in your company one day? Am I good enough?'

After Regan took his shot, Rosa called him over.

She said, 'Meet Princess Tatiana Vytenis, who could have been a ballerina had she worked harder and turned up for her lessons. Do you know each other? I can see you do. Ah, wait, don't you have Una McBride in common?'

She spoke fast, making no concession to Regan's preference for English. On first meeting, she and Regan had conversed in French until she blinked at one of his phrases and demanded, 'Where *did* you pick up the language?'

When he answered, 'On Grand Street, the Bowery end,' and filled in the details, she'd bent double with laughter, telling him, 'I learned mine in a steam laundry in Bow. London, East End. It employed Frenchwomen because they were the best laundresses and so I became bilingual without trying. When I was plucked away to study ballet, it was all Russian and French.' She'd been Connie-Rose Marshal until the dance school's principal rechristened her. 'Just as waiters need to be French, ballerinas have to be Russian.'

It was Rosa Konstantiva, not Connie-Rose, who told her lover to, 'Let Monsieur Dortmeyer take some more photos. Edward is an illustrator fresh from England,' she explained, which Regan knew already. 'Like all vocational artists, he dreams of daubing in oils because, as we know, regular work and a wage is *sooo* unutterably bourgeois. How do you want me?' Rosa blinked at Regan through Cleopatra eyes.

'Let's get a slice of theatre life, all-revealing.'

'You want me to take off my robe?'

'Up to you – only you should know, whatever the light, whatever I do in the darkroom, candlewick always looks like damn candlewick.'

'I suspect you might be very clever in a darkroom.' Rosa stretched on tiptoe, putting her lips so close Regan saw the brush marks of her lipstick.

He said, 'You can speed things up, you can slow things down. It comes down to chemistry.'

'Mm. What are you doing later?'

'Dinner at Mère Richelieu's, then back to my workbench.'

'That's where we're all having dinner. Join us.'

He heard her friend Edward snort, 'Bloody charlatan.' As for Tatiana, her expression was that of a fishwife whose corns had been trodden on. He could almost imagine she was jealous. Which she had no right to be, on a night out with her fiancé. Where was the charmer, by the way? Regan took a couple more shots, then went to the bar and found himself standing next to Gérard's double, who was asking for white rum. A large measure.

The show hadn't been that bad.

Regan asked for bourbon, was told it wasn't available. 'Beer, then. Cold... any chance?'

'*Encore un autre.*' Gérard's double had tipped back his rum like water and slammed his glass down, unaware or not caring that Regan was ahead of him. Regan cancelled his beer and swung away from the bar. His camera case smacked against the man. His apology went unheard. The fellow was downing a fresh shot and staring hard at a magazine page, which was a full-length portrait of Tatiana.

'God darn,' breathed Regan as suspicion collided with the evidence of his eyes.

Gérard had a brother, and the brother loved Tatiana. Or wanted her, or both. He stayed close, and when at last they were all trooping out of the theatre, he continued following the man. Everyone in the crowd was gazing up at the moon which was drifting, smoky-orange, into eclipse. Keeping close as Gérard's double lurched up to Tatiana, Regan heard a brief exchange.

'I will love you to the end of life – why won't you believe it?'

And her reply: 'I don't want your love, Armand. You trailed me to Dr Jolivet's, then betrayed me to your brother and mother. I despise you.'

'I did not betray you! Gérard told Maman.'

'But who told him?'

'Not I. I swear it.' Armand clasped his hands, and Regan could almost believe he was begging for his life. 'I got nothing from that place – all I did was read the name-plates inside the lobby. I left almost at once and followed you, hoping I might talk to you, but I lost sight of you when you ran from the bridge.'

'I don't believe a word of it.' She raised her hands, warning him away. Warning she'd scream if he touched her. 'I'm going to tell Gérard tonight what you did to me. You will wake up tomorrow as an outcast from your own family.'

Regan felt the penny drop. This miserable excuse of a man had harmed her.

She'd had enough, she was burrowing into the crowd, and a minute later Regan saw her with her fiancé, walking away uphill. Regan took Armand by the elbow. 'You've had your moment, fellow.' Only when the couple was out of sight did he cast off the brother, who seemed to have no fight in him, and join Rosa's party heading towards a late supper. On Place du Tertre, however, he made his excuses and peeled away. The moon was the colour of tawny port. He could have dinner any time, Regan told himself, but photograph a total lunar eclipse over the domes of the basilica of Sacré-Coeur? That was a once in a lifetime opportunity.

As he crossed the square, Regan saw Tatiana and Gérard again. They were standing under one of the globe gaslights and… was he imagining it? They were arguing.

Chapter Thirty-Two

'If I'd known I was being brought to watch a half-baked maul without structure or plot, I wouldn't have bothered. Let's go and eat, though Les Ambassadeurs is a faint hope. It's after midnight.'

Gérard strode away, leaving Tatiana to follow or not, as she chose. It was all right for him, he was wearing trousers and flat shoes. The chance of talking over a dinner table was ebbing, and she didn't rate her chances if she broke her news in the car. It was a compact vehicle, the passenger seat set slightly behind the driver's seat. She'd have to fling her news at the back of Gérard's neck.

She hurried after him. 'What about dinner here on the square? Everyone else is going to Mère Richelieu's.'

'Haven't I made it clear? Your dancer friends are not my type.'

'What I meant was, the Lapin Agile might be quieter than normal.'

'We could try Les Ambassadeurs after all. They know me so well, they might lay a cover for us.' Gérard nodded, approving his own idea.

'I don't feel up to eating in front of attentive waiters.'

'When do you feel up to eating anywhere, Tatiana?' They came to a stop beneath a lamp and he tucked his thumb and forefinger under her chin. Though his tone was amused, his eyes were not.

A pulse filled her throat. 'I have to tell you something. Gérard, you have to marry me and soon. If you care for me and your good name...' she trailed off.

The change in his expression warned her even before he spoke. 'Tatiana, I don't want to marry you.'

'You don't want...' she echoed stupidly. 'You do. You have to.'

'I don't want to marry you. I made the decision in Vienna, though in my heart I had made it before.' He tried to step past her, but she gripped his lapels. Sighing, he went on, 'It's not your fault, but this engagement was a mistake. We aren't suited.' And after what seemed like a protracted pause: 'I'm sorry.'

'You have to marry me, Gérard, because I'm pregnant.'

He stared down at her with intensifying disgust. 'That is stooping low, Tatiana. Don't imagine you can blackmail me. I'll drive you home.'

Chapter Thirty-Three

He had parked his blue Peugeot Quadrilette on the corner of Place du Tertre and rue Norvins, and as Tatiana waited for him to unlock it, she lifted her gaze to the moon glowing pink behind the domes of Sacré-Coeur. In all the conversations she'd rehearsed, she had not anticipated this. The chilling of Gérard's manner now assumed its true significance. He'd been falling out of love and steeling himself to tell her. Telling him she was pregnant had made it easier.

He guided her to the passenger side, an unloving hand on her shoulder, then walked to the driver's side. She noticed he stood for an interval before getting in and starting the engine.

'Can't bear to be in a car with me, Gérard?'

A lurch of speed threw Tatiana forward. She didn't think he had drunk anything at the theatre, but perhaps he'd downed a shot or two earlier, fortifying himself for his announcement.

Her cry of 'Slow down!' had no effect. Wind knifed through the unglazed sides of the car. 'You're right, I was blackmailing you,' she cried, looking straight ahead in case she provoked him to go even faster. 'It's just that I love you so desperately and I need you. I *am* having a baby. It isn't a lie – please, Gérard, slow down!'

They left Place du Tertre behind, heading along the eastern arm of rue Norvins. 'I don't want to marry you,' Gérard ground out. 'Not now and not— *Oh, mon Dieu!* A figure stepped from a doorway into their path and the impact crumpled the little car. As Gérard braked, a human form slewed over the bonnet, a white, aghast face imprinting itself on Tatiana's vision. Then the windscreen shattered.

'Gérard, stop! It's Armand!'

He came to a halt in a burn of tyres and the icy, controlling aristocrat vanished. He began hurling out a fractured prayer: 'Please, God, no. Please, God, no. I cannot... *Dieu, aide-moi!*' God help me.

Tatiana leaned forward to open the passenger door, but her fingers had turned to putty. She started to climb over the open side of the car, only to pull back as she saw an arm and a white hand flung out in front of the wheel arch. 'He's on the ground. I don't think he's moving.'

Gérard grabbed a map book from the door pocket and knocked hanging fragments of windscreen onto the bonnet. She felt he was buying time.

'What was Armand doing? He must have seen your headlights.'

'Shut up. Just shut up and let me think.' Gérard opened his door, cursing because shock – or fear – made him weak and it slammed shut on him twice. They heard the rake of shutters being thrown back in a house nearby, someone calling, 'What's going on out there?' The impact had woken at least one resident. Gérard stayed with one foot on the running board, frozen with indecision until they both heard the shrill pipe of a whistle.

'Police,' Tatiana whispered. 'They can help. They can bring an ambulance.' She fumbled with her door handle again, but the impact must have buckled the frame. 'I'll say it wasn't your fault, he was suddenly there in front of us. Gérard?'

'Shut your mouth.' The words came down like a blade. 'Get behind the wheel.' Indecision left him. Gérard got out and she heard his shoes crunching on glass. He didn't stop – he must have stepped over Armand. A moment later, he'd wrenched open her door and was pulling her out, uncaring that her dress caught, that her shoe snagged under the driver's seat. 'Gérard, take care!'

'Get behind the wheel,' he commanded. 'We'll say it was you.'

'No. No, I won't.'

Armand lay on the cobbles, arms wide and his coat-tails spread like wings. His shirt collar was twisted, as was his neck. His head rested in a slight depression where the rain of a few days ago had left a shallow well. The water was wine-dark. She whimpered, 'Oh dear, sweet God. Armand.' Kneeling down beside him, she cradled him, hardly aware of blood staining her dress. His empty eyes stared past her into the night. 'What were you doing? What were you doing?' His head jinked to the side, coming to rest at a hideous angle.

'Get up. He's beyond help.' Gérard marched her, a hand in the small of her back. 'Tatiana, listen. If I'm convicted I'll lose my job. My rank, future, everything.'

'You'll still have me. And our child. Gérard? *Our child.*' From this moment on, she would give no ground. For her sake and the baby's. He need never know he was not the father. Her secret, shared with Constanza and nobody else.

He didn't answer – he was forcing her towards the driver's door. She dug in until one of her shoe heels snapped off. A van was approaching from the direction of Place du Tertre.

'Gérard, they won't believe I was at the wheel. Not in evening shoes and long gloves!'

'I'll say it's your first time driving, that I was ill, you were taking me home. Or to hospital. Yes, that's better. An emergency – they won't hold you to blame. You, a young, pretty girl. You'll get a fine, a small one, perhaps a warning.'

Two gasps later, she was in the driver's seat and Gérard was leaning into the car, his breath like sandpaper on her face. Headlights filled the interior. She heard the slam of heavy doors, the bark of questions. Police. Gérard kept a clamp on her arm and she heard him call, 'Messieurs, there has been a terrible incident. Can you help?' Panic and desperation had vanished. Gérard was back in control. She grabbed his arm, pulling him towards her.

'If I do this for you, you marry me.'

'Later, *chérie*. We'll talk.'

'Now, Gérard. Say you will marry me or I swear, I'll tell them you were driving.'

'Yes, yes all right.' He might have been speaking to a whining child.

'At the Hôtel de Ville on 26 October. You will marry me. Say it.'

'Yes. I will.'

'Swear it.'

'I swear.'

'On your honour – on your mother's eternal soul.'

A pause. 'On my mother's eternal soul. I will marry you.'

She sat, gripping the wheel, only now aware of the scarlet blots on the front of her dress. Staring through the shattered windscreen at a moon in the ruby climax of an eclipse, she told herself, 'I won. I got my way and a man is dead.'

The next voice she heard was Regan's.

'Tatiana? There's a body in the road.'

'It's Armand de Sainte-Vierge. He's dead.'

'Wait. I'll check.' Regan disappeared from her view, but was back within a few seconds. 'Yup, I'm afraid so. Why are you behind the wheel? You weren't driving.'

'I was. It was me.'

'No. I was on the corner of Tertre and Norvins and I saw you both get into the car. Don't tell me cockamamie stories. What's the bastard making you do?'

Regan had braced his arms against the car and was leaning in. His eyes were pools of fury.

Like an automaton, she repeated, 'I was driving. Regan, will you get a letter to my sister Katya. Roland Javier may know where... I can't think... she and Harry will be in London. Or maybe not. I wish I were there with them. Regan? Please. I need help.'

'Tatiana, don't let that man stick the blame on you. The law won't let you off with a smacked wrist. Sweetheart? You listening?'

She never got to answer because the next moment she was pulled from the car, pushed against its side by men wearing flat-topped helmets, button tunics and black capes. Someone wrenched the jade circlet from her forehead and she heard beads scattering across the cobbles. Her name was demanded. They asked if she was drunk.

'Gérard!' she cried in terror. 'Gérard!'

He'd gone.

Regan tried to intervene, but there were six uniformed voices to his one. She was taken to wait by the police van until another vehicle, with grilles for windows, arrived. She was pushed inside into the company of several agitated women and a man in handcuffs. The women, who were dressed in the gaudy finery of streetwalkers, bared their teeth at her.

*

At the police station, her fingerprints and a statement were taken. At some point in the early hours, she was remanded to Saint-Lazare prison in the tenth *arrondissement* to await trial. For several days afterwards, she held to the unshakeable belief that Gérard would come. Would use his influence to make things right for her. He did not come.

She was told that another man, a foreigner, had given evidence that suggested she was not driving that night. That her friend, Monsieur de Sainte-Vierge, had been at the wheel.

Was that true?

No. She stuck stubbornly to her story. She had been driving and had accidentally killed Armand de Sainte-Vierge.

During the first two weeks of her remand, she was allowed one visitor: her mother, who did nothing but weep. Irina left Tatiana a linen handkerchief and a tiny bottle of cologne, immediately confiscated. She was provided with a solicitor who persuaded her to plead guilty, assuring her that her youth and previous good behaviour would win her an easier sentence. Evidence had emerged from more than one witness that Armand had spent the evening of his death drinking heavily. That would weigh in Tatiana's favour if she made the guilty plea. She listened, she assented. Gérard had promised on his mother's soul to marry her and she would keep her side of the bargain. Her love for him had died under that blood-red moon, but they would – *must* – marry, for her unborn child's sake.

'Hopefully, by the time you come to trial,' her lawyer said, 'the judge will consider you've served enough of a sentence. It's unfortunate that Monsieur de Sainte-Vierge has no memory of the impact, or of the minutes before, and cannot give evidence in your favour.'

So long as he remembered his vow. That's what she clung to.

Solitary hours and little contact with the outside were part of the punishment at Saint-Lazare. From the turning of the first key, Tatiana knew she was not in prison to reform, but to imbibe society's disgust. Vermin and a cold, overcrowded dormitory. Fellow inmates who, once they realised who and what she was, behaved savagely. Nuns made up the bulk of the staff. Some were kind, some cruel, but they all judged her.

From newspapers that found their way to her, she learned that her 'fall' was providing fuel for salacious commentary. She'd spent the evening at the theatre, watching a modernist ballet, and so she became a byword for the degenerate, arty set. Much was made of Armand's war service, his honourable discharge and the mental wounds he had suffered. There were plenty of so-called friends eager to describe her capricious, selfish ways in lavish detail.

Some friends held fast. Rosa must have set up a rota because rarely a day came without a fresh letter. Kind notes came from Roland Javier and Pauline Frankel, and from other, surprising sources: Larissa and Madame Markova, Marianne du Gard, Madame Léonce from the apothecary's, even Monsieur Aristide, proprietor of the English Tea Parlour on rue Cambon – but after some poison-pen missives squeezed in alongside, Tatiana refused to open any more.

All her energy was invested in the life in her womb, the child she had learned, finally, to love. As wretchedness turned to bitterness, she named those who had deserted her. Gérard topped the list. After that came her mother. And Yana, who could have helped Anoushka send a card, if not come herself. Katya and Harry. And Constanza yet again absent in her hour of need. Her 'set', the youthful illuminati who could not find their way to the tenth.

Regan wrote. For him she made an exception, though she glowered coldly at his letters which, because they were partly written in English, went through the prison censor's office. In every one of them, Regan urged her to 'state the truth' and promised to speak at her hearing, if he could persuade the police to take him seriously. He'd written to Katya at a London station hotel and asked the management to send the letter on, as it was his understanding that Katya had already left. Meanwhile, had Tatiana told the authorities that she was 'in the family way'?

Thanks to the censor's zealous eye, she got a transfer to the *Maternité*, a wing for pregnant prisoners and those with babies. Better food, extra blankets. A room shared with only three others, paradise after the bear pit of the dormitory. She ought to be grateful, but Regan's interference put her in jeopardy, for what if one of the staff or another prisoner tittle-tattled to the press and Madame la marquise found out she was pregnant?

Her twenty-third birthday passed unmarked on 18 October. Her trial by police tribunal fell on 26 October, which she'd once believed would be her wedding day. And on that day, Gérard came.

She saw him in the public gallery, his gaze sliding along the line of prisoners, briefly touching her then on to the next. She was unrecognisable. The lice that had hurled themselves at her clean scalp on day one had led her to ask to have her head shaved. And so she looked little different from the prostitutes awaiting their sentences and who had been shaved in punishment. Regan was in the gallery, with Rosa, their eyes boring into her.

Tell the truth.

She saw her lawyer arrive. Late. His gaze passed over her too, and she saw him check his papers, as if he feared he might have come on the wrong day.

Only when her name was called and she was hustled into the dock did he look up. Gérard finally recognised her too. It was a small courtroom and she read all too plainly both men's horror at the shorn and bony creature she'd become. She tried a brave smile, but her mouth wouldn't obey.

From the gallery, Regan shouted, 'Tell them you weren't driving, Tatiana.'

Gérard gave him a sidelong glance. He then seemed to signal to her lawyer and cold fear lodged in Tatiana's throat. Surely, the two men didn't know each other.

When she was asked if she pleaded guilty, she had no voice to answer.

'She wasn't behind the wheel,' Regan projected into the silence. 'You there, lawyer, do your damn job!'

The courtroom guards moved, Gérard helpfully pointing them in Regan's direction. There ensued a fracas, Regan defiant even as he was strong-armed out, shouting, 'God damn you, the man responsible is here in court.'

When reinforced doors were shut behind Regan, the judge again asked Tatiana if she pleaded guilty to driving recklessly, of causing the death of Armand de Sainte-Vierge. She hesitated. Her lawyer nodded. *Yes.* As they'd agreed. But Regan had woken her to a different possibility.

Gérard came to the front of the gallery. Placing his hand over his heart, his eyes blazed a promise. 'On my mother's eternal soul,' he mouthed to her. 'I will marry you.'

She answered the question. 'Yes, Monsieur.'

'Speak up,' the judge ordered.

'Yes. I plead guilty.'

Relief spilled over Gérard. He smiled.

The judge sentenced her to a further six weeks' imprisonment.

Gripping the edge of the dock, she wept, 'No, you have to let me go! I've served enough time!' Then in desperation, 'Gérard, don't abandon me!'

A figure pushed Gérard aside, lips pulled back in snarling hatred. It was Clothilde de Sainte-Vierge, who screamed, 'Tatiana Vytenis, I curse your existence and hope – *pray* – that one day you will know what it is to lose a child. Drunken trollop! They should throw away the key and let you rot!'

Not even the marquise's hatred stunned her as much as Gérard's response. He put his arm around his mother and drew her close. Tatiana now saw with absolute clarity. He had what he'd come for and for her, for Tatiana, there was nothing but indifference.

Taken to a waiting van to be returned to Saint-Lazare to begin her term as a convicted criminal, atrocious pain ripped through her. She felt the burn of blood on her legs, her body fighting to eject the life within, while her mind prayed, pleaded, begged for it to be spared.

Her body won.

Part Three

Chapter Thirty-Four

On Monday, 11 December, a pilot door was unlocked within the gates of Saint-Lazare prison and Tatiana stepped out. As she took her first, free breath a punching wind took off her headscarf, revealing a scalp of copper curls as downy as the floss on a silk weaving floor.

Re-knotting the scarf under her chin, she scanned the crowd on the forecourt. She wasn't the only one getting her freedom this morning. Family members, boyfriends and not a few pimps were on hand to collect the newly released. Clutching an oilcloth roll that contained her possessions, Tatiana searched for a friendly face. Her mother would be here, surely. Or have sent Yana at the very least. Tatiana nurtured a hope that Katya might have hurried home. But she saw nobody she knew. The world had branded her a heartless killer and seemed bent on showing its contempt.

'Tatiana?'

Not recognising the masculine voice, she cautiously raised a hand. At once, a corner broke off the crowd and moved towards her. Men and women, notepads folded back, pencils poised. Questions flew at her like machine-gun fire.

'How does it feel to be out?'

'How does it feel to have lost your looks?'

'Did the streetwalkers inside teach you any tricks?'

'You killed your fiancé's brother, how d'you feel about that?'

'How drunk were you?'

'Is it true your mother didn't visit you?'

'We heard you collapsed and were taken to the prison sanatorium. Tatiana?'

She shoved her hands to her ears, dropping her parcel, as notepads were rammed in her face. She smelled the morning coffee on the reporters' breaths. The previous night's alcohol, the sweat and the soap. Somebody ripped off her headscarf.

'Did they pluck you like a chicken? I hope they left a few tail feathers for your boyfriend to find.' The man saying it chuckled at his own wit. He wrote as he spoke, so close his coat buckle pressed against her. Helplessness swept her. In her mind, she cowered behind curtains while half a room's distance away her father screamed in his death throes. Armand was there, pinning her against the wall, hoarsely insisting, 'I'll love you to my life's end.' She would have fallen, except that she was jammed upright by the press pack.

'Take your hands off her. Now.' A new voice. Male.

'Do as he says, you pigs!' A woman's voice. Fearless.

A sound like raw meat being slammed against wood produced a cry of pain. Violent profanities added to the mayhem. The stubbly jowls of the pressman closest to her gave way to a different face.

Regan Dortmeyer looped an arm around her and the mob opened out before him, because he was kicking shins and knees. Someone else was swinging a handbag, making contact with the sides of faces, the tops of heads. Tatiana couldn't see who was wielding it, other than that the hand controlling it wore a blue kid glove.

Regan hurried her to where a taxi waited. He pressed her into the back. Someone flung themselves in beside her and rapped on the glass with a blue-gloved hand. 'Driver, rue de Rivoli. *Chez* Angelina, and don't spare the horses.'

Una McBride.

Regan climbed in beside the driver and the vehicle pulled away. He turned and waved to her through the glass. His eyes fastened momentarily on her butchered hair, showing neither pity nor disgust, for which she was grateful.

'Where's his camera?' Tatiana's lungs felt crushed. 'He could sell my release to a dozen journals.'

'He left it at home,' Una said, taking Tatiana's hand. 'This moment is about you and you alone. Welcome back to freedom, Princess. We're taking you for brioche and hot chocolate.'

Tatiana shook her head. The cotton-knit dress and coat she was wearing had been provided by Roland Javier, so she wouldn't have to emerge in prison rags. Chosen from last year's collection, the dress would bolster any woman's confidence. But it was rumpled and soiled now. 'I'm not dressed for a Rivoli café.' She couldn't stop herself tugging the remnants of her hair.

'Try this.' Una fetched a parcel from the footwell. Out came a coat of vicuna wool, soft as whipped caramel. Its buttons were deer horn. 'Madame Frankel chose it from this November's midseason line, and I would trade my soul for one. She thought it would cheer you up.' Una flowed into fashion writer mode: 'Amply sized, but we're showing generous coats this season. Note the picture buttons and the absence of a belt.'

Tatiana shuffled off the coat she had on and put on the new one. Instant warmth, like sliding inside a hot-water bottle. Somebody had sprayed the lining with a subtle perfume. Tatiana hoped she had never in the past been insolent to Pauline Frankel, but couldn't convince herself of it.

'Here's my present.' Una placed a box on Tatiana's knee. The hat inside was a shade of coffee. 'From Bonwit Teller, New York, based on one by Caroline Reboux.'

Tatiana turned it in her hands. It was little more than an upside-down plant pot with a band of grosgrain above a downturned brim.

'May I?' Una put the hat on her, adjusting it until she was satisfied. 'We have remarkably similar head measurements. I'm twenty-two inches and one-eighth.'

'Twenty-two and two-eighths. When I have hair, that is.'

'It'll grow back before you know it.' Una rapped on the dividing glass. Turning to see Tatiana transformed, Regan did a double take. Tatiana would have laughed, but joy had seeped from her soul. Not one letter from Gérard, not even a line on a postcard. She was the damn fool who had served a prison sentence for him, allowed him to get off scot-free and break his vow. Armand had warned her. So had Agnès de Brioude, in her way.

'I lost a baby in prison,' she whispered.

Una's clasp became a squeeze. 'You have been through hell, and all for a man who isn't worth the scrapings off your shoes. Regan told me what he did to you.'

Tatiana said, 'I thought you and Regan had fallen out, after you filched his photographs.'

Una gave a huff. '*Et tu*, Tatiana? When I called on him, the first person I saw – bar Rosa – after getting back from America, he turned on me like a junk-yard dog. If I wasn't blond and cute, I wouldn't be here now. Sure, I was as high as the Eiffel Tower the night I left, but I did not, repeat *did not*, steal Regan's work. Nor did Griff.'

'Then who did?'

'As I said to Regan in pleasurable expectation, "Search me, honey".'

Tatiana turned away, staring out at passing facades, recognising Avenue de l'Opéra and the entrance to rue Molière. What day was today? Monday or Tuesday? A weekday, at any rate, to judge by the delivery vans on the road. It crossed her mind to stop the cab. There was something she needed to give back to Gérard, and pride demanded she do it in person.

But rue Molière flashed by. Una was chattering about a rich New York fashion wholesaler she'd met during her trip home – Artie Shone, who wanted to set her up, 'As an agent, buying couture for him in Paris.' Tatiana *must* meet him.

Tatiana let it all gurgle over her until they were cutting through Place Vendôme, passing the Ritz. 'Have you seen Constanza?' she interrupted. 'She didn't come to see me. She can't still be in Argentina for a funeral?'

'Funeral in Argentina?' Una *had* seen Constanza Darocca. But in New York. 'On 5th Avenue, while I was hat-shopping.'

'That's not possible.'

'One never mistakes *La Darocca*. Not a girl to fade into the crowd.'

'Did you speak?'

Una hesitated. 'I didn't want to intrude. She seemed to be in a happy world of her own. Is she a very close friend?'

'My best. If she went from Buenos Aires to New York, it explains why she doesn't know what happened to me.' They were turning into rue de Rivoli, arcades to the left, the railings of the Tuileries gardens fluting silver and black to the right. 'Did Regan tell you I was pregnant?'

'No. He's tight-lipped, you know? First cousin to a clam. Here's Angelina.' The taxi was pulling up.

'I was five months' gone, it was more like a birth than a miscarriage. Not that I knew what a miscarriage should feel like… Katya has had two. My poor sister. It was a boy. I can't tell you… the sisters took him away.'

'Sisters? How come—'

'The holy sisters. Saint-Lazare is staffed by nuns. Two of them were kind in a brisk sort of fashion.'

As Tatiana unleashed her pent-up story, Una mouthed an instruction to Regan, and the taxi took another turn around the block. Tatiana was aware of being ravenously hungry. She raged at herself. How dare she be hungry, alive and free?

Hot chocolate and brioche stopped her shaking, but her nose kept snatching stale whiffs behind the masking perfume, and which she realised came from her skin. Legacy of living between walls marinated in mildew. She must have grown used to it.

'Can you take me home?' she asked. 'I must take a bath then rest a little before I get back to work.'

'You need to rest a lot,' was Regan's response. 'Let press interest simmer down before you appear on a catwalk.'

'I need to work,' she repeated. 'And to sort out my future. I cannot spend my life bouncing between question marks. First, can we go to Avenue du Bois de Boulogne?'

Regan's expression turned wary. 'Isn't that—?'

'It is,' she agreed, 'and if you don't take me, I'll walk there.'

Una's opinion was 'avoid at all costs' but Tatiana was adamant.

Chapter Thirty-Five

Winter had scoured the avenue's wide verges during Tatiana's weeks of incarceration. Every tree had been laid bare, which allowed an unimpeded view of the Sainte-Vierge mansion. As she stepped out of the cab, checking her shoes for scuffs and other signs of her shame, a man, suited, hatted, dressed for business, came out.

'Gérard!'

He appeared not to hear and proceeded to a waiting car. Tatiana recognised the solemn family Peugeot, the driver holding the door. Gérard was inside before Tatiana could get near.

'Gérard!' This time, she knew he'd seen her, but the car slid away.

Una came up. 'Note how the nicely tilted Homburg complements the line of cheek and jaw. Upper lip sporting the *de rigeur* and impeccably groomed moustache. What was Gérard's war record?'

'Logistics and supplies. Procuring feed for the horses and mules.'

'Behind the lines. Figures.'

The Peugeot must have turned in the road, because Gérard came past again. Tatiana looked away.

Una had no such qualms. 'Hang on,' she said. 'Didn't he used to come into Callot?'

Tatiana nodded. 'I met him there. He came in one day to—' To fetch Armand away. Remorse broke over her. How much of Armand's death was her fault?

The door of the Sainte-Vierge residence opened and Gérard's mother hobbled out, supporting herself with a cane. The loss of a son lay in every line of her face. The hornet temper had not softened, however. She brandished her stick at Tatiana.

'You dare show yourself?'

'Watching the darling boy leave for work,' Una whispered.

'Madame.' Tatiana walked forward. 'I have something for you.' From her dress pocket she took a scrap of handkerchief, which was tied in a knot. The marquise stared at it.

'I won't have you bothering Gérard. Leave him in peace, if you know what's good for you.'

It felt like a threat, but what could be done to her that hadn't already been done? Tatiana undid the knot, revealing the Sainte-Vierge engagement ring. 'Take it,' she said. 'I have no use for it.'

Madame de Sainte-Vierge snatched it, then held it up to inspect it. Presumably in case Tatiana had levered out some of the pearls, or damaged it in some way.

'It's in the same condition as when Gérard presented it to me,' Tatiana said tartly. *Unlike me.*

The marquise gave a grunt. 'Now leave, or I'll have my staff call the police.'

Una chipped in. 'You're telling us we can't stand on the public highway?'

The marquise bathed Una in disdain. 'I know who you are. A seagull that follows the couture steamship, diving for scraps. Stand where you like, except on this avenue.' Her contempt settled again on

Tatiana. 'Send back anything else my son gave you, or I'll have you arrested for theft.'

'You are unfailingly gracious.' Una gave Madame de Sainte-Vierge intense scrutiny, reminiscent of a short-sighted dowager peering through opera glasses. She mimed the opera glasses so convincingly her victim frowned in confusion. 'Poiret?' Una asked, having thoroughly inspected Madame de Sainte-Vierge's day dress. 'Genuine or knock-off?'

'Una, not now,' Tatiana begged.

'How dare you!' The marquise's face went perfectly red.

'Knock-off,' Una said with satisfaction. 'But good. Whoever did it, keep her close.'

'Go, get away. Criminals – murderesses – have no place here.'

'I am no murderess,' cried Tatiana. Armand's face behind a shattered windscreen flashed through her mind. 'I wish with all my heart that I and Gérard could undo that night. But he hasn't told you half of it. Gérard has lied, and as for Armand, he… he took advantage when I was—' Tatiana's words erupted in a scream as the marquise brought her cane down on her shoulder with all the force she could muster.

Una grabbed the marquise's weapon arm while Regan, who had been waiting by the taxi, ran up and made a shield of himself in front of Tatiana.

The marquise struggled in Una's grip. 'Dirty, foreign trollop! Gérard told me how he was trying to break from you. You, godless drunkard, punished him by driving at the war hero who was my younger son. Burn in hell, Tatiana Vytenis. Burn in hell.'

Regan bustled Tatiana to the taxi and climbed in beside her, leaving Una to get up beside the driver.

'You blocked my attempts to help you,' he muttered. 'I stood next to Armand at the theatre bar, watching him down white rum like it was his last drink on earth. I'd have gone on the witness stand and told one hell of a story.'

Tatiana stared blindly out of the window. *Burn in hell!* 'Why has Gérard blackened my character? Isn't it enough to have discarded me?'

Regan answered. 'There were once two men in a lifeboat, and enough fresh water for one. When the lifeboat arrived on shore, there was only one man in it. Human nature. At least, now you know. If you'd married him, imagine how it would have ended.'

'He'd have neglected me, hectored me, but he'd have been forced to look after me. *Us.*'

'Maybe. Did that old witch break anything?'

Her shoulder was smarting painfully but nothing could match the lacerating wounds of Gérard's betrayal. 'I want to die.'

Regan sighed. 'You need to sleep, Tatiana. In your own bed for seven nights before you make any decisions about life.'

'Seven? Not possible.'

'Five, then. Then call on me. You'll find me where I was before, in Pigeon's loft.'

On rue Rembrandt, Regan escorted Tatiana to her door. 'I won't intrude, but I will call later, to check up on you. Happy reunion.'

There were no happy reunions. Only the cook was in the flat, with her coat on in the strangely tidy kitchen. She told Tatiana that her mother, 'Madame la Princesse', had left Paris with her granddaughter. 'Gone to Enghien-les-Bains for her nerves.'

Enghien was a watering spa, a few miles north of Paris. 'Yana's gone with them?' Tatiana asked.

'Most assuredly. It was her idea, to get your mother away from those oafs lurking in the shrubs.'

'Which oafs? What shrubs?'

'The press, outside in the street. Thankfully, one of your neighbours is a retired judge and he had a court order drawn up, keeping them away. You have no idea what it was like, running the gauntlet of newspapermen twice a day.'

Tatiana had a powerful idea of what it felt like.

'Mind you,' the cook went on, 'Yana was little better, showing your mother every mention of you in the papers, every picture, until Princess Irina was sunk in shame and unable to eat a bite. The little girl couldn't sleep for nightmares. I was asked to stay on and look after you on your release, but I cannot say it will be convenient.'

'Mama didn't visit me in prison. Nor did she write. Why not?'

The cook shrugged. How should she know?

Perhaps her mother had written… the nuns had given Tatiana letters, which she'd refused to open. The most compassionate of them, Marie-Nazareth, had packed them along with her personal belongings. Which Tatiana had dropped on the wet cobbles outside the prison. 'So you won't look after me, Madame?'

'I am choosy whom I work for.'

Tatiana had never really looked at their cook closely, perhaps because they'd only ever met in a steamy kitchen. 'I wish you would stay,' she said, promising herself she'd make amends for any neglect.

'No. I have to take care of my reputation. Besides, what's the point of cooking for you? You don't eat.'

Tatiana drew back. 'I won't detain you any longer then, Madame. Good morning.'

By the kitchen clock, it was just gone eleven. She wandered through the flat, feeling numb. A few minutes at the drawing-room piano revealed that her fingers were clumsy. Skating over arpeggios reminded her of Benjy Crouch and gin, and her attempts to kill her baby. Suddenly afraid of the silence, she telephoned Katya's flat.

The housekeeper took the call, telling her that Madame and Monsieur Morten were still abroad, still being elusive, though a letter had arrived that morning with some news. Would Princess Tatiana like to see it?

'If you don't mind. I'll call for it later.'

After rooting out some banknotes in her mother's writing desk, Tatiana put on her new coat and hat. Outside the house, she looked right and left but the street was empty. Her neighbour's intervention had proved effective. From rue Rembrandt, she walked to Boulevard Malesherbes where she spent most of her money at the apothecary's shop. Three bottles of Sirop Roze. The proprietor, Monsieur Léonce, served her swiftly, his eyes skimming her as if he'd been warned she carried a notifiable disease.

It was unseasonably cold for early December, a grey-brown sky promising more rain, and icy rain at that. Her vicuna wool coat was proof against it, a reminder that there were people who still cared about her.

Five days, she told herself as she continued on down Malesherbes. *Five days' sleep and then I will act.* The trays in the *traiteurs'* windows pulled at her, with their ready-made dishes. With the loss of her baby, her appetite had come out of hibernation and she wished she'd retained enough money for eggs and bread. The cook had better have left something for the next day or two. Until she got her job back, she was officially a pauper.

She then remembered her reason for coming out in the first place. Dragging herself to rue Goya, she rang the bell of the Morten residence. Madame Roche had the letter ready, and while she was polite, she shut the door as soon as she could.

Head bent, Tatiana retraced her steps down Boulevard Malesherbes. Rue Cambon wasn't far. The English Tea Parlour would be open, where Katya had an account.

Monsieur Aristide fingered his suspiciously black moustache when Tatiana asked for a 'table for one'. Was he going to refuse her? She thanked him humbly for writing to her in prison and that seemed to make a difference. He bowed. 'A table for one it is.'

He put her by the front window, half hidden behind a folded-back shutter. Understandable. While working for him, she'd behaved dreadfully. Spilling tea, cheeking the customers. She'd eventually walked out mid-shift, flinging her waitress's cap behind her. She hadn't cared then. All that had mattered was that she'd had an appointment to have her long hair cut, and an interview at Callot on Avenue Montaigne, to become a mannequin. Her great chance. A chance she'd stolen from Katya. Heartless and ambitious, though beautiful enough to lure Gérard de Sainte-Vierge's discerning eye. And now? Brought low. Dependent on others for kindness she herself had never shown. She ordered tea with lemon, sandwiches and cakes. 'To go on my, um, sister's bill.'

'On Madame Morten's account. Very good, Princess Vytenis.'

She read Katya's letter as the wind typed in sleet on the window. It was dated from a week before and made clear that Katya and Harry had left London some considerable time ago, travelling north. '*Ma chère* Madame Roche,' Katya had written, 'Monsieur Morten and I are finally leaving Manchester, where we have been staying for many weeks while the next stage of our journey is arranged. We are bound for Gothenburg in Sweden, though first, we'll call at Islay, which is one of a cluster of Scottish islands. The Hebrides, they're called, and we mean to taste the special waters. I am not looking forward to the crossing – Scottish seas are wild as wolves. My husband doesn't care. It's the Viking in him. He says the Vikings traded with Russia long ago, and that I probably have their blood. Tatiana certainly does, with her red hair.'

Tatiana sniffed, 'Golden, thank you.' Were these 'special waters' an elixir to promote fertility? 'The Hebrides' was a new name to Tatiana, though she recalled their ship passing between mist-shrouded isles on their voyage from Sweden to France at the close of 1918. The last part of their journey from Russia had taken them around the North Sea. Why was Katya striking out on that dangerous route again, but in reverse?

Katya offered no clues, and none as to when she intended to return. Tatiana folded the letter as a waitress brought her food.

Cramming a salt beef and cucumber sandwich into her mouth, she looked across the road to Chanel's five-storey emporium. Three winters back, she'd watched workmen hefting wardrobes, mirrors and hanging rails into that building. The sight had made Katya more determined than ever to carve a career in fashion. The same spectacle had made Tatiana feel deprived and desperate. Lo, the difference between them! Coco Chanel was one of the wealthiest women in France and it was no secret how hard the woman worked. How hard Katya worked. Work was the key.

It would fill the void. Her little baby boy… could she have saved him? Eaten properly, rested her body? Another sandwich went into her mouth and she reached for a third. How could she break the news of a lost baby to Katya? Perhaps, after all, it was a blessing her sister was far away.

Comfort was Monsieur Aristide's cake. He had provided enough for three… had he noticed how thin she'd become? Tatiana was reaching for a chestnut cream macaron when she became aware of a man on the other side of the tea-room window, staring in at her. Overstrained nerves were to blame for her scream, which brought Monsieur Aristide to her table.

'Who is that?' he demanded.

'I don't know his name.' Though Tatiana recognised the pressman whose belt buckle had pressed loathsomely against her in the maul outside the prison. He was grinning, showing discoloured teeth and he mouthed a word at her. *Justice*. Aristide surged outside and the man walked smartly away, leaving a circular mist of breath on the glass.

Chapter Thirty-Six

At home, Sirop Roze sent Tatiana to sleep. She woke to the telephone and clear light streaming through a gap in her curtains. It took half a minute for her to orientate herself. Satins and crisp cottons, a wispy fragrance of citrus and rose with a base of something perversely masculine. Habanita, her signature perfume. She was in bed, in her own room.

A chair was shoved under the door handle. She must have done that. It took her ages to wriggle it free, but the phone kept ringing.

It was Regan. 'Rosa gave me your number. I wanted to check you were all right.'

'Five days,' she said unsteadily. 'We agreed I'd be left to sleep.'

'Forgive my impatience. How's the family?'

Gone, fled to exile, she told him.

'Should I come over?'

She'd pushed a chair under the handle of the apartment door too. That's when she remembered the man with the graveyard teeth the other side of the tea-parlour window. Regan's company would be welcome but she had a task to perform first. So she told him, 'No thanks.' She was cold. There was no heating on. 'I'll call Rosa when I'm ready.' Returning to the bedroom, she pulled back her curtains, blinking as steely brightness bowled in. Diamond frost on roofs and chimneys, treetops turned to sugar crystal. The phrase 'wedding-veil day' slipped into her mind.

It was mid-afternoon, if her mental clock was correct. Shivering, she walked into the kitchen and checked the real clock, which made no sense. It couldn't still be morning, unless she'd slept for almost twenty-four hours? She telephoned Rosa, an extravagant way of finding out.

'Eleven fifteen, Tuesday, 12 December, my love. Why don't you come here, let me look after you?'

'Soon, Rosa, I promise.' Time alone mattered, though she wasn't sure why. On impulse, she telephoned Constanza's flat.

'She's still abroad, Madame,' Constanza's maid informed her. 'Mademoiselle Darocca was called home to Buenos Aires, for her grandmother's funeral.'

'I know that but a mutual acquaintance saw her in New York, not so many days ago.'

There was a smooth pause before the maid acknowledged the possibility. 'She may have stopped off on her return. Yes, I recall that was her intention.'

'So she's on her way back to Paris?'

The maid could not say.

Hanging up, Tatiana went into the bathroom and turned on the hot tap. It ran cold, so she boiled some water in the kitchen to create the shallowest of baths. Before getting in she looked in the mirror which had caught steam. 'Oh, good God!'

Prison had put two years on her. Her skin had a grey whisper and her eyes were those of a scared rabbit. A piece in *Vogue* back in the summer had stated: 'From the age of fifteen to twenty-five, a woman's beauty is a matter of chance. From twenty-five and beyond, it is a matter of effort.'

When had she last consumed a healthy meal from beginning to end? As she lay in the shallows, and the water pooled in her concave belly, she answered the question: five years ago, December 1917. The first Christmas after the Bolshevik revolution, when Vera's husband had come home from war. Though scarred physically and emotionally, he'd been overjoyed to be reunited with his wife, while Vera's frozen fear had melted at his return. The festivities had gained a taste of old-regime merriment. Roast goose and baked carp, glazed pork and apples, sweet almond cakes… Tatiana had joined in with unrestrained appetite, forgetting that she was an eligible beauty of eighteen and ought to be watching her waistline. A day into the New Year, at four in the morning, a unit of the newly formed Cheka had hammered on the door. A servant had opened it. They had come for Mikhail. Stumbling from their rooms in slit-eyed confusion, the family had watched Vera's husband being dragged away. Never heard of since.

'And I stopped eating,' she informed herself. 'As if starving myself would bring him back. I thought it was my fault because of what I did on their wedding day.' Attention seeking. Pulling the veil off the mirror, so Vera saw herself in her wedding dress. Bringing down a curse. Self-denial had been the one thing she could offer her traumatised sister in recompense, even though Vera had forgotten the mirror incident. Later, Tatiana had blamed her aversion to food on the need to keep thin for her job. But as she interrogated the veiny backs of her hands, a different motive put itself forward. 'Look at me, don't look at me.' She still craved attention but dreaded anyone seeing behind her carapace, uncovering her rottenness. Vera was still interred within the vastness of Russia, if she was alive at all. As for Mikhail, who knew? How, under such circumstances could she, Tatiana, nurture herself?

Regret and pity became mourning for the baby whose fall from her body felt like the loss of her second self. She howled from the pit of her lungs. For Mikhail, for Vera, for darling Anoushka who would never know her parents' love. For a baby boy Tatiana would never hold in her arms. 'A little at a time,' she promised, sponging her eyes. 'Good food. Small amounts, but no more cakes, no more cocktails. No more medicine. I'll try.'

She dry-brushed her skin, massaging her body with peach kernel oil, wincing at the angles and undulations of bone. Wiping a hole in the steam on the bathroom mirror, she regarded her mutilated hair. Una's optimism that it would quickly regrow was precisely that. Optimism. A couple of months? Three, four? She couldn't hide here that long, she'd starve. Another decision, no more procrastination.

Stroking body oil through her curls, she combed them flat, replicating Una's style. A dash of face powder, kohl and red lipstick made her feel more presentable. It was too cold to go out bare-headed but she couldn't ruin a hat by putting it on an oiled head. Her accessories drawer yielded a head ornament of stiff gold lace. Fastened about her brow, it entirely swallowed her shorn hair. She added gold tasselled earrings. The effect was 'Mata Hari' though best not to dwell on that poor creature's fate.

Putting on her black dress and the new coat, silk stockings and shoes with a confident heel, she telephoned for a taxi, putting the fare on her sister's account. Her last act was to dab Chanel No. 5 behind her ears, forgetting until she'd done so that Gérard had given her the perfume some days before he'd proposed. Would she ever understand why a man, so frantic to marry her, had thrown a hand grenade into her life and walked away?

Outside on the pavement, she told the taxi driver, 'Rue Duphot, please. Maison Javier.'

'Front entrance, Madame?'

'Side entrance. I'm not shopping, I'm going to work.'

Chapter Thirty-Seven

'My dear, dear Tatiana, no, no, I'm sorry. There is no role for you here this season.'

She had cornered Roland Javier in his studio, interrupting him at work, sketching. He raised a hand to fend off her disappointment. 'It grieves me, but I must place the well-being of this house ahead of personal feelings.'

Tatiana pressed on. 'I belong here. This business is as much Katya's as yours and I take a pride in it too.'

He reminded her of the times she'd sashayed in late. Of her wayward behaviour on the catwalk, her giddy moods. Too late, he told her, for declarations of loyalty.

'But I've changed. Give me a chance, and I'll earn your confidence, I promise.'

Roland sighed. 'Your arrest and conviction cannot be dusted under the carpet.'

'I've paid my dues.'

'It is to do with perception.' He put down his pencil and came to her. Not much over five foot five, Roland had to look up into Tatiana's face. 'It is about what our clients think. What the press will say.'

'What about the customers I bring in? The ones who come to see silly, fickle Tatiana and end up buying theirs and their daughters' entire wardrobes from you?'

With a sigh that came from deep in his chest, he walked to a sofa, passing a group of wax mannequins in muslin *toiles*. His retreat offered Tatiana a moment in which to study the figures. They offered a glimpse of the spring–summer line which would be revealed in February next year. Nothing very striking. Yes, all right, *toiles* were only muslin mock-ups, but to her eye they looked like things the wardress nuns of Saint-Lazare might wear under their habits. Shift dress after shift dress.

Born out of the Great War, the drop-waist shift had become the prevailing style, but Roland had pared it down further. His necklines were high, shoulders demure. Waists had descended almost to mid-thigh. 'What colours are you showing for spring?' she asked, knowing he'd respond.

'Camel,' he answered, 'as in the coat you have on. *Café crème, maron crème, guimauve.*'

Coffee, chestnut cream and marshmallow. Perhaps he had a standing order with Monsieur Aristide. 'Katya would call your palette "timid".'

He returned the shot. 'Bright colours are rarely stylish. In my opinion.'

Tread softly, Tatiana counselled herself. Challenging the *maestro* was not the way to worm her way back. What contribution had she ever made? Apart from her physical presence during fitting sessions, when she'd complained of back ache while fantasising about her next encounter with Gérard. 'I beg your pardon. You and Katya have differing strengths.'

Appeased, Roland invited her to sit next to him. By the looks of it, he did his paperwork on the sofa. There were shoe boxes stuffed to bursting with bills, a telephone with its cord stretched to the limit. Administration had been Katya's domain.

Tatiana listed the wealthy women who had visited the salon out of curiosity and become loyal regulars. 'They heard that the Russian princess who once served them their tea was employed here. You know I bring in custom, Roland.'

'Brought. Past tense,' Roland countered. 'Only yesterday, Madame Renée Lefleuve asked to be assured that she would *not* run into you here. Besides, the midseason line, which we are showing at the moment, was finalised while you sat behind bars. None of it will fit you.'

'But I can be part of the spring–summer collection.'

Roland reached for her hand. 'I am a Spaniard, and the fact that I speak French as a second language sometimes makes me too much blunt. Better, I think, to speak the truth than to do the little dance that only deceives. You cannot come back.'

'But I need to! And by the way, your memory's at fault, Roland. You were producing the midseason *toiles* in September, and at least seven of the models were made on me.'

'I had them refitted, for the other girls.'

'Who is showing Constanza's things? I'm the same size as her.'

'Ah.' Roland nodded. 'Her sudden leaving was awkward, but a family funeral takes precedence even over couture. I have withdrawn the dresses she was to wear.'

'Then let me show them!'

He shook his head. 'We have reduced this collection to a manageable size, Madame Frankel and I. After all, it's only a midseason bagatelle.'

Bagatelle, a mere nothing. As, it seemed, was she. Tatiana rose. 'I'm to starve, then?'

He rose too and met her eyes. 'My dear girl, you have your dividend payments every quarter, as well as your family to look after you, no?'

No as far as family went. The dividend would come, in time, but it was never high. She'd only been granted a handful of shares in the company.

He nodded in appreciation of her head adornment. 'How regally Russian you look, and the coat is perfection.'

'Madame Frankel sent it. You admit I'm still a decent coat hanger?'

On cue, the lady herself hurried in, looking harassed. She hesitated on seeing Tatiana, but came up and they kissed cheeks. She too commented on the coat. 'You like it?'

'It's divine. Such a kind gesture.' It was on the tip of Tatiana's tongue to ask Pauline to intercede, but the other woman had turned to Roland.

'Have you any idea where the last of the ochre poplin might be? We had a few lengths left, but can I find any?'

He threw his hands up. 'My dear Madame, I am not keeper of the scrap bag. Do you imagine I sit here stitching patchwork quilts and rag rugs?'

'Roland, I don't think that at all. But we've lost the offcuts, as we lose everything these days.' Pauline Frankel scowled at the sofa and its shoe boxes, then consulted Tatiana. 'You know the fabric I mean? A difficult colour, I call it "sulky yellow" but Katya persuaded the duchesse de Brioude to have a dress made from it, straight off the catwalk. The first time the duchesse wore yellow since her husband was killed at Verdun.'

Tatiana nodded. 'I know the dress, I have one the same.' *Had.*

'Well, the duchesse's lady's maid brought it here this morning, something about a pet dog getting into her room and chewing it.'

'And they want you to repair it. But you can't find any spare fabric. Katya would know where to lay her hands on it.'

'I'm sure,' Pauline said drily. 'And if you know when she's due back, I hope you'll tell us. But if your version of the dress isn't precious to you, I'd appreciate it so much if you'd allow me to plunder it.'

Tatiana explained that, unfortunately, she had lent the dress. All at once, she remembered. To Constanza! That sulky shade had looked spectacular against her friend's brunette skin. 'I could ask her maid to locate it.'

'Thank you! The duchesse de Brioude is such a valuable customer. Are you…' Pauline gave the impression of seeing Tatiana properly for the first time, 'coming back to work?'

'She is not,' Roland said firmly, and accompanied Tatiana to the door where he said, 'it is not personal. Simply that your presence would damage us.'

She wanted to shout, 'I'm innocent!' but what was the point? Her past behaviour had left her with no credit in the bank. Nobody, with the exception of Una, Rosa and Regan, was prepared to give her the benefit of the doubt. Tarred and feathered.

She might have slunk home, but as she crossed Cour du Comte, she thought – damn them. Vytenis money founded this firm. She entered the main building. Nobody was about, though lunchtime was over and the mannequins would soon be on their way in. She glanced into the salon. No calla lilies now, it was all silver branches and trailing wintergreen. She read the midseason programme which oozed blandness, like a page from a rainwear catalogue. Perversely, the collection was called 'The Eternal Flame'.

It made no sense, unless the name had been announced to the press before Katya left. After which Roland had jettisoned all Katya's ideas, leaving 'Eternal Flame' to hang like the name board of a demolished house.

Tatiana felt angry for the sister who poured her soul into her work. '*Bright colours are rarely stylish.*' Really? Their Russian home had been rich with the Persian and Aubusson carpets their father collected. Katya's eye had fed on Orthodox cathedrals, icons and the work of the imperial jeweller, Fabergé. 'And all you can come up with, Monsieur, is sodden mushroom, moth wing and drizzle,' she mocked. Roland Javier needed a wake-up call. He needed a red-hot poker applied. She needed her job back.

Tatiana crept upstairs to the empty *cabine* where six busy-looking dressing tables stood alongside two bare ones. Hers and Constanza's. Mail had been placed on hers, three letters, different sizes. Opening the first of them, she read:

'You deserve to die by the guillotine for what you did, dirty foreign harlot. You should die of leprosy or some other putrefying disease—'

'Ugh!' Who wrote words like that? Clothilde de Sainte-Vierge, came the instant reply. Perhaps. Perhaps not. Tatiana tore up the letter and dropped it, with the others, into the wastepaper basket then sat down at her dressing table and opened a drawer. For a while, she stared at powder compacts and perfume bottles, a packet of silk stockings and a pair of velvet knee garters, plum leather shoes she'd forgotten ever buying and a very wizened apple. In the deepest drawer lay a half-drunk bottle of Sirop Roze. Tempting. But no.

'Oh, hello.' There was her favourite yellow and russet silk headscarf. Putting it to her nose, she got an echo of her former self: almond shampoo and setting lotion. She moved to the next dressing table along.

Constanza's drawers were a jumble of indigestion powders, perfumes, greasepaint and screw-top jars of kohl, all the same lead-grey shade, all part used. A confetti of nightclub cloakroom tickets suggested an evening bag had been emptied. Tatiana wasn't sure what she was looking for. Unless for clues as to Constanza's real motives for leaving Paris. Not to bury a grandmother, that was for sure. Summer,

1919 she'd lent Constanza a black dress and coat. Her friend's darling *abuelita* had died and she'd had to catch the fastest boat for Buenos Aires to get home for the memorial service. Constanza's swollen eyes and hollow cheeks had been no sham on that occasion. But this time? Her other grandmother ran a second-hand dress shop in Marseilles, and they didn't get on. Lies, lies.

In the dressers' storeroom, the autumn–winter collection was hanging ready for showing in an hour or so. Roland had said he'd withdrawn Constanza's outfits, but what did that mean? Cut up, unpicked? Or hung up and forgotten? A search along the hanging rails threw up nothing. But when Tatiana opened one of the wardrobes, she jumped back, as if scorched. Here was 'The Eternal Flame': amber, red and orange fabrics and a coat of papal scarlet that could only be worn by Constanza with her black hair and indecipherable beauty.

Tatiana slipped an evening dress off its hanger, exclaiming at its weight. Its cotton base was embroidered with coils of red and gold beads. Craftspeople must have laboured for weeks over this. Russians, possibly, as fine embroidery was one of the skills refugee aristocrats had brought here. She went to a mirror, holding the dress to her. A label inside the neck read 'Flamme'. Flame. It was exactly the right size and length. From the shoulders down, it looked fabulous. From the neck up, it sucked the life from her cheeks. It needed Constanza.

An idea struck her.

Nobody wanted Tatiana, but what if Constanza happened to return?

Chapter Thirty-Eight

In a storeroom was a collection of wigs that had been ordered when Maison Javier first opened its doors, intended for those mannequins reluctant to cut their hair. Attitudes had since changed; short hair was everywhere, the wigs were redundant. Tatiana reached for the blackest with a fringe and bangs that would graze her cheekbones. Very 'Hollywood vamp'.

At Constanza's dressing table, she dug out make-up. First, a bulb of the new Max Factor greasepaint, 'A complexion in a tube'. Constanza favoured a tint she referred to as 'yacht varnish'. Smoothed right up into the hairline, it took away Tatiana's prison pallor, making her look as though she'd spent six months on the Riviera. Coty powder in brownish rose, patted on with goose down, sealed the foundation. Smudged kohl and Rimmel mascara gave her eyes an exotic slant. Brown-red lip colour from a tiny glass jar, three layers, imitated Constanza's voluptuous bow. A few drops of her own perfume, then Tatiana put the wig on.

It certainly wasn't Constanza Darocca looking back from the mirror but it wasn't Tatiana either. Tatiana unboxed the silk stockings from her drawer, gartered them on, then put on Flamme which she'd brought in with her. No choice but to wear the plum-coloured shoes, as otherwise it would be the boots she had on.

Her last action as she heard voices on the stairs was to squeeze inside the wardrobe where the mannequins hung their robes and wraps and pull the door after her, though not entirely closing it. She heard Marianne du Gard first, complaining about the ice on the pavements. 'They'd better have turned up the radiators in the salon. Everyone is forgetting their job these days—' Marianne sniffed loudly. 'Goodness, I haven't smelled that musky perfume for a while.'

A response came in Mary-Jo's precise elocution. 'It's Habanita. Don't tell me *she's* back.'

The cupboard door was pulled open. Tatiana froze in mortification.

A hand reached in, pulled a silk robe off its hanger. The door was shut again. Hard, muffling the voices in the room.

Tatiana congratulated herself sourly. She was shut in. She might suffocate. The wig itched unbearably, but she couldn't raise her arms to scratch.

Chapter Thirty-Nine

Katya was sure she'd caught cold sailing between Kennacraig and Islay. They'd arrived on the island the previous day, having spent just short of three months in Manchester waiting for the Kremlin official, Abel Yenukidze, to renew contact. Separated from the trappings of normality, living like a pair of wealthy recluses, despair had gripped Katya. Had Yenukidze lost his power and would Vera's fate sink with him? Then, at last, a wire had come from Harry's father.

Abel Yenukidze had approved their visit to Russia. Even better news, a meeting with one of his deputies would take place in Petrograd and not Moscow, thus cutting out an entire, exhausting, leg of the journey. In Petrograd – formerly St Petersburg – they would be found accommodation and 'the item for expatriation' would be put into their hands, once the agreed payment had been satisfactorily rendered. Half the payment for Vera's freedom was to be a consignment of fine English cloth. That was easy. The other half required this visit to Islay, off Scotland's west coast.

The sea crossing to Port Ellen had been rough. Their ship had carried a cargo of wood tar and the fumes below had been unbearable, so Katya had stood on deck with Harry for the whole voyage. They were lodging in a house above Port Ellen harbour, and she'd spent a day resting in bed, listening to the rain casting relentless prayers at the window. Today, she'd got up, not wanting to miss out on a tour of the local whisky distillery.

To anyone observing them, they would look like foreign tourists enjoying a day out. Who would guess that this foray had a life-or-death purpose?

She sneezed violently, quickly mouthing to Harry that she was fine. Their kilted guide promised her that a glass of aged single malt would cure her.

She *thought* that's what he'd said. 'I don't understand his English,' she muttered to Harry as they were ushered into a vaulted room full of oak barrels. Harry whispered in reply, 'Don't call it "English".'

'What is it, then?'

'Scots-English and Gaelic. I only understand half of it myself.'

'Ask him to speak slower.'

'I have done, and he is.' Harry appraised her. 'I'm afraid this is all too much for you.'

She was *fine*, she repeated and borrowed Tatiana's phrase. 'I'm absolutely A1.'

'Mistress?'

It was their host, pouring generous measures of amber liquid. Offering the first to her. When they all had a drink in hand, he raised his glass. '*Slàinte mhath.*'

Harry replied, '*Slàinte mhòr*' and translated for Katya, 'Good health. In Russian?'

'*Na Zdorovie.*' She put her nose to her glass. Strong, but not unpleasant.

'The Scotsman's medicine,' Harry smiled. 'Don't sip, drink it. Try not to choke, it's not good manners.'

She downed the liquor and grabbed Harry to stop herself folding. 'My word! If that doesn't cure me, nothing will.'

Laughing, their host opened a glass-fronted cupboard filled with bottles bearing the distillery label. Katya understood he was asking if they'd like to take some home.

Harry was the negotiator, the one whose emotions were always in check while hers flapped like a flag in a north-easterly. She'd committed one cardinal sin already, writing to her housekeeper and to her mother, outlining her travel plans to both. That she'd done so out of guilt and homesickness only proved her fallibility.

'What we're doing is dangerous, more so for you than me,' Harry had admonished when she confessed. 'One thing I've learned, Katyushka, is never raise expectations so high in others that you cannot then retreat from them.'

They wouldn't retreat, though, would they? They were signed up to this madness.

'Six bottles, sir? Aye.' Their host beamed as Harry took out his cheque book. 'A six-bottle crate can be fetched right away.' Funny, Katya thought. One glass of Islay malt, and she was mistress of the language.

Harry shook his head. 'Sorry, not six.'

The distillery manager looked crestfallen.

'Not *six* bottles,' Harry repeated. 'Six hundred.'

Chapter Forty

Ear to the keyhole, Tatiana urgently wished the parade would start and the dressing room empty, so she could get out of this damn wardrobe. Marianne and Mary-Jo had been joined by Larissa, Françoise and Suzy. Her knees had locked in their half-bent position.

At last, she heard the commotion that always preceded the five-minute call. The room door opened and closed, then again, then a third time. Then silence. Tatiana pushed the wardrobe door. It wouldn't budge. She fiddled with the catch, without success. Finally, she knocked with her knuckles. 'Let me out!'

She had only to wait a few seconds. There was Mary-Jo, one hand on the door handle, the other holding her mascara brush in petrified astonishment. Larissa Markova had a foot up on a chair, lacing a suede walking boot. She resembled a photographic still.

'Constanza, what in heaven's name?' Mary-Jo's face grew round with bewilderment. 'We thought you'd be away until after Christmas.'

'Thought I'd give you all a surprise,' Tatiana said, approximating Constanza's husky accent.

Larissa finished with her boot and stepped back. Cynicism edged her smile. 'Clever Constanza, finding the fastest boat in the world. Buenos Aires is a three-week sailing each way, isn't it? And you only set off six weeks ago. Your family can't have seen much of you.'

'I went, I came back.' Tatiana stayed in character. 'I was missing you so badly, Larochka.'

'Did you get the dress?' Mary-Jo whispered.

'The what?' Tatiana stepped out into the room.'

'Isn't that why you went – to find the perfect dress?'

'Shame on you, it was her grandmother's funeral,' Larissa reproved. 'Not a shopping trip. So… you're out. Back, I mean.'

Larissa had seen through her charade. Mary-Jo wouldn't stay duped for long. Tatiana adjusted her wig in Constanza's mirror and couldn't resist asking, 'Is all well here? Monsieur seemed *muy alterado* when I spoke to him earlier.'

'If that means "upset", he is,' Mary-Jo burst out. 'One "darling" princess in jail and another idiot princess leaving without notice… Don't give me that look, Larissa. "Truth needs not the ornament of words".'

'Then stop talking,' Larissa advised.

'You can't deny, things aren't what they were. We're all looking for new jobs. Wait a moment…' Mary-Jo peered at Tatiana. 'You aren't Constanza. You're—'

'Ta-da!' Tatiana struck a showgirl pose, one hand curled above her head. 'The jailbird herself.'

'Why are you wearing Constanza's dress?'

'Because I don't want to look like myself. I'm borrowing a different personality.'

'You can't.'

'Why not?'

Mary-Jo hadn't an answer. She had an opinion, though, a strong one. 'Nobody wants you back. We won't work with you.'

'Speak for yourself,' said Larissa.

'We'll walk out.'

'Again, speak for yourself.' Larissa went up to Tatiana and inspected her make-up, like an art critic. 'Clever. I've no objection to you coming back to work. My objection is to spoiled girls who think they're *above* work.'

'I've changed,' Tatiana said.

'Does the leopard change its spots?' demanded Mary-Jo. Madame Markova came in, jerking in shock at the sight of Tatiana, and not for an instant taken in. 'What games now?'

'Monsieur Javier said I could parade Flamme.' Tatiana twirled, her red hem flaring.

'When?'

'An hour ago. You don't believe me?'

'I'd like to but you have been in prison, Princess Tatiana.'

'For reckless driving, Madame. For supposedly hitting a drunk man in the dark, not for fraud, or embezzlement.'

Hearing Mary-Jo tutting in disapproval, the *chef de cabine* ordered the English girl to join the others downstairs, then turned to her niece. 'Larissa, go ask Monsieur Javier if he has indeed given permission for Tatiana to make an appearance.'

'If I must.'

As Larissa left, Tatiana regretted that she hadn't hidden in one of the storerooms downstairs. She could have slipped into the salon without this interrogation.

While they waited for Larissa's return, Anna Markova gave Tatiana silent and detailed inspection. 'You make a good brunette,' she said at length. 'We should never have dropped fire colours from the collection. What we're left with feels all a bit...'

'Insipid?' Tatiana nodded. 'What's come over Monsieur? This midseason collection has all the panache of afternoon tea in a hostel for retired spinsters.'

'Do spinsters retire, Princess? I thought marriage was the only cure for the single life.'

'You know what I mean. Without Katya, this house has lost its spirit. Without me and Constanza, it's lost its devilment.'

'"Devilment" comes a very poor second, in my view, to poise, manners and deportment.'

Larissa came back. 'Well?' her aunt demanded.

'Monsieur says, "She goes on with my permission." Tatiana is allowed to join us.'

Madame Markova hadn't expected that, but she shook aside her doubts. 'In that case, I'll get the coat that goes with Flamme.'

Alone in the dressing room, Tatiana and Larissa stood awkwardly. Tatiana finally managed a gruff, 'Thanks. I take it you didn't speak to him?'

'No.'

'You didn't have to do that for me.'

'No,' Larissa agreed, 'except I owe you an apology of sorts. The night you were arrested, I was the last to leave the theatre. Rosa went, with the cast, to eat. I collected up my music and I couldn't resist playing a few notes on the piano in the pit.' Larissa shrugged. 'A few notes became a few bars. In the end, the janitor shooed me out. As I came out of a side door, your fiancé's brother accosted me.'

'Armand?'

'Yes. I couldn't shake him off or stop him blathering on about how he would win you away from his brother. He wanted my help.' Larissa looked down, foreshortening her face, showing that her butter-blond waves were innocent of dark roots. Then up came her unemotional gaze. 'I told him to go after you. I even told him which way you'd gone. I shouldn't have, as he was so obviously drunk. I smelled spirits as he stumbled away.'

Tatiana's throat hurt. She massaged it, to find her voice. 'Did you tell that to the police? I got a lesser sentence because Armand had been drinking.'

'I wish I could claim so, but no. I don't know who spoke for you, unless it was your American friend. I'm sorry, Tatiana, I was advised not to get involved. I haven't got my full residency papers yet, you see. I was fearful the police might look too closely at my documents.'

Madame Markova returned with a wine-red coat over her arm. 'You draw it behind you, dragging on the floor.'

Only a dozen ladies had come that afternoon. A couple of men, husbands presumably, sat engrossed behind the newspapers the salon provided. Boredom reigned. But as Tatiana made her way down the catwalk, a sizzle cut the air. The tinkling *divertimento* Benjy Crouch was playing suddenly gained tempo. Tatiana felt the force of eyes on her. It was like walking into a wall. Breath thickened in her lungs. What on earth had she been thinking of? She wasn't ready.

Somebody touched her arm, and she realised the piano had fallen silent. She gasped, 'Benjy? I don't know what to do.'

'Tatiana? I thought we had a new girl! You're not looking too well.'

'Tell them to look away. I can't bear them staring at me.'

'Shh. It's all right.' Benjy took her arm, got her out, sat her down in the antechamber, fetched iced water. Upstairs, Larissa and Anna Markova helped her into her own clothes, but she wouldn't let anyone take off her wig. Nobody must see her prison crop. Roland Javier met her in the front lobby, his face immobile with fury.

'You defied me.' He told her to go, never to set foot in Maison Javier again. Larissa and her aunt were also summarily sacked, and no tears or pleadings could soften his fury.

'You've turned into a monster, because Katya's away,' Tatiana shrieked from the door. She was making things worse, but she was a stranger in her own body. Raging and helpless.

'We all have layers of character, Princess Vytenis,' Roland answered. 'Some we show only rarely, like the family dog baring his teeth when intruders break in.'

'I'm sorry. For what I've done today. It was stupid.'

'Sorry to have failed to win approval. Sorry to have made a fool of yourself. But sorry to have ended the careers of two good women with families to feed?' Roland shook his head. 'You don't have that in you. As the barren grape lacks pips, so lovely Tatiana lacks compassion.'

'That's not true! I do care.' *Too much, and it's killing me.*

'Look at yourself.' Roland pulled her back into the lobby to a grand, Venetian mirror. 'See a spoiled girl who kills a man on a night out with her aristocratic lover, and sheds not a tear.'

Pauline Frankel found them. She looked grave. Madame Markova would certainly have sought her out, beseeching her help.

'Please.' Tatiana gripped Pauline's arm. Mary-Jo, Suzy, Isabelle and Françoise were watching from the stairs, captured by the drama and directing hatred at her. Upstairs, from the *cabine*, came the sound of heartbroken sobs. 'Make him give Madame Markova and Larissa their jobs back.' Tatiana's voice cracked. 'I tricked them, it wasn't their fault. He's doing it to punish me. Being a vindictive bully, as all men are.'

'That's enough, Tatiana. I will handle this matter. Please, just go. *Leave!*' Pauline shouted as Tatiana opened her mouth to argue. 'Do you not understand how fraught everything is with your sister gone? If only you might have taken her place, instead of being the brat who throws the tea things off the table.' Pauline all but pushed Tatiana out onto the pavement. 'Get yourself married and come back and order your clothes from us when you're a wealthy matron – if we're still in business.'

The door slammed, leaving Tatiana the wrong side of it, gasping with mortification. *If* Maison Javier was still in business?

One of the disorientating things about prison was that seasons moved on without you. She'd missed the gentle run-up to winter, the shortening days and tumbling leaves. Night had fallen, streetlights were on. Every surface glistened with the ice-cold rain that was falling. She had no hat, and the borrowed wig would be ruined if she didn't cover it. Raising her arm at the approach of taxi headlights, she secured a ride home. But as she told the driver 'Rue Rembrandt', a little voice snickered that she had no money, and no longer had the right to throw taxi fares on the Maison Javier account.

'Sorry, my mistake,' she said, stepping back from the car. 'I'm expected somewhere else.'

Muttering about females who couldn't make up their minds, the driver pulled away. The greasepaint she'd put on her face earlier was running, in danger of ruining her beautiful new coat. It was crucial she find somewhere to shelter. The solution was obvious, and close by.

Chapter Forty-One

She'd always kept keys to Gérard's apartment in her favourite leather handbag, which she had with her now. The night she was arrested, she'd taken an evening purse, holding change, a lipstick and a handkerchief. None of which had found its way to prison with her. As she took out the key she hadn't used in a long while, it crossed her mind that Gérard might have changed the lock. He hadn't.

Letting herself in to the communal hall she pressed the timer light, summoning the courage to put her foot on the stairs. Was this the second blunder of the day? She could have sought shelter in a café.

The truth was unavoidable. She wanted to see Gérard, and he was upstairs. She'd seen a glow behind his shutters, and he was not a man to leave lights on in an empty flat.

She would be the last person he'd expect to see. But it was time he looked her in the eye. Today's antics had made something clear to her. Tatiana wanted to be declared innocent. She wanted Roland, Pauline, her former colleagues and even Madame de Sainte-Vierge to say of her, 'She was wronged, she sacrificed herself.' The timer light went off and she walked upstairs in darkness. The dusty smell of old carpet and damp wallpaper tickled her nose. The communal areas here were unkempt, as they were in ten thousand other shared Parisian buildings, and it had often surprised her that Gérard hadn't kicked up a fuss.

Perhaps he didn't want to pay his share of the upkeep. Or didn't want strangers coming in and noting who came and went from his flat. Unrelated thoughts assailed her as she climbed. She must write to Sister Marie-Nazareth and ask if any of her personal belongings had found their way back to the prison. She must dig out the yellow dress Pauline Frankel had asked for, proving she could rise above petty resentment. What was Regan Dortmeyer doing? Working, probably. If she stayed with Rosa, as invited, she'd see him on the square.

Inward chatter kept her moving. Tatiana hung her coat on the newel post outside Gérard's flat. She could hear music, an aria sung by a male voice. She unlocked the door and stepped into the lobby.

'Greetings, chaste and pure dwelling place, wherein lives a soul innocent and divine,' sang the mellifluous tenor.

Oh yes? Few chaste or innocent pursuits had taken place here. Not in the bedroom, at any rate. She took off her boots and walked on soft feet to the living room. Gérard was in a chair, his eyes closed, cradling a cut-glass goblet in his palm. A half-full decanter by his elbow reflected the smouldering coals in the fireplace, which along with a lamp was the only light in the room. The shellac disc on the gramophone winked as it turned, the needle arm oscillating with a crackle. It was hypnotic. Gérard had removed his jacket and hung his tie over the back of his chair. The tiepin she'd bought him was still attached to it. She recalled agonising over what would please him most, before deciding on a gold bar with a red-jasper bead.

His ribs rose and fell in time with the music. That was one of the unexpected differences between them. While she clung to the edge of sensory pleasure, afraid it might consume her, the so-controlled Gérard liked to drown in music. Head tipped back, eyelashes making dark sweeps on his cheekbones, he tore a fresh strip from her heart.

All she had given him, all she had thrown at his feet, hadn't been enough. He had begged her to put a noose around her neck, then pushed her off the scaffold. She murmured his name.

'Mmm.' His eyelids flickered.

She arranged her dress and smoothed her wig. 'Gérard, my treacherous love.'

He sat up, almost spilling his drink. 'You,' he stuttered. 'When did you get home?'

'Two days ago, or three. It's a bit of a blur. But why are you asking? You saw me – you walked past me.'

'Walked past you? I'd never dare! Constanza, my matchless darling.' The seducing smile spread across his lips. It knocked Tatiana speechless.

Constanza and Gérard? Clues tumbled, too late, into her mind. Constanza's spiky response to news of her engagement. Constanza, trying to apprehend Gérard as he arrived at the Javier cocktail party, having been absent all afternoon. At the dentist, yet with no subsequent sign of pain or discomfort. A yellow button on a pillow in the bedroom of this flat.

Tatiana could have wept. Or picked up the decanter and broken it over Gérard's head. Instead, she walked to where he sat. Making her voice deep, she asked, 'How good is it to see me?' Hitching up her dress to reveal the garter rolls holding her stockings at mid-thigh, she straddled him.

He shut his eyes with a soft groan, saying, 'I've been dreaming of you… wildly dreaming… and all the time you were nearer than I knew.'

'You know where I was, Gérard.'

Eyes still closed, he stroked her breasts, her waist, hips and thighs. Relearning her shape. His fingers halted at the sudden warmth of skin as he lingered on the garters, lowering his head to look. He'd bought them for her, velvet-sheathed elastic, scattered with gold hearts. He studied them, then looked up at her face. A shiver ran through him. 'Tatiana?'

'Uh-huh.'

'I wasn't expecting… You've – you've dyed your hair.'

She climbed off his knee. 'You thought I was someone else.'

He denied it, scraping up a smile that was entirely automatic. 'I was far away. Suddenly, here you are.'

'Here I am.' How far should she let this go? Until she had a heartfelt apology, or her revenge. One or the other. She put on a lost, sad voice. 'I've missed you so much.'

He took her hand, his pupils darkening as he got to his feet. His nostrils flared. He wanted her. After all he'd done to her, he was ready to rut.

Never again. No man would ever take her the way Armand had. She reached for his tie, releasing the gold pin and folding it in her palm. 'Gérard, why didn't you meet me outside Saint-Lazare?'

'What? The railway station?'

'The prison. When I was released, I looked for you.'

She felt his recoil. Shame? No. Distaste.

'I had no idea when you were being let out.'

'You didn't write on your calendar: "Tatiana comes out of jail, having served my sentence for me"?'

A nerve twitched in his cheek. She waited, but he clamped his lips. She carried on in her false, jokey way, 'Aren't you going to ask who came to meet me?'

'Your mother, I hope. Your sister too. Is Katya back from her jaunt?'

'I was met by two Americans who aren't even my closest friends, but who felt sorry for me. Oh, and there was another bunch of well-wishers.' She described the press pack.

That pierced his guard. 'Who alerted them?'

'Nobody – they knew my release date. They have diaries, unlike you. Gérard, do you have the first idea what prison is like?'

He was more concerned by what she might have told the press. 'I'll stamp on it – I'll make telephone calls. Damn it, Tatiana, I won't see my family name on newsprint ever again.'

She leaned forward, as if to kiss his neck, and felt him recoil. Her wig was slipping and she pulled it off to show her savaged hair. 'This is what prison does.'

'You look…' he couldn't find words.

'Like Joan of Arc at her trial? A sheepdog clipped for the summer? Or what about, "matchless"? Or is your eloquence all for Constanza now?'

He shook his head, but there was more derision than shame in the gesture.

'Prison takes your soul,' she said. 'All the more if the time served was on somebody else's behalf. I need to know that my sacrifice means something to you.'

'I think I know something of sacrifice. I lost a brother.'

She knew what he was seeing – Armand's broken body on a nest of moonlit glass. 'You killed him, not I,' she said. 'In prison I lost my hair, my dignity and my livelihood. I cannot work or buy food for myself. My mother has fled in shame, taking my niece with her, and the worst…'

No.

Describing her miscarriage would win her the last word, but she wouldn't bring her child into this sordid mess. She'd told Gérard she was pregnant the night of the accident, but he hadn't responded. He had lost his right to know. But she hadn't finished with him. 'You made a promise, a binding one.'

He recovered enough to clip his voice into a formal shape. 'Did you not understand when I told you, as firmly as kindness allowed, that I did not wish to be your husband? As for who killed my poor brother, has your memory deserted you along with your grip on reality?'

'My memory is sharp. On 5 October, I put my hands on the driver's wheel and took your crime to save you.'

'*You* were driving that night, my girl, not I. Overwrought from the breaking of our engagement, you ignored my warnings to slow down. You'd been taking a cocktail of medicines and alcohol in the days leading up to the tragedy. One of your colleagues verified that you were swigging pink elixir like water.'

'Who? Constanza? Thank you for not calling her "friend".'

He shrugged it off. 'You can bleat your innocence but nobody will believe you. A tin-pot Russian princess with a past, accusing a Sainte-Vierge. *Me*.' His offended dignity flared into life. 'A man who works alongside this country's leaders. You'd do well to leave Paris. Find another city in which to tout your dim little flame.'

'You swore on your mother's soul you would marry me.'

'That's it. That's the proof.' He tried to push her away, but she held his shoulders. His face twisted with contempt. 'You are incurably mad. I feel sorry for you, or I would, were you not my brother's killer.'

Tatiana now appreciated Regan's grim parable about the two men in the lifeboat. Her mistake had been to think Gérard incapable of such gross and unmanly treachery. She turned the jewelled tiepin in her hand so its point faced out. One more question. 'Did Armand tell you that he drugged my drink at the Café Select? It came to me while I was in prison that he must have done so... jail gives you ample time to think. He drugged me so I couldn't fight back. Armand raped me.'

Gérard's lips slid open. *He believes me.* She saw it, there momentarily before denial smashed down.

He shoved her violently. 'Lying slut. My brother was as broken as a man could be, but maimed as he was in his mind, he had more honour than you know the meaning of. Drug you? Rape you? He wouldn't know how, though I wouldn't put it past you to have amused yourself by tempting him. A little challenge, hmm? Something to make Tatiana the centre of attention for a minute or two?'

She drove the tiepin right through his cheek, into his gums. As he clutched at his face, letting out agonised yelps, she stepped back. 'I'd hoped for a show of courage, Gerard,' she said with all the scorn she owned. 'But you are a treacherous gut-worm.' She snatched up the black wig. 'I hope never to see you again.'

Threats and howls followed her out of the flat. Tatiana retrieved her coat and folded it against her breast. Her heart was swimming in adrenaline. She made herself walk down the stairs, afraid she'd fall otherwise.

It was still raining and she was soon chilled to the marrow, oil dripping off her uncovered hair, greasepaint dripping down her neck. She wasn't a mannequin anymore, nor a fiancée. She was simply Tatiana making her way home.

Chapter Forty-Two

Friday, 15 December

Katya and Harry

The voyage from Scotland to Gothenburg proved less daunting than Katya had feared. The wind was with them, the seas as gentle as December in the northern hemisphere allowed. She hadn't been sick. Much. They had a few days as guests of Harry's father and stepmother to look forward to. Harry would at last meet his little half-brother, Bjorn. He was offhand about it, laconic as always, but Katya knew how much it meant to him. Having lost a younger brother, Christian, in the war, he often admitted to a gaping hole in his life.

She would hide the pain of seeing Harry bounce a small child in his arms. Her body had rejected two chances of motherhood. She hoped that Elsa Morten would refrain from asking when Harry and she were starting their family. Katya liked Harry's young stepmother, but tact was not Elsa's signature virtue.

A horse cab was waiting at the portside. Harry helped Katya in and loaded their bags. He would escort her to his father's house, then return to complete paperwork on the cargo they'd brought with them. Crates of Islay whisky and bales of best-quality wool-worsted from his

Manchester mills. As he closed the door of the cab, she knocked on the roof and they lurched away. Passing rows of wood-clad buildings powdered with snow, Katya recalled a previous time in Gothenburg. Then, she and her family had been fugitives without means. Harry had helped her. In a horse cab just like this, she'd begged him to lend her money, though he was a stranger who owed her nothing. There'd been no place for pride.

She spoke her thoughts and he smiled in tribute to the memory. They'd been thrown together at a time of intense personal and political crisis.

'Let's not think back,' he said. 'In a week, we'll be in St Petersburg.'

'Petrograd.'

'Buying your sister's freedom. I wonder what our friend in Port Ellen would think if he knew the use his beloved whisky was being put to.'

Chapter Forty-Three

Tatiana passed a succession of days in fits of sleeping that followed no pattern. Sunday, 17 December announced itself in the distant chime of bells. She slid out of bed with a foul headache, so hungry, she had to cling to the furniture as she searched kitchen cabinets for food. Getting home from rue Molière the other night, she'd expected to find a policeman waiting. She had expected retribution, but Gérard was holding back. Perhaps he feared another scandal. She wondered how long it had taken him to pull the tiepin from his cheek. She felt no regret. Gérard and Constanza. It kept hitting her: *she and I, sitting in the Tuileries gardens.* Constanza fishing secrets from her. Booking her in with Dr Jolivet. Constanza putting the Sainte-Vierge engagement ring on her own finger 'for safe keeping'.

In a store cupboard, she discovered a waxed paper bag of raisins, which she ate in two handfuls. Post had piled up at the front door. Bills for her mother. A note from Pauline Frankel, expressing regret at the unhappy conclusion to her time at Maison Javier. Reminding her about the yellow dress. 'Remember, anger fades where there is kindness and goodwill.'

A note from Regan, a masterpiece of brevity. He wrote simply, 'Call me.'

A wordier, more affectionate instruction from Rosa to call at Place du Tertre. This came with a 'P.S.' from Una:

'How about dinner at Ma Richelieu's? Or we could meet by the Seine and hurl our hearts into the water.'

Tatiana telephoned Rosa who reproved her for hiding away, then fetched Una to the telephone.

'I stabbed Gérard,' Tatiana said after the pleasantries, clarifying over Una's gasp, 'Not fatally.'

'Thank God – not that he doesn't deserve it. Let's meet so you can dish out the gore. Tonight, at eight?'

While her bath was running, Tatiana found the button she'd picked off the bed in Gérard's flat and tried to remember if she'd ever worn the dress there. Turning off the taps, she tested the temperature before slipping into its embrace. No, she was sure she never had.

'*Tatiana darling, it's adorable. Only I can carry off that strange yellow. I have the complexion for it.*' Constanza had coveted the dress. She must have worn it to meet Gérard. Lain with him on the bed, lost a button.

Enough, enough. Tatiana put her head under the water, drowning the chatter.

Chapter Forty-Four

Walking into Mère Richelieu's, Tatiana saw Una straight away. Rather, she spied a bicorn hat in a striking shade of blue with a tangerine cockade. Una sat alone at a table, working a pencil, deep in concentration.

Handing her coat to the man who washed the pots, absently tipping him with her last twenty-centime piece, Tatiana crossed to Una's table. 'You look busy.'

'Hi, just putting thoughts on paper.' Una's gaze flickered over Tatiana's mouse-brown dress with black ribbon trim, then to her head. 'Whoa, have you dyed your hair?'

'Wig.' Tatiana had got soaked walking home from Gérard's flat, sparing both her coat and the hairpiece. *Priorities*, she'd told herself. 'Can I see what you're drawing? Unless it's secret and you have a guilty conscience.'

'I have no conscience at all.' Una pushed the pad across the table. 'Glass of red?' There was a half-full carafe and a spare glass. Without waiting for an answer, Una poured.

Una had drawn a series of day and evening dresses, coats and hats. For spring and summer, judging by the short sleeves and scoop necks. Tatiana tilted the sketchbook to see them all. 'You're a fashion designer now?'

Una shook her head. 'I'm trying to pin down the look for next season, based on the last three. Are skirts slim or wide? Belts or no belts. Collar or no collar? Colours – bright or subdued? Are we showing knees or being prim?'

'This is for your journalism?'

'Maybe. Or I may be branching out.' Una explained, 'My column's syndicated coast to coast in the States. Boston to Portland, Oregon and all points between. I ought to be rich, but I signed a bad contract. Don't you get tired of earning hobby money?'

'I'm not earning any at all.'

'I want to make my pile, and while I was in New York, I got a good contact. Sit, sit.' Una flapped her hand, encouraging Tatiana. 'I think I told you, his name's Artie Shone.'

Tatiana took her seat. 'What does he do?'

'Wholesale, Paris gowns for department stores all over America.'

'How can an American make Paris gowns?'

'By getting hold of French designs and copying them.'

Tatiana put her knuckles to her head. 'Has being Katya's friend taught you nothing?'

'It's taught me plenty, not least to marry a loaded, handsome textile magnate if at all possible. What I'm doing is not piracy. It is the *psychic* version of piracy.' Una dropped her voice to a mystic rasp. 'I envision what each house will show this coming spring, using my special powers of insight.' Her voice snapped back to normal. 'Two months is how long Artie needs to put out a collection for the smaller retailer. The deal is, I send new ideas, he makes a line of dresses that are Paris-ish and I get a commission on every one that's bought.'

'Will that make you a pile?'

'Could do, though to be truthful, my eye is on the major stores who reproduce couture designs on license. And it transpires that Artie wants an agent here in Paris. A lady who can attend the shows, buy a few models from each house and ship them to him.'

'You're that lady?'

Una turned down her mouth, like a child taken home from the fair. 'For reasons that are wholly obscure to me, I'm barred from most couture houses in Paris. Hey, would you care to—'

'No.' Tatiana cut her off. It was hot in the café where a massive glaze-tiled stove shimmered with haze.

'I was going to say, choose your dinner. You are eating with me? I like your dress, but what's with the black trim? Not mourning for creepy Armand?'

Tatiana glanced down at herself. 'I was cold... though not now. I'm wearing a flannel shift.'

'As your friend, all I can say is no, no, no.'

'And thanks, but... um, I wasn't intending to eat.' Tatiana was cleaned out. It was one thing putting her tea-parlour bills on Katya's account, but she wasn't ready to scrounge off Una McBride.

Una's response suggested she really had psychic powers, or empathy at least. 'Shame, because I've ordered the casserole, and you know they serve enough here for a platoon. I hate sending back a plate unfinished, but if you're not hungry...'

'Well, if you're sure.'

'Sure I'm sure.' Una called to a waiter to lay an extra place. 'Hear me out about my new venture. It's kosher and there's enough money for us both.'

Over the last weeks, Tatiana's affection for Una had matured. Before, she'd been grateful to Una for being around when needed. For having solid medical skills hidden under a layer of froth. Now, she profoundly loved the girl. But trust? Even Katya didn't fully trust Una.

She said, 'I don't need a job.'

'Maison Javier is keeping you on?'

'No. We had, er, creative differences.'

Una tipped her head, measuring the effect of Tatiana's wig. 'That's some look you've got going, but with your complexion it's like topping a cauliflower with caviar. If you mean to find work with another house, you should go back to your natural shade.'

'Maybe I'll go blond, like you.'

'Honey, nature gave you Titian curls, and one day you'll go grey. So enjoy them while you have them.'

Wanting to take the spotlight off her future, Tatiana asked Una if she was still living full-time with Rosa.

'Yeah, I love it on the square. Rosa's show is doing great – in artistic circles, at least, the man on the Montmartre omnibus doesn't really get it – and she always brings a quiver-full of bohemians home at night, or we gather here. I sleep better up on the butte and dream better too. Hey, she has a room spare, small but…' Una tailed off as she saw Tatiana's expression fold into 'maybe'. 'Just a thought. It'd be fun.'

As they waited for their dinner, Tatiana studied Una's sketches in more detail. Una had a deft touch. But then, she'd been copying Parisian couture since the end of the war. Katya had told her that Una had begun by sketching the female guests at the Ritz Bar, and reproducing their outfits for herself. People noticed and she'd started offering the service to others. When Harry had first introduced Una to Katya in 1919, she was building her client list and using the atelier of a notorious copyist, Madame Claudine of rue Duphot, a few doors down from where Maison Javier now had its premises. Claudine's had closed in 1920, leaving Una with unfulfilled orders. An ill-wisher had reported her to the *Syndicale*, the governing body of couture which came down hard on copyists. Una had slipped back to New York, staying away long enough for trouble to blow over – but not long enough for the industry to forgive her. That was why she was barred from fashion houses. She was seen in the same light as a clothes moth. A costly nuisance.

Their casserole arrived in a vast tureen and Tatiana's concern switched to the ladle Una was picking up. 'Not too much for me.'

Una served her a manageable portion. 'Never overfill an empty stomach, but enjoy every mouthful. We're going to get your health back.'

'What if your crystal ball is cloudy, Una?' Tatiana said after they'd eaten in silence for a while. 'What if you say to your Artie Shone, "No trumpet sleeves this season", then you find that the catwalks are blasting with them?'

'I won't get paid. He'll drop me. I'll go hungry. Thing is, life isn't life without risk. Agreed?'

'I don't know.' Tatiana savoured her wine, an everyday *vin de table* and her first alcohol in three months. Una's plans bothered her. The girl was talented. Why couldn't she be content with dealing the cards straight? 'You had Pigeon Boccard in your pocket, didn't you?'

Una's head shot up, her wine glass halfway to her mouth. 'My stars, he doesn't fit in anyone's pocket.' She rested her upper lip on the rim. 'All right. You got me. He'd show me what he took and I paid him a dollar every time I memorised a print.' She winked an eye, making a camera click with her tongue. 'Total cost per season, around eighty dollars. I did sketches from memory, and sent them on a fast boat to this guy in New York. *He* paid me fifty dollars for every dress he put into production, total earnings around two thousand dollars per season.'

Tatiana whistled. Eight thousand dollars *a year*? That was the sort of money her brother-in-law paid himself.

Una laughed dryly. 'I should say, "Total potential earnings". The cheques dwindled, maybe fifty dollars a season if I was lucky. Short of sailing to New York and demanding a look at the schmuck's account books, I had no way of knowing if he was playing straight. I needed a business partner I could trust, and now I have Artie who is as iron-hulled as the USS *Monitor*, but don't share it around. Paris is bursting with girls like me, all looking for the next buck. Honey, fess up, you need a job. I need someone who can get into the couture shows. Doors open for you the way they don't for me.'

'You asked a moment ago, what's life without risk? Well, I'm a risk. A few days ago, I stabbed my faithless former lover with a tiepin. Before my world fell apart, I had a chance to step into Katya's shoes.' Tatiana raised her glass in mocking toast to herself. 'I didn't have the guts. There's no sharper lesson than getting exactly what you asked for. No responsibility. No work. No love. Nobody wants me, Una.'

'Darling, that's simply not true. There's me. Katya and Harry. Oh, and what about—'

'Constanza has taken Gérard from me.'

'No! When?'

'I don't know, she's left town. Where was it you saw her again?'

'Um... 5th Avenue. I was about to say, "What about Regan?"'

'What about him? He'll leave Paris too. Katya and Harry might as well be on the moon. My mother is hiding out at a second-rate spa. Everyone who's meant to love me runs away.'

'Shame you gave the ring back. You could have lived on it for a few months.' Una made a sound suggesting Tatiana had missed a trick. 'A girl I knew sent a ring back, baked in a madeleine. The faithless one bit into it and broke his tooth. We called it, "À *la recherche du dents perdus*".'

Tatiana suspected a joke, but her mind was blunted. She stared down at her plate. She hadn't eaten much, for all she was hungry.

'You are valued and loved, Princess Tatiana. And if you don't believe me…' Una gestured towards the door. The café was sucking in customers like a whale pulling in krill. Somebody had lodged the door open to cancel out the great, vibrating stove. *If you don't believe me…* 'Ask him.'

Regan had walked in.

Chapter Forty-Five

He and Una kissed cheeks, after which he extended his hand to Tatiana. 'Name's Dortmeyer, how do you do?' At her nervous giggle, he grinned. 'Bless me, it's Tatiana.'

'I'm going out later to haunt a churchyard.' Tatiana dared him to answer.

'Sit down,' Una invited him. 'Eat with us.'

'Sure. Thanks.'

His presence brought an awkwardness. For Tatiana, at least, as the days since they'd last seen each other were stained with Sirop Roze, which he'd warned her against. His arrival was fortunate in one way, however. She could make her excuses and leave without hurting Una. Only, she lost the chance when Edward, Rosa's lover, passed them on his way to the closet. Una broke off from her panegyric on the business acumen of Artie Shone and grasped his sleeve. 'Not so fast, Eddie. I've been trying to nail you down forever. That commission with *Ravissante* I got you, illustrating the Christmas special? I'm waiting for my commission.'

When Edward muttered an excuse and kept going, Una followed him.

'I wouldn't put it past her to barge into the gents with him,' Regan remarked with a dry smile. 'Tatiana, have you thought more about what you want to do with your life?'

'I hardly think about anything else, but the truth is, I'm broken.'

'Physically?'

'And socially.' She held his eye, challenging him to deny it.

All he did was nod. 'Let's finish dinner, then I'll make you coffee at mine. Sometimes it helps to throw ideas around with a detached third party.'

'That's you? Detached?'

'Uh-huh. Maybe I can see a path you haven't thought of.'

'I've only ever been one thing. A clothes horse.'

'That's kind of my point.'

In his studio, Regan heated water and poured it over coffee grounds. It wasn't just the wig, Tatiana looked more frail than when she'd come out of jail. OK, the light in here wasn't all that forgiving. The unshaded bulbs blanched the hell out of everything. But still.

While they waited for the coffee to brew and he washed out two tin mugs, he watched her viewing the prints he'd pinned across two walls.

'All yours?' She accepted a steaming mug, shaking her head at his apology for the steerage-class crockery. 'You must have reshot everything that was stolen.'

'Mostly. Till I got side-tracked by an idea for a book. "The Night-Haunts of Paris". Edgy culture goes down well with a certain kind of American. An erotic shiver from the safety of the porch rocking chair.' He drew her attention to scenes taken in Mère Richelieu's and backstage after Rosa's first night. He'd been to the Lapin Agile, another brasserie on Place du Tertre crowded with artists. There were shots of dancers at the Folies Bergère, and scenes at another café she knew well.

'Isn't that the Select?' Crowded tables on a Montparnasse pavement. Some of the figures might be her now-invisible friends. She didn't want to be reminded of her last visit there. Armand talking in his seamless monotone. Staring at her. Constanza pouring champagne paid for by Gérard. Constanza mixing martini cocktails to her own special recipe. Armand sliding a drug into hers.

'Recognise that?' Regan drew her attention to a panorama of Paris, taken from a height. She moved on gladly.

'You went up the Eiffel Tower! How very *touristique*.'

'You mock, lady.'

'It's a nice picture.' The Seine, a shining slug trail, and the twin towers of the Trocadero palace on its north bank. There was Pont d'Iéna and Port Debilly. Regan's view of the city resembled chunks of iced wedding cake separated by roads and parks. The detail was pin sharp. 'It must have been a day without mist.'

'Cold but bright, perfect conditions. What do you think of that?' Regan drew her to a picture taken with the camera pointing straight down. It made her scalp crawl.

'I know,' he said. 'Afterwards, I practically crawled back behind the cage work.'

'You climbed *outside* the tower? What if you'd fallen?'

Her genuine dismay pleased him, which revealed to him that he was as much attracted to her as ever. 'If I'd fallen, the US consulate would have had the duty of sending me home in boxes.' He polished his knuckles on his lapel and blew on them. 'Whoever cleared me out did me a favour. Course, I never managed to reshoot at Maison Javier.'

Their gazes fused. He'd always known she had green eyes, but with that fake hair, dark as Cajun spice, they gleamed like gemstones. She gulped coffee, turned her back. Walked along his wall like a visitor at a gallery. Abruptly, she stopped, as if stung.

She'd reach the picture he would have produced as evidence in court, had she not scuppered him by pleading guilty. Regan took it to a side bench and switched on an angled lamp. 'Come and see it properly.'

Reluctantly, she joined him. She was looking at a large-scale photograph of Place du Tertre: rooftops, night sky and a vast moon nudging the domes of Sacré-Coeur.

'The night of the eclipse.' Tatiana shifted the lamp to pull the shine off the surface. 'People say it's a time of ill luck, and I agree.'

'I had to get that shot of the basilica. Cheesy, but when else would I capture anything with such impact? Sorry.' *Impact*. He saw her hunch into herself. 'I was about to take it when you two stepped into frame. Gérard must have heard me shifting my feet because he stared full at me. That's when I squeezed the shutter. No flash so you can't make out much, but look there.'

The lower part of the picture was a medley of dark tones. Gérard could be made out at the driver's side of the car. 'Where am I?' Tatiana pulled a face. 'I've dissolved into the shadows.'

'You were in the passenger seat by then. I saw you get in and lover-boy go to his side. He stood there awhile, trying to see who I was before he got in and drove away. I was always your best witness, Tatiana.'

'But you can't prove it was Gérard who hit Armand. After all, he could have stopped further on, let me take the wheel… it could be a different night.'

'Not with that moon. There hasn't been a blood moon like that in my lifetime.'

'But the picture's black and white!'

'Black and white to you,' he said, and fished around for a magnifier. 'Take a look and you'll see it's actually made up of halftones. Thousands of tiny dots, for every colour a different pattern. I could prove that moon was pure, goddam strawberry.'

She looked through the magnifier then put it down and walked away. 'Go to the police, then. What will it change?' When she added, 'Gérard works for the Ministry of Finance. He's an aristocrat, a wealthy man,' he heard nothing but defeat.

His arms ached to close around her. In that oversized coat, she had the fragility of a fawn. 'I agree, this picture won't cut it in court, and maybe it's too late anyway. You made your plea and served your sentence. But what about going to the press? Journalists don't require the same level of proof as the police.'

She was shaking her head before he'd finished. 'Gérard has already called me delusional. He'd turn on me like a jackal, because he has too much to lose. He'd have to tell his mother that he was behind the wheel, and pretty much ran from the scene. She'd want to know if it was an accident or if Armand deliberately stepped in front of the car and it would all come back to me. Last May, Armand drugged me and you can guess the rest.'

'Armand was the father of your child,' Regan said softly.

She gave a nod. 'I don't think Gérard can admit the truth. I don't think anybody could.'

'Tatiana, you need to start thinking of yourself.'

She gave a choking laugh. 'That's generally what I do. Regan, leave it.' She moved to the door. He got there first.

'For one, you're not going home in the dark on your own. Two…' there was a 'two' and probably a 'three', his desire to keep her here till morning overwhelming everything else. He could deal with her having a past. Everyone had a past.

She said in tones of finality, 'I can't go to the papers because I don't come across well. I sound cold, as if I think I'm entitled to hurt and do as I like. Even Roland Javier, who has the softest heart in Paris, thinks I'm a flint-hearted jade. I'll be pilloried and things will be worse than they are now.'

'Can they be?'

'Yes! This is not my first brush with injustice.'

'You mean what happened to your family? That was Moscow.'

'And this is Paris, where judgement wears finely pressed shirts and expensive cologne, but is every bit as blind. I'm innocent of the crime I was convicted of, but that doesn't make me good.'

'Nobody's good.'

'But I do awful things, I use people. I tried to eject my baby.'

'You didn't go through with it.'

'But I tried. You won't make me like myself, Regan! I'm trash. I make love when my body demands it. Even before Armand put whatever in my cocktail, I was drunk. Not tipsy, Regan. Not "nicely oiled". Drunk. He got to use me because I couldn't fight him off. Couldn't stop him putting a child inside me, and afterwards, all I could think about was how to hide the shame and the consequences. To keep Gérard at all costs.'

'I don't need to know.'

'You do, while you insist on bleaching my soul. I let my fiancé's brother have me—'

Regan hauled her up to his level, kissing her until she stopped talking. When he let her go, the gemstone eyes were full of tears but as remorseless.

'Armand's mother called me a whore,' she said. 'She's probably right.'

He wouldn't let that stand. 'I lived in a whorehouse. The women were among the smartest people I ever knew, but with a few exceptions they had no choice. You have a choice. You've said it, Tatiana. You need work and you want to be loved. So – do yourself a favour. Find a job, and fix on a man willing to pay the price of fidelity.'

She wouldn't answer and he took her home, saw her safely inside. That done, he got back in the taxi, bribing the driver who wanted to go off shift to take him back to Place du Tertre. Lights still burned in Mère Richelieu's window.

Una was there still, her garish hat the centre of a carousing scrum including Rosa, her dancers and theatre staff, and the eternally sulking Edward. Drawn in, plied with wine, Regan managed a moment with Una. He unloaded his latest run-in with Tatiana's demons.

'I'd give anything to know how to make her happy.'

'Being happy means different things to different folk,' Una responded with the wavering precision of someone who has seen the bottom of two wine carafes. 'For some women it's a home with a white picket fence, a faithful husband and a clutch of children. For me, it's a flat overlooking a Paris park, my bills picked up by an enthusiastic yet frequently absent lover. For you… only you know. For her, it would be to wipe out the last ten years and start again, clean.'

'Where does she get her self-destructive addiction from?'

'How about, "Seeing her darling Papa bayoneted to death by thugs for trying to protect his wife and daughters." She blames herself for it. Don't ask me why. And don't ask Princess Tatiana Vytenis to think like the granddaughter of Irish immigrants from the Lower East Side.'

'Hell's Kitchen. Lower East Side is where we dreamed of escaping to.' He spread his hands apart, as if measuring an expanding mystery. 'She loved a man who would have hanged her from the town-hall clock. What kind of crazy is that?'

'She thought she was going to be Madame la marquise de Sainte-Vierge. Safe as houses for the rest of her days. Honey, this is Paris. Position isn't a matter of life and death, it's far more important. Don't fall deep. She'll open you up like a tin of anchovies, pour out the goodness and chuck the rest away. She won't mean to, but it'll happen.'

'If that's how it is, I don't want to be here.' Regan's inner eye made a flash inspection of his studio, and the work he'd accumulated. 'I'll use up my film stock, then I'm out.'

Part Four

Chapter Forty-Six

Overnight on Friday, 22 December, snow fell on Paris. For Tatiana, the day began with dead-cold radiators. She was attempting to lay a fire one-handed, keeping a shawl around herself with the other, when a knock shattered the peace. It was the concierge, wearing hat, gloves and two coats, who informed Tatiana that the heating was off because the coal merchant refused to visit.

'He won't fill the bunkers unless you pay everything outstanding,' the woman said. 'Your sister Madame Morten usually settles, but with her away, and your mother too…'

'How much?' Tatiana had never in her life seen a coal bill.

'In all, about 700 francs, a little more perhaps at this time of year.'

'Do we need so much coal? I could use an electric fire.'

'But *I* like the central heating on, Princess Vytenis, and you use hot water, I imagine?'

Tatiana agreed yes, she did. 'Does that need coal, then?'

What did you imagine, the concierge's expression implied, that the boiler ran on fresh air and bird droppings?

As she closed the door, Tatiana reflected she'd been saddled with the costs of maintaining an exclusive apartment while her family disported themselves in hotels. Where, no doubt, the coal bunkers were always full. A sense of grievance sent her to the telephone and, with the help of the operator, she called every large hotel in Enghien-les-Bains until she was connected to the Jonquil, where they recognised her mother's name. She was told that Princess Irina Vytenis was currently not in residence. Visiting friends in Switzerland, but returning to her suite on Christmas Eve. That was three days away. Tatiana hadn't known her mother had any Swiss friends.

'Is her maid with her? Yana Egorieva.'

Indeed. The maid had accompanied the princess. In the informant's voice, Tatiana detected a note of relief.

'What about my niece?' she demanded. The little girl had accompanied her grandmother abroad, the hotel employee told her, though she had been somewhat under the weather. A throat infection.

Alarm bells rang. Anoushka had been a very premature baby, prone to fevers. 'You're certain they'll all be back on Christmas Eve?'

'As sure as I can be, Madame. Princess Irina Vytenis has already ordered dinner for that night.'

Tatiana wrote 'To Enghien' in her diary, over the days of Christmas. The post brought happier news. Her portion of Maison Javier's quarterly dividend had been paid into her account. At just over 2,000 francs, it was down on last quarter's pay out, though to most working Parisian girls it was a windfall. She could satisfy the coal merchant at any rate.

She had a sudden craving for bread and butter, which required a trip to the shops. The city was muffled and silent, like a bell clapper wrapped in hemp. Snow deadened everything but the creak of her boots as they broke the virgin surface. She'd forgotten her gloves, keeping her hands in her pockets. Something she'd been taught that only vulgar people did.

Still, there was hardly anybody about to see and judge her, though at the junction with rue Murillo, she became aware of a man keeping pace behind her. He followed her to her favourite baker's, hanging back so she could never see his face. She bought a long loaf, fresh from the oven, which kept her hands warm as she headed for home through the park, unwilling to walk back the way she'd come, as it would involve passing the man. Her lungs were chilled, her breath short. She'd lost her fitness. She'd return to her ballet, she decided, after Christmas. Rosa had invited her to join her for the holiday celebrations but Tatiana had declined. Even had she not been planning to visit her mother, Regan would certainly be one of the party, and last time they'd met she'd shown him the scarred interior of her mind. He'd now seen her physically and mentally naked, which was more than Gérard ever had.

Parc Monceau was a pageant of crystal-glass fantasy trees held together with black wire. The park's architectural follies were furred with snow, paths indistinguishable from lawns. All this beauty came at a price. The temperature had plummeted.

Her thoughts turned practical. Regan was right, she needed work. Her little windfall would not last long. But when she thought about it, her mind crowded with all the skills she didn't have, all the tasks she was bad at. It wasn't as though she hadn't tried. She'd telephoned the *directrice* of Callot Soeurs, where her career had begun, and asked if they were hiring.

'I'm afraid our books are full,' had been the reply. 'But how lovely to hear from you.'

'May I come in and talk? My "look" has changed since you last saw me.'

'Perhaps not immediately.' Much was packed into those syllables. 'We're rather busy with Christmas upon us. Goodbye, Princess Vytenis.'

It had been the same at all the other houses she'd called, only the responses were blunter. When, finally, she telephoned Worth on Avenue de la Paix, and got a barked, '*Non!*' she'd given up. She'd understood the hostility better after she picked up a back copy of *Le Petit Parisien*'s illustrated edition, left behind by their cook. It featured a cartoon of 'Tatiana' slinking out of the gates of Saint-Lazare in a racy flapper dress, stockings gartered below wildly rouged knees, high-heeled shoes tied at the ankle with ribbons, a long cigarette holder held to disdainful lips. 'Free to re-join the party while her victim's family mourns'.

Gérard had doubtless stifled scandal in the serious newspapers, forgetting that gossip thrived best at gutter level. *Le Petit Parisien* and its right-wing cousin, *Le Petit Journal*, had circulations that knocked the respectable press into a corner. She could not imagine ever recovering from this.

What was left? The click of curtailed conversations wherever she went? Should she do as Gérard had suggested, and leave Paris? Find a fashion house willing to take her on in London? Madrid? New York, even?

That was when she saw the man again, ahead of her on the path. He must have doubled back and entered the park by another gate. Terror gripped her. She recognised the belted coat, the Homburg hat. No eyes... strange, empty sockets added to the nightmare impression that she was being stared at by a skull. *It was Armand.*

Chapter Forty-Seven

She'd reached the Rotunda gates, the midpoint in her walk home. Ahead lay the ornamental lake, glaring brightly under the winter sun, and it was this that had stopped her seeing the apparition. It was maybe twenty paces away. She strained her ears for reassurance that others were near.

All she heard was the click of expanding ice, the clatter of pigeon wings as a flock took off nearby. Dropping her warm loaf in the snow, Tatiana measured the distance to the Rotunda. She ran.

A frozen puddle was her undoing. Her feet went, pulling a scream from her. Her fall sent pain through every bone, especially her hands which took the brunt. Hearing scraping breath beside her, she pushed herself up. Her wrists gave way and she fell face down.

'Leave me alone,' she sobbed.

'Tatiana, look at me.'

'I don't want to!' She'd seen enough. But the voice sounded human, so she eased into a sitting position. It was not Armand, but Gérard, wearing his brother's hat and coat. His eyes looked bruised, as if he hadn't slept for days. 'What do you want?' she demanded.

In reply, he angled his cheek towards her, showing a purplish swelling. It looked very sore. 'I've had to take time off work, and visit a doctor who poked and prodded.' He winced at the memory while she thought grimly of Dr Jolivet.

I could tell you something about prodding. 'Go to the apothecary on Malesherbes,' she advised breathlessly. 'Madame Léonce will make a poultice for the infection.'

He clenched his fists. 'I don't want fucking witchcraft, I want to stop looking like a plague victim. I stink of the surgical spirit my mother plasters on me five times a day. I want you to know how it feels to have your looks stolen.'

'I know how it feels, Gérard, and if you think a little prick in the cheek makes us even—' Was that someone approaching? She shouted, 'Over here, help!'

A male voice answered. 'Madame? *Que diable—!*'

Gérard backed away, jabbing a finger as he warned her to keep away from him and keep her mouth shut. 'I had some journalist scum follow me to rue Molière. Out for a story. I'm warning you, don't speak to him or I'll turn you in to the police for more than dangerous driving. You know what I'm referring to.'

'Say it out loud, Gérard.'

'I've said all I mean to.' He jabbed again, but ruined the effect by slipping, having to save himself. With a last, loaded, glance he disappeared around a corner fringed by shrubs. Tatiana looked up to see who had come to her aid. What she thought at first was a beret worn at a slant was thick dark hair. A leather carry case was slung across the man's chest. 'Regan!'

'Tatiana? Was that who I think it was?' He cupped his hands round his mouth. 'Hey, Sainte-Vierge, come back and talk. Or is it only undefended women you're interested in?' There was no response.

'He followed me,' Tatiana said shakily. 'I thought he was Armand returned from the dead. I'd have preferred that.' Her hands hurt. A lot. 'How did you know?'

'That I'd find you here? I didn't – I was working. The bridge and that folly over there all in white lace, that's my final location... why am I talking? You're in pain, sweetheart.'

She nodded, bending her wrists to make sure nothing was broken. 'Will you help me home?'

Chapter Forty-Eight

As Regan let them into her flat, she noticed him shiver. 'Heating's off,' she explained. 'I paid for coal this morning but I don't know if it's arrived. We could light the drawing-room fire, and the kitchen stove.'

'We? I'm guessing you don't know how to lay a fire.'

'I haven't felt the need.'

'Or is the truth that you don't know how to replenish a coal scuttle or find kindling? Where's your store?'

Tatiana daren't admit she didn't know that either. 'Somewhere in the bowels of the building?'

'I'll go check when we've seen to your injuries.' Regan took her to the bathroom. Putting the plug in the sink, he ran cold water. 'Hold out your hands. That looks nasty.' She'd sheared skin from the undersides of her wrists. As Regan plunged her hands into the water, bloody grit floated off. 'We need to clean the wounds.'

She wondered if he was remembering being in this tiny room before. She'd fallen naked to the floor in front of him. Last time they'd been together, she had called herself 'a whore'. Where did those violent cadenzas spring from?

'Towel?' he asked.

She directed him to the airing cupboard at the end of the hallway. He came back saying, 'Antiseptic?'

'No.'

'Be a brave soldier.'

She sighed and nodded at the wall cabinet.

He moved items aside until he found a brown bottle – TCP. He pulled cotton wool from a dispenser, then paused, something else in his hand.

'Don't peer,' Tatiana chided. 'A lady's cabinet is very personal.'

He showed her an almost empty bottle of Sirop Roze. 'Early on in my career,' he said, 'I was employed by a mortuary to photograph its occupants. Yeah, I've done all the glamorous jobs. One victim sticks in my mind, a young mother found dead in her bath.'

'This is not the moment.'

'She'd been taking pink syrup for chronic tooth pain. Got addicted, took too much.'

'I'm not addicted.'

'We all say that.'

'The night I fell asleep in… in here, I was very tired.'

'Uh-huh. Medicine, gin and hot water. Quite a cocktail to drink in the tub.'

'I told you before, most of the gin ended up in the water.'

'Just as well, Princess, or you'd have blown your last bubbles before I broke the door down. OK, shake the water off your paws.'

'It hurts.'

'Not as much as it will in a moment.' Regan tipped the brown bottle onto a wad of cotton wool, releasing an astringent tang. 'Ready?'

'No, but do it anyway.' She yelped as he pressed sodden cotton wool on her left wrist and again when he repeated the action on the right. 'I won't be able to do anything for myself,' she moaned. 'Not even fill a saucepan with water.'

'Hasn't Rosa invited you to hers?'

'Several times. I'm not sure I can cope with her constant visitors. I need peace right now, and anyway, I'm going to stay with my mother over Christmas.'

'Why don't I move in here till then?'

'You? Here?'

'Sure. I'm handy round the home. I'll find your coal, crank up the heating. I can cook too. I do a damn good steak, the only good thing I learned from my dad.'

'But it would be outrageous! I mean, alone with a man who isn't a relative. My reputation.' She blushed, knowing what was passing through his mind. 'I mean, it would compromise my efforts to restore my reputation.'

'How about I take you to wherever your mother is?'

'She's in Switzerland at the moment. I don't know why, though I did wonder if she was trying to find Katya and confused Switzerland for Sweden. I haven't had so much as a postcard from either of them.'

'Happy families.' He found a roll of muslin bandage and wrapped her hands, telling her she looked like the star of *The Girl and the Mummy*. A film he'd seen in New York a few years back, which had made his girlfriend at the time scream in fright.

'She must have been a nitwit,' Tatiana said crossly. 'I can't stand the stink in this room. Will you make me a hot drink?'

'Yes, ma'am. Go lie down on the sofa.'

The odour of TCP wafted along with her to the drawing room. She asked Regan to bring a blanket from her bed and he wrapped it round her. When he brought the camomile tea she'd asked for, he helped her with her wet shoes and stockings. His touch so clinical, there was no time for it to feel intimate. She snuggled into the sofa cushions and must have slept, because she woke calling for him. No answer. He'd left, without saying goodbye. Sorrow seeped in. Since jail, his unpolished appearance had offended her less. And he had a knack of being around when she needed him.

Still, what did that amount to? Everyone left in the end. But when she heard the flat door click, she called out eagerly, 'Regan? Are you back?'

'I've been talking to your concierge.' He stepped into the room, holding up grimy hands. The smell of coal dust cut through the haze of TCP. 'I told her there's a crazy on the loose, following good-looking women, and to keep the front door locked at all times. She gave me a soulful look and said, "*C'était la guerre*".'

'She blames everything on the war,' Tatiana said. 'Prices, the state of the gutters, even the weather.'

'Your coal was delivered two hours ago, but she was having trouble coaxing the boiler back to life, thinks the coal was damp. We got it going between us. I've brought some up, too. You look pinched around the mouth, sweetheart. I honestly don't think Gérard will trouble you again. He knows he's been seen and recognised.'

'I'm not afraid of Gérard,' she said, glad to discover she meant it. 'If he'd wanted to hurt me, he had his chance. He's afraid I'll take my story to the newspapers and wanted to remind me that he's still the puppet master and I'm still dancing on the end of a string.'

She watched Regan build a fire in the grate and light it. Fast, assured. He must have done this a thousand times.

'You told me once you were the "bossy-boots" in your family.'

'I was the oldest boy. The man of the house.'

'Did your father leave you?'

'Nope.' He sat back, sweeping up ash residue with a brush that was absurdly small in his hands. 'He didn't leave us. He was never really there.' Regan hung the dustpan and brush back on its brass tree and stood up. 'He was a chef with a merchant shipping line, at sea most of the time, and he'd come home just long enough to knock my mother up, then sign up for another tour. He didn't send money home either, because they weren't married.'

A breath slipped from her throat. 'You're…'

'Out of the bottom drawer, and that's putting a gloss on it.'

'It wasn't disapproval.'

'No? What, then?'

'Shock, that a man could be so callous.'

'My mother was a fool. He only got to do what he did because she took a step backwards when he knocked at her door. She was too eager to please. Desperate to demonstrate to the neighbours there really was a father to her children, though they knew the truth well enough. But for Grandma O'Regan, we kids would have gone on the Orphan Train.'

'What's that?'

'A train packed full of foundlings and unwanted cherubs from the big cities. Sent away to be adopted by kind folk in the countryside.' The way he skewed 'kind folk' conveyed his feelings on the matter.

'You had a bad childhood.'

'Only when my father came home. Rest of the time, it was poor but full of love. I know which I'd rather be without when it comes to money and love.' He smiled. 'I'm going to go clean up, then go out and forage.'

'You don't need to,' she said, but he wasn't listening. *Go out and forage.* Did that mean he intended to stay? The prickly version of Tatiana thought: he'd better not imagine he can make himself at home. The girl who hated being alone hoped he would.

*

When he came back, she asked him to run her a bath. It would unlock her muscles, help her over her shock.

'Sure. The water should be hot by now. How will you get your things off?' He looked at her bandaged hands. 'Buttons, you know?'

Perhaps he could help? 'If you keep your eyes closed.'

'How am I going to find your buttons like that?' He tried it as the bath taps ran, and almost pulled her down. 'I'm lousy at balancing with my eyes shut. Did I tell you before, I get vertigo?' He undid a couple of them and her dress slid off her shoulders.

She gripped its neckline between her teeth. Through a mouthful of stretch cotton, she asked if he'd always suffered vertigo.

'It's inner-ear damage from the guns in the war. It comes on when I shut my eyes, though I'm fine in pitch dark. Work that out.'

'So what are we going to do? I mean, in and out of the bath. Me.'

'How about you pretend I'm a lady's maid and I pretend you're my brother Eric. I've helped him out of a frock before.'

'Your brother wears dresses?'

'He's a priest in Manhattan. At his first mass he was so nervous he fainted in front of the altar. My brother Dominic and I hauled him into the vestry and we got him out of his cassock.'

'I'm not sure I can see you as a lady's maid.'

'Maybe you should close *your* eyes. It's not as if I haven't seen you naked before.'

'That was different.'

'Same bath, same bathroom. We going to trust each other, Tatiana?'

Stepping out of her dress, Regan placed it somewhere it wouldn't get wet. She heard him testing the water. 'Bit hot,' he muttered and turned on a single tap.

Trust. He could have no idea what it was costing her to stand like a mannequin at a fitting, knowing the hands touching her were not professionally disinterested.

'You're clenching your jaw,' he said, his voice a husky burr. 'Arms up.'

She hadn't worn flannel underclothes again after Una's reaction to the mere idea of them. Her silk-satin slip was easy to pull over her head. She shivered from the unsettling novelty of standing in front of a man in only a flat brassiere and 'step-ins', loose-cut knickers. 'I can do the rest,' she insisted, but he pulled her close to unfasten hooks and eyes. It was confusing, because she'd never quailed from physical love. Gérard had never had to seduce or trick her into intimacy. Why did she feel so exposed now? Because her body had lost its bloom? Vanity, in other words... When she nestled close to Regan, it was to hide her lack of curves.

She would fill out again, but for now she was a catch most fishermen would throw back. Regan's breath deepened against her forehead. His muscles were shot through with wanting. She felt his arousal and sensed he was fighting for control. She kept her eyes closed. He undid the drawstring of her knickers and she let them fall. An erotic flame rose inside her and every follicle shouted in awareness of Regan's closeness. When a strand of his hair tickled her shoulder, she gasped and put her arms around his neck. Her lips parted.

'You can kiss me,' she whispered.

Instead, he picked her up in his arms. 'Ready?' He meant the bath. 'It won't scald me?'

'Trust me. Keep your hands clear of the water. Don't want your bandages floating off.'

He lowered her in. The temperature was perfect, as her sigh confirmed.

'Do I add anything? Rose oil? Asses' milk?'

'There's peach-kernel oil in the cabinet,' she told him. 'Put a little in.' Hearing the cabinet door, she dared to open her eyes. His back view told her nothing but she caught a glimpse of herself in a mirror tile, her skin rosy against the slipper end of the bath, her hair russet with moisture. Still short as a schoolboy's. She closed her eyes again. Yana made their soaps for them from castor and almond oil, and always added a dash of scent. As Regan washed her using a soft cloth, notes of hyacinth, rose, jasmine and musk stroked her. This was the most outrageously carnal thing anyone had ever done to her, and all without the haste of lust. Without compulsion or invasion. She'd drown on the unfinished desire building inside her. Surely he would kiss her, or even get in with her. Though that wouldn't work... she really would drown.

'Arms up.'

To her intense dismay, he helped her out and wrapped her in a towel. He dried her tenderly and asked if he might go into her bedroom again, fetch her something to put on.

'There's a robe on the door.' *That was it?*

He left, came back, helped her on with the robe, tied the belt. 'Open your eyes.'

He was so close she could see the dots of shadow on his chin and jaw. Such dark hair, he'd need to shave in the evening if he was going out. She put her lips to his. He moved his head back, a finger to her mouth.

'I promised to look after you, not take advantage.'

'You wouldn't be.'

'I'm old fashioned. Go sit by the fire. Mind if I use your bath?'

'Fine. There might be enough water for another, if you wait a bit.' Rejection brought back her crisp, formal voice.

'Listen,' he said, 'first time I ever ran a bath and let out the water again without another person hammering on the door, shouting "me next!" I was into my twenties.'

'So long as you don't mind smelling of roses.'

'It'll be a first.' He pulled off his clothes and got in.

Wide shoulders, bands of muscle. In the subdued light, water pearling his nakedness, she learned that his flesh was darker pigmented than hers, but not by much. His face, neck, the backs of his hands, had deceived her. They must be sun- and wind-burned. She lingered, intending to ask if he wanted a change of clothes, unsure where she'd find anything to fit him. From Katya's flat? Harry and Regan weren't so differently built and the housekeeper would dig something out. She could telephone. The suggestion died on her lips. All she could do was feast on him until, abashed, she backed out of the room.

When Regan emerged wrapped in a towel, she blinked at the arrowhead of hair that travelled from breastbone to navel, and hurried to fetch him Yana's second-best dressing gown. It was Yana's favourite dragon-blood shade, made to fit an expanded girth.

Regan took one look at it. 'I'd prefer to go naked.'

'It's the only thing in the house anywhere near your size. But if you want to go home…' She could suggest telephoning for a taxi. Always an unarguable dismissal, the offer of a cab. But she didn't want to.

'I'll buy a shirt and stuff while I'm out foraging. There must be a men's outfitters nearby.'

'There are several on Boulevard Malesherbes.' She tried and failed not to sound eager. 'You will come back?'

'Sure. I'm going to cook you dinner.'

Chapter Forty-Nine

She marvelled that someone packed with muscle could move around a kitchen with such quiet assurance. Regan had come back with a string bag of provisions including wine and a bottle of bourbon. He'd been to the butcher's for filet mignon, thick chunks of tenderloin steak which he braised on a skillet, checking the middle with a skewer to keep them rare. He served this with pureed potatoes and steamed spinach, bringing two plates into the dining room where Tatiana had set the table.

'Candles, nice touch. À *la table*, Madame,' he instructed, laying the plates down. 'Hope you're hungry.'

He'd cooked for his own appetite and Tatiana quailed at the quantity. Reading her hesitation, he said, 'Eat what you can. I'm not a "clear your plate or you don't get dessert" kind of guy.'

'There's dessert?' She watched him open the wine. A red Burgundy, a little chilly but he poured it high over the glasses to oxygenate it.

'Dessert is Algerian dates.' Regan had seen them in the grocer's window and pounced. 'To be eaten with a bleu d'Auvergne and bourbon whiskey to follow.'

She warned him she rarely made it to the cheese course. 'Don't be offended.'

'I'm not given to offence,' he assured her. 'I cause too much of it to object to other people's faux pas. Enjoy.'

She surprised herself by eating half her beef. Regan put the leftovers in the meat safe in the larder. She needed to get some more ice, he told her.

'What for? It's cold enough outside, surely.'

'You put ice under the meat safe lid. It's what stops food going off.'

'In Moscow, in winter, we collected ice from the river's edge to store under the house for the summer. It was one of our jobs. We weren't brought up helpless. Well, not entirely.'

'There's ice on the lake in the park. Shall we go get some?'

She shuddered. 'I won't go back there. Not until it's bursting with families and English nannies once more. I don't think I'll ever walk near the Rotunda again.'

They drank bourbon in front of the fire and Tatiana directed Regan to the cupboard that held the chess board. She hadn't played for years. Moving pieces with the exposed tips of her fingers, she demonstrated her competence by taking Regan's bishop. She laughed. 'You're surprised I'm any good? My father taught us. Katya and I played each other until we knew each other's moves so well, there wasn't any point.' She played a gambit, sacrificing her knight and bishop.

'Who would win?'

'Of the two of us? Me.' Sliding her queen in vertical attack, she took his undefended queen.

He swore then apologised. 'I've only ever once been beaten at chess by a woman.'

'Not the screaming girlfriend?'

'No, someone else. It was our third date, at her place.'

'What did you do?'

Turning the board around, gathering up the pieces so they could play again, he said, 'Her name was Janet-Marie and I married her.'

They turned it into a joke, but this was new territory.

'You never speak of your wife.'

'Former wife. We were a mistake. Daughters of millionaire press moguls don't take up with jobbing photographers, but Janet-Marie had to prove that to herself. What about princesses? Who do they take up with?'

'They don't "take up" with anyone. They become formally engaged and advantageously married. If you don't watch your rook, Monsieur Dortmeyer, I'll have that too.'

He concentrated on his moves and, after a drawn-out battle, he claimed the game. 'Best of three?'

'Let's leave it one–all.'

'Good thinking,' he smiled. Then yawned. 'So, where do I sleep?'

'You can have my bed.' She blushed as silence greeted her remark. And blushed deeper at the ink-stain dilation of his pupils. 'I mean, I'll sleep in my mother's room.'

His eyes did not leave her. 'Goodnight, then.' His look smouldered. As if she were beautiful still.

Over the rattle of carved wooden pieces being put away, she whispered, 'Unless you'd prefer a different arrangement. No, forget it. You've already said you don't want me.'

'I said nothing like it,' he objected. 'What I *don't* want is to take the daughter of the house to bed while her mother's away. I was the spoilsport, stopping the neighbourhood Romeos doing the same to my sisters. I don't do what doesn't feel right.' Sliding the box lid over the chessmen, he said, 'Make me understand what you loved about Gérard.'

'That he loved me, I suppose. He's a man women want, even if they pretend otherwise.' She wouldn't name Constanza, but that's where her thoughts went.

'And that's it? He was a catch?'

'He is! He's polished. Good in bed. Well, you did ask! He made me feel safe.'

Regan bristled. 'Didn't he dump you when you were ill? Una told me. You caught the Spanish flu, which killed half the people it touched. He brought you home in his arms, found your niece's first birthday party was going on, laid you on the floor, made some excuse and fled. How can a man who breaks the most fundamental rule, the protection of those he loves, make a woman feel safe?'

'I've had nightmares since before I came to Paris,' she answered. 'I'm afraid to breathe most of the time. His position and name would have built a fortress around me.'

'Some fortress. Anyway, why live in a fortress when there's a world?' Regan knelt beside her and took her hands, carefully retying the ends of the bandages which had come loose. 'If impregnable security is what you hanker for—'

'Yes?' She buttoned her breath.

'Then I'd be the worst person in the world for you. I should go.'

She stopped him by linking her arms around his neck. Kissed him, her lips hesitant. From the age of fifteen, she'd carried her beauty like a flame, scorching all in her path who were not her equal in worth or status. Humbled at last, she offered herself in chiffon kisses. He felt so different from Gérard: a wider jaw, rough with evening beard growth. His lips were fuller, the hair on his upper lip minimal. She smelled the bourbon, tasted it too.

'You aren't playing fair,' he growled as his hands closed around her, one sliding inside her robe. He found the swell of her breast and she opened her lips. They kissed until, wordlessly, she led him to her bed. They made love feverishly the first time, then languorously, once the pulsing blood had calmed. The second time felt daring, as they no longer had the mask of passion. Regan worried he'd hurt her.

'You didn't.' Tatiana didn't know how to voice her surprise. Mutual desire and liking had drawn them together. No force, nor promises. He'd taken her to heights of pleasure she had not known her body could reach, and only as she lay shuddering in his arms had she owned that for the first time she had made love without any wish to wield power, or court veneration for her looks.

'May I take your silence as approval, ma'am?'

She told Regan to 'shush', and put her lips to a different task, which quickly robbed him of the capacity to ask questions or even think.

She woke first the next morning. Regan was asleep on his stomach, and she spent a minute staring at him. The skewed bed covers, the blatant reality of male limbs flung untidily against her magnolia sheets. '*Là-là-là*, what would Yana say? Or Mama. Actually, Mama wouldn't speak. There would be a gasp followed by a thud as Irina Vytenis fainted. Everyone else would call her mad. Except Una, who would gasp, 'Oh my stars!' and then point out that though Regan Dortmeyer was cute, he had no money.

'Two people can't live as cheaply as one, whatever they say, honey.'

'It's only an interlude,' Tatiana answered the Una of her imagination. 'He's going home and I'll be one of his happier memories of Paris.' Pushing her arms into her robe, she stomped to the bathroom. Her bandages were unravelling and she ran a sink of warm water, letting them soak until they came off, revealing welts outlined with swollen skin. After she'd bathed herself and put sticking plasters over the wounds, she went to the kitchen and brewed China tea. It would have to be drunk black and without lemon. Perhaps Regan would help her shop for essentials. At least the flat was warm, since his finessing of the boiler.

She wandered into the lounge, smiling at the chairs pulled up in front of the ashy fire, the chess board waiting to be put away. Gingerly, she carried their bourbon glasses to the kitchen. She was still very, very badly injured. Or so she'd insist when Regan woke. He had left a shopping list on the side, and she read through it then, on a whim, she took the page into the drawing room and pulled back the drapes and opened the shutters. More snow had fallen overnight. She found a pencil and, turning Regan's page over, wrote a list of her own.

Reasons NOT to marry Regan Dortmeyer:
1. Too poor.
2. No connections.
3. Low status.
4. Artist/artisan.
5. Never visits barber/tailor.
6. No education.

She let the objections flow, wanting them out of her head. She then raised her pencil intending to write: Reasons *to*— but a soft thwack on the windowpane took her out onto the balcony. Below, in the middle of rue Rembrandt, a man stood ankle-deep in snow, staring up at her. Her first thought was 'Gérard'. But this man was too roughly dressed to be a Sainte-Vierge. He tipped up the brim of his hat and waved to her.

It was the journalist who had intimidated her the day of her release, then sought her attention outside the English Tea Parlour.

Chapter Fifty

She could wake Regan, send him forth to confront the man. But there were the neighbours to think of. It was one thing for an unmarried woman to invite a man to her apartment, something else to have him stumble out the following morning in his shirt.

She could close the shutters and go back to her list.

Or she could summon up the courage she was so keen on acquiring and face this foe. All right, she decided. If he was still there after she'd dressed, she'd go down and ask what he wanted. Having donned the armour of her black dress, a thick jumper and woollen stockings, she went back to check. He was still there.

He shuffled forward as she wedged open the front door so it wouldn't clash shut behind her. He touched the muffler at his neck with a gloved hand, then used the same glove to wipe the end of his nose. Then he held out his hand.

She put hers behind her back.

'Princess Vytenis.' His voice was that of a heavy smoker. 'My name is Patrice Denois, and I am a writer for *Le Petit Journal*. I have a proposition.'

'That rag! I won't talk to you. Go, or I'll call the police and you'll discover what it's like in a Paris jail.'

An amused grimace answered her. 'No point threatening me with police vans and prison,' he grated. 'I've seen the inside of both. The police don't like me and I don't like them. Know why?'

She shook her head, clasping her arms around herself as the cold penetrated.

'Because they lie and I like pointing it out. The night of the eclipse… 5 October. I was on Place du Tertre. I'd watched a ballet, *Le Père Négligent.*'

'Rosa Konstantiva's.'

He nodded. 'Degenerate rubbish, as I wrote in my piece denouncing it. That doesn't matter. The point is, I followed the dancers from the theatre, along rue Lepic to Place du Tertre, which is how I saw Armand de Sainte-Vierge. He was alone, muttering to himself. Unable to walk a straight line. I asked him if he needed help.'

'Did you tell the police he was drunk?'

Denois nodded. 'Minutes after I spoke with Armand, I witnessed his death.'

Tatiana didn't believe that part. Nobody had witnessed the accident, so her lawyer had told her.

'I should say that I witnessed him dying,' Denois amended. 'He was not killed outright but expired on the ground in front of the car.'

Tatiana hadn't known. But maybe that was a lie too. 'On what part of Place du Tertre?' she demanded.

'Armand de Sainte-Vierge did not die on the square, but on rue Norvins. I assure you, Princess, I saw it. Having spoken to him earlier and offered help – which he refused – I went to a house on Norvins where I'm well known. I was in the front bedroom when I heard the squeal of brakes and the impact. I pushed open the window and shouted to know what was going on. I saw a body on the road, in the car headlights. I saw Gérard de Sainte-Vierge get out of the driver's seat, step over the body of a man I now know to be his brother, and go to your side of the car. I watched him force you to change places with him.'

She recalled a voice shouting to know what was going on moments after the impact. The memory had disappeared in the anguish and violence of event. 'Why did you say none of this at the time?'

Denois spread his hands in an apology of scant depth. 'A policeman who tips me off from time to time told me you'd admitted to being the driver. I thought, "If she sacrifices herself for love, she's a fool who doesn't deserve help." Another reason: the house on rue Norvins which I visited is not one I wish my wife to know about. You understand?'

Coldly, she nodded. 'And now, you smell a juicy story.'

He grinned, exposing every whistling gap in his teeth. 'You want justice, Princess? Give me your side of things and my publication will do its work.'

Tatiana bent her knees. A second later, a swiftly formed snowball hit Patrice Denois full in the face. 'Damn you. How could you keep quiet? I lost my—' She nearly said 'baby'. '… my livelihood and reputation in prison.'

'Here's your chance to even the score.' Denois flicked snow off a coat thick enough to repel an avalanche, and gazed pityingly at her hair. 'Sainte-Vierge has another woman, did you know?'

'Thank you, I do know.'

'But do you know who it is?'

'Again – yes.'

He turned up his lip. 'I doubt you do, but I could name her.'

Tatiana once more brandished the threat of calling the police and retreated, slamming the door behind her.

*

Upstairs, she counted to a hundred before going into the lounge to check if Denois had gone. Footprints made a line towards the park gates. Good. Tiptoeing into her bedroom, where Regan still lay deeply asleep, she put on an old coat and a fur hat. She'd go out and buy fresh bread. Hopefully, with better results than yesterday. Maybe she'd surprise Regan by cooking the eggs and mushrooms he'd bought.

It was as she stood in line for bread at the bakers on rue de Courcelles that she remembered the list she'd left in the drawing room. Reasons not to marry... She went cold. *He hasn't woken*, she promised herself. *He won't go into the drawing room.*

Back home twenty minutes later, she went straight to the bedroom. The bed was empty, though the mussed sheets had been put back in place and smoothed out. 'Regan?' She tried the kitchen, hoping, expecting...

He wasn't there. The drawing room was empty too. 'Regan, where are you?'

She found her list, though not where she'd left it. It was on the dining room table where she could not fail to see it. He had added another item.

'No. 7. Never looks back.' He'd signed his name, adding, 'So long, Tatiana.'

Chapter Fifty-One

The following day, Tatiana stood by the river, the wind scouring her face and throat. *Low status*. How could she have thought it, far less put it on paper? She'd written to Regan, explaining that she'd been extracting evil thoughts from her head, like rotten teeth. She'd pushed the apology under his door.

She'd included a line she hoped would dispel the hurt he must be feeling. 'I would not attempt to catalogue my own woeful inadequacies. It would be too long a list.'

Regan had not replied. He hadn't called.

Christmas was a wink away, the year almost played out. Nineteen twenty-three held no special promise. A flat number without mystery. By the end of today, she'd be with her mother and niece. If she could find the energy to get to the railway station and on to a train. She hadn't eaten in hours.

I'm killing myself, she admitted to the rude, brown torrent of the river. Would that be such a bad thing? Yes, she answered. Die, and you'll never see Anoushka again. The thought of never hearing herself called 'Tatie-Tatya' again was too much. Sobs broke from her and she was thankful that only birds, battling the wind, witnessed her breakdown.

When she'd mopped her cheeks, she turned over her hands. The wounds to her wrists were still painful, at the ugly, vivid stage of healing. They didn't seem infected, though they probably would have been had Regan not—

She shook her head and put her gloves back on.

She walked home along Avenue d'Ièna whose pricy shops were dressed for Christmas with candles and fairy lights. Crêpe paper boxes filled the windows. On impulse, she went into a toyshop and bought a porcelain bisque doll for Anoushka, with real, curled hair and a picture hat. She wrapped it up at home, along with perfume she'd bought for her mother and some embroidery threads for Yana. She was spending her dividend fast. How she ached for those childhood family Christmases, when all had been well with the world. Ached for Katya and Vera, for Mama and Papa. Life had started to unravel on Vera's wedding day. And my malice began it, she reminded herself.

Before setting out for the train, she made herself eat an apple and a piece of the cheese Regan had bought. At two that afternoon, with a bulging suitcase, she caught a train to Enghien-les-Bains, excited and apprehensive in equal measure. She pictured Anoushka unwrapping the doll and was actually smiling when she reached the Hôtel Jonquil and rang the bell at the desk.

Her smile was extinguished when she learned that her mother had not returned.

'Madame la Princesse has extended her stay in Switzerland for an unspecified duration,' the manager in dark tails and white tie informed her. 'She has asked for her rooms to be kept.'

'Rooms' plural. How much was her mother's long exile costing? Tatiana took in the overblown belle époque decor in the hotel lobby, relieved to see that it needed fresh paint, and that some of the plaster mouldings were cracked. With luck, the prices would reflect the neglect. 'Where exactly is my mother?'

'Berne,' came the reply. Princess Vytenis had made friends with a Swiss family, kindly people who had taken a shine to Anoushka and invited them to stay. 'I have an address, Madame, if you were intending to write.'

'Why does my mother never write to me?' It wasn't a fair question to put to a stranger, and the manager blinked before contradicting her.

'Princess Irina Vytenis writes many letters. Her maid is always trotting off to the post office.'

'Not to post any to me, Monsieur, I can tell you that much.'

She could have stayed in her mother's suite and eaten the dinner Irina had ordered, but the prospect of sitting alone at a table was nightmarish. She caught the train back to Paris, and it broke down for three hours. She arrived home in pitch darkness, exhausted. In the hall, she stared at the telephone. There was still time to spare herself a solitary Christmas Day. What was worse, being alone or sitting at a dinner table that might include Regan?

She dialled the operator and recited Rosa's eight-digit number. The call was answered by Rosa's housemaid who told her that 'Madame' was about to go out. 'I believe a table has been booked at the Rose Noire. Did you wish to join the party?'

'Who is going?' Tatiana asked nervously.

Mademoiselle McBride and several gentlemen, came the answer.

'And Monsieur Dortmeyer?'

'I don't believe he's one of the party, Madame.'

When Tatiana clumped the receiver back on its cradle, her mind was made up. She wasn't going to spend Christmas nursing a bourbon between bandaged hands. She would join Rosa's fun. What's more, she'd stop off at Place du Tertre and invite Regan to be her escort. The worst he could do was slam the door in her face.

As she hurried to get ready, she quoted Una. 'What is life without risk?'

Chapter Fifty-Two

She took 'Solfatare' from her wardrobe. Its name, redolent of volcanic gases, described the pewter-grey, sulphur-yellow and amber beads that patterned the dress in random swirls. This was an evening dress she'd helped her sister design a year ago, when Roland's vision for the business and Katya's had begun to diverge. Even then, Katya had been trying to draw her closer, and this dress had been her excuse.

After Roland rejected Solfatare as part of the collection, it was to Tatiana that Katya had turned for reassurance. 'Apparently, it reminds Roland of a lampshade commissioned by the newly rich wife of a tinned meat manufacturer.' Katya had been delicate at the time, pregnant and heading for the first of her miscarriages, though of course they hadn't known that. 'Una warned me that working with Roland would be like singing in a four part-harmony, in which he takes the other three parts. We're supposed to be equals, but everything I present is too flamboyant or vulgar or expensive, or all three. Perhaps I should give up and concentrate on motherhood.'

Had she reassured her sister? Not a bit of it. Tatiana had responded by saying, 'Remind Roland who funded the business. Stop letting him push you around.' I resented her weakness, Tatiana admitted as she stepped into Solfatare and moved to the mirror. On her angular body, the splashy pattern made perfect sense. Lampshade? Roland

Javier needed a pair of spectacles. One other version of this dress had been made for Agnès de Brioude to wear at a gala evening at the Elysée Palace. Tatiana had a feeling Katya had subsequently destroyed the pattern and the *toiles*.

Black elbow-length gloves concealed her hands. She rejected the black wig. Tonight, she'd go out as herself. At 10.30 p.m., her taxi stopped outside Regan's building. She asked the driver to wait. There was no light on in the upper window, but maybe Regan was in his darkroom? Or at Mère Richelieu's. Of the two, she'd prefer him to be at work as that would spare her a possible public rejection. In the end, there was no answer to her knocking, so she called next door. Mère Richelieu herself broke the news.

'Gone home to New York, *ma choux*. He left first thing. I'll miss him,' the old lady sighed, 'but he left me some lovely photographs as a memento.'

Chapter Fifty-Three

Katya Morten squinted through the dark at the receding lights of Stockholm. Her eyes clung to the brightest of them, an illuminated Christmas tree, which made a fast-disappearing beacon as their ship headed into open water. She gripped the rail, mesmerised by snowflakes caught in the glare of the ship's lanterns. Like fireflies, they soared then died in the roiling black waters.

Harry coaxed her away from the side. 'You might be wearing the best my factory can produce, but it won't keep the snow out with this wind driving it.'

'I'm afraid.'

'Don't be. The crew has crossed this water hundreds of times, they're born to it. And these ships are built for Baltic conditions. It'll be calmer once we reach the Gulf of Finland.'

'I'm afraid of what we'll find at the other side.'

'We'll find Estonia, darling.'

After six days in Gothenburg with Harry's father and stepmother, and another three nights in Stockholm at the Swedish capital's best hotel, they were making the 24-hour crossing to the port of Tallinn. They'd then take a train into Russia, to Petrograd. Into the territory from which Katya had fled three years before. To do business with men who lived by no known code of honour.

Chapter Fifty-Four

In the Rose Noire's lobby, Tatiana handed over her coat in return for a pink chit. From the cloakroom, she made straight for the stairs, ignoring the ticket counter. In her world, gentlemen bought tickets, pocketing a disc or receiving a stamp on the hand as proof that they'd paid. Tatiana wasn't going to have anybody ink her hand. As for paying to enter the Rose Noire, which in the past had sucked her in like the sweetest sherbet… No.

Walking down the stairs, she heard a piano. Benjy's set was always about now, elevenish to midnight. She prepared her smile. If an usher asked to see her entry token, she would say, 'It is Princess Vytenis, joining friends at their table.'

In the event, she was bowed politely on, her glimmering dress and a Russian cigarette in an ebony holder her passport. Confidence is king. Or queen. She never smoked, and the cigarette was unlit. It was one Constanza had given her long ago. The holder had been a gift from an admirer whose name she'd forgotten.

Twinkling lights hung in swags across the industrial ceiling. The Rose Noire was more factory than *palais*, but that was its attraction. It was the top C of fashion; here you could dance to the new wave in jazz and watch society change in front of you. It drew people of every class, and from across the world.

She was being stared at. At first, Tatiana imagined people were seeing the recently released convict. But no. It was Solfatare that was creating the ripple. Nobody had yet recognised her, thin as a candlestick with kohl-rimmed tragedienne's eyes, her hair pomaded close to her head. Her ballet training made her progress to the piano a performance in itself. Benjy was playing a fast foxtrot but he must have felt her gaze as he looked up, and when she was close enough to hear him, he asked, 'Come to create some mayhem?'

'No. I'm a reformed character.'

He laughed. 'How very disappointing. Is that who you're looking for?' He nodded towards a table crowded with chattering young people. Her former colleagues, flute glasses picking up the light, a silver champagne bucket in the centre. Isabelle, Françoise, Mary-Jo, Suzy and all 'the boys' – with the poignant exception of Armand de Sainte-Vierge.

Mary-Jo spotted her. Tatiana went up to their table, only to see the English girl nudge Françoise. Tatiana knew her presence was being received like that of a beggar woman in a first-class metro carriage. They were going to cold-shoulder her. Or worse, scatter patronising words without offering her a seat at their table. It did get worse. Fake smiles turned to hard appraisal. The men frowned at her hair, the women at her dress.

A poke in the back was her saviour. 'Hey, you walked right past us, snooty princess! Oh my Lord. What galaxy did that dress fall from?'

Tatiana had never been so glad to see Una.

Rosa's party was the usual throng, including the English lover, whose full name Tatiana discovered was Edward Whittle. Unpronounceable to her. Most of Rosa's cast and backstage crew were present, a theatre chest upturned, contents spilled merrily along with friends, spouses and sweethearts. They went wild about Solfatare and Tatiana was grateful to the point of tears.

'You heard about Regan?' Una asked.

Tatiana pretended she hadn't.

'He's scooted back to New York. The *Centennial State* sailed this morning. I guess the picture agency was threatening all sorts, but I'd have put money on him staying a few more weeks. Didn't you become quite good friends?'

Tatiana's distracted imagination gave her Regan denting her bed with his powerful body, his hips and buttocks wrapped in white sheet like a Roman slave. That night was the only one in recent memory when she hadn't felt afraid and abandoned.

'Did you, um, speak to him before he went?' she asked Una.

'Uh-huh. Gave him drawings to deliver to the office of Mr Artie Shone who is back in New York and wiring me every other day.' Una's tongue appeared between her wine-red lips. 'Artie still wants a buying agent here, so my offer of a job still holds.'

'Everybody dance, come on.' Rosa pulled Edward from his seat. Benjy had finished his set and the resident band was on. Their first number was Jerome Kern's 'Whose Baby Are You?'

'On your feet, Tatiana,' Rosa ordered. 'We have spare gentlemen, it won't do to stay on your backside. Besides, I want to see how that dress moves. One of Katya's?'

Tatiana nodded and cold fear ambushed her. Katya was in danger. Lost somewhere, afraid. Just as quickly, she banished the thought. Silly and superstitious.

'Come on.' Rosa chivvied her party from their chairs. 'Allez-oop!'

It was cooking on the floor, the air sticky with body-heat. Her partner, Rosa's principal male dancer, didn't care. He was in a passive, smiley state due to the strongly scented cigarettes he'd been smoking. Disinclined to twirl or kick up his feet, for which she was thankful. When she rested her wrists on his shoulders so he couldn't grip her hands and hurt her, he didn't notice. The abortive trip to Enghien-les-Bains, the shock of losing Regan and Mary-Jo's wind-dried smile, had all sapped her. It felt good to lean against an expert dancer. But as she thought it, her arm was wrenched from its resting place. A voice in her ear demanded, 'What's this about? Who brought you? Why are you draped over this man?'

Tatiana swung around, knowing whose eyes she would meet. 'Gérard, I can dance with whoever I like.' He had grasped her lacerated wrist but she wouldn't show how much it hurt.

'Now just a moment—' Gérard broke off. A rictus flickered in his cheek, drawing her eye to the swelling that still marred it. It was hard to be sure under the festive lights, but he seemed to flush, his moustache turning down as he realised who she was. 'Tatiana?'

'The very same. You're here to meet Constanza, I suppose?'

'That dress belongs to my cousin Agnès!'

'Wrong again. You thought I was her? I'm flattered. Why are you here, Gérard? You used to say you hated this place.'

'I do. I'm meeting, um…' Clearing his throat, he nodded contritely at Tatiana's partner who was finding the mix-up hilarious. 'Your pardon. Mistaken identity.' The band had finished 'Whose Baby' and were vamping the intro to the next. Tatiana's voice soared over the dance floor.

'Mistaken, *mon cul*! You and Constanza are partners in treachery. Since when, though? I have a right to know.'

Gérard clearly wanted to get away, but he was blocked by dancers, some of whom were listening avidly. 'Stop this, Tatiana. You're embarrassing yourself.'

'Since when, Gérard?'

He put up his hands to parry the question.

'Since early last spring,' came a silken voice. A voice filled to bursting with self-satisfaction. Constanza.

'Early spring?' Tatiana echoed. 'But Gérard and I only got engaged in May.'

'Mm. We've been together longer than that. I beat you by several months, Tatya.' Constanza must just have arrived as she hadn't taken off her shoulder cape. It was thrown back to reveal the honey lustre of her skin. She wore a dress of cranberry silk velvet with diagonal insets of red satin. It had a daring neckline, more plunging than any Maison Javier would ever produce. Tatiana felt she was seeing this woman for the first time. 'He can't have been engaged to both of us!'

'Certainly not. Only ever to me.'

'I wore his ring… He put it on my finger at my ballet class. Ask Rosa.'

Constanza extended her left hand, displaying the Sainte-Vierge ruby. 'He never meant to marry you, but didn't know how to break it off – the poor man is too soft hearted.'

'I don't believe it. Why would he announce our engagement and proceed with wedding plans unless he loved me?'

'He didn't make plans though, did he?' Constanza said. 'He let you make them, then delayed. Delay after delay. You didn't get the message.'

'You have no soul, Constanza. You tempted my fiancé away from me.'

'I had no need to,' Constanza said, her voice curling. 'Your trouble gave him his exit, letting him see you for what you are.'

Her trouble. Her pregnancy? It hit like a fist. She'd confided her most intimate anguish to Constanza, who had poured out sympathy and steered her to the 'obvious' solution. 'You. You, Constanza. You talked me into—'

Constanza flashed a finger against her lip. 'Don't be a fool, Tatiana.'

'You had me harm my unborn child.'

'I didn't tell you to do that!' Gérard was trying to move Constanza towards their table but she was having none of it. She launched into a parody of Tatiana. '"I can't tell him the truth, but I can't have a baby! I'll starve myself and pretend it's all a bad dream." Why wouldn't you marry Armand? Such an obvious solution, considering it was his baby you were carrying and my God, that boy sweated you. I did you a favour the night I sent him back along the river. Had you used that moment intelligently, you'd be Madame Armand de Sainte-Vierge and we'd have been sisters-in-law.'

'What d'you mean?' Tatiana whispered. '"Sent Armand back along the river". After my engagement party?'

'Hardly that.' Constanza sneered. 'Just a party. You got left behind and I sent Armand to find you.'

'Did you tell him to force himself on me?'

'Perhaps. Certainly, I helped him along. They call it a Mickey Finn in America. A pinch of chloral hydrate. Quite harmless.'

Constanza, mixing her own, special martinis for them all. No, please no. Tatiana couldn't believe one woman would do that to another. But Constanza was holding her eye, no attempt at denial. '*You* spiked my drink, not Armand?' It explained everything she'd experienced on the bridge, the heavy legs, her lack of will when Armand pounced. 'My God, Constanza, what rancid stuff are you made of?'

Something shifted in Constanza's eyes. 'You are on dangerous ground, Tatiana.'

'Armand's baby?' Gérard spoke at last, and as though he had been punched.

Tatiana turned on him. 'So Constanza kept one secret! I imagine it was she who told you of my visit to Dr Jolivet? I accused Armand. Don't look at me in that way, Gérard! I told you what happened with Armand but you wouldn't listen. Now d'you understand? Your lovely Constanza procured me so your brother might violate me. He made me pregnant. She's held that knowledge to herself. I can't think why. Perhaps you know... they say that the worm is cousin to the snake.'

Gérard looked as if he might speak, then changed his mind and ushered Constanza away. Tatiana saw them join Mary-Jo and the others.

Una was at her elbow and hustled Tatiana to the ladies' room, turned on a cold tap. 'Put your wrists in the water. It'll calm your heart rate.'

When Tatiana made no move, Una took off the black gloves. 'Jesus, what happened there? You didn't try to cut your wrists?'

'A kitchen accident.'

'You tried to peel your wrists?'

'Never mind. Those two. They're not just having an affair, they're—'

'Engaged.'

'You knew?'

'Not till now, when I saw their eyes go to each other. OK, done.' Una dried Tatiana's hands. 'I told you I spotted Constanza on 5th Avenue. What I didn't tell you was, it was in Bergdorf Goodman, in...' – she took a steadying breath – 'in the wedding section.'

'Doing what?'

'Trying on the stock, what else? For all I knew, Constanza was putting on wedding gowns for the hell of it. Lots of girls do it. Don't you?'

'No, never.'

'OK, you're different but I promise, I *swear*, I had no idea she was stealing your fiancé.'

'She lied about a dying grandmother to buy a wedding gown in New York?'

Una squeezed a sound from her throat. 'I guess even Consty doesn't have the gall to buy one under your nose. Know what? Somewhere in her heart, she wants to be you. Wants what you have.'

'But I have nothing, Una.'

Rosa invaded their sanctuary. 'What's going on, girls?'

'Love,' Una said succinctly. 'The bad kind. I'm taking Tatya home.'

'Not yet.' Tatiana broke past them both. She marched out, across the ballroom to the table where Gérard sat nursing his shock and Constanza quaffed champagne with an air of tarnished triumph.

Chapter Fifty-Five

'You unprincipled slut!'

The band was between numbers, and the club was as quiet as it ever was on a busy night. Everyone heard Tatiana's judgement on Constanza. She turned to Gérard. 'You're as bad. You threw me under a train and you'll do the same to her.' Her words split apart in the air. 'You'll back away when your mother points out that a part-Argentinian mannequin with a grandmother who sells second-hand dresses in the port of Marseilles, is not quite what the Sainte-Vierge family ordered.'

Tatiana saw Constanza's face alter and grasped the advantage. 'You're right to be worried. It doesn't do to be too confident with Gérard. He may yet have another one lined up. Eh, Mary-Jo?' The unexpected swipe caught the English girl off guard. Mary-Jo shrank from Constanza's sudden head-turn. Tatiana put her face close to Gérard's. 'There's an eyewitness to your brother's death. You're a step away from a conviction for false witness.'

'Waiter,' Gérard summoned a passing staff member. 'This woman is drunk. Please escort her out.'

The Rose Noire paid its waiters badly for long hours, and Gérard's command was met with a muttered, 'What do you think this is, a nun's teashop? Everyone is drunk, M'sieur. Take her away yourself.'

'I'll see you in the gutter,' Tatiana repeated. 'I have no mercy left in me.'

Gérard got up and made himself as tall as he could. He said, 'Nor I for you. Cross me, and I will report you for attempting to murder your unborn child. Constanza will corroborate, and there are other witnesses including the apothecary you tried to coerce into selling oil of rue.'

Constanza stood too, with the snarl of the cornered vixen. 'Not to mention Dr Jolivet and a certain piano player.' She looked for Benjy, but he'd long ago wandered off into the backstage realms. 'I know he obtained gin for you. Two years' prison, Tatiana, for attempting an abortion. What can you accuse me of in return? Falling in love. Oh, and borrowing a few dresses from you. Speaking of which, I'll have my maid drop them off.'

The band began a smooth waltz called 'Is Everybody Happy?'

'Gérard, shall we?' Constanza held out her hand to him, the one with the ring on it.

'Sweetheart, we're going now.' Una came up behind Tatiana and gripped her, rowing her towards the door like a cumbersome boat. Rosa followed, bringing handbags and wraps, and stopping at the cloakroom.

As they walked out into a night of dense, chill mist, Tatiana felt her fury give way to a grief so intense she feared it might shatter bone. Luckily, Rosa had rallied her dancers and two of them caught her as she staggered towards the wall of the building. They supported her to a waiting car.

Chapter Fifty-Six

Christmas Day on the Baltic

Towed into Tallinn's harbour, a doughty tug breaking the ice ahead of them, their vessel bucked in and out of troughs. It was eight in the morning, a glacial sun wresting control from the dark. Up on deck, Harry put his arm around his wife. 'You're the bravest woman I know. A week from now, we should be on our way home.'

'Paris for New Year.'

'Not sure about that, but in time to see the snowdrops in Parc Monceau.'

'What are they doing at home, do you suppose?' Katya asked.

'Laying out breakfast. Trying not to think about the presents piled under the tree. Paris is an hour behind.'

'Anoushka will be so excited. It's the first time she's old enough to understand what it's all about.' Katya pulled a face. 'I hope Yana won't spoil it. She had no family and sometimes I think she's jealous of Anoushka. Don't listen to me, I'm not making sense.'

'You are. That woman has become altogether too dictatorial, and when we're home, we'll do something. My fault. I insisted you take Yana back into the family, but I hadn't predicted she'd take over Anoushka. The next weeks and months will be difficult enough without

Yana Borisovna Egorieva trying to keep possession of Vera's child, body and soul. Darling, are you warm enough?'

She nodded. They both wore wolfskin gloves lined with silk and wolf fur *ushankas* with flaps covering their ears. To coats of heavyweight tweed they'd added quilted oilskin gilets. A Baltic December could kill. In their battered trunk was a second set of outer clothing, along with blankets and tins of condensed milk, a portable form of nourishment. They were taking no chances. No chances with the Russian border authorities either. It was too late in the year for them to sail direct to Petrograd, whose home waters would be frozen solid. They would take a train overland through Estonia into Russia, travelling as Herr and Fru Morten, Swedish citizens.

Katya confided, 'Last night, I dreamed we docked in Petrograd and somebody shouted, "It's that traitor Princess Vytenis! Arrest her at once!"'

'Dreams lay out our fears like a deck of cards,' Harry soothed. 'I don't suppose you were a familiar face in the St Petersburg docks when you were growing up.'

'Call it "Petrograd" Harry!'

'I will, never fear.' He produced peppermints from his coat pocket. Sucking them helped distract the mind from the ship's rolling. But Katya was not to be torn from her worries.

'I cannot think why there wasn't a letter from Mama at your father's house. I gave her that address before I left and told her very particularly, "Send letters there, or they'll chase us across Europe".'

'I'm sure she nodded, agreed and immediately forgot.'

'I wrote it down for her, Harry. Something's not right… Mama was never strong, but nor was she silent. And I keep thinking about Tatiana.'

'Well, I doubt Tatiana's thinking about us.' Harry's expression hardened. 'Chances are, she persuaded Gérard to go ahead with the wedding and is on the Riviera, having a protracted honeymoon. Sunshine and palm trees.'

'I feel she's not happy.'

'You "feel" she's unhappy?'

'I do.' Katya reared back to avoid a plume of salty spray. 'Didn't you feel a connection to Christian, and know when he was in danger?'

Harry thought about it. 'He and I were as close as brothers could be, but did I read his emotions when we were apart…? No. I'm too thick-headed. I'd love to know how Morten et Cie is faring. Have customers paid their bills, is the cloth I ordered before we left of proper quality? I remain,' he shrugged, 'blissfully ignorant.'

'It must be blissful,' Katya agreed. 'When I telephoned Maison Javier from your father's, I got the impression things weren't going well. The phone line was awful, but I'm sure Pauline said that cash flow was tight.'

'They're working round the clock on the next collection. Expenses will be high.'

'I asked how Tatiana was and Pauline said, "Fine—"'

'That's good.'

'"Fine, as far as I know." Then the line went dead.'

'When you consider how much snow fell on Gothenburg that week, it's remarkable you got a line to France at all.'

Katya sucked her peppermint. As she made a bleak acquaintance with the steel-and-iron clutter of Tallinn's docks, worry set around her eyes. Unlike Harry, Katya had no faith in Tatiana's ability to manage Gérard de Sainte-Vierge. She sent out a prayer. 'Let this journey bear fruit, so we can get home as fast as humanly possible.'

*

In New York, it was almost as cold. At around four in the afternoon of December 31, Regan paid his first visit to family having docked the day before. His mood was matched by the stark colours of East 15th Street, where his sister Vicky lived in a tenement flat. Dirty brick. Waist-high snow piled along the middle of the road, which in the falling dark glistened blue. As he went up the front steps of Vicky's building, a resident came out and held the door for him. Three flights up, he found his nephew, Creane, home alone.

'Uncle Regan! When did you get back? Mom's been going crazy, telling Aunt Maureen and Aunt Elsie you must have died, or been murdered or something. She's gotta have wired you ten times at least.'

'Why so many times?' Getting nothing more from Creane beyond, 'You know what Mom's like,' he ditched the subject. 'Is my big sis still at work?'

His nephew nodded. 'Till five.'

'How about you ask me in for a cup of coffee?'

'Sure.'

Creane took him into the small kitchen and looked helplessly at the stove. 'Mom doesn't like me using the gas when she's not here.'

'You must be fifteen years old now.'

Creane nodded.

'Old enough to turn a knob on a stove.'

'Maybe.'

Regan sighed. 'I'll make my own. Get back to your studies.' Schoolbooks littered the kitchen table and Creane returned to them with surprising eagerness. When he sat down with his coffee, Regan made no attempt to open a conversation. Creane was deep in a schoolbook entitled *History of Industrial Nations*. Regan would bet his last dollar that a comic strip lay camouflaged inside.

Only when his nephew stretched his neck did Regan break the silence. 'So what's the big story among the world's industrial nations?'

'Uh?'

'Your study book…' Regan jutted his chin. 'What's it tell you?'

'Oh…' Creane gurned. 'Nothing much.'

'Some fat spine it's got, to tell you nothing. How about the section on "Maggie and Jiggs"?'

Creane flushed, then grinned. He fished a newspaper cartoon from between the pages. 'Why didn't you say?'

'Why didn't you?'

'It isn't actually "Maggie and Jiggs".' Creane turned it so Regan could see that the title was *Bringing Up Father*. 'Don't tell Mom you saw me reading it, OK?'

'Hope to die.' Regan drew a finger across his throat.

'Only she hates it. Says it rots the brain.'

'I guess she doesn't like it,' Regan mused, 'because it's our family biography.' The 'Jiggs' character of the cartoon was the archetypal hod-carrying Irish immigrant. The story went that Jiggs had struck lucky on the sweepstake and his wife, Maggie, was desperately trying to 'bring him up' in the world, to suit her new station in life. Too close to home for Vicky, who was in perpetual flight from ancestral memories. When Creane opened a maths book with a sigh that suggested he meant to do some actual study, Regan took up the cartoon. This issue had Jiggs out carousing with his old gang, and the cops were pursuing him through the city for some violation. Meanwhile, a dolled-up Maggie was trying on dresses in a fashion salon saying, 'Why, I wonder where my husband can be? He's supposed to be driving the Cadillac over to pick me up.'

Could be me and Janet-Marie, Regan reflected. Me and Tatiana? Uh-uh. That repugnant list. Reasons not to marry Regan. Side note: I do not recall asking you, lady. 'Low status. No money. Never visits tailor. Or barber.' Fine. All true… *ish*. But what self-regarding vanity had stirred her to pick up a pencil in the first place? Because she was all body and no heart. Sure, he'd got her letter of apology. He'd stuck it in the nearest dustbin.

'Why are you scowling?' Creane let his math book flop shut.

'Just thinking… I could do a photo montage in the style of "Maggie and Jiggs".'

'Yeah? Like a movie?'

'No, still photos, telling a story.' Actually, it wasn't a bad idea, but where would the market be? Was there a market for him at all? This morning, buying film at a photographic supplier's on the corner of 4th Avenue and East 23rd Street, he'd toyed with the idea of giving up freelance photography. He could open a studio, do weddings and bar mitzvahs. Paris hadn't lived up to her promise. He'd shown his material to Frank Chapman, boss of Worldwide Pictures and the man who had sent him to Paris, and the reaction had been flat.

'They're good,' Chapman had acknowledged, 'but… how to put it… derivative?'

'Are you kidding?' Regan had exploded. 'Derivative of what, for Jesus' sake?' He'd brought images of a quirky, rarely seen Paris. Nooks, side alleys, the underbellies of bridges; the famous light doing things with architecture only light was allowed to do. Was Chapman running him down to strike a lower fee? Screw that. A second-class ticket home had reduced Regan's bank balance to almost zero. Plus, he was technically homeless as he'd given up his Hudson Street walk-up when he married Janet-Marie. Home for the foreseeable future was a tenement room in Hell's Kitchen that smelled of last Thursday's stew and unemptied wash pots. The prospect of life coming the full, crappy circle had started a fire burning in both sides of his head. He'd got out of Chapman's office, afraid he'd say what couldn't be unsaid.

'Is the spare room still free?' he asked his nephew.

Creane wrinkled his nose. 'I've got it, I grew out of mine.'

'What about your old room?'

'Full of boxes. It would have to be the sofa, and Mom won't let you set up a darkroom, she can't take the smell.'

'I'd rent workspace. You'd be OK to share this flat with me again?' He'd lodged here on and off after his marriage foundered.

'I guess, if you don't leave your boots in the hall. Mom says she wishes she had a dollar for every time she fell over them.'

'So do I, if it would make her happy.' Jeepers. His sister might have talked him up a bit. It was right his nephew should be unaware that Regan had been helping Vicky out for years with a monthly allowance. He didn't expect to be ticker-taped every time he set foot here, but to be branded a nuisance? 'Why's she been sending me wires?'

'You don't know about Mrs Dortmeyer?'

'You're talking about my wife?'

'Ex-wife, I thought.'

'Don't be a smart alec. What about Janet-Marie?'

'She—' The slamming front door was Creane's reprieve. Regan tethered his impatience and rose to await his sister. He forgot the low ceiling, crashing against the light shade. Dust floated down. Creane noticed it.

'Mom's slacking.'

'She still working full-time?'

'Yup.'

'Then maybe you're slacking, kid.'

Vicky was a finisher for a big furrier's company a few blocks away, hand-stitching silk linings in sable coats. Close work, badly paid. On her salary alone, she'd never have afforded this place.

'Whose boots are these?' The familiar, careworn voice demanded from the corridor.

'He'd better have knocked the snow off, the no-good guttersnipe,' Regan boomed in reply. The kitchen door bounced open.

'Mercy, it's you!' His sister's body made an electrified shape in the doorway. 'When did you get here? Thanks for the warning! You're too important now to send a wire?'

'Hi, Vicky. Creane was saying something about Janet-Marie.'

Victoria Dortmeyer unbuttoned her mackintosh, pulled off her neck scarf as if she suddenly couldn't breathe. As she hung her coat and hat on a hook, her eye took in Regan's cup. 'Did Creane get coffee for you?'

'I made it. Don't worry, I didn't let him get close to a naked flame.'

'Only, he turns the gas too high and it pops.'

'Sure. Gas has a mind of its own.' Regan looked closer at her. Pretty much unchanged, though at thirty-three, she shouldn't be turning grey. Vicky packed a lot of worry into a small life. When he'd first fled from home, Vicky, then fourteen, had been left behind to nurse their grandmother, prop up their mother and younger siblings while waiting hand and foot on that pig, their father, who at the time had been 'between' other families and other women. Pregnant at seventeen from a fling with a neighbour's boy, she'd been thrown out by Ludvic. Regan had taken care of her and the baby and he always would. Her navy dress was neat, but worn under the arms and at the hem, and the sight of it grieved him.

Before Paris, it wouldn't have crossed his mind that the baggy blouson shape put pounds and years on her. Nor did he like to admit that the first thing he'd noticed on walking in was how dowdy this apartment was, how functional. But after twenty-four hours in Tatiana Vytenis's place next to Parc Monceau – watered silk, ornate plaster and the flowing use of pastels – a snob had been born. You better convert back, he told himself, because Paris is over.

Vicky told Creane to take his work to his room. 'Your uncle and I need to talk.'

'The light's no good in my bedroom, Mom. Anyway, I know what you're going to tell him.'

'Go. Now.'

Creane went.

Regan waited. Vicky began fussing, washing his cup at the sink. 'I don't remember a winter this cold.'

'They're always this cold, Vicky.'

'Uh-uh. There'll be pigeons frozen to the railings by morning.' She backed up her prediction with a shiver. 'You get a streetcar here?'

'Nah, I walked.' In Paris, he'd gone everywhere on foot so he could cut through parks, or go by the river. He would miss the Seine, that endless lava flow of light and shadow, carrier of secrets and private tragedies. Where he'd first seen Tatiana.

Tatiana, who'd lain in his arms, fragile as spun sugar. Pouring herself over his heart like hot gin on a cold oyster. Who'd then taken a pencil and made a list. Let it go, he told himself. Vicky was speaking. Or rather, clearing her throat around the subject of Janet-Marie.

'Creane wouldn't say,' he interrupted.

'Are you drunk, Regan?'

'No – nothing but coffee in my coffee.'

'You just said, "Tatiana wouldn't say". Who is Tatiana?'

'I said "Creane".'

'You think I can't hear now? You think it's easy for me to speak about Janet-Marie?'

He shook his head. 'What's she done?'

'Regan, she's dead and her father has been trying to get you. I gave him your Paris address, but he couldn't get an answer.'

'I moved out,' he said numbly. Dead? 'How?' He had stopped loving Janet-Marie at about the same time he'd stopped hating her but this… this was un-graspable. He sat heavily and his sister sat opposite and told him what she knew. It had happened the previous month. A pleasure trip in an aeroplane that had ended up in the Potomac River.

Chapter Fifty-Seven

Janet-Marie's father, Lemuel Slinfield II, was usually to be found on the fifteenth floor of Manhattan's Fuller Building. Known for its shape as the 'Flatiron', the building housed a number of publishers. None bigger than Slinfield & Gish, whose stable of weekly magazines and business journals had a circulation of millions.

Regan wasn't looking forward to this visit and on leaving Vicky's, he'd bought time by calling on Elsie and Maureen at their 2nd Avenue flat. Teachers at the same public school, both were at home, getting ready the family feast they were putting on the next day.

Their cries of 'Regan!' nearly burst his eardrums and their hugs would have dismembered him if he hadn't insisted, 'One at a time!' They asked, did he know about poor Janet-Marie? And though he said he did, they repeated all that Vicky had told him. In the belief that food was the universal balm, they force-fed him almost a whole, fresh-baked apple cake.

Prising himself away with a promise that he'd be their surprise guest next day, he'd walked to the Marble Cemetery, a step away from where they lived, and laid flowers in front of his mother and grandmother's memorial plaques. He silently imparted his news, until the flat-voiced wind reminded him of his duty. He took a streetcar to 5th Avenue. To the Flatiron.

Where he was kept waiting. Daddys' girls are usually married to two men at once, and Regan and his father-in-law had never been destined to get on. Regan had cut his photojournalism teeth in dives and bars, while Lemuel Slinfield supported prohibition, believing strong liquor to be the root of other people's evil. Though his popular magazines oozed gossip and sleaze, Lemuel despised a man who sought it out and photographed it. His revenge had been to appoint Regan to a political magazine called *Era*, telling him to 'make it popular' only to fire him three months later for doing just that. The firing had coincided with Janet-Marie's divorce suit.

As he waited, Regan tried to work out why his father-in-law should be so eager to get hold of him. The only thing he came up with was that Lemuel had found a way to blame him for Janet-Marie's death. When a personal assistant in a black dress and oversized lace collar invited him to 'come through' he discovered he was spot on.

'If you hadn't screwed over my daughter, she would never have got on that goddam aeroplane,' Lemuel Slinfield bulleted before Regan was halfway across the carpet. Behind a lacquered desk, Slinfield's arms formed a triangle with his bald head. He'd made Regan feel scruffy even at his own wedding and was doing the same now in pinstripe and a Harvard tie, a silk handkerchief making three sails in his top pocket. Nothing could diminish his air of desolation, however. When he sneered at the camera case across Regan's shoulder, saying, 'She said you loved that thing more than her,' his voice tore streaks in the air.

'I never screwed Janet-Marie over, sir, and you and Mrs Slinfield rejoiced when she left me for a man rich enough to buy his own plane.'

'To fly in those conditions, out over Chesapeake Bay... it was as good as murder.'

'I won't argue with that.' Regan understood that Janet-Marie and her new husband had taken off from an airstrip in Maryland for a jaunt over the bay. It was mid-November, and conditions had been bad before they started, turning atrocious as the water opened out below them. A misjudgement of height and the little plane had gone down in the Potomac. The bodies had been retrieved. 'I'm so very sorry, Lemuel. It was a waste of her life and you've every right to be angry.'

'I'm suing the bastard's family. I'll drag his mother through the courts for having a criminal jackass of a son.'

'Sure.' Regan waited while Lemuel's rage spent itself. 'Sorry you couldn't get hold of me in Paris, sir. I'd have come home for the funeral.'

'We kept it small. Close family only. So… how's it with you? How was Paris? "The city of lights",' his ex-father-in-law intoned. 'They switched them back on yet?'

'Pretty much. You wouldn't really know there'd been a war. Restaurants and nightclubs are full, fashion is back in full swing.'

'Whaddya know about fashion?'

'More than I did. What really shows is that women outnumber men near enough three to one.'

'How come you didn't get snapped up, then? I hear you're on the skids. Need my help?' It was Lemuel's favourite technique, to floor you with a punch of generosity just when you were hating him most. 'Need a hand up?'

'No, sir, I don't.'

'No' wasn't a word Lemuel heard very often. And today, it opened a door. 'This…' Lemuel threw a magazine down in front of Regan. 'What d'you see?' It was *Ravissante*, the US edition, priced at 80 cents.

Regan glanced at the colour-tinted front-page image. 'The girl is wearing Molyneux.'

'How d'you know that?'

'The line. Timeless elegance, skirts long to the calf. But mostly, the girl. It's Hébé, one of Molyneux's top mannequins.'

'Well, I'll be.' Lemuel Slinfield sat back. 'I need a man in Paris to run it. It was doing great then, I don't know, the team went off the boil. Circulation's dropping like a stone. The editor I've got now is a bozo so you couldn't be worse. Whaddya say?'

Had the shadow of Janet-Marie not been in the room, Regan would have laughed. If he said yes, the offer would be instantly withdrawn. Say no, the offence would cut deep. He said, 'I'm done with Paris.'

Lemuel nodded bitterly. 'You don't want to leave, now things have shaken out for you, ha?'

Ha? Regan had no idea what he meant.

Without leaving his chair, Lemuel Slinfield summoned his assistant and told the woman to drag the corporate lawyer up from the thirteenth floor. 'I have him do family law too,' he informed Regan. 'That way, I get my money's worth.'

'Why do you need a lawyer, sir?'

'I don't. It's you who needs one.'

The lawyer arrived as fast as the elevator allowed. It was he who explained to Regan that Janet-Marie Plover, formerly Dortmeyer, née Slinfield, had not changed her will from the one she had made on her marriage to Regan. 'You're her sole beneficiary, sir.'

Chapter Fifty-Eight

New Year's Day, 1923 was the most memorable of Regan's life. All seven Dortmeyer siblings gathered around Elsie and Maureen's table, the first time they'd all been in one place since their grandmother's funeral. His brother Eric, released from his clerical duties for the day, said grace. Regan looked at each of them in turn. Vicky, the prodigal with the fatherless child, middle-aged before her time. Maureen and Elsie with their own buried troubles, now wedded to their careers, finishing each other's sentences. Dominic the liner steward, boasting of girls in every port – though that was to shock Eric, Regan judged. And the youngest, Gracie, hungry for her life to start, without the first idea how to be anything but an overworked, underpaid milliner's assistant. And himself, the black sheep who had married a tycoon's daughter and, out of the blue, inherited all her money. As yet, he hadn't told them.

Vicky and Elsie served the soup course while Maureen kept everyone supplied with sweet German wine. At first, conversation limped. They were too conscious of Janet-Marie's death, shimmying round it until Regan told them, 'I feel I've lost an old friend, not a wife, and that's how she wanted it. So let's drink to her, and pass on.'

After that, talk slipped towards comfortable common ground. Old friends, news of distant cousins. Who had married who, or run off with who else. What happened to this neighbour, to that school friend.

'You remember Mr Prasolov who taught his parrot to swear in Yiddish at his Ukrainian neighbour? So his neighbour bought a mynah bird and taught it to swear at Mr Prasolov in Ukrainian.'

Regan gave Gracie a hat he'd brought her from Paris. Overwhelmed, she forgot to breathe and almost fainted.

'Who chose it for you?'

'I did. Hidden talents.' Over the turkey dinner, Regan broke his news. 'I'm rich.' Money, shares, real estate. 'It'll take a few months for it to go through the legal grinder, though I have a suitcase of cash to dip into.'

You could cut the silence until Creane asked *how much*? Vicky told him to stop being ghoulish.

'*Never* discuss a deceased person's money.'

'But I need to know. Uncle Regan can sponsor me through college and I won't have to feel grateful, like you're always telling me I have to.'

'When am I telling you that?'

'If I take it,' Regan interrupted them.

'Why wouldn't you?' Creane looked bewildered.

'Regan, before you refuse this bequest, think what good you could do,' Eric slid in. 'There are organisations helping the kind of brats we used to be which are in need of money.'

Dominic grinned. 'Let Father Dortmeyer spend it for you. You going to live in that fancy Dakota building all on your own, Regan?'

'Maybe.' Regan had been trying to ignore the fact that Janet-Marie's duplex was also coming to him. What would the neighbours say, when he arrived with more camera equipment than suitcases? He imagined Tatiana there with him, taking in the park view, imbuing the rooms with her perfume, her spirit. He shut out the thought.

'How about I move in with you?' Dominic suggested.

'Yeah, he'll need a doorman.' Gracie begged Regan, 'Take me to Paris. It's my dream.'

'I'm not going back.' Regan had been adamant on that point with Lemuel. No fancy jobs or editorships would lure him.

While her sisters cleared the plates, Gracie disappeared and returned with a magazine. It was the November edition of American *Ravissante*. 'Isn't that fit to die for?' She snuggled up beside Regan on the sofa, pushing the magazine under his nose. 'The dresses, the room. The flowers. It's why I have to go to Paris. To see it for myself. It's a show at Maison Javier.' She pronounced it 'May-zon Javvy-er'.

Regan stared at a picture of Tatiana. *His* picture, the one he'd snatched as she ducked behind calla lilies and stuck her tongue out at him. That hat, framing her kitten face. There was another of her, in the wedding dress, stretched out on the floor. He'd teased her, hadn't he? 'The bartered bride'. She'd had no idea that day what lay ahead. That was only half of what knocked his breath back. The shots were part of a four-page spread and every one had come from his Speed Graphic. Worldwide Pictures was credited, but Regan's name wasn't there as photographer. That honour had gone to another name entirely.

Matthias 'Pigeon' Boccard.

Chapter Fifty-Nine

2 JANUARY 1923

Regan was outside Worldwide's office as the janitor unlocked. It was the first day back after the holiday. Icicles like walrus teeth hung from guttering and streetcar lines and the streets were empty but for teams of snow sweepers. The janitor let him into the lobby, and Regan paced until Frank Chapman arrived.

Registering Regan's presence and his mood, Chapman quipped, 'Santa Claus didn't come? I heard different.'

Regan shot down the attempt at humour. 'We need to talk about my work. We can do it nicely or we can do it here.'

'Let's keep it nice. Come on up.'

The air in Chapman's office soon reeked with expletives and the bluster of a man on the back foot. Yes, Chapman admitted, Boccard had sold Paris views and fashion shots to *Ravissante*, claiming the work as his. Could Regan prove that was untrue?

'Do I need to? You know my style, Chapman, so don't play dumb.'

'It's Boccard's name on the contract.'

'Because you put it there. I can have the fashion house write you a letter, and every mannequin sign an affidavit at the bottom. Or I can find Pigeon Boccard and stand on his neck till he squeals.'

Chapman raised his hands. 'Let's calm down while I consult the attorney. I mean, who owns copyright now?'

'You gotta ask?'

'I'd say it's whoever holds the negatives. You need to get them. But why bother? Aren't you rich as Rockefeller now?'

Regan supposed news of his amazing windfall was flying around New York. He didn't care. Just wanted to know, where was Pigeon Boccard? Where was the swindling bloodsucker?

Chapman told him: Pigeon had gone back to Paris.

Regan made a decision about his future before he realised it. He took a motorbus to the Flatiron and had his name sent up to Lemuel Slinfield. Twenty minutes later, he was back in Slinfield's office, uttering words that changed the course of his life.

'I'll do it.'

'Do what?'

'Take the editor's job in Paris.'

'Too late. I changed my mind. I'm gonna sell the damn magazine, it doesn't fit in my stable.'

'How much? I'll buy it.'

A week later, having had five suits, two pairs of shoes and a new overcoat made – all packed in a burnished set of leather luggage – Regan was on board the SS *France*. First class, as befitted the owner and editor of *Ravissante*, Paris and New York.

He docked eight days into the new year, 1923. His first port of call, Place du Tertre. Pigeon's door was unlocked. Regan went straight in. He had Pigeon pinned to the floor before the Frenchman could snatch breath.

'Havana? You damn liar. When I thought you were sailing away, you were lurking round the corner, waiting to steal my work. You took it to New York. To my own back yard. How stupid is that?'

'You're the fool, Dortmeyer,' Pigeon ground out. Regan was pressing on his chest, one palm on top of the other. 'Going out to eat breakfast, leaving your work spread out for anyone to take. You deserved to lose it.'

'I trusted you, you schmuck. We owed each other.'

'*Bien sûr*, and I gave you my studio, rent free.'

'And one time in Harlem, I got between you and a mobster's handgun. For God's sake, why did you do it?'

Pigeon huffed, an attempt at nonchalance. 'When I offered to help you find fashion work, you made out that I had sunk in your estimation.'

'You surely have now. On your feet.' Regan got up, and while Pigeon painfully righted himself, he took stock of the prints on the studio wall, recognising most. There was his shot of the underside of Pont des Arts, and the cheerful nuns in the Tuileries. The kissing lovers were there, and the shot he'd taken in the mannequins' room at Maison Javier. Tatiana astride the windowsill, laughing but with the glint of wild distraction in her eyes. He ripped that one off the wall.

'I'll give you five minutes to restore everything of mine, Pigeon. Every last negative.'

'And then what, huh? Prove they're yours!'

Regan took hold of Pigeon's left wrist in a vice grip, pushing up the Frenchman's sleeve to reveal a watch with a worn strap. Regan broke the leather with a twist of the fingers.

'That is assault. You foreign savage!'

Turning the watch over, Regan read the inscription. '"Rémy-Gausac, J-L". You took this off a dead French soldier. We were camped outside a flattened village and you'd been taking pictures of my unit. I saw you bending over the lad's body, but you assured me you were retrieving the watch to send it back to his family. I'll track them down unless you make a pile of my stuff. Now.'

'All right, all right. Permit me to say, you have mislaid your sense of humour.'

It took Pigeon almost an hour to box up all the negatives, contact sheets and prints he'd stolen from Regan. As Regan went to the door with his arms full, Pigeon attempted a truce.

'There's a new editor coming to *Ravissante*, I heard. Some idiot they're sending over from America.'

'That right?'

'How about I put in a good word for you, *mon pot*? Pass work I don't need over to you?'

'You're all goodness, Pigeon. Be sure and send that watch back to its rightful home, you got that?'

Ravissante's offices were at the rue de Rivoli end of rue Cambon, convenient for Chanel and the English Tea Parlour. Where, he'd been warned by Lemuel's attorney, the staff spent too much time. 'To a man and woman they believe working at *Ravissante* is some kind of paid holiday,' the attorney had confided. 'And they'll all hate you. Good luck.' Entering his new office, leaving his taxi running at the kerb outside, Regan told the girl on reception to call the editor down. 'Tell him his replacement is here.'

The girl folded her arms. Regan hadn't yet unpacked his new suits, and his hair was rough from wrestling Pigeon. She smirked. 'Go tell him yourself.'

Regan sacked her on the spot. He had no sympathy for the editor he was booting out, either. Having forged his own career on a hungry belly, he despised freeloaders. At least he'd provided a taxi for the man.

By the time evening shadows were filling the street, Regan had made himself at home in an office that was the last word in grown-up, art-nouveau styling. His desk was a monster of highly polished bird's eye maple. He had telephoned the hotel he'd booked into, which happened to be the George V, and had a valet bring over a change of clothes. He'd managed to get his hair cut at a barber's on Malesherbes. Tonight, he would dine without checking the prices on the menu, then go to sleep in a luxuriously appointed suite. Half the time, he wondered if he would wake and find himself on a hard bed in Hell's Kitchen.

Early next morning, having read the previous ten editions of *Ravissante* cover to cover, he acknowledged that a few months ago, the magazine had been witty, original and well-produced, as Una had once told him and 'using photography in a really interesting way'. Not now. Recent editions were woeful. No wonder the Paris side of things was haemorrhaging money. He summoned the staff journalists to his office. Only two made the trip up the stairs. The others had yet to arrive for work, apparently. Who, Regan asked the twitchy pair in front of him, was ready to graft, starting now? He got no takers, so he dismissed them. When the others wandered in at ten o'clock, he dismissed them too. In the post room, he scribbled a short note to Una: 'Freelance opportunity at *Ravissante*, call in person. *Soon as,*' underlined. He didn't sign his name, but had an errand boy take it straight away.

Part Five

Chapter Sixty

January 1923

Tatiana had been staying at Rosa's since her clash with Gérard and Constanza. She had spent Christmas Day there, a cosseted queen. Rosa monitored her eating, preparing nourishing broths and fruit compotes. Una had collected her clothes from rue Rembrandt, assuring the concierge that Tatiana was safe but withholding details of her whereabouts.

After a late breakfast on 11 January, a Thursday, Tatiana got up from the table having eaten a two-egg omelette. She took her plate to the kitchen, passing Una in the hall. Her friend was brushing her hair in front of the mirror, a handbag at her feet.

'Going out?' Tatiana asked.

'Rue Cambon. I got an intriguing invitation ten minutes ago and I'm hoping it's not a prank.' Una had oiled her hair into its former, sensible shape, and looked like a pixie training to be a schoolteacher.

'How about I come with you?' Tatiana had the urge to get out of the house. 'I could bring the dog.' Rosa had acquired a borzoi bitch at Christmas, an ill-advised gift from an admirer, and it had become Tatiana's job to walk her. Her name was Pavlova.

'Um, sure. Maybe not to the actual meeting.'

'To rue Cambon, no further. You don't mind? People don't gawp at me so much these days.' Tatiana's hair had grown to an acceptable length. A hairdresser had shingled it against her neck. Sheened with beeswax and rosemary oil, it glowed, and if people stared when she walked around Montmartre, it was because the colour was an exact match for Pavlova's red-bronze coat.

Una passed Tatiana the dog lead from the hall stand, then fixed a studious-looking beret to her head. 'My meeting's at *Ravissante*, and from what I've heard and read lately, it sure could do with some help. And I could do with a new challenge. I'm bored writing for the syndicate. Finding new ways to say the same thing, week in, week out: "Stop the presses! Madame So-and-so has been seen wearing her hat at a fifty-five degree angle. Last week it was already at a dangerous forty-eight degrees." Hey, Pavlova,' Una stroked the dog's silky head, 'you're sniffing my gloves, just as I sniff opportunity.'

They walked to the Abbesses metro. Una received her share of looks, but Tatiana got the most. She'd chosen a coat of black velvet embroidered with China roses in metallic thread and a matching hat that left her hair visible. At the station entrance, Una said, 'Elevator or steps?'

'Elevator, but you'll have to distract Pavlova while I get her in.' Abbesses was the deepest station on the network and its two hundred spiralling steps would have been beyond Tatiana even without a dog to carry. She had started ballet again, but had been put down a class. She got tired quickly.

On rue Cambon, they separated, Tatiana and the dog strolling to the English Tea Parlour where Monsieur Aristide welcomed her with his customary caution, though he made a fuss of the dog.

'A corner table, near the window, Princess Vytenis?'

'Um, thank you.' The same hiding place as before, it seemed. 'May Pavlova have a bowl of water?'

'But of course. Tea and her very own cake, if she wishes.'

'Water is enough. But I'll have cake – if you don't mind?'

'Why would I mind, Princess?' Aristide was resplendent in a black morning coat, a watch chain straining across his plum silk waistcoat. Since her last visit, he'd gained appreciable weight. Christmas? The end of flour and butter rationing in 1920 had made the production of croissants legal after a wartime ban, and as a seasonal treat, Aristide baked them filled with praline. Everyone knew that he tasted his own wares. He regarded Tatiana with droll cynicism. 'Why should I object to so famous a lady enjoying my humble offerings?'

'I'm not famous, I'm notorious. And I was rude to you when you employed me. I ask your pardon for that.'

'Ah, you were not suited to life in an apron.'

A waitress brought tea and a plate of bread and butter, a selection of iced cakes and a new speciality.

'English scones, served with butter and *confiture de fraises*.' Strawberry jam. As her tea was poured, Tatiana opened the book she'd brought with her, *Notre-Dame de Paris* by Victor Hugo. She'd have to wait at least an hour for Una to finish next door. Her friend would haggle over this opportunity, whatever was being offered. It was Una's nature.

Aware of somebody staring at her through the window, Tatiana jerked her eyes from her page. A stout woman was looking in. Anna Markova. Tatiana half rose to invite her to join her, but she hurried away.

A worse snub was coming. Two new customers were being shown to the table next to her. Aunt and niece: the marquise de Sainte-Vierge and Agnès, duchesse de Brioude. Tatiana quickly shifted so her back was to them. They might not have noticed her had her waitress not returned with water for Pavlova, apologising cheerfully, 'It took me a while to find a suitable bowl for so elegant a creature, Princess Vytenis.'

'Vytenis? Damn. What's she doing here?' was sputtered from the neighbouring table.

'Aunt, please,' a softer voice muttered. 'This is a public place.' Tatiana heard Agnès de Brioude quietly requesting that they be moved to a different table.

'I will stay here,' the aunt thumped back. 'Let *her* move. I don't know how she has the effrontery to trespass on my lunchtime retreat. The conceit. The insolence.' Tatiana felt her sleeve being tugged. 'And don't pretend you cannot hear. You know I am a regular customer, young woman. You served me often enough when you were employed here.'

'Not that often,' Tatiana said coldly. 'Whenever you came in, I made a point of escaping to the kitchen.' It had been Armand who had demanded that she or Katya take their order, sending the plainer waitresses away. 'One thing I do recall, Madame, was spilling tea over you the first time we met.'

The marquise cut across her. 'One does not "meet" waiting staff.'

'Tante Clothilde,' remonstrated the duchesse, 'this is undignified. Princess Vytenis wishes to continue reading her book.' Dark eyes regarded Tatiana more coldly than in the past. Of course, Agnès would believe her to be Armand's killer.

The aunt and niece removed themselves to the furthest away table. Tatiana said to Monsieur Aristide, 'I bring storms with me, like the God Zeus. I don't mean to.'

'Sure you do not enjoy wreaking havoc, Princess Tatiana?'

'I did once but it grows tiresome, like walking against the wind with your umbrella blown inside out. I'll go if you want.'

'I hope you won't, or it will be said that I turned you out to placate the marquise de Sainte-Vierge, and that would set a dangerous precedent. Within six months, she would be taking her tea here all alone. I will refresh your pot—' The tinkle of the entrance bell took Monsieur Aristide's eyes to the door. 'A friend of yours, I think.'

It was Anna Markova, and instead of a cool, 'How are you, Madame?' what burst from Tatiana's lips was, 'Why did you scuttle away when you saw me?'

'Scuttle?' Madame Markova shook Tatiana's hand. 'That would defy the laws of physics. I saw you, and suddenly remembered there are things I've been waiting to return to you.'

'Things I left at Maison Javier?' Tatiana had known since Christmas that both Anna and Larissa had been given their jobs back. Larissa had told Tatiana the news over cocktails at Rosa's.

'Monsieur apologised for overreacting. He was very upset at the way he'd treated us.'

'But not at the way he treated me?' she'd remarked, and Larissa had looked as though she'd liked to disagree, but couldn't.

Madame Markova laid two envelopes on the tablecloth. One was plain brown, the other ivory with a nice grain. Both had been screwed up and smoothed out. Tatiana knew exactly what they were. Seeing Madame Markova eyeing the scones and the glistening jam, she made a gesture of invitation. 'There's too much here for me. If you're not hurrying back?'

'You're sure? Thank you.' Anna Markova moved the letters closer. 'They were rescued from the waste bin in the *cabine*.'

'Where I'd thrown them. They're poison-pen letters.'

'How do you know? They're still sealed.'

'I ripped up a third one, which was vile. Bad things come in threes.'

'Not always. Shall I open them?'

Tatiana sighed. 'Does Roland know you're here?'

'N-no. I don't have to report all my actions to him and, anyway, I'm in your debt. You spoke up for me and Larissa.'

'Having got you into trouble in the first place.'

'You could have fought for your own job but you pleaded for ours. That shows good character.'

'I doubt these letter writers think so.'

'I'm so very angry over this business with Constanza and your former...' Madame Markova came to a stop.

'Yes, what do you call the fiancé who has thrown you over? Let's not talk about him.' Tatiana cast a covert glance towards the marquise as she picked up the ivory envelope. 'All right. Let's see what my well-wishers have to say.'

The letter had been sent from the Paris suburbs, by a priest. Driven to write, he explained, as it pained him that a young woman such as Tatiana – a princess, no less – should squander her life in vainglorious and immoral pursuits. 'Let this terrible reversal reveal to you that vices such as drinking, driving and dancing unchaperoned lead only to sin. I will pray for you.'

Madame Markova cleared her throat. 'I suppose he means it kindly.'

Tatiana tore into the brown envelope. 'Let me guess... a moral reformer, disappointed that I wasn't guillotined.'

It had come from Armand de Sainte-Vierge, and was dated the day he died. 'I-I can't read it.'

'Shall I?'

'No – thank you.' Tatiana closed the letter inside her book. 'Please, help yourself to cake.'

As Madame Markova tucked in, Tatiana resorted to asking about Maison Javier. Anything to dispel the shadow that had fallen over her mind. Fortunately, Madame Markova had plenty to say. The spring–summer collection would be launched in a month's time.

'You know how hemlines have been dithering the last couple of years, unsure whether to go up or down? Roland has made up his mind. Down, almost to their mid-war length. Simple shapes as one would expect, but the colours, the patterning!'

'What about them?' Tatiana asked.

'There aren't any. Roland slumbers on, in colourless sleep. The tragedy is, this is his second attempt at a spring–summer collection. The first was everything we'd dreamed of. Cerise, peacock, buttercup yellow. Apple green, which I haven't seen on the catwalk since 1914! Straight shapes, but fabulous detail below the hip line. Not so ideal for us plump ladies, but perfect for you. Just as we were rehearsing the running order, he had the whole collection locked away in Katya's office and now we're back to plain-and-simple.' Madame Markova dropped jam onto her scone, and a dollop of cream. 'The November midseason was a financial disaster. Sh! Don't repeat that. I'm afraid the spring–summer will be too.'

'What has got into Roland?'

'I wish I knew. Your sister is so badly needed, Tatiana. Madame Morten wouldn't have let the fire go out! Did you know, she telephoned Roland but the line was so bad, they could hardly hear each other.'

Tatiana hadn't known. Katya had yet to call her.

Madame Markova sighed. 'Roland needs to rediscover his genius.'

'He needs America,' Tatiana said slowly, thinking of Una McBride and the as-yet unseen Artie Shone. 'It's where the money is.' She skimmed jam on a scone. 'Paris must sell in New York and London, because without foreign money, couture cannot cover its vast costs.'

'I don't know about London, but Monsieur considers New York to be a nest of copyists. He'd rather see his designs on a rail in Bon Marché than in an American department store.'

Tatiana said grimly, 'He may live to see it.' It would destroy Katya's dream, the years of hard work. It would spell the end of the lives they had come to take for granted. Their home, their clothes, freedom to travel. The future they all wanted for Anoushka. As poverty's spectre rattled its manacles, Tatiana absently gave her scone to Pavlova, whose nose had been following the scent of jam. 'It won't happen, if I can help it.'

'What can you do?'

'I'm a Vytenis and we fight when we're in a corner.'

'You sound like your sister, but Katya would have a plan.'

That was true. Katya would not be sitting over a pot of cooling tea. But had she been more like Katya, Tatiana was miserably aware, this entire situation might have been avoided.

'I must fly.' Madame Markova lumbered to her feet. 'You won't repeat any of this?'

'You have my word.' They shook hands and, at last, Tatiana was able to read Armand's letter. The first line hit like a gunshot.

'My darling love, I waited with roses outside your workplace. You strode past me.'

She had no memory of doing so. Had she cut him? Mercifully, 5 October had disintegrated into dry crumbs, nothing remaining of the earlier part of the day. She forced herself to read on:

'I will see you with my brother at the ballet tonight. You are entrapped by him, and nothing I or my mother can say will change that.'

There followed an angry remonstrance against her pride, immediately contradicted by rambling apologies. He was so in love... could not sleep... had treated her abominably. Loved her too savagely... could not hope for forgiveness... a reference to his assault on her, presumably. 'Sometimes I am not myself – the war. Had you met me before that carnage, you would have known a different man.' Something was crossed out and unreadable, then: '... I have no wish to live if I cannot have you.'

Tatiana felt her windpipe twist. Please, *please* let this letter not have been a cry for help.

'Gérard can be the instrument of my death. That car he's so proud of... he always needed to be the winner, even when we were boys. Don't trust him, my beloved. Not in life or love. He sees dependency as weakness and love as a burden. I am so sorry.'

Armand had signed himself 'The loser'.

Shaking, she returned the letter to the envelope. It bore no postmark. He'd written it perhaps in a taxi or a café and delivered it by hand. It had lain, unopened, on her dressing table for more than three months, gestating its secret.

She signalled for the bill and roused Pavlova who had curled under the table to sleep. When the waitress came, she gave her Armand's letter. 'Would you give that to the duchesse de Brioude, but not in front of her aunt.'

Chapter Sixty-One

Tatiana walked the dog up and down rue Cambon to order her thoughts before entering the lobby of *Ravissante*. She'd spent longer over tea than she'd intended, but Una must still be in her meeting, otherwise she would have joined her. It was too cold to stand about and Pavlova was shivering – so Tatiana persuaded herself. The inside of a magazine office would be the perfect place to recover from the shock she'd just received.

Typewriters on desks. Telephones with tangled cords. People bent over pages. The world of work. Almost on a whim, she had decided to become the Paris agent for Artie Shone. Assuming the job was still available. Assuming Una had not invented the man, which wasn't beyond possibility. In that role, she could help Maison Javier regain profitability. It was the only way she could think of to keep one step ahead of the nightmarish guilt that Armand's letter had unleashed.

As she looked around for an escalator, she murmured to Pavlova, 'I'd have to sail to New York every few months, I suppose.' The idea was attractive.

She couldn't persuade Pavlova to get into the cage lift, so they walked up one flight, where she found a door marked 'Editor'. A mirror on the landing gave her a chance to reassure herself that her coat and the snuff-brown dress beneath passed the test of elegance. Fawn leather gloves and, of course, Pavlova on the end of a tan leather lead… everything harmonious. Even – and this she knew was a touch obsessive – her perfume, Habanita, was smoky with sandalwood, Virginia cedar and oak moss.

She heard the rumble of the lift on its way up. A moment later, a mature secretary, hair in an iron-grey chignon, stepped out. She greeted Tatiana with stony politeness, then gave Pavlova a look of dislike. 'Ha. Is the dog here for an interview too?'

'No and neither am I.'

'You have an appointment, yes?'

'Again, no. I'm a friend of Mademoiselle McBride.' Tatiana could hear Una speaking behind the editor's door, though not what she was saying. 'Should I wait?'

The secretary flashed a cynical smile. 'Go right in. Join the party. *Americains*,' she added, as if that explained everything.

Knocking and going straight in, Tatiana saw Una perched on one end of a big desk. Una had thrown off her coat and cardigan and was waving her bare arms. Her legs, beneath a pleated sports dress, swung as she talked. Her attention was on the open door of an adjoining office, from where came sounds of somebody opening and slamming filing cabinet drawers. Una was rattling away to this invisible person, an edge of hysteria to her voice. 'How about "The A to Z of couture", beginning with Madame Agnès who makes scrumptious hats, finishing with the House of Worth?'

'That isn't A to Z, that's A to W,' returned a deep voice, which made Tatiana's fists ball up in shock. Tension on the lead made Pavlova whimper and put her paws on Tatiana's embroidered middle.

'*Petite*, get down, you'll wreck my coat. Una, is that who I think it is?'

Una jumped to her feet and came over, mouthing, 'Thank God. I've been cudgelling my brains but he blasts every suggestion.'

'Una, *who* is in the next office? It can't be Regan Dortmeyer!'

'It's him, large as life. But this is desperate. Here's my opportunity to carve a name both sides of the Atlantic, and can I scare a decent idea out of my head? I cannot. Help.'

'What's he doing?' Tatiana hissed. 'When did he come back?'

'Shoot, I don't know. Stop gabbling. We need a theme. One of the journalists Regan sacked destroyed all the pages before he left – poured ink over the layout – and the February edition is due out next week. Regan is starting from scratch.'

'What's his role?'

'God, basically. He bought the whole damn magazine.'

'Bought? He has no money.'

'All I know is, he wants ten earth-shattering ideas…' Una stared at Pavlova, then pitched her voice towards the adjoining room. 'How about "Fashionable ladies and their dogs"?'

Back came: 'Fashionable ladies all have the same kind of dog, overfed and flat-faced. Babe, I need to set the Seine on fire, not shine a torch into a dirty puddle.'

Regan came out of the side room, white-shirt arms loaded with cardboard boxes which he deposited on his desk. He stared at the dog and once, briefly, at Tatiana. Antipathy bounced in his eyes. Without speaking to her, he dialled a short number on his telephone. 'Madame Saule?'

'The dragon down the corridor,' Una whispered.

'Have you fixed up a printing schedule?' Regan asked into the phone. 'You have? The press-room manager is all set for overnight, Thursday 18. And that's the best he can do… all right, Madame. If you say so, I believe you.'

Replacing the receiver, he spoke as though Una had heard both sides of the conversation. 'It gives us a full week. We compose pages by Monday, galleys by Tuesday night, typeset end of Wednesday. Plates made Thursday daytime—'

'Whoa,' Una stalled him, 'we haven't any editorial or pictures.'

'We have tomorrow and the weekend.'

'Nobody can create a magazine in a weekend, Regan. You're going to have to pull the February issue.'

'Forget it. Advertising has been sold.' He pointed to the boxes on the desk. 'They're full of artwork, and we've been paid for the space, so we're committed. Besides, readers who can't find *Ravissante* on the stands will buy a different magazine. We could lose half our circulation by March.'

Una turned to Tatiana. 'What would you want to read in the next issue?'

Tatiana was absorbing the startling change in Regan's appearance and said the first thing that came to her. 'That I'd made a comeback, all forgiven, that the fashion world had ground to a halt without me.' Regan wasn't simply changed… Gone was the comfortable dress-down. Today it was wide-legged trousers, a crisp poplin shirt and pearl-grey braces. And his head… the tangled curls had given way to a clippered crop with a side parting. Curiosity slipped the leash. 'Regan, you've become someone else!'

He didn't answer. She tried again. 'How come you're an editor now?'

Finally, he acknowledged her. 'Princess Vytenis. How kind of you to call.'

A sharp cough announced that the dragon secretary had come in. 'Vytenis? Had I known, I would never have let this person into your office, Monsieur.'

'She's with me, Madame Saule,' Una put in. 'And she isn't "this person", she's Tatiana and has given me the most stupendous idea.' Leaning down to stroke Pavlova, Una said, 'We should use *Ravissante* to relaunch Tatiana.'

'Out to sea?' Regan asked, after a pause.

'Low punch,' Tatiana snapped back.

'But I'm a low-status person, after all.' He folded his arms. 'How is that going to help me get a magazine out and selling, Una?'

'Because,' Una said patiently, 'everyone in Paris knows who Tatiana is and, whether they like her or not, they'll want to read her story.'

Regan's glance stripped a layer off Tatiana. 'Our advertisers would accuse me of sullying their brand.'

'You've lost none of your charm,' Tatiana observed.

Una returned to her perch on the desk. 'OK… We should dedicate the entire February issue to one fashion house. An exclusive preview of one spring–summer collection.'

Regan waited for her to add more. 'Sell it to me.'

'Maison Javier.'

'Won't work,' Tatiana said firmly, repeating what Madame Markova had told her, only to grind to a stop as she remembered she'd promised not to say a word. 'That mustn't leave this room.'

'Old news, honey.' Una kicked her legs and a shoe flew off. 'After you headed off for your tea, I bumped into that English girl, Mary-Jo. Slinking out of Chanel, all furtive, so I guess she was trying for a job. She told me much the same thing. Roland Javier is sabotaging his own firm. People are suggesting that his war has finally caught up with him. I'm not sure how.'

Tatiana had an idea what that meant. Katya had told her how Roland had volunteered to serve as a stretcher bearer in 1914. As a Spanish national, he had been ineligible to fight and had spent months in the mud of the Somme, dealing with dying and mutilated men. Such sights never left the mind. Horror could ambush you at any time, but could it affect business judgement too? 'He is certainly behaving erratically.'

Regan spoke at last, having heard Tatiana out. 'I'm sorry for it, but if his company is sinking, it's not the moment to splash out on a feature.'

'That's right, desert the sinking ship,' Tatiana hit back.

'Pot, kettle. Oh, hang on, you didn't desert Maison Javier. You were kicked out.'

They glared at each other.

'Stop bickering,' Una cried. 'What is it with you two? Mary-Jo thinks Roland's lost his balls. Well, she didn't say "balls" because she's mealy-mouthed. She said "mettle". Roland created a magical spring–summer collection but he daren't show it. Without Katya behind him, he's crawled back to—'

'Beige,' Tatiana filled in.

'He needs somebody to help him see what he's throwing away. Tatiana is that person.'

'I don't think so,' said Tatiana. 'In fact, I'm the last person he'd listen to.'

'Let me get this right…' Regan walked to the window, pausing to trail a hand over Pavlova's neck. The dog had been staring at him hopefully. 'You want *Ravissante* to feature a disgraced mannequin wearing the discarded output of a fashion designer who has lost his… mettle.' He thrust his hands in his trouser pockets.

'But that's the point.' Una swivelled so she was facing him. 'Not the beige collection, the one he's scared of showing. What if we got hold of it?'

'McBride, are you crazy?'

Una went up to Regan, stretching to put her hands on his shoulders. 'You know perfectly well that I am – but who else would think of doing it?'

'Nobody, for good reason. The couture police, whatever they call that department, would arrest me. And you.'

'Roland would never forgive you,' Tatiana warned. 'I've seen him in a rage. He cannot bear to be tricked or made a fool of.'

Una's eyes clung to Regan. 'This is the idea you've been searching for. Something other than the usual simpering flim-flam. We're all sick of invented facts passed off as insider knowledge. I should know, I've invented most of them. Tatiana plus Javier gives us cast-iron credibility.'

Regan topped her. 'Theft of copyright. Anyway, how does it help readers to fall in love with clothes they can't have?'

'But they could, and then it wouldn't be theft,' Una insisted.

Regan cocked an eyebrow. How come?

'Tatiana, tell Regan about Maison Javier's boardroom structure.'

They both looked at her, Una encouragingly. Regan stonily. Tatiana had no idea where this conversation was going, but cleared her throat. 'Uh… there are three directors with equal voting rights. Roland, Pauline Frankel and my sister Katya. Only, Katya isn't here.'

Una clapped triumphantly. 'But a clause in the company documents states that if Katya is unavailable or incapacitated in some way, your mother assumes her voting rights.'

'How do you know that?' Tatiana was aghast. Nobody had mentioned it to her.

'Before she and Harry left, Katya sent a taxi to bring me to her flat. There were papers all over the table, and we spent almost the whole night reading them. Katya wanted somebody on hand to advise your mother if she was called on to attend a board meeting and make a decision. I agreed to be that person.'

'You said nothing.'

'I was embarrassed. It should have been you Katya turned to, and I didn't want it to spoil our friendship.'

Tatiana flicked a hand to imply, 'Never mind.' Her mother, Katya's representative on the board? 'No wonder Roland and Pauline are desperate for my sister to come home.'

'If you could persuade your mother and Madame Frankel to champion the abandoned collection,' Una persisted, 'Roland would have to listen. The workforce is demoralised and bewildered, they don't understand why he created something spectacular, only to reject it. Pauline and your mother could force him to reinstate it.'

'What do you think, Tatiana?' Regan's expression remained cold, but a frown between his brows suggested an idea fermenting.

'Katya put her soul into that business,' Tatiana said slowly. 'We put our family money in too, and I can't let it collapse just because one man is having… I don't know…'

'Nobody blames Roland,' Una said. 'Maybe he's having some kind of breakdown. Men behind the battle lines would go from being cheerful and talkative one day to being completely numb the next. I nursed any number of them whose minds had shut down. This captain, he was on leave one time, and he asked for a glass of beer in a bar, and he could not pick it up. His mind couldn't make that simple decision. He found himself God knows how long later, walking along a road, no idea how he'd got there.'

'This is Roland's "glass of beer" moment?' Regan suggested.

'He'll be devastated if he wrecks everything he's worked for,' Tatiana said. 'Maybe it would be doing him a favour, pulling him back from the brink.'

'So you force his hand?' Regan asked. 'You get your mother together with Pauline Frankel to show him where salvation lies? Trouble is, I haven't time for that. The press-room manager is all set for overnight, Thursday 18.'

Tatiana nodded, saying crisply, 'You're right. My mother isn't even in France, and we don't know if Pauline Frankel would agree anyway.'

Una wouldn't give up. 'We could acquire the collection, then get their permission after we've written up the magazine.'

'Break and enter?' Regan came back from the window. 'Take Maison Javier's collection?'

'No, no,' Una answered. 'Not the whole collection. Only the most gorgeous items. Hey,' she chided, 'where's the man Pigeon told me used to chase police wagons to get the shots nobody else could? You gone soft, Dortmeyer?' Smiling at the flash reaction that provoked, Una turned to Tatiana. 'You got keys to Maison Javier?'

Tatiana shook her head.

'But Katya would have,' Una persisted. 'They'd be at her flat?'

They would, Tatiana agreed. Una's idea was typically lacking any thought for the consequences. Steal and photograph a collection for a magazine, without their owner's permission. There might be a lawsuit in it. Then again, siding with Una might challenge Regan's granite indifference. She heard herself say, 'Let's do it. What is the theme?'

Una asked for some thinking time and left the room. For what felt like an hour but was probably only ten minutes, Tatiana stood awkwardly trying to think of something to say, petting the dog, picking Pavlova's red hairs off her coat. Regan remained at the window, staring resolutely out at the street. They both visibly relaxed when Una came back.

'Theft,' Una told them triumphantly. 'Tatiana, you snatch a haul of high-priced couture as men in uniform… *ruthless* men in uniform… give chase. You tear off through the streets of Paris, through the night, racing up steps—'

'*Walking* up steps,' Tatiana chipped in. 'I couldn't run.'

'Over walls, across bridges…' Una nodded excitedly. 'Posing every twenty minutes or so, while Regan snaps and I dash off razor-sharp copy.'

'I can't "snap" at night,' he said crossly. 'I need to set up shots.'

'Oh, fuff,' Una waved away the technicalities. 'Get an illustrator. Coloured pencils work anywhere. We dedicate the whole magazine to this one story. "Notorious Princess-thief liberates the gowns they did not want you to see". I love it.'

Tatiana anticipated Regan's response. Dedicate a whole magazine to a woman I now hate?

He met her gaze. 'Would you do it?'

'Damn right she would, to save Maison Javier.'

'Una, I'm asking Tatiana.'

'I… I would. If I thought Mama and Pauline would back me.'

'Say they won't?'

'Mama will agree once she understands she'll lose her income if Maison Javier collapses. Pauline, though… She's loyal to Roland.'

'She's not blind,' Una argued. 'She has a husband who broke his back and will never walk again. She can't afford failure.'

Tatiana shook her head. 'She stood by as Roland sacked me. No. I've a better idea.' This was laying her head on the guillotine, trusting the blade wouldn't fall. 'You steal the collection for a night and do a stunning set of pictures. You mock-up a feature and show Roland and Pauline and dare them to say no.'

'And if they do?' Regan asked.

'Then it's "Fashionable ladies and their dogs".'

He digested that and Tatiana imagined him testing out the possible outcomes. Saying yes would rescue her from an empty diary and fruitless brooding over Armand's goodbye letter. Afraid her silence would provoke him, she went to him and whispered, 'Disliking me never stopped Pigeon Boccard taking extraordinary pictures. Loathing sharpens the eye.'

At the name of Boccard, small pits appeared each side of Regan's mouth. Tatiana had no idea if she'd turned the key in the right direction until he said, 'It would have to be tomorrow. You heard the deadlines.'

'We're on?' Una came to life.

But he'd moved from the general to the specific. 'We need to get the clothes, write copy and get an illustrator to come along because you're right, it can't all be photography. Readers like to see details, and outdoor photography can't do that. We need a sketcher who won't have a tantrum because he doesn't have his desk, chair and a pot plant.'

'Rosa Konstantiva's Edward.' Una was scribbling notes. 'I already got him some work here, on the Christmas issue. It was good and he owes me.'

'He wants to be a fine artist,' said Tatiana. 'To paint in oils.'

'Some dreams are made to be broken,' Una came back. 'He trained as a courtroom sketcher, and somehow, every face he draws looks tense, or guilty, or both. He'll be perfect and he doesn't need much sleep either.'

'So long as he can work to my brief.' Regan suggested they plan operations over dinner at Mère Richelieu's.

Tatiana hesitated, unsure whether 'they' meant all three of them.

Una solved the dilemma. 'Tatya, why don't you take the dog home, have a rest, and join us at eight?'

Tatiana accepted her dismissal, muttering, 'Go home, while the big people discuss plans,' and feeling resentful until she reached the metro at Madeleine where Line 12 would take her direct to Abbesses. Tiredness caught up with her. She needed to conserve her strength to be any use at a fashion shoot.

Not that it would be like any fashion shoot she'd ever taken part in.

Chapter Sixty-Two

As Tatiana descended the station stairs, matching her step to Pavlova's, her mother walked through the front door of their apartment, home at last. She had not returned to the Jonquil from Switzerland, but come direct to Paris.

As she picked up a parcel and letters from the mat, Irina felt the cramped hours of a train journey in her knees. Thank goodness Yana had returned with her; she couldn't have travelled all that way on her own with a child in her care.

It had been by no means easy to persuade Yana to come back at all. It was said there was someone for everyone… in Berne, where they'd stayed as guests of the well-heeled Birchmeier family, Yana had met a man. A shopkeeper, a widower.

Yana interrupted these reflections, saying gruffly, 'Go sit in the drawing room, Irina Petrova. I will give the little one her lunch and prepare something for you. Soup will be best.'

'Still ordering me about in Russian,' Irina murmured, but obeyed anyway. Yana and this man, a butcher, were intending to marry and that would end twenty-five years of service to the Vytenis family. Irina couldn't see any good coming of it. She was equally disturbed by the drawing room's lack of flowers, the reek of absence. Her eye fell on the chess board, left out on a low table near the fireplace. Her heart skipped. Had her daughters been here together, playing as in the old days? She was ashamed of abandoning Tatiana but Yana had told such alarming tales of what might unfold from her daughter's conviction. 'The police will come,' Yana had predicted, 'and take you away for questioning, Irina Petrova. Then the do-gooders will snatch away Anoushka because of all those pills and powders you swallow. They will lock her in an orphanage and you in a hospital.'

So she'd fled and it had taken the sensible Birchmeiers to assure her that she needed to go home. To face her terrors. Where did one start?

Not knowing where her three daughters were in the world was a dreadful anguish. Irina sat down and closed her eyes. When Yana returned to Berne and her butcher, she'd be alone, wholly responsible for Anoushka. She had written to Katya, at the Swedish address, and to Tatiana. Neither daughter had answered. She had not written to Vera as nobody knew where her darling eldest daughter was, but she prayed each night for her restoration. Strangely, she felt Vera's presence the strongest.

When she opened the parcel she'd found on the doormat, out spilled letters. A dozen at least. Irina recognised her own handwriting and the blue envelopes she used. They had been parcelled up by the manager of the Hôtel Jonquil, and he had enclosed a card: 'Found by the chambermaid after your departure for Switzerland, Madame la Princesse.'

'Yana?' The letters had no stamps. It was very strange. Irina called again, but Yana was busy and did not respond.

Of the other letters, all were bills, except for one whose stamp bore the profile of a monarch Irina recognised as King Gustaf of Sweden. That one was from Katya.

'Dearest Mama, I can't imagine why you haven't written to me, but I must tell you why Harry and I left Paris. It is only fair to prepare you.'

'I did write, I did,' Irina insisted to the empty room. Her chest tightened as she read Katya's message, until she could hardly breathe. 'Yana, quick.'

This time, the maid came to her. Seeing what was spread over the sofa cushions, Yana's cheeks altered colour. 'Where did those letters come from?'

'From the Jonquil. You were supposed to have posted them.'

Yana snatched Katya's letter from Irina's hand. 'It is in French. What does it say?'

'Katya and Harry are sailing across the Gulf of Finland, to the port of Tallinn, and on to Russia.'

'Are they mad?'

'To bring Vera home.'

'Rubbish.' Yana's cheeks burned beneath eyes hard as glass. 'Vera is dead. Katya should be whipped for tormenting you.' She gathered up all the envelopes, dropping them into the pocket of the apron she'd put on.

'These letters were never taken to the post office,' Irina accused. 'They have no stamps!'

'Do not hold me responsible for the failings of the postal service. Go rage at the postmaster, not at me.' Yana lit a fire, poking it to a good blaze and fed it with the contents of her apron pocket. By the time Irina had consumed a bowl of soup and taken her afternoon sleeping grains, the episode had grown as soft-edged as the pillow Yana slipped under her head. The next day, when she asked for her letters, Yana insisted there were none, only bills from the chimney sweep and the window cleaner.

Katya and Harry

The train from Tallinn shuddered and skirled as the brakes were engaged. Katya glanced at Harry. His profile, the part visible below the rim of his *ushanka*, suggested he was approaching the final stage of their journey in a sternly focused frame of mind. He'd accompanied his father on enough business trips for this slow roll into Petrograd's Vitebsky station to have become routine. It was she who was peering nervously through the steam at the platform signs written in a script that felt foreign, for all it was her own language. She'd felt sick since the Estonian–Russian border, and begun to wish she'd stayed safely at home. In Russia, she was a criminal aristocrat and fugitive.

By the time Harry had pulled down their hand luggage and assisted her to the platform, her pulse was beating inside her ears. When she pulled on her round-topped *kubanka*, the beating seemed to fill it.

Harry checked their tickets and travel permits. 'Do you feel thoroughly Swedish, Fru Morten?'

'I hope nobody asks me to speak.'

'We've agreed, I'll do the talking.' Harry took out the bills that proved his ownership of the freight stowed in the train's rear wagons. 'Ready?'

She nodded.

Against the stream of passengers, they walked up the platform to the freight wagons where Harry tipped a man in a military-style coat to offload their cargo first. Eight large wooden crates. Female porters heaved them onto trolleys, wheeling them along the now empty platform, through the barrier to some unknown holding bay while Harry and Katya were directed to the station superintendent's office. There, an hour crawled by with their breath hanging white on the air. A fire in the stove had been left to die. They were thinking the same thing. What if Russian customs seized their irreplaceable cargo of whisky and cloth? They'd have lost their bargaining chips for Vera's freedom.

'I'd forgotten what cold is,' Katya whispered. 'Harry – do you think she knows we're coming?'

'Vera?'

'Do you think she's waiting for us here in St Petersburg?'

'Petrograd,' he growled lovingly. 'Stop speculating. And remember, men in uniform don't like questions.'

As well as being icy, the waiting room was dirty. Cigarette ends littered the floor. Katya remembered this station when it had been a grand statement of French-inspired architecture. It still had its art-nouveau interior, something she recalled her brother-in-law Mikhail speaking of. He'd dreamed of one day building a Parisian-style home for himself and Vera. It would be a joy to inform Vera that Anoushka was alive and thriving, but what to say about the husband she had loved more than her own life?

After another hour's wait, an official escorted them to a different office where they were informed that the Kremlin had been notified of their arrival, by telephone.

Did that mean they were expected to travel on to Moscow after all? In Moscow, she was known. Katya began, 'Please, can you tell us—'

'Thank you, comrade,' Harry replied, mowing down her question.

Two underlings led them to a corridor where they found their crates lined up like a barricade. They counted. All eight, present. While one subordinate stood guard, the other checked the contents against Harry's dockets and the customs bills that had been telegraphed from their last border check. The first crate opened contained Islay malt, and at the sight of so much liquor, the Russian drew in an audible breath. He held a bottle up to the light.

'*Viski*,' Harry translated.

The man looked slyly at him.

'Better not,' Harry said in Russian. 'The Kremlin also has a copy of the manifest.'

A more senior official arrived and barked out orders. Every crate was opened and inspected. Their dockets were stamped, and Katya and Harry were informed that they would be shown to their accommodation to await Comrade Pavluk. 'From Comrade Yenukidze's office in the Kremlin, and who will take these goods on to Moscow. We will contact you on his arrival.'

'How soon?' Katya imagined Vera watching a clock somewhere, cold and anxious.

The official smiled inscrutably. 'I hope you will find your welcome in no way lacking.'

Katya nodded. She'd promised to let Harry do the talking, and to hide her aristocratic birth behind lowered eyes. The clothes she'd chosen for this part of the trip supported her pretence that she was the docile wife of a Swedish businessman.

'Comrade Pavluk is not yet in Petrograd?' Harry queried in his text-book Russian.

'He is on his way,' the official assured him.

'And the individual he is bringing with him? In exchange for these valuable goods… you have word of that person?'

'I know nothing of any other individual, only that you are our guests until Comrade Pavluk's arrival.'

'Very good,' Harry replied. There was no other answer.

A horse-drawn cab transported them through the dark. Snow lay thickly. Buildings each side of the road were boarded up and crumbling, some burned out. The beautiful city of the Tsars had taken a savage beating.

Their accommodation in a shabby grand hotel was adequate, their dinner, when it arrived, starchy but plentiful. They settled down to wait. Lying in Harry's arms, Katya whispered in Russian, 'Vera is on her way but what will her state of mind be? She's been in prison four whole years. Will she blame us, do you think?'

'Katya, we mustn't presume anything. Hold back from hope, it's safer.'

'I can't believe we've come all this way on false promises.'

'No? This is Russia, my love. They want our luxury commodities, but they are still our enemies.'

Chapter Sixty-Three

Over a late dinner of lamb escallops, Una and Regan hammered out the details of the photo shoot. They'd start tomorrow night, Friday, and go on until dawn. Tatiana let them talk.

'Last night was dark as a coal hole and the moon's waning, so tomorrow won't be much brighter,' Regan said. 'We'll do interior shots, then get to our first outside location around 8 a.m…. Una, will you be Tatiana's dresser? She'll need someone standing by with a coat and blanket.'

'Sure, and I'll keep the boys in check.'

They were hoping Rosa would hire out her male dancers to play the role of the police and create the illusion that the fashion thief was running from the law. Rosa was to join them shortly. *The Careless Father* had ended its run and she was now staging *Doctor Faustus*, which was thirty minutes shorter.

'They'll need an alarm call,' Una said. 'I don't know many dancers who'll get up at dawn after a performance.'

'Let 'em stay up all night,' was Regan's solution. 'The question is, what do they wear?'

Una had the answer. 'Rosa has them in uniform for a scene when they come on as devils, to drag the wicked doctor down to hell. Plenty of drama in that.'

Tatiana stiffened. She'd seen Rosa's new ballet three times, but on the first occasion, five swaggering policemen in leather coats and caps leaping on stage had paralysed her in her seat. When they fell on their victim, manhandling him off stage as he screamed and fought, she'd thought she might be sick. She concentrated on her food, in case Regan thought she was making a fuss, the way she used to in front of the lens.

'Here she comes.' Regan stood to greet Rosa, who tonight was accompanied only by Pavlova and Edward Whittle. She was in high spirits, having seen a full house and taken three curtain calls. Regan ordered wine for her, brandy Alexander for Edward, then asked his favour, getting it out ahead of Una who was busy blurting out their secret plan.

'The boys are not mine to lend,' Rosa answered, though she thought their escapade hilarious. 'If you pay them, I'm sure they'll say yes. Just be aware that the boots they use on stage are for dancing. They'll have to have different ones for the street.'

Regan's answer carried conviction. 'I'm counting on a dry night tomorrow.'

Regan had already approached Edward to be on-set illustrator, and the two men went to a separate table to plan. While Una and Rosa chatted brightly over the din of conversation, Tatiana eavesdropped on the two men, lacking the self-assurance to walk over and plonk herself down beside them. Regan and Edward were sketching out a story in cartoon-strip form. She was the lead character and her role would be to wear stolen dresses, look scared and act desperate. Shouldn't be hard, she told herself.

'Who is actually going to break into Maison Javier and steal the clothes,' she heard Rosa ask Una.

'Myself, Regan and Tatiana,' Una answered.

Me? Tatiana gaped. First she'd heard of it.

Chapter Sixty-Four

The night of Friday, 12 January was mild, the moon pickled in mist. Shortly after midnight, Regan pulled up outside Maison Javier at the wheel of a hired car. He had three passengers: Tatiana, Una and Edward Whittle. Una calling Regan their 'getaway driver' did little for Tatiana's nerves. The urge to reinvent herself, to challenge Regan's coldness, had worn off overnight.

'Pull into Cour du Comte,' she suggested from the back seat. 'There'll be less chance of us being seen.'

A minute later, the four of them were moving through shadows. Una had called at Katya's the previous evening and borrowed a spare set of keys, giving Madame Roche the plausible excuse that she needed papers from Katya's office for Irina Vytenis to sign. Una had noticed something odd on that errand, and had told Tatiana about it.

'I cut through the park and went by your flat. The shutters were open. Would you have left the place like that?'

It was possible, as Tatiana had left for Rosa's on Christmas Eve in no calm state of mind. When all this was over, she'd go to check, she said.

'I can't see the damn lock!' Una was stabbing the key at the atelier door.

'Give it to me.' If they were caught, Tatiana guessed that Regan and Una would be sent home to America, Edward back to England, while she, as a previously convicted felon…

Regan shone his torch beam on the lock and made her jump. Tatiana turned the key, and then they were inside.

'Where has Roland hidden the goodies?' Una didn't bother whispering. Other than the light cast by Regan's torch, the building lay in utter darkness.

'Katya's office, I was told.' Tatiana's voice had sunk inside her.

The lock of Katya's office was stiff but the key turned with some jiggling. It was like stepping into a crowded train carriage at the busiest time of day. Hanging rails were pushed together at cross angles, draped with dust sheets. Una squeezed inside and went to the window, rattling the shutters to check they were tightly closed.

'It's safe. Put the light on,' she said. Regan did so, switching off his torch to rest the batteries.

Katya's desk had been pushed to the side, chairs and other items stacked on top. 'She'd hate us all in here,' Tatiana muttered. Una was near enough to hear.

'Love her as I do, her absence has led to all this. Ready?' Una whipped the dust sheet off the rail nearest to her. 'My stars!'

Deep, lustrous colour. Cerise, azure, ochre, fire.

'The workmanship,' Una breathed as she picked out a sports dress whose front featured the letters 'MJ' composed from gold vermicelli. 'Madame Frankel will have hired in extra hands.'

Tatiana agreed. 'Those craftspeople ask a fortune.'

'Assuming they've been paid,' said Regan. 'They're running out of cash, you said.'

'Yet Roland hides it away.' Tatiana resisted the instinct to pose. Edward was busily sketching her. He'd said as they drove here, 'Just be natural. My pencil is as fast as my eye, and my eye is as fast a camera.'

Watching him blow pencil debris off his page, Tatiana said, 'I'm angry with myself.'

'Why?' Over dinner yesterday, Regan had finally given up glaring at her. It didn't mean that he'd thawed. His tone was offhand.

She said, 'Katya offered me a role here and I rejected it.' She gestured at the clothes rails. 'I could have prevented this.'

Una disagreed. 'You'd have ended up in a daily tussle with His Spanish Majesty, hammer and tongs, Pauline in the middle.' She was lifting hangers, selecting every tenth garment or so. 'Oh, boy, are these amber?' Una held up a dress of toasted-orange crushed velvet, studded with beads.

'Bakelite.' Tatiana took the dress and held it against herself. It had been cut for Isabelle or Mary-Jo perhaps. It would show all her leg from the knee down, but when she moved, it swung like a pendulum. 'I could dance in this.'

'Me too.' Una took it back. 'And it's more my size.'

'We're bringing them all back when we're done. No actual stealing, Una, no copying.'

'No copying, honour bright.'

Edward was still at work, picking out coloured pencils wedged under the baker's boy cap he wore. Regan had left them. They found him in the courtyard, setting up his tungsten filament lamp, using the building's electricity supply.

His first shot was of Tatiana emerging with clothes draped over both arms. The thief at the start of her adventure.

'Good acting. You look truly scared,' he said as he turned his film pack around for the next shot.

'I'm not acting. You didn't get the name "Javier" in the picture, I hope?'

'Course. I made sure of it. It's what it's about. And you, of course. It's your face everyone will look at.'

She didn't feel he was delivering a compliment.

They loaded the garments Una had selected into the rear of the hired car, a Renault type AG1, the model familiar to Parisians as a 'Taxi de la Marne'. This one looked dented enough to have been one of those that ferried infantry soldiers to the first battle of the Marne in 1914. Regan sat behind the wheel, Edward up front next to him, the women in the back. Regan had laid the tungsten floodlight at their feet, warning them it would be hot. And so, accompanied by the stink of scorched metal and with thousands of francs' worth of couture on their laps, they made their way to their next location, Mère Richelieu's. It was a few minutes short of 1 a.m.

One vehicle was not enough for the full cast and Regan had commandeered *Ravissante*'s delivery truck to ferry the dancers around, along with the man who drove it. It was parked outside Mère Richelieu's, its driver nodding behind the wheel.

Regan unloaded his gear while Una selected dresses for Tatiana to wear inside the café. The story Regan and Edward had thrashed out was that of a young girl, repressed by her father, who breaks into a couture house, and 'liberates' clothes to wear at a series of raffish locations. Meanwhile, her father informs the couture police, who then chase her across Paris. A silly plot, but Regan wasn't setting out to be William Shakespeare.

'Where do I end up?' Tatiana asked as she picked up the trailing lead of the tungsten light Regan was carrying into the tavern.

'By the river,' was the curt reply. 'Pont Neuf, where we first met. Remember?'

'No,' she said, though she did.

Inside the café, Rosa and her male troupe were crushed around a trio of tables, singing along to the piano player. The dancers all wore their final-act leotards, with loose trousers belted on for decency's sake. Muscular and fit, they quaffed watered wine as they unloaded their heads of the performance that had finished three hours earlier.

'Regan wants you to dance. Your choice who with.' Una took Tatiana to a storeroom, helping her put on an evening dress. Green georgette, its crinkled surface overlaid with glinting *paillettes* – dragon scales, Una called them. When Tatiana made a pirouette, they became a thousand mini heartbeats.

For the next hour, she played the role of the ingénue out on the town, dancing with a series of partners. Rosa's principal male dancer, Laurence, taught her the Breakaway, a variation on the Charleston. Not having danced for weeks – months – she balked at being jammed up against male hips. But adrenaline took over, and by the time she'd changed into the toasted-orange dress, her limbs were loose, her cheeks flushed.

'Hold that,' Regan would insist every few minutes. When he was satisfied he'd taken a good range of shots and Edward had filled pages with quick-fire sketches, Tatiana was allowed to change back into her own dress and they dined on kitchen leftovers the proprietress heated up for them. Afterwards, they retired to Rosa's to drink coffee, play cards or doze. Tatiana was roused some time later by Regan's hand on her shoulder.

'It's first light. Time for the next adventure.'

She stumbled to the Renault. Una was half in, half out, hanging dresses on a hook in the back. The boys had changed into their final-act costumes. Coats, some of black leather, others made from theatrically stained oilskin, an assortment of knives and fake guns pushed into their belts. All wore leather caps, and a grimness had settled on them. Either from the lack of sleep or because they had fallen into character.

'What's up?' Una, stepping back from the taxi, saw Tatiana frozen to the spot.

'It's them. The Cheka.'

'They're Laurence, Louis, Sim, Martin and Georges.'

'They came to our home. They murdered my father. Bludgeoned him... they took Vera.'

Una put her arm around Tatiana. 'This is a game. She'll be fine,' she assured Edward who looked as if he was catching some of Tatiana's reluctance. It was chilly in the dawn mist. Directing him to 'Buck up, get in the cab', Una gently pressed Tatiana into the back seat. To Regan, who joined them, she whispered, 'Men in leather coats... brought back memories.'

Regan leaned forward, touched Tatiana's wrist. 'If you don't want to do this, say.'

Tatiana lifted her face, struck by the unfamiliar smooth outline of his hair. His eyes, boring into hers, were liquid black. To dispel the pressure building inside, she answered, 'I'm to run away from these men in terror... that's what I've been doing in my sleep for years and I never get to the end of the dream. Maybe this time I'll find out what it is.'

Chapter Sixty-Five

Their first stop was rue Foyatier, the inhumanly steep stairs that scaled the butte de Montmartre to the basilica. The funicular railway, running alongside, was silent.

Regan positioned himself near the top, getting a shot over the heads of the boys to focus on Tatiana 'escaping' down the stairs, the tail of her gown flying behind. From Montmartre, they drove through silent streets to the centre of Paris. In the Tuileries gardens where the Louvre palace made a grey silhouette, Regan set up on a path. He had Tatiana run towards him, pursued by the 'police'. He'd marked spots where they were to freeze in motion. Tatiana did as directed, turning to stare back at her pursuers. She pictured herself in a movie still, the kind pasted outside the cinema in the Latin Quarter, until a flock of pigeons flew up in a blur of wings.

She heard Regan chuckle, 'Perfect timing.'

Edward finished his sketch as Tatiana changed into the sports dress with the MJ cypher. Una held a sheet in front of her, makeshift privacy. After that, it was a dash east along Quai du Louvre to the Gothic church of Saint-Germain-l'Auxerrois. Regan got on the taxi roof to vary the angle, while Tatiana acted the role of a sanctuary-seeker, gripping the railings that sealed the church off from the cobbled plain in front. He had Laurence and Louis stand in front of the van's headlights, casting elemental shadows. Gripping the icy railings, Tatiana tried not to hear, in the idling grind of the van's motor and the banter of the men around her, any kind of threat.

'Down to the river,' Regan ordered. A real policeman was walking past, his feet slowing in suspicion. Una went over to compliment him on his alertness to duty, smoothing down his hackles like a pastry chef icing a bun. 'We'll be less obvious down on the wharf,' Regan said as they piled back into the taxi. 'Tatiana?'

She nodded. She didn't care where they were going, just that she got through the next stage without breaking down. A fugitive memory was stalking her, impossible to pin down.

'We won't get the clothes back to Maison Javier before they open,' Una observed. She was peering out of the cab window at the strengthening light.

'We locked the office behind us,' Regan said, so casually one might think he regularly stole the props for his photo shoots. 'It would be unfortunate if someone at Javier decided that today, they were doing a stock take.'

'They won't,' Una agreed, equally at ease. 'We'll break back in tonight, though I'm afraid that lovely dark-orange dress will have to stay with me. Those Bakelite beads weren't sewn on quite firmly enough, some of them are hanging off.'

They had come to Quai de l'Horloge, to the wharf where Regan had photographed Tatiana that very first time and where the river sounded like a million hammers beating on felt. Tatiana pulled her glance away from the slates of the building where Dr Jolivet had probed and poked her. On the bridge curving above her eyeline, she had pressed herself into a stone bastion and considered jumping off. She knew herself better now. She hadn't been seeking death, but escape.

She pulled the edges of her coat closer. It was made of *duvetine*, a downy fabric intended for early spring. Vapour rising off the river was thick enough to taste, and the frosted cobbles bit through her shoes. Standing about unsuitably dressed was the mannequin's lot, but this was extreme.

Una was up on the embankment, directing the boys, while Edward sketched from the bridge. Where was Regan? Tatiana saw him beyond the first arch of the bridge, on the river path. He would be captivated by the lip of the wharf, the shifting mooring ropes, the horseshoes of light on the water. When he called her, she walked forward. He asked, 'Ready for the next scene?'

'I suppose so. I'm freezing.'

'Let's warm you up, then. Go back to your mark and, on my signal, run towards me like a hare out of the traps.'

'It's too slippery to run.'

'Take care, then.' He sounded clipped, impatient.

She returned to her position by the stone steps that ran up to Quai de l'Horloge. He still thought her spoiled and weak-spirited, it seemed.

Above her, she heard Una yell, 'OK, boys, go!' Immediately, there came wild whoops. Looking up she saw figures in leather coats, staves and knives held aloft, swarming towards the stairs.

It shunted her back to the night the Cheka raided their home. Not when her father was murdered, but when they'd come for her brother-in-law. A cussed old servant, Konstantin, had opened up to them and they'd swarmed through the house, breaking glass-fronted cupboards and mirrors as they passed. Screams had come from every direction, the loudest from the room Vera had shared with her husband. Tatiana, cowering in her doorway, had watched Mikhail being hauled between leather-clad men. Vera clinging to his waist. They'd beaten her off. Mikhail had seen Tatiana, had communicated silently; *Get back.*

Too late. Two men had peeled from the group, pushing her into her room. Her terrified cries had brought her father, and he'd pulled out a pistol, threatening the men who then fled. Then, to her indescribable distress, her papa had struck her for the first time ever, furious that she'd exposed herself to danger. Exposed them all, because by saving her, he had marked them out as rebels.

Eleven months later, they'd come back, killed him, taken Vera.

From the embankment, Una shouted, 'Tatiana, take care, they're coming to get you!' As Martin and Sim leapt athletically off the steps, something snapped inside her. Tatiana careered towards the bridge and Regan, but her numb feet couldn't hold to a straight line. A shout penetrated her confusion.

'Careful, you're too close!'

All she knew was she had to get away. Suddenly, she was plunging off the edge of the wharf. She broke the stone-hard surface of the river, into unimaginable cold. Her ears filled with roaring. Panic – she inhaled. Her coat pulled her down. Lights behind her eyes. The splash of a second body hitting the water sent a shock wave against her eardrums. She flailed, trying to rid herself of the coat, but it clung to her like a lover. She thought – *I'm dying.*

The next sensation was of the coat being dragged off. She kicked and got her head above water just long enough to snatch a breath before sinking again. Somebody put their arms around her. They were locked in dance; they would drown together. Though her eyes were wide, she saw only darkness and phantom lights inside her head.

The imminence of death pulled memories into focus: Moscow, the day the Cheka had returned. She, Tatiana, hidden in a window embrasure, behind the curtains. Broken glass under her feet, glass embedded in the window frame because before they broke down the door, Cheka thugs had fired shots from outside in greeting. Paralysed, she had stared out at the glittering wilderness that was their November garden, while on the other side of the curtains, butchery took place. Her father's, her sisters' and mother's screams joined the pinheads of light in which she was drowning. Her father was dead, Vera was dead, Mikhail dead. Armand was dead. Her baby, dead. All her doing, and now she was being pulled down to a hell that had always been a hand's breadth away.

She felt herself floating up into the stratosphere. Light grew brighter and all at once, she was gulping air and coughing out water. *Alive*, she told herself. She had to be because she'd never felt pain like it. Someone held her hips, lifting her out of the water. She was rolled over the slimy bullnose of the wharf.

They laid her on the cobbles, where Una knelt beside her and massaged her ribs, to rid her body of what she'd swallowed.

Chapter Sixty-Six

Regan allowed one of the dancers – Laurence, he thought – to wrangle him out of his drenched jacket and shirt. Gratefully, he pushed his arms into the coat held out for him. His own, which he'd hurled away in the moment before he dived into the river. Their party was split: those clustered around Tatiana, and those trying to help him. He wanted to say, 'I'm fine' but his teeth were knocking together. 'Get blankets round her,' he coughed to Una, who was wiping Tatiana's mouth with a handkerchief.

'Sure. Someone help me off with her clothes. We'll put my coat on her.'

He stepped forward, no false gallantry. This wasn't the moment to look away. 'You can stop sketching,' he snarled at Edward.

'Damn well won't. We'll use this image to end the story.'

The story. He'd forgotten that idiocy. It crossed his mind that, perhaps for the first time ever, he'd abandoned his camera. It was somewhere in the mist, might even have fallen face first, onto its lens. He didn't care. He only cared about Tatiana. His feelings for her were like a fire in a matchbox: a contained disaster and spectacularly hot.

'There's enough muscle here to carry her to the car,' Una was telling him. 'Let's get her to Rosa's and into a steaming bath.'

Tuesday, 16 January

Rosa's bedroom had become Tatiana's, as it had a fireplace. Rosa allowed Regan to enter as Una was there to chaperone them.

That had to be tongue in cheek, Regan thought, as Rosa herself had only just emerged from the room she was temporarily using with Edward and Pavlova. It was four in the afternoon. Four days since Tatiana's near-drowning. He'd brought her the galley proofs that would become *Ravissante*'s February edition.

She was sitting up against pillows, pink-eyed and pale, but with a faintly beatific smile that instantly halved his anxiety. He'd feared she'd catch pneumonia or get some horrible gastric infection from swallowing water. But she must be tougher than she looked. Regan arranged the galleys on the bedspread. 'I trust they meet with your approval.' He knew he was sounding like a municipal clerk. Nobody must guess that his feelings for Tatiana had revived. Actually, they'd never gone away. That damn list was still in his thoughts, though, curdling like vinegar in cream.

'Too bad if she doesn't like them,' Una chirped. 'The presses roll on Sunday. That's when the balloon goes up with our backsides lashed to it.'

'There aren't many pages.' Tatiana didn't seek Regan's eye. She hadn't thanked him yet for saving her and she was in a muddle of gratitude and shame. She'd fallen into the river like a bumbling drunk.

'Well?' Una was twitching with impatience.

'You must have been up all night,' Tatiana said, buying a few moments.

'Two nights straight.' Una mimed pulling out hair. 'Don't you see it in our bleary, bloodshot eyes? Only sixteen pages, but—'

Regan's patience burst. 'Quit talking, Una, let Tatiana look.'

Tatiana had leafed through hundreds of fashion magazines in her life but never had she seen anything like these proofs. Under the masthead ran the teaser: 'We steal the secrets of the spring–summer look for 1923!'

'That's a big claim,' she said anxiously.

'Don't see the point of making small ones,' Regan answered.

The galley proofs came in pairs, laid out to show how the printed magazine would appear. The front cover illustration was of herself sneaking out of Maison Javier with a thief's mask over her eyes. Edward had used tawny-gold for her hair. The back page carried a full-page advertisement for Habanita perfume. Everyone knew that was her favourite. Everyone? Don't be ridiculous, she admonished herself. Your friends, colleagues and hairdresser know. And then she remembered – 'The clothes! They need to go back!'

'Done,' said Una. 'I even took the keys back to Katya's flat.'

'All the clothes?'

'Not the coat that's keeping company with the fishes in the Seine, nor the dress you were wearing. But most everything else.'

'Most?'

'Before you ask, nobody saw us break back in. Our secret is safe,' Una said, 'until we reveal it.'

'Until *Ravissante* hits the stands,' Regan corrected.

The inside-front page listed the editorial staff. 'R. Dortmeyer, Editor'. Una was credited as a 'Special Correspondent'. Reading the page-three editorial, Tatiana mewed in dismay. 'You've named me. "Tatiana, fashion thief, in a daring heist of Maison Javier's upcoming collection, the style secrets they did not want you to see." That's my fate sealed.'

The storyline was delivered in the breathless hyperbole of crime reporting. Edward had reverted to his hard-nosed courtroom style. He was really talented. In the centre pages, Regan's photographs stood alone, uncluttered by editorial or advertising. There she was, face and figure in razor-sharp detail.

Not quite as thin as I was. The last photo was of her running towards the Pont d'Iéna, a blurred form just about discernible through the arch. 'You took this as I staggered towards the edge?' she accused.

'It happened so fast,' Regan replied. 'I had you in frame, then you seemed to swerve. I shouted, but I also pressed the shutter release.' He rustled up a brief smile. 'Admit it, it's one hell of a frozen moment.'

'Frozen is understating it!' She pushed the proofs away. Edward's final illustration was of her in the river, one arm raised like a sinking Statue of Liberty. 'Has Roland seen these?' She looked from Regan to Una.

'No, and we should make an appointment to show him.' Regan began packing the proofs away.

Tatiana wanted to pull the bedclothes over her head. Rosa's telephone was ringing and the sound made her aware how frayed her nerves were. 'What if he only sees that we stole his property?'

'Then there will be no February *Ravissante* and probably no March, April or May either.' Regan became businesslike. 'Una, d'you want to take these galleys to Pauline Frankel and show her first?'

Una made a face. 'She kind of frightens me.'

'Get outta here! Take her to the Ritz Bar. Tatiana, we need your mother involved.'

'I don't know where she is.'

'She's at home,' said Rosa, who had entered the bedroom noiselessly. 'That was Larissa Markova calling. Tatiana, your concierge has been trying to reach you and didn't know where to go but to Maison Javier – they had the sense to ask Larissa. Your mother's home, with your niece.'

'Home? But that's wonderful.'

'Mmm.' Something suggested that 'wonderful' was not the word Rosa would have chosen. 'Apparently, yesterday evening, your mother locked herself in her bedroom and is refusing to come out.'

Chapter Sixty-Seven

Regan took her to rue Rembrandt in a taxi and offered to wait outside.

'No, come in.' She couldn't leave a man who had thrown himself into the river to rescue her out in the evening air. 'You'll be useful.'

'Good to know.'

Inside the flat she called, 'Mama?' When that brought no response, she tried, 'Yana?'

No response there either. Tatiana pushed open Yana's bedroom door. The room was empty, the bed unmade. She looked into Anoushka's room. Empty too. A chill rippled through her. 'Regan, would you check the drawing room? You know—' she stopped.

'Where it is? Uh-huh. I was here before.'

Her cheeks burned. 'Of course.'

'Which is your mother's bedroom?'

'This one.' It was next to Tatiana's own room. She tapped. 'It's Tatiana. Mama? Where's Anoushka?'

No answer.

The door seemed to be locked from the inside. So she knocked harder. 'Mama, please speak so I know you're all right.'

This time, she discerned a sound. Tatiana pressed her ear to the door and picked up the squeak of bedsprings. A sigh? 'Mama?'

'Tatya?' The voice on the other side was wary.

'It's me.' To prove it, she said, 'Tatiana Ulianova Vytenis, born 18 October 1899.'

A metallic click, and the door opened a crack. 'Has she gone?' The question tumbled through the gap.

'Who, Yana?'

Regan confirmed it. 'No sign of her. I checked her room. Cupboards, drawers, cleaned out.'

Tatiana gently opened the door. 'You don't have to be afraid.'

'Is Katya home?' came the quavering question.

'No, but I am.'

'She's bringing Vera.' Irina stood in the middle of her bedroom. Her dress was rumpled, her silvery hair tumbling messily from its pins. She looked haggard. 'Katya wrote, promising to bring my darling home with her.'

Oh, dear God. Tatiana quailed. Her mother had never ceased believing that one day Vera would return as abruptly as she'd gone. She often dreamed of it, and would wake hysterical with joy, only to be savagely crushed. 'Mama, where is—?' She didn't complete the question as she spied Anoushka crouched against the bedroom wall. ''Noushka, my pet, my little bee. What has happened?' Tatiana hunkered down in front of her niece, tipping the small chin up with her fingers. Blank eyes. Tatiana felt the wrench of fear. *I left her in the charge of two unfit women.* 'Tatie-Tatya's here, darling.'

The child stared up at Tatiana with eyes as candid as paint daubs. 'Yana isn't my mama.'

'No, indeed. She is not.'

'My mama died in Russia. And my papa.'

'She has poisoned the child's mind, but she won't take her from me. Never!' Irina spoke so piercingly, Tatiana expected to see Yana in the room. There was only Regan, arms folded, his back against the wall.

'Mama, are you saying that Yana intended to take Anoushka from this house?'

'I had to stop her!' It all came out. Yana had accompanied Irina and Anoushka from Berne to Paris reluctantly, having engaged herself to a man there. She'd even set her wedding date. 'She tried to make me come home alone and leave my granddaughter behind.' Yana had wanted to adopt Anoushka.

'She told me I was a bad grandmother, that you and Katya had abandoned the child and that she and her new husband would be better parents. When I told her that Katya was bringing Vera home and Anoushka would have her real mother again, she said I was mad. She drugged me, gave me more veronal than I need just to sleep, and told Anoushka she was taking her away. But the concierge called in and saw what Yana was doing. Anoushka ran in here and I was enough awake, thank God, to lock the door.' Irina noticed Regan then. 'Who is this?'

'It's Monsieur Dortmeyer, Mama. He... he saved my life. Twice. Once here and at the river.' Tatiana raised her eyes to Regan's. He raised an eyebrow in return.

'Is he staying?' Irina asked.

'I don't think so.' Tatiana queried with a glance. Regan said nothing. Not a flicker.

'He must. He looks strong,' Irina insisted. 'He won't be afraid of Yana and her butcher.'

'Butcher? Good God, what are you saying, Mama?'

'Yana is to marry the man who supplies the Birchmeiers with meat. They met at Christmas, when he delivered a pair of geese. We will tell Vera nothing of this when she comes. Promise. It will distress her.'

'I won't say a word.' She's lost her wits, Tatiana thought desolately. Vera coming home, Yana abducting Anoushka, a Swiss butcher and his geese – this was drug-induced delusion.

'Would you like to sit down in the drawing room, while I light a fire?' Regan offered his arm to Irina, which was graciously accepted.

Later, as the room warmed up and they drank tea, Irina expanded on the news she insisted Katya had written. 'She and Harry crossed the Gulf of Finland to Tallinn. That is the capital of Estonia. Do not look at me as though I am stupid, Tatiana. I am not.'

'No, Mama. But perhaps you're mistaking Tallinn for the Scottish isles? I happen to know that Katya and Harry were staying in Scotland, and visiting a place called Islay. Katya wrote as much to her housekeeper.'

'Tallinn,' Irina repeated stubbornly. 'They were on their way to Russia. To find Vera.'

Tatiana fed and bathed Anoushka, dressed her in brushed-cotton night clothes. From the other side of the door, Regan asked if the bourbon he'd left behind was still around.

'In the kitchen cupboard. There's plenty left,' she answered, making a face. Actually, she'd knocked it quite hard after he'd left. Hopefully, he wouldn't notice. She put her niece to bed, reading a storybook until Anoushka fell asleep, clutching her comfort blanket. Tiptoeing away, Tatiana heard tranquil voices from the drawing room. Male companionship always had a sedating effect on her mother. Irina ought to have borne sons, not daughters. Tatiana pledged never again to leave her niece to her mother's unsupported care.

The shrill of the telephone kept her in the hallway. It was Una, calling from the Ritz, where she had been with Pauline Frankel until a few minutes before.

'Maison Javier, tomorrow at nine,' Una informed her.

'You mean—'

'Pauline and I spent two hours in the ladies' bar, me selling her the gospel of *Ravissante* like a street-corner preacher.'

'You showed her the galleys?'

'Sure, and at first, she hated what we'd done but I talked her down, and then she looked at it afresh. Three glasses of Moët brings out the party girl in any woman.'

'She's going to back us?'

'Well,' Una's tone was not encouraging, 'she has a lot on her mind. She confided that she won't be able to pay all her staff at the end of this month without an injection of cash. That's as bad as it gets in couture, like a cab driver being refused gas. Lose your seamstresses, you might as well roll up your tent. Then a miracle happened.'

'Go on.'

'Two of the most powerful fashion buyers in New York walked into the bar. That's not the miracle, there is only one hotel in Paris where the top store buyers stay and that's César Ritz's place. Only he died. Where was I? Oh, the miracle. Two buyers walked in, who acquire for Macy's on 34th Street. You with me?'

Tatiana nodded, not a useful response in a telephone conversation, but Anoushka had stumbled out of her bedroom, the blanket she wouldn't let go of clutched to her tear-streaked cheek. Tatiana crouched and held out her arms, while still speaking into the receiver. 'Did you introduce them to Pauline?'

'I did,' Una replied. 'They were cool with her. I finally got them to say why. Seems they tried to buy Javier dresses in the past and kept getting the "no" from Roland. They came to see the midseason in November and walked out. That's what Maison Javier is up against, a high-pitched buzz of apathy. So I let slip they'd be in for a stupendous treat come February.'

'Can you get them to the collection show?'

'That's down to Roland, isn't it? I showed Pauline the galleys again after that but I don't think she saw them. Meeting those buyers brought home to her where the problem lies. She presides over the most technically perfect atelier in Paris, but if the customers won't eat vanilla ice cream, there's no point feeding them vanilla ice cream. She's fixing a meeting with us and Roland, tomorrow morning.'

'Nine o'clock, you said. But will he see us?'

'She's going to say it's with the company accountant and will bar the doors so he can't escape. Talking of which, did you unlock your mother? Can you bring her along? And Regan, is he still there?'

'Um, yes.'

'Wow. Will he stay the night?'

'Why would he?'

'Why indeed. Imagine the two of you waking up under the same roof. Crazy. Did you tell him you love him yet?'

'How much champagne have you drunk, Una?'

'As much as I needed and not a sip more. Sure you love him. It was the first thing you said after you'd honked half the Seine out of your lungs onto my shoes.'

Anoushka was pulling on Tatiana's arm, a perfect excuse to end the call.

Chapter Sixty-Eight

Regan bid them goodnight at eleven, to return to his hotel. Or was it 'hostel'? He gave Tatiana the impression he was staying in a windowless hutch in some down-at-heel location. 'George's place', he called it. Tatiana wondered why *Ravissante*'s new editor was not worthy of better. She certainly didn't credit Una's assertion that he'd bought the magazine. A man who didn't even own a wallet, but jammed his money in his jacket pocket?

But she was too fatigued to do more than toy with these thoughts. They were to rendezvous tomorrow at the English Tea Parlour, an hour before their meeting at Maison Javier.

Next morning, Tatiana was the first up. She made tea for herself and her mother, checked there was hot water for washing and ordered a taxi. Irina flatly refused to come with her. 'I am not strong enough to speak to strangers.'

'Roland and Pauline are not strangers. And I'll be there, and Monsieur Dortmeyer.'

'I cannot. I know you think me weak.'

'I think you selfish and unimaginative, Mama. Why did you leave Paris when I needed you?' Resentment, festering for many weeks, burst free. 'You could have come to court or visited me in Saint-Lazare. Once would have been enough.'

'I was afraid,' Irina confessed.

'Of the shame?'

'Afraid of the police. Of men in uniform. I'm not brave, Tatya.'

'Nobody is, until they practise. Go back to bed, sleep some more. God knows, you never seem to get enough.'

But when she saw Tatiana dressing Anoushka in outdoor clothes, Irina caved in. Anything was preferable to being left alone. What if Yana returned with her butcher in tow?

'If this Swiss fiancé really does exist,' Tatiana said impatiently, 'she's on her way to a new life with him. Good luck and good riddance. As for you, *ma mère*, I'm not sure I want to be seen in public with you. I may be bad, but you're a deserter.'

'When did you grow so cruel, my child?'

'When a key turned on me, and I was left to the mercy of a pack of jail-hardened prostitutes.'

'Don't speak so!' Irina pressed a handkerchief to her face. Grim-lipped, Tatiana fetched her mother's coat and hat.

On rue Cambon, they found Una and Regan at the table Monsieur Aristide reserved for his most favoured clients.

'We've ordered brioche, coffee and chocolate. Good morning, Princess Vytenis.' Una shook hands with Tatiana's mother then bent to kiss Anoushka. 'Why, *ma petite*, don't you look the finished article.' The child was dressed in a frock coat and short boots. Her flaxen curls lay over her shoulders, and she clutched the doll Tatiana had bought her on Christmas Eve. She'd discovered it at the end of her bed on waking.

Tatiana said, 'From now on, Anoushka's glued to my side.'

Una winked at Regan. 'No better chaperone than a kid, ha?'

Regan ignored her. He took Irina's coat, then did the same for Tatiana. The galleys were in a portfolio by his chair.

Irina glanced about. 'Tell me again why we are here?'

'For breakfast, Madame,' Regan said. 'Then we're meeting Roland Javier.'

'Maison Javier is in financial trouble.' Tatiana used the lowest voice in her register. 'I didn't want to say it before, but we have to persuade Roland and Pauline to alter direction before it collapses.'

'Shouldn't we wait for Katya to come home? She's—'

'Never mind Katya,' Tatiana interrupted. 'This meeting affects our future, so please do as I say. Do you understand?'

'I understand that until yesterday, Yana dictated to me and now you have taken her place.'

'But from vastly different motives.' Tatiana explained how a crisis at Maison Javier could wipe out their income. 'We'd have to move – oh, no, *Pchelka*!' Anoushka had been about to feed her doll with hot chocolate. 'Her mouth is only painted on.'

Regan asked the waitress to bring a 'doll cup'. The girl came back with an egg cup on a tiny saucer.

'It's empty,' Anoushka told Regan, unimpressed.

'No it's not. It's full of invisible drink. See?' He stuck his finger in, and drew it out fast, exclaiming, 'Ouch!'

Anoushka laughed. Tatiana hadn't heard anything so beautiful in a long time. She smiled at Regan, who looked at her gravely before turning his head away.

Walking into Maison Javier five minutes before their meeting required several deep breaths. Last time she'd set foot here was the day she'd been sacked. 'Roland knows I'm coming?' Tatiana whispered to Una.

'Um, only if Pauline told him.'

'Fabulous.'

At least the mannequins would not be in for some hours. In the reception area, they were greeted by the *directrice*, Lilliane, who conjured up an ingratiating smile for Irina, which fluttered as it moved to Regan and died as it encountered Tatiana. However, she beamed at Anoushka.

'What a beautiful doll.'

'Tatie-Tatya gave her to me,' Anoushka lisped. 'She was for Christmas but I didn't see her until I woke up today.'

'We have some very big dolls upstairs, made of wax, dressed in lovely clothes. Would you like to see them?'

Anoushka nodded eagerly.

'I'll entertain the little one while you're discussing business.' Lilliane directed them to an office across the courtyard where, she said, Monsieur Javier and Madame Frankel were waiting.

Chapter Sixty-Nine

'If I say no, you may not run this issue, that I will sue you, what will be the outcome?'

'I'll lose money and face,' Regan replied to Roland's question.

'Ha. You will eat a good deal of humble pie.' Roland was leafing through the galleys a second time, having done so at speed after Regan first presented them to him. Nobody was smiling. Funny, how polite everyone becomes when they're tense, Tatiana thought. Except Mama who simply looks pale and afraid. I shouldn't have worried her about the business failing.

'We want your blessing to run the issue,' Regan said. 'We also want you to meet Una's American contacts. If you won't let those buyers spend their dollars with you, they'll spend them elsewhere. You need to reinstate the collection that inspired Una, Tatiana and me to turn thief. It's not too late to stem your losses, but it soon will be.'

A flush rose in Roland's cheeks, familiar to Tatiana. 'What business is this of yours? You are not a director nor an employee. Nor even a friend.'

Regan looked to Tatiana. He was going to let her answer.

She gathered herself. 'There are three voting directors here, Monsieur. You, Madame Frankel and Katya, represented by my mother.' She pointed to each in turn. 'If my mother and Pauline vote against you, your decision won't count.'

Roland bowed his head. 'It is always a pleasure to see Princess Irina Vytenis, and to be reminded of the articles governing this company. Pauline,' he said, turning to his colleague, 'you wish to do as our friends recommend? Abandon the collection your workrooms have been engaged on for weeks, waste all that time, money and fabric and throw us into retreat?'

Pauline Frankel nodded. 'It's a risk, but so is playing safe. We need our customers back. We need new ones, American ones. So yes, I would vote to reinstate your first collection, Roland.'

'Princess Vytenis?' Irina had slithered into reverie. 'You would use your position as Katya's proxy to vote for a radical change of direction?'

Irina opened her mouth a couple of times before anything came out. 'I... I don't do anything radical as a rule. But if selling clothes to America means I continue to receive my dividends, and can stay in rue Rembrandt where I have known some happiness, then I would vote for it. My daughter Vera is coming home, you understand, and I must appoint a new housemaid and a cook as a matter of urgency.'

'Mama, not now,' Tatiana begged.

Roland sighed. 'Tell me, Princess Vytenis, is this your unbiased opinion?'

'You're leading the witness,' Regan objected.

'I am allowing Princess Vytenis to reach her decision without pressure or prejudice,' Roland replied.

To their surprise, Irina asked for a pencil and paper. 'When I don't know what to think, I make a list. My mother taught me to do so, and I taught my daughters the same.'

'It's true,' Tatiana said, then caught Regan's eye and stumbled into miserable self-consciousness. To cover it, she passed a notebook to her mother. Irina began to write, biting the end of her pencil. At last, she looked up.

'I have made two lists. It is how I do it. The first list is for everything I do not wish to be true, and the second is what I wish for.'

'Like a prayer,' Pauline Frankel suggested. 'State it out loud and shame the devil.'

'That is right.' Irina smiled for the first time.

'Will you reveal what you've written?' Roland invited.

Irina did so. 'One: I must not be poor again. Two: I must never again live in a flat up six flights of stairs with no lift. Three: I must always take care of my daughters and Anoushka. Four: I must stop taking so much veronal—'

'Mama, this isn't what we want.' Tatiana's toes creased with embarrassment.

Irina raised a hand. 'Three.'

'You've already done three and four.'

'Five, then: to become the person I was before my darling Ulian was killed.'

Roland invited her to read her second list. There was only one item on that. 'For my darling Vera to come home to me. Lists are not always useful.' Irina began to cry softly.

'More than that, they're damn destructive.' Regan spoke with a heavy edge and Tatiana was suddenly gripped by a need. While the others stared in bemusement, she went to Regan and knelt by him. Not in supplication, but so she could look into his eyes.

'I made a list. I laid out all my prejudices on paper. I meant to burn it, but you should be glad I didn't. You needed to know what I am.' She waited for him to speak, to say he understood and that it didn't matter. When nothing came from his mouth, she crumpled and would have left the room had not Pauline Frankel raised her up.

'I'm not sure where this leaves us,' Pauline said, passing a handkerchief to Tatiana. 'I suspect Roland will get his own way as he usually does. And so, I resign. I won't stay on a ship that is being wilfully sunk...' – her voice wobbled, the emotions of the moment catching her out – 'sunk by its captain.'

'Who talks of sinking?' Roland begged Pauline to please sit down. 'You too, Tatiana. These tears are most distressing. Monsieur Dortmeyer is speechless; he cannot have expected a beautiful woman to kneel at his feet. The only person ever to kneel at mine is my tailor.'

They smiled, grateful for the joke which broke the tension. When they were all around the table again, Roland restarted the meeting, but after a minute he went and stood at the door and cleared his throat. 'I was at the bank yesterday, agreeing a loan to finance our next collection. Allow this ship to sink? No, indeed. I have poured too much into Maison Javier to allow that. Ladies, Monsieur Dortmeyer, follow me and let me show you something.'

Filing out behind Tatiana, Una whispered, 'What did you put in your list? Was it about Regan?'

'Yes, awful things about him being poor and unschooled,' Tatiana admitted. 'Describe his face. I daren't look.'

'He's got his back to us. Men aren't good with public emotion. That's why it works so well.'

Roland led them to Katya's office. The rails were as they'd been the night they broke in. Roland removed the cover from one with a flourish. 'What you see, Monsieur, Mesdames, is Roland Javier's spring–summer collection for 1923. See? I am not immune to reason. And certainly not to tears. If you all truly believe that my first collection will save this house, I yield. On the condition that Pauline withdraws her resignation.'

Pauline Frankel was staring at the rainbow colours. 'If you mean what you say, I will.'

'I mean it, Madame Frankel. Do you wish me to make a list?'

'No,' Pauline laughed. 'I never knew they could be such powerful, dangerous things.'

'Monsieur?' Roland spoke to Regan, who had said nothing for a long while and who appeared to have been punched. 'I do not suppose readers will like what you have done with *Ravissante* but that is your affair. So long as you put in a prominent statement that it is done without the permission of Maison Javier, you may publish. Tatiana,' Roland's voice took on a softer hue, 'are you aware that Constanza Darocca is leaving us, to be married?'

'I can safely say that I know more than I wish.'

'Perhaps you would consider taking her place here.'

'You're inviting Tatiana back?' Una answered for her. 'She accepts.'

'I find this place is less exciting without her.' Roland held out his hand. 'Friends again?'

Tatiana accepted the hand clasp, but it was a brisk reconciliation as a child's voice reached them from the corridor.

'Grandmama? Tatie?'

It was Anoushka, searching for them. Time to go.

As they walked across Cour du Comte, Una murmured, 'Roland hadn't changed his mind about the collection. He was all set to dig in until he realised he might find himself shut in with four weeping women. I can outcry anybody when the spirit moves me.' Una looked back at the atelier. 'Where's Regan?'

'I think he stayed behind to talk to Roland. Una, he wants me back.'

'I'm not sure, honey.'

'*Roland*, not Regan. I'll be a Javier mannequin again. I can start over.' Tatiana went to her mother and said stiffly, 'Well done, Mama. You did well.'

'What did I do?' Irina asked, bewildered. 'Except answer the question I was asked.'

Chapter Seventy

Katya and Harry

Playing cards and biting their nails, they were like caged rats by the time the summons came. The same horse cab followed the snow furrows back to the railway station.

'Do you think we're being deported?' Katya suggested.

'I don't see why,' Harry answered. 'We've been perfect guests. Invisible, never complaining about the inadequate heating.'

'What if this is all a nasty joke?' All week, trucks filled with police in matted *ushankas*, gun barrels slanted, had been their primary experience of Petrograd's population. Katya had sat for hours at the window, hoping the next truck would bring Vera. 'What if we're sent home, because all they want is our cargo?'

'Then we'll know, in an hour or two.'

Taking no chances, they'd brought their personal luggage with them. As they unloaded it from the cab, the official who had met them on their arrival was waiting. He glanced at the worn valises and their elderly trunk as if trying to square these with his belief in Harry and Katya as wealthy foreigners.

They were taken to the railhead depot. In a room which might once have been a dining area for customs officers, they were reunited with their crates. Policemen stood guard, chins ratcheted high. A different official took over from the first, and enquired if their stay had been to their liking.

Harry complimented the hotel, then asked, 'Are you the Kremlin representative?'

The official explained that he was a mere intermediary. 'Comrade Pavluk, aide to Comrade Yenukidze, is on his way.'

On his way from a location in Petrograd, or from Moscow, two days' travelling distance? It was not made clear. Harry rocked on his heels, grinding his frustration underfoot. 'I trust nothing has been removed?'

He was reassured. The crates' ultimate destination made pilfering unthinkable. 'Comrade Yenukidze is still a man of some importance in the Kremlin.'

Still of *some* importance… that wasn't what Larissa had implied when giving Katya the names of her Russian contacts. Not Larissa's fault, of course. Politics here had a snake-like character, motionless until they bit.

'The odd bottle of whisky will go astray between here and the Kremlin,' Harry murmured to Katya when he was sure they couldn't be heard. She'd said nothing since stepping out of the cab. Half the morning ticked by before Comrade Pavluk was announced. A slight man, dominated by his overcoat and a thick moustache. He had hard, small eyes and a handshake to match. One of the two female functionaries accompanying him requested Katya and Harry's papers. The woman eyed Katya as she read out what was written on the visa. 'Ekaterina Ulianova Morten, of Russian birth.'

'Correct.' Katya coughed to subvert the tell-tale inflexion in her Russian. They don't care who I am, she assured herself. I can endure this.

The crates were unpacked on trestle tables. Two hundred lengths of men's suit cloth, the best Harry's English mills could produce. Six hundred bottles of Islay malt, all checked against the duplicate import bills Harry had presented a week earlier. The papers were taken away to be stamped.

'Everything is in order?' Harry asked Pavluk, who was walking slowly in front of the trestles, apparently memorising what he saw. Katya jumped compulsively every time the Russian came close. Clenching her jaw was bringing on a headache.

The papers were brought back, stamped and dated. Comrade Pavluk took one set, Harry was given the other. Folding them inside his coat, Harry said in a neutral voice, 'We have honoured our side of the transaction. My wife and I would like to take possession of the item promised in return.'

'I know nothing of that.' Pavluk ordered the crates to be repacked.

'Wait a moment.' Slow colour invaded Harry's cheeks. 'Agreement was reached at the highest level. A consignment of goods, for the enrichment of the Russian people, in return for Vera Ulianova Starova being handed into our care. I hold you responsible for honouring that promise, Comrade Pavluk.'

'As I said, it is nothing to do with me. Others are bringing Starova to you.'

'She is coming – you swear it?' Katya couldn't help herself. At Harry's flash of warning, she began coughing.

But too late. 'You speak Russian with a French accent.' Pavluk came to stand in front of her. 'What was your upbringing? Those of aristocratic birth have no legal identity in Russia now. Any who have not been imprisoned and set to work for the benefit of the people, have been killed.'

She lowered her eyes, saying in a small, bleak voice, 'We came here in good faith, comrade. We wish to leave in the same way, to spread word in the rest of Europe of the dignity and justice of the people of this great country.'

Pavluk grunted. 'What is your relationship to the prisoner?'

Before she could answer, men entered. Katya recognised their leather coats, the black animal-hide hats. Worse yet, she knew one of them and he recognised her.

He had commanded the squad that had murdered her father and dragged Vera away, still clutching her newborn baby. Katya had tricked this same officer into giving her access to Vera in the Lubyanka prison, and she'd stolen tiny Anoushka from under his nose. Katya had left her sister to her fate, and whatever vengeance this man chose to mete out.

He grinned at her and his eyes burned with triumph. *At long last*, they seemed to say. Saluting Pavluk, he produced a wooden box about the size of one of Harry's father's cigar boxes. 'Comrade – the prisoner, Starova, as promised.'

Pavluk presented the box to Katya. Disregarding Harry's warning, she opened it, releasing a cloud of grey-brown ash. It took her a moment to understand.

Harry caught her. 'Don't give way,' he said against her ear. 'I didn't expect this but there's nothing we can do.'

Pavluk informed them, 'Travel warrants have been drawn up for you and you will leave on the next Tallinn train.' Ash speckled his coat and he brushed it off in displeasure. 'These police officers will put you on board.'

'When did Vera die? When did you kill my sister?' Katya screamed at Pavluk. 'Did you know of this? How could you be so cruel and call yourself human?'

Harry took over. Grabbing two of their travel bags and leaving the rest, he marched her out of the depot, across the snow-packed yard to the station. Nobody got in their way as they were flanked by grinning Cheka. Barriers swung back. A steward raced to open the train door. Within five minutes, they were on their way home.

They had failed.

Chapter Seventy-One

Ravissante's February 1923 issue was launched at the end of January and sold out within a week. Regan immediately set about planning the March issue. He kept Edward Whittle as illustrator but decided to bring in another photographer. He was edging the magazine back to a more conventional format, feeding the readership with fashion scoops they couldn't get elsewhere. Una, meanwhile, beetled between early couture shows and all the smart parties where she eavesdropped, flirted and took notes.

Tatiana eased herself back into work. Madame Markova put her on the opposite side of the room to Constanza who was staying for the spring–summer launch, which would take place on 22 February. Anna Markova persuaded the *directrice* to re-choreograph the daily parade so the two women never waited downstairs together.

Françoise, Mary-Jo and Suzy had left for other houses, which improved the atmosphere and stripped Constanza of natural allies. With her marriage to Gérard set for the end of March, she was in a confetti storm of preparations and hardly acknowledged anyone – except Tatiana, who she resented in direct proportion to the wounds she had inflicted. Larissa assumed the role of Tatiana's defender, being neither intimidated nor impressed by Constanza and taking pleasure in showing it. Larissa's friendly overtures stemmed more from her loyalty to Katya than anything else. Or so Tatiana judged. Still, she'd take friendship from whatever source. She wished she could be more forthcoming when Larissa asked if Katya had written, sent a wire or telephoned. Larissa's dismay whenever Tatiana replied that she'd heard nothing was unsettling. She didn't mention her mother's repeated assurances that Katya had gone to Russia, nor did she mention Vera's name.

At home, life had assumed a placid routine. Tatiana had appointed a Breton cook-maid, Madame Tanguy, who epitomised 'plain', but went about her tasks with good humour, showing no desire to be commander-in-chief of the household or to adopt Anoushka. Tatiana had also engaged a nursery maid, allowing her to leave Anoushka with a clear conscience. Zara was a refugee from Moscow who spoke French and Russian, and was coaching the little girl in reading, music and numbers, in preparation for 'proper' school next September.

All in all, life was on the up. Happiness should be her next ambition, Tatiana often thought. But she was still the ex-convict. Her mother still fretted about everything, while refusing to drop her insistence that Vera was about to return. And Regan was busy making his mark in rue Cambon. Tête-à-tête with Una much of the time, in his office or the press room. Tatiana still wasn't certain where he was living; he hadn't felt it necessary to tell her.

January ended on a thaw and Paris emerged like a grey gosling from a white egg. In the park, the once-sparkling trees dripped morosely on to exposed paths. Snowdrops and yellow aconites sang in the grass, so it wasn't all gloom. Two days into February, Tatiana's mother received a wire from Gothenburg.

H and K arrived safe stop K unwell more follows stop.

'Did it only say "H and K"?' Larissa asked when Tatiana gave her the news. They had been summoned to the atelier with the other mannequins, for a fitting. Roland had created some last-minute ensembles, inspired by his daily walk through Parc Monceau from his flat on rue de Courcelles. With the revised collection show nineteen days away, he was still adding to it. Rumours were flying that Pauline Frankel was on the verge of a nervous breakdown.

Not only was it a Saturday morning, it was 8 a.m., practically the early hours for a mannequin. Marianne, Isabelle and a new girl, Petronelle, squinted at their reflections in the mirrors, yawning and sighing as fitters moved around with tape measures and notepads.

Tatiana stood impassively. She had vowed never to complain about her work again. '"H and K". That's all it said,' she whispered to Larissa.

'Just the two of them?' Larissa queried, adding a sigh. 'It was always going to be near impossible.' She turned away from Tatiana's searching look.

At 11 a.m., they were offered a twenty-minute break. When they returned, they found an assistant draping the mirrors with muslin.

'What nonsense is this?' the senior fitter was spluttering. 'How can we work if we can't see back and front?'

Madame Markova was summoned, and she explained, 'Mademoiselle Darocca is coming in for the final fitting of her wedding gown. Mirrors… reflections… ' she clicked her tongue. 'Humour her, it makes our lives so much easier.'

'I thought Constanza was buying her wedding gown in New York,' Marianne said as she undid her robe and returned to her position.

Isabelle knew better. 'She couldn't find what she wanted, and decided it had to be Javier.'

'Of course.' Marianne flashed Tatiana a pitying glance, which should have warned her, but her thoughts were on Harry and Katya. And so, when Constanza arrived and was helped into the calla lily wedding dress, shock caught her like the back swing of a club.

'What Constanza wants, Constanza gets,' Larissa whispered. 'Smile. Grant her no power.'

Tatiana closed her eyes. Her fitter unpicked an underarm gusset and released a fraction of a centimetre of buttercup-yellow seam. She could not block out Constanza's chatter, however.

'I shall not walk to my beloved holding a lily. I shall carry a deep-red rose, to match my ring.' It was easy to imagine Constanza displaying her left-hand knuckle to the room.

Confirmed when Larissa commented, 'We've seen it already, *chérie*.'

'And not only on your hand, *ma choux*,' Marianne followed up. 'It gets around, that ring.'

'May we please uncover the mirrors,' the senior fitter pleaded. 'You really don't believe it's bad luck, Mademoiselle Darocca?'

'Oh, but it is,' Tatiana heard Larissa say. 'The bride who sees herself in the glass before her wedding day sees the woman her husband will be stuck with for the rest of his life. It is too terrible a knowledge.'

'It *is* bad luck,' Tatiana whispered. Only her dresser heard her say, 'On my sister Vera's wedding day, the servants covered all the mirrors but I exposed the one in her room as our mother fixed on Vera's veil. Our lives were shipwrecked from that moment on.'

Constanza gave a tinkling laugh. 'You are shy today, Tatya, with your eyes shut. Do you not wish to see the gown on me?'

'Not especially.'

'Seeing you in yellow reminds me, my maid did not return the dress I borrowed. Silly creature. But I have it. It's in the *cabine*.'

'I don't want it.'

'Neither do I. Josette,' Constanza instructed her fitter, 'it's on my dressing table with all my other jumble. Bring it.'

Josette returned within a few minutes, and rather than stand holding the parcel, Tatiana ripped it open and let the ochre-yellow dress unroll itself. 'You might have ironed it, lazy-bones,' she said, turning at last to look at Constanza. Yes. Spectacular in the dress, but Tatiana no longer felt any jealousy. Anger, but none of that visceral, sexual pain. Aware that Constanza was watching, she inspected the ochre dress, curious to see which button was missing. None were. All sewn firmly in place. Even the spare one, attached to an inside seam.

Somebody had lain on the bed in the rue Molière flat in a dress like this, one of only two ever made, and had shed a button. A giggle bubbled between her lips.

'What's funny?' Constanza demanded. 'What have you got to laugh about? You're only here because Roland Javier pities you.'

Tatiana laughed so hard she couldn't get the dress back in its parcel and had to hand it back to Josette. 'Take it to Madame Frankel,' she said. 'With my compliments. Tell her she can plunder it to her heart's content.' Nobody noticed Larissa move to the mirror nearest to Constanza and twitch away its muslin veil.

Constanza, suddenly seeing herself reflected head to toe, let out a demonic scream.

'Oops,' said Larissa.

Chapter Seventy-Two

On the death of his English wife, Harry's father had left England and returned to his family home in Gothenburg. He had brought his heavy English furniture with him and been very comfortable until he married his second wife. Swedish Elsa preferred French style. Out had gone the country-manor sideboards, making room for Louis Quinze antiques imported from Paris. The steely northern light had faded these interlopers and now they looked as though they had always been there. It made the house feel welcoming. Under other circumstances, Katya would have enjoyed her stay. But she had been ill. Bronchitis had made the journey home from Russia a misery. Leaving without Vera was the death of hope. The Kremlin had played them for fools, acquiring hundreds of pounds' worth of British produce in return for... ashes.

Her depression was affecting her marriage. She and Harry had not made love since Petrograd, and most days he accompanied his father to the Morten paper mill upstream on the Göta Älv River. 'I am here when you are ready to look at me again,' he'd said last night as she turned from him.

This morning, the pain felt almost unbearable. She was sewing diapers, helping Elsa who was expecting her second child. If there were a medal for suppressing pain, I should get it, Katya thought.

'Madame?' Elsa's housemaid came in, relating something in Swedish that was beyond Katya's grasp. Her heart sank as the girl handed Elsa a note. Most likely from Harry or his father, warning of a late return home. Katya liked Elsa but her domestic chatter and maternal concerns overwhelmed her.

Elsa frowned. 'It's from the luggage office at the railway station. There is lost property to collect. I cannot imagine… oh, wait. Baggage dispatched from Russia. "Fru Morten" is you, not me.'

Katya put down her sewing. 'I can guess what it is. When Harry hustled me onto the train in Petrograd, we left four of our bags behind. I didn't imagine they'd ever be sent back.'

'My Harald says that the Kremlin is cautious in its dealings with neutral countries like ours,' Elsa said. 'They also love to surprise. I'll send Tomas to the station.' She was referring to the manservant who doubled as chauffeur, but Katya asked if she might go herself.

'There's no need,' her hostess insisted. 'Tomas knows his way!'

'I'd like a change of scene. Sorry, I don't mean—'

'It's all right, Katya.' Elsa smiled. 'It is hard to be a guest for so long and you want to be at home.'

Actually, Katya dreaded the return to Paris. She hadn't written to anybody or picked up a telephone, though Harry had sent a wire assuring her mother that they were alive, if not well. She regretted bitterly having sent that earlier letter, pre-empting Vera's rescue. Dread of breaking the news to Irina was a large part of her reluctance to go home. Her mother would never accept Vera's death.

The car was ordered and within forty minutes, Katya was at the railway station lost-luggage desk. As there was nobody in attendance, she sat down on the end of a bench to wait. She wasn't alone. A man was pacing, glancing at his watch, occasionally breaking off to rap impatiently on the counter. A woman Katya took to be his wife sat at the other end of the bench, her shoulders drooping in meek forbearance. She had a threadbare coat and darned gloves, a black scarf knotted tightly behind her head. When the pacing man exclaimed furiously in Swedish, and marched out, Katya expected the woman to follow.

When she stayed put, Katya looked at her more closely. Something in the sharp, still profile compelled Katya's gaze. *Don't think it.* The woman's boots were canvas strips wrapped around her feet and tied off at the top. Wisps of hair escaped the headscarf, like the spikes of a fraying wicker basket. She appeared tall, as were many Nordic women. *Don't hope*, Katya pleaded with herself. But without Harry, there was nobody to urge caution. She asked in Russian, 'Have you been waiting an awfully long time?'

The woman looked at her. Instead of the haggard misery Katya was expecting, she saw blue eyes burning in a malnourished face.

'A long, long time,' the woman answered in Russian.

'Vera?' Katya rasped.

Chapter Seventy-Three

Wednesday, 7 February

The consensus in the fitting room was that Constanza's shriek as she saw herself in the mirror had more to do with being made a fool of than with dread of a curse. Tatiana felt she'd earned the right to laugh with Una about it, however, and took herself to rue Cambon. It was midday, the world at lunch. The street door of *Ravissante*'s building was wedged open, and she walked up. Lingering outside Regan's office, she heard a familiar vocal duet.

Una and Regan, speaking English, though she'd noticed they didn't so much speak as battle. Even when they agreed with each other. A New Yorker's habit?

Regan was saying, 'I'm bringing in fresh talent for the next issue.'

'Sacking me, you snake?' Una demanded.

'Hell, no. A different photographer, a new slant. The February issue made waves, but it won't stand a repeat.'

'Totally agree. It would be like retelling a joke and expecting everyone to laugh again.'

'I mean to establish *Ravissante* as a vessel of bona fide, inside news. A fresh insight every month.'

'Again, totally agree. Does that mean Tatiana gets bumped?'

Did she have any friends left? Tatiana wondered. Her elbow accidentally collided with the door and she gritted her teeth in pain.

'I'm going to keep her out of the next couple of issues,' Regan was saying. 'For her sake.'

Una: 'You're right. Mustn't fuse your brand with hers.'

'My brand? Excuse me while I laugh,' Regan replied. 'Tatiana considers me a barely washed peasant.'

'She went down on both knees to apologise, in public. What more do you want?'

'That charade was for Roland Javier's benefit. In her eyes I'm low status. Poor, obscure, plain and little. "Little" socially, at any rate.'

'You've read *Jane Eyre*?' Una sounded incredulous. 'A boy from Hell's Kitchen?'

'Is there a law against it?'

While quoting Charlotte Brontë, which had been his sisters' favourite novel and passed around until it fell apart, Regan moved to pull open the door. Una stopped him. She mouthed, '*Tatiana's out there*. I can smell her perfume.'

'I know,' he mouthed back. 'She doesn't get forgiven that easy.'

Una nodded and put a finger to her lips, saying loudly, 'I don't consider you plain or obscure, Regan. And if I hadn't temporarily given up men for the sake of my career, I'd prove it to you.'

He answered, 'Wow, sugar. You wouldn't care that I have to hire myself a suit and a good pair of shoes?'

'Hired? You don't say! They fit so well.' In a low voice, she said, 'I've been hearing rumours that you're loaded. That you didn't borrow from a bank to buy this joint, you paid cash.'

'Who said that?' he asked just as quietly.

'Artie Shone. He knows everyone in New York including your ex-father-in-law.'

'Maybe he got the wrong end of the stick.'

'Nah. But you don't want Tatiana to know, right?' Una raised her voice, almost to a shout. 'Shucks, don't they pay you, Regan?'

'Only my keep, and even then, my boss is late wiring the money. Say, Una, could you lend me twenty francs so I can take Tatiana out tonight? Now she's no longer engaged, I can ask her. I'd like to give her the opportunity to apologise again.'

'I'll see what I have in my bag. A whole twenty? Would ten do?'

They crept away from the door, and when Tatiana stumbled in, cheeks aflame, it was to see Regan pushing a scruffy ten-franc note into his pocket. When he asked if she'd care to take pot luck with him that evening, she almost flung a refusal at his feet. But the suspicion she was being hoodwinked spurred her to answer, 'Lovely. I'm rather fond of Maxim's.'

'Tell you what, I'll take you to my favourite diner. Were you outside the door a long time, Tatiana?'

'No, just arrived,' she said. 'Hello, Una. Fancy lunch? I have a story that'll have you in pieces.'

That night, she thought hard about what to wear. She was still on the back foot with Regan, but something had changed in him too. He'd either pardoned her behaviour, or no longer cared so deeply.

As for her, her feelings had undergone a revolution from the moment he'd rescued her, bleeding, from Parc Monceau then soared higher when he'd held her head out of the Seine. But what did that mean, exactly? She had loved Gérard so intensely, she'd traded her liberty for his sake. Would she do the same for Regan?

The difference was, he'd never ask.

She checked herself in her bedroom mirror. Her dress was sea green with inserts of old silver lace. Callot Soeurs, from her time there. A green ribbon around her brow set off her hair. Plain earrings, no other jewellery. She stepped into mid-height shoes and threw on an opera cape, then called goodnight to her family and went to wait for the taxi that would convey her back to Regan's office.

He was waiting by the side of the road, wearing a dark-blue suit, as well cut as the previous one she'd seen him in. Hired? Hmm. She said little as their taxi took them by the Seine, and only when they crossed to the Left Bank did she ask where they were eating.

'Chez Antoine. A little place I got fond of when I was living in the fifth. That all right?'

'Perfect.'

It was indeed a little place, with steep steps down to a candlelit vault. They both had to dip their heads, and Tatiana steeled herself not to think of prison cells. Regan caught on to her silence. 'Cat walked on your grave?'

She told him: 'Saint-Lazare smelled like this. Damp mortar and stale air.'

'We'll go. Come on.' He got up, too fast, and hit his head. He swore.

'Sit down,' she said. 'Lean forward.' She rubbed his brow. 'I'm not a brittle, highly strung female. You don't have to tiptoe around me.'

'Nor you round me. Don't ever prostrate yourself again.'

'I won't. It was a once-in-a-lifetime event.'

The meal was simple but delicious. Fresh grilled sardine, tomato salad and omelettes. Wine in pitchers. They talked about *Ravissante*, and he described the print-room politics, which were bloody and costly. They discussed Maison Javier, and when she described the Machiavellian currents at work in the *cabine*, he offered to trade. The evening passed quickly and when he carefully counted out money to pay the bill, she looked away. Afterwards, they strolled around the Latin Quarter, where every building was a clutter of peeling shutters, sagging roofs and bent chimneys, and the dome of the Panthéon resembled a puffball against a violet sky. Talking all the way to the Quai de Montebello, they stared at Notre Dame in Gothic splendour across the river.

Leaning against the embankment wall, Regan's arm crept about her waist. 'I'm in love with you, Tatiana,' he said. 'Can a New York ragamuffin say that to a princess?'

She stared at the inky water. This was so unexpected, bursting without preamble. 'Is this a game you and Una have invented?'

'Nope. Want me to unsay it?'

'I'm not sure.'

'You think there's too much of a gulf between us?'

'There is a gulf,' she answered, after thinking it through. 'Being a Russian princess doesn't mean much in Paris, but I grew up expecting to marry somebody of my own class who could support me in comfort.'

'Yeah? I grew up expecting to marry a nice girl who worked in a dry-goods store. I'd father nine kids in a two-room apartment. Guess what, I'm not going to do that. What I'm asking is, will you put down the script and improvise? I promise you one thing. Every time I look at you, I will feel awed by my luck. I'll never go stale or go searching for the next fling. We'd take care of each other. Not a Shakespearian proposal, but I mean it.'

'I don't know,' she said quietly. 'I just don't know.'

'You worry about position? Poverty?'

'I'm terrified of poverty. I can't bear being an object of pity.' She hugged her opera cape tighter. It wasn't thick enough, she was growing cold. 'It was one of the reasons I wanted Gérard so much.'

'To throw a granite castle up around you. Tell me this. If I were Regan, Marquis von Dortmeyer, would that change anything?'

She was glad of the chance to laugh. 'That's the kind of nonsense Una would come out with. Can we go somewhere warm for coffee? Can you afford it?'

'Sure, so long as you don't want cream or sugar.' There was a café over the road. As they sat over small cups of strong, black coffee, he brought out a little square box and her heart flipped as he revealed a ring with a yellow-gold stone. He held it between his thumb and forefinger.

'It's like a cat's eye,' she said. 'What is it?'

'Er, glass I think. Did I tell you, my youngest brother Dominic is a liner steward? At Christmas, he brought some swanky crackers off his ship that didn't get pulled in the state dining room.'

'Oh. From a cracker.'

'A quality one.' He got up from his chair, then went down on one knee next to hers. 'Shall I put it on you? Call it an opening bid, till I save up for something better.'

She didn't know what to say. Daren't say yes, daren't say no. In her confusion, she held out her right hand. Regan slipped it on the first finger.

'Wrong hand, but it looks pretty.'

'Please get up,' she begged. 'Everyone's staring.'

He got them a taxi because she'd promised her mother she'd be back before midnight. On the journey, she rested her head on his shoulder, and he kissed her lightly. She knew he was holding back.

She asked if she was forgiven for writing that list.

'Sure. Now I know more about it. There was supposed to be a second one, right? Listing my perfections.'

'I was interrupted before I could begin it.'

'Do you forgive me for letting you fall in the Seine?'

'It wasn't your fault I slipped,' she said.

'I made you run when I knew it was dangerous. I let my anger cancel out my duty to look after you.'

'You're forgiven. I'm glad we're friends again.'

'Friends. Sure.'

As they turned up Boulevard Malesherbes, meaning 'five minutes to home', she tried to tell him that she still needed time to erase memories of hurt and rejection. It didn't come out well, she mentioned Gérard's name three times, and Regan sighed. So, for good measure, she kissed him, deeply.

When the taxi pulled up on rue Rembrandt, he cupped her face. 'I'm here for the next three months. I mean to build up *Ravissante* then install a new editor. No rush, Tatiana, but I don't know if we can just be friends after that kiss.'

Chapter Seventy-Four

22 February 1923

Fashion correspondents and buyers turned up en masse for Maison Javier's spring–summer collection. The invited elite were in the salon, sipping champagne at little tables. Those queuing for admittance were the hopefuls without tickets, rehearsing their pleas or waiting to dash inside while the gimlet-eyed saleswomen were looking elsewhere.

Walking up the line, Regan heard French being spoken along with cross currents of British and American English. This street, this hour, was the place to be if you were anything in fashion. Tatiana's return had been trowelled into public consciousness by Una who, as the celebrated voice of *Ravissante*, now penned syndicated columns in several European newspapers and journals. She had written:

'Tatiana is once again Maison Javier's premier mannequin and will sparkle in this season's most daring shade, "buttercup yellow". She will grace the spring–summer show on rue Duphot alongside Constanza Darocca. Formerly friends, now avowed enemies since the raven-haired seductress filched the fiancé from under Tatiana's pert, Russian nose, they will tread the catwalk together. Never has a walk been so aptly named. Not to be missed.'

Regan was photographing the queue at the door. The pictures would go into *Ravissante*'s April number, in the 'Out and About' section under Una's byline.

Behind him a voice erupted. 'At last I have found him, the man who owns a dog yet barks himself!'

Regan lowered his camera and regarded the squat figure in a raincoat and battered hat. 'Pigeon.'

'What is Lemuel Slinfield's son-in-law doing with a camera in his hands?' Pigeon gave Regan's tailored torso a sardonic once-over. 'Yes, I know of your great stroke of fortune. You are rich enough to never have to work again. You know what they say of wealthy artists... the sharper the suit, the duller the work.'

'Then you must be very good at your job, Pigeon. What are you doing on my patch?'

'I am here to offer my services. I find myself somewhat at leisure.'

'It's got round that you've been selling your fashion shots to couture thieves.'

Pigeon prepared a blustering denial. Then all at once, the wind came out of him. 'Let me take pictures for your magazine, my friend. My name will tell the fashion world that you are serious.' He patted his camera. 'I come ready to let bygones be bygones.'

For a moment, Regan wavered. He wasn't a man to clutch hard to grudges. But in touching his camera, Pigeon had exposed his left wrist, and there was the watch he'd stolen from a fallen compatriot, its strap newly replaced. 'No deal,' Regan said harshly. 'Today, I'm giving a young, up-and-coming man his chance. Actually, you know him.'

'Who?' Pigeon looked left and right, his eye passing over Isidore – Petit-Pigeon – who was encouraging some girls in the queue to bunch closer to fit in shot. Pigeon's lip curled as he watched Isidore step back to judge his composition. 'That?' he demanded. '*That*, to eclipse me? A little boy with a Box Brownie?' Pigeon spat. 'I will wire Lemuel Slinfield to inform him that his editor is making a mockery of his magazine.'

'Do it,' Regan advised. 'But don't wire, book a telephone call and remember the time difference. Call nice and early, eight in the morning his time, before Lemuel's had his first cup of coffee and be sure to mention my name plenty of times.' Regan's attention was drawn by a motley group swelling the end of the queue. Mostly men, a few women, notebooks in their breast pockets, they struck a dud note among the squirrel-furred, minked and silver-foxed fashion crowd. Press.

Pigeon saw them and his smile returned. 'Here to record Tatiana's first tottering steps back into public life. Something not to be missed!'

Tatiana happened to look out of the *cabine* window at that moment. Seeing Regan glance up, she waved. Then held her position as he raised his camera. He'd told her that his late, former wife had resented his love affair with photography. For her part, she'd take a man any day who preferred a camera to other women.

Months ago, she'd hurled flowers at him, hoping to hurt him. What could she throw now? She searched the pockets of her robe, but the handkerchief she found would make a poor missile. Nor would she throw the ring which she hadn't yet removed from her right hand. Instead, she bathed him in private scrutiny. She regretted his smartened-up appearance, because it robbed her of the honour of loving the tousled stray he'd been.

'Tatiana, stop dreaming. I want you dressed in good time.'

'Of course, Madame Markova.'

Joining her at the window, Anna Markova let out an amused grunt. 'Does he photograph in his sleep?'

Tatiana blushed as Larissa and Marianne, seated close by, paused in their preparations to hear her answer. 'How would I know what the man does in his sleep?'

'No, indeed,' murmured Marianne. 'If I spent a night with Regan Dortmeyer I wouldn't waste it sleeping. Does he have a girl?'

'Maybe.' Tatiana went to her dressing table. Securing her hair under a knotted stocking top, she opened her make-up box and studiously ignored Constanza who had arrived a few moments before, and whose unblinking stare seemed determined to prise out her secrets.

Tatiana shaded her eye sockets with kohl stick, then darkened her lashes with a mascara brush. She'd been washing her face in almond milk recently and had her flawless complexion back. No need for powder. Her final touch was to gloss her lips with beeswax.

'I can lend you a lipstick, if you're worried you look colourless.' Constanza sat down at the neighbouring table, the one that had belonged to Mary-Jo.

'No thanks.'

'Nail varnish?'

'No. I buff my nails *au naturel*. What's your shade?' Tatiana looked at Constanza's hands. "Fire Hydrant"?'

'It's "Flame".'

'You always did look good in red.' Tatiana said it as pleasantly as she could. She wasn't going to play up to Una's hopes of claws on the catwalk. All she wanted, alongside echoing applause and the well-bred stamping of feet, was for today's show to pass serenely. To attend the after-show party with Regan, and pick up the conversation that had ended, unresolved, with a kiss in a taxi.

'Did Roland give you that?' Constanza pointed at the cushion-cut yellow stone on Tatiana's right hand.

'This? No, it's… out of a cracker, but Monsieur Javier is happy for me to wear it.'

Larissa, who was doing ballet exercises in the space behind them, came to Tatiana's side.

'I've noticed it too. Show me.' When Tatiana extended her hand, Larissa gave a half laugh. 'Must have been a gold-plated cracker.'

Constanza asked sharply, 'It's a topaz, I suppose? Costume jewellery.'

'It's a yellow sapphire,' Larissa informed her. 'Very rare. My uncle was a jeweller, so I know my gemstones.'

Constanza thrust the Sainte-Vierge ring towards Larissa. 'Tell me about this.'

'What can I tell you?' Larissa went back to her stretching. 'Sago pudding with a blob of raspberry jam in the middle.'

'It's priceless, ruby within pearls.'

'Then why ask my opinion, Consty?'

Constanza turned on Tatiana. 'Gérard told me you stabbed him! You should go back to prison. As for giving Armand's letter to Agnès de Brioude – now the family must live under the shadow of suicide. You are malignant, Tatiana.'

'They needed to know.'

'What, that he was desperately in love with you, and that you could have helped him? Don't flatter yourself that you are forgiven. You will always be the drunkard who killed a war hero.'

Tatiana took perfume from her drawer, fitted an atomiser spray and wove a generous halo around herself. 'Go to your own table.'

Constanza batted away the fragrant mist. 'You know this is my final day? Gérard and I marry on 21 March, the first day of spring. For our honeymoon, I am taking him to meet my father in Argentina.'

Tatiana looked her in the eye. 'I hope your grandmother's second funeral wasn't too upsetting… except you weren't in Buenos Aires, were you? Why lie about New York? So childish.'

The dressers were rumbling the clothes rails into the room and Madame Markova was clapping her hands. Avoiding each other's eyes, Tatiana and Constanza slipped off their robes. Their dressers handed them chiffon scarves, to cover their faces and prevent make-up ruining costly cloth.

Tatiana's first outfit was a sports dress of primrose wool, its sleeveless bodice decorated with a bold, capital 'T' in old-gold satin. Roland had used the cypher 'MJ' across this collection but the 'T' was a stamp of approval for Tatiana. A sign she was back in the fold. Constanza wore a similar drop-waist dress in red, but without any decoration to the front. Flashing a look at Tatiana, her jaw moved. She was grinding her teeth.

Once their numbers were fixed to their wrists, all six mannequins trooped down to the antechamber and waited, sipping iced water.

'Sounds like a barn,' Larissa commented.

'A barn with diamonds.' Madame Markova peered out to check the crowd. 'Buyers yell so! They're terrified a rival might get first rights to something they want.'

They all knew that as they made their appearance, they'd be assailed by shouts of 'Mam'selle, turn this way!' 'Mam'selle, I need to see the back view again.' Or when the din ran high, simply, "Ahoy, Mam'selle!" It wasn't unknown for the more ruthless buyers to manhandle the clothes or push into the mannequins' waiting room or even pursue them upstairs.

Lilliane Germond hurried in. 'Petronelle, Larissa, Marianne, beginners in one minute. Move fast, turn and come back. No loitering. We think we have copyists in, but we can't police every corner.' Lilliane looked harassed. 'There are some odd-looking press people at the back. I believe we have you to thank for this, Tatiana, but don't let them distract you. In a moment, Monsieur Javier is going to ask for quiet.'

'I can't hear the piano.' Tatiana frowned. They'd rehearsed all week with Benjy Crouch.

'He came, he saw, he walked out,' the *directrice* informed her. 'He refused to play with that racket going on. One of my girls will put on gramophone records.'

On cue, Scott Joplin's 'Cakewalk' struck up. Joyful, determined music to set the tone. The first three mannequins danced out, leaving Tatiana waiting with Isabelle and Constanza. Isabelle retreated to the opposite side of the room.

Constanza came right up to Tatiana. 'Who told you I was in New York, not Buenos Aires?'

'Una McBride saw you in a department store, shopping for wedding clothes. It's not my business if your lies eat you up, Constanza. I'm glad you have Gérard because you cancel each other out. I'd hate to think of a decent man or woman ending up with either of you.'

Constanza attempted a chuckle. 'You know why Gérard asked you to marry him? You were a decoy. His mother wanted Agnès de Brioude for him but he was in love with me. She would keep throwing them together so he used you to deflect attention, knowing Madame la marquise would object violently. You're everything wrong. A damaged, self-obsessed crane fly who isn't even Roman Catholic. The night before he asked you to be his wife' – Constanza frowned down at her ruby as if checking its lustre still held – 'he begged my pardon. "Don't be jealous, my darling. Let Maman suppose me besotted with Tatiana so that when I break it off, and bring you home to meet her, she'll be so relieved she'll overlook your foreign birth."'

'You looked on while we became lovers?'

'You never were lovers!' Constanza flashed back. 'Oh, he slept with you. It was necessary, to maintain the fiction and you, *you* were wild for him, all a-tremble whenever he so much as looked your way.'

'You're telling me he faked his passion? I don't think so, Constanza.'

'He got through it by thinking of me. Always called you *'chérie'* or *'ma chère'* in case he forgot himself and spoke my name.'

'Men who cheat always do that,' Tatiana said coldly. 'But I still don't believe you. Everything you did to harm me stems from desperate jealousy. You know in your heart that he loves somebody else.'

Constanza laughed. 'Convince yourself, if you must.'

'Oh, not me. Somebody who trumps both of us.' The first, and the last, time she had visited Gérard's family home, she had sat down on the stairs, her eye caught by a portrait. 'Agnès, before her marriage,' Gérard had told her at the time and Tatiana had suggested he might have liked to marry his cousin himself.

'Agnès outranks me.' A qualified denial, because the question had caught him out. Tatiana knew the truth. A few days ago, she had eavesdropped on a conversation between Pauline Frankel and Agnès herself. The duchesse had been thanking Pauline for sending back her favourite yellow dress. Perfectly repaired.

'That shade of ochre, does it sound vain if I say it flatters my complexion like no other?'

'Not at all, Madame la duchesse,' Tatiana had heard Pauline reply. 'But will you solve a conundrum for me?'

Tatiana had edged forward, had seen Agnès incline her head. *Of course.*

'Your maid brought the dress to us saying that your little dog had chewed it. We were expecting a pile of torn rags and I searched high and low for remnants of matching fabric. But all that was wrong with it—'

Tatiana gave a laugh that made Constanza start. 'All that was wrong with it was that a button was missing. She had her maid invent a story about a dog, to cover her indiscretion.'

'What are you gibbering about?' Constanza rolled her eyes, implying that Tatiana had finally tumbled over into insanity.

'Conny, wake up. By becoming enemies, we've done Gérard's bidding. He pursues his real quarry while you and I scratch each other's eyes out. It's what illusionists call a "misdirection trick". Gérard loves Agnès.'

'That dowd? Don't be ridiculous.' Constanza yanked Tatiana's shoulder. 'Look at me. Look at the future marquise de Sainte-Vierge.'

'He'll call off your wedding.' Tatiana was as sure of it as she had been of anything in her life. 'A week before, a few days… he won't go through with it.'

'You are pitiful. You think he'd treat me as he did you?'

'I do. The next marquise will be his cousin if she'll have him. You know, don't you, that Gérard killed Armand?'

'Your word against his.' Constanza's eyes hardened defiantly. The door swung inwards to admit Larissa and Marianne, who warned that it was 'a jungle, not a barn, out there' and that poor, novice Petronelle had been taken captive by some buyers from Bonwit Teller, working as a pack.

*

They had it right. Buyers were competing with journalists to draw first blood, to a background of ragtime turned up as loud as the gramophone allowed. Tatiana looked for Regan who had said he'd watch from a niche, out of the way. She couldn't spot him. Flowers, lights, crystal stemware, fur coats discarded, hats retained, gold neck chains. Everywhere she looked, it was glittering, expensive chaos. Petronelle was pinioned halfway along the catwalk by a woman in a black mink coat and another in white fox. The mink woman was rubbing Petronelle's cyclamen pleats between her fingers, demanding, 'Is it knitted cotton, or is there silk in it? Cotton or silk, we need to know, what proportion?'

Other buyers were barracking the Bonwit Teller contingent, telling them to sit down. The *directrice* added her voice. 'Please, Mesdames, return to your places.' Petronelle looked perfectly intimidated.

Tatiana saw Una in the front row. Ha, somebody was enjoying themselves, anyway. Next to Una, an empty chair and next to that in black and lilac polka dot, Agnès de Brioude. Tatiana's eye slid to the row behind, picking on a mousy girl who was taking advantage of the scrummage, sketching Petronelle's dress. Tatiana strode over to her. Ignoring the girl's injured, 'Hey!' she swiped both pad and pencil, broke the pencil in two and returned to the catwalk with the sketch pad held aloft.

Roland Javier intercepted her, urging her on by singing a line from the Marseillaise, '*Marchons, marchons!*' Tatiana raised her arms to display the gold 'T' on her front. She shouted to the buyers, 'Catch me if you can!' A woman in the front row nudged her neighbour.

'*Tatiana.*'

Her name rumbled through the crowd.

She heard, 'Hey, Tatya, hey Doudou, welcome back!'

Doudou? Searching for the source of the impudence, she saw a row of faces that even now polluted her dreams. The press pack that had bayed on her release from prison.

She didn't realise she'd run for the exit until she hammered into a solid wall of muscle.

'You have to face them,' Regan said. 'You won't forgive yourself if you don't.'

With the attention now fully on Tatiana, Petronelle made a run for it. The *directrice* got on a chair and roared out: 'Is this Tatiana, or the goddess of the hunt, strayed from Mount Olympus?' She beckoned ferociously for Tatiana to come back to the catwalk.

Regan gave Tatiana a push. 'You can't leave the poor woman declaiming like Ellen Terry to an audience of drunks. Go. Slink. Sashay, whatever it is you do.'

The oratory continued: 'Timeless, fluid wool-weave allows Tatiana to glide like a swan. To run like Atalanta, or leap like Hero into the waters of the Hellespont.' That brought laughter from those who had lapped up February's *Ravissante* and the picture of Tatiana in the river.

'Over here, Tatiana!' cried a voice.

'This way, Princess,' came another.

'Where's my *vendeuse*? I want that dress. Hey you, that's my *vendeuse*. Give her back!'

'I want no. 4! Somebody mark down that I asked for it first!'

'How does it feel to be a free woman? Ever think about Armand de Sainte-Vierge?'

Tatiana ran down the catwalk. The 'T' dress flared around her as she performed a dozen *fouetté* turns. The copyists who had crept in disguised as buyers' assistants got down a few hopeful lines. Buyers scribbled on their programmes, and the vultures cawing for blood were thwarted as Tatiana escaped at a sprint.

When she came out again in crocus yellow and turned a cartwheel on the catwalk, the leering press caught the wink of a jewel on her right hand but could make nothing of it. Regan noticed Pigeon setting up a shot. The parasite must have schmoozed Roland Javier, or one of the saleswomen, to get inside.

But when Roland himself came to stand beside Regan, he was unaware of Pigeon's incursion. 'But not surprised. Everyone seems to have got in.'

'You need security on the doors, Monsieur.'

Roland shrugged. 'Lilliane is usually deterrent enough. I'm told Chanel's shows are rowdier even than this, and that Patou's resemble a public holiday at a railway station.'

'Chanel doesn't do too badly.'

'Couture earns no money,' Roland told him seriously. 'It is why Mademoiselle Chanel makes perfume.'

'So make perfume.'

Roland clicked his fingers. 'And send it by tanker to America?'

'You're getting the idea.'

Roland jerked his head towards the press with their slanted notebooks. 'Next time, I will hire the guards who bar the doors of Montmartre cabarets—' He broke off. 'What is he doing here? Constanza, I suppose.'

Gérard de Sainte-Vierge was being shown to the seat next to Agnès de Brioude, whose cool smile suggested she had saved it for him.

Roland tutted. 'A ladies' man! Is it the way Monsieur de Sainte-Vierge has combed his moustache, or does he look even more smug today than usual?'

Intensely smug, Regan agreed, and felt a twinge. Tatiana no longer cared for the swine, by her own declaration. And she was wearing his, Regan's, ring, yet he felt far from secure. Did she love him the way she kissed him? He'd been invited to the after-show party at Maxim's, and if they got a quiet moment, he'd ask her straight.

How would he feel if she answered with a straight no? 'I'm going to step outside,' he said. But before he could, events shifted.

Chapter Seventy-Five

Enjoying a moment's rest in the antechamber, Tatiana listened to 'Maple Leaf Rag' spilling through from the salon. The door opened, and Petronelle once again scrambled past her, her rumpled skirt hitched up for ease of running. Constanza lolled in a boudoir chair, her expression dark. She was wearing the *pièce de résistance*, the latest Javier wedding gown.

Tatiana's final showing was an evening dress, neck-to-hem with gold and buttercup sequins, in a snakeskin pattern. The skirt fell to the knee, with a fantail train at the back. She wore it with a Russian *kokoshnik*, a starred headdress that made her appear six feet tall. No more cartwheeling or pirouetting.

An assistant brought in the veil for the bridal gown, asking Constanza to please stand.

Scowling, Constanza got to her feet. Her dress was watered silk and ivory chiffon with metallic embroidery. Medieval in shape. The gold lace veil fitted to the head, then pooled like lava around Constanza's satin heels. Her bouquet of white calla lilies had been brushed with gold leaf. Tatiana glanced at the ring on her own finger. *Out of a cracker? A rare, yellow sapphire must have cost Regan everything he owned. Damn the man for being so—*

'Tatiana?' Madame Markova had a talent for interrupting. 'Monsieur Javier has switched the running order. The bridal gown will now be the penultimate event and you will finish the show— Now what?' She clicked her teeth and went to Constanza who was haranguing the girl who had fitted her veil.

'There is no time for histrionics,' Madame Markova scolded.

Constanza came right back, shouting, 'Tell this creature I won't go out looking as if I've been dressed with a pitchfork. No, you will not fetch a mirror!' she shrieked at the young dresser. 'How many more times?'

Larissa came in, setting the carpet aflame in scarlet taffeta. 'Bad luck, Consty. Your fiancé's out there with—' Seeing Constanza's chin go up, Larissa glided towards the stairs, winking at Tatiana as she passed.

Madame Markova moved Constanza's train away from her feet. 'You're going out next so please put your emotions to one side. No angry brides, please.'

'Tatiana is next,' Constanza corrected her.

'Change of sequence, orders from on high. You're out next,' Madame Markova repeated. 'Smile and obey.'

'I'm not doing it. I cannot.'

Madame Markova stood back. 'This is your final triumph, Constanza, something to tell your children about in years to come.'

'Did you not hear? Are you stupid? My husband-to-be is out there. He can't see me in this dress.'

'This isn't the dress you're getting married in,' Madame Markova said icily. In the hierarchy of the salon, she ranked one stage below director-level. She brooked insolence from nobody. 'Stop tugging at your neckline. Head high. Come along.'

'I cannot let my fiancé see me in a bridal gown. Any bridal gown.'

'Then we will ask him to leave.'

Constanza hurled her flowers. 'Damn this dress, it's hideous anyway.'

'Is there trouble?' Roland walked in, blinking as a dresser scrambled to retrieve Constanza's bouquet.

'Her fiancé is in the audience,' Madame Markova explained.

'I am aware.'

'So obviously, I'm not going out.' Constanza folded her arms.

Roland instructed the dresser to kindly request that Monsieur de Sainte-Vierge leave the salon. He then offered Constanza his arm. 'We will go together and everyone will laugh at me, for you are so much taller.'

'No. Get this dress off me.' Constanza began pulling it off. Madame Markova seized her hands.

'I've had enough temperament for one day.' She dumped the flowers in Constanza's arms and pushed her to the door. 'Take her arm,' she told Roland. 'You – go,' she instructed Tatiana. 'Take up the rear. Let's get this over with.'

Gérard's was the first face Tatiana saw. The dresser was trying to get his attention, no doubt to ask him to step outside, but he was ignoring her. Who was that by him? Ah, Agnès de Brioude. Constanza saw her too and stopped dead.

'Move, before every copyist in the room has sketched you from all sides,' the *directrice* begged. Tatiana overtook Constanza, keeping her expression haughty under the heavy *kokoshnik*, until she noticed Regan. She smiled and, daringly, blew him a kiss. The press pack got clear aim at her.

'Got the smell of prison off you yet, Tatiana?'

'D'you think it's fair you get to parade in pretty clothes while your victim lies in his grave?'

Manufactured rage. Patrice Denois, he of the gargoyle features, was taking avid notes. He had offered to clear her name. For a price, no doubt. 'You want to know who killed Armand de Sainte-Vierge?' she yelled in his direction, and would have singled out Gérard but the press pack, weary of hurling taunts from the sidelines, chose then to invade the catwalk. Notepads were shoved up to her face.

'Were you drunk the night you killed Armand?' was bellowed beside her ear.

'I was not driving that night. I don't drive!' she cried. 'Your friend Denois is right – it wasn't me.' She might as well have shouted at a bank of whirring machinery. A hand dragged her gown off one shoulder. She felt sequins breaking, tumbling between her breasts and screamed so violently, she tasted blood.

'I am innocent. The guilty man is there!' She pointed at Gérard. He saw her.

Patrice Denois demanded, 'Say that again, Princess. Tell us who was driving.'

But she couldn't. She was being shoved from side to side and her fantail train, caught under many feet, had become a hazard. Any moment, she'd fall and be trampled. The needle was pulled off the gramophone record and the music stopped. Roland Javier shouted for order.

'Ladies and gentlemen, return to your seats. Show my girls some respect.'

The crush had become a beast with no master and those walling Tatiana in were also fighting to stay upright. She snatched for breath. Little lights fired in her head. She knew it as oxygen deprivation. Which was why, when she saw Gérard in front of her, she reached for him in relief. He slapped her hands away.

'Don't threaten me, girl! I warned you.' He lunged, meaning to take her by the throat, but grabbed her *kokoshnik* instead, wrenching it from its pins while she screamed at him.

A blinding flash went off in front of her. Like a bundle of sticks whose binding has been cut, the crowd fell away and she lugged in a huge breath. An arm hooked around her waist, and she was half dragged, half carried to the other side of the room, leaving a trail of sequins on the carpet.

'Who are worse, newshounds or fashion divas?'

'Regan Dortmeyer,' she gasped, 'did you photograph me when I was being murdered by barbarians?'

'Not guilty. It was Pigeon. I used my Speed Graphic to beat a path to you.'

She thrust her hand towards him. 'I don't know where you got this ring from, but take it back.'

'I refuse. And you owe me. I just saved your life again.'

'Damn you.' Drunk on adrenaline and oxygen deprivation, she grabbed a hank of his hair and kissed him. When she drew away, she said, 'Is there anything you won't stoop to?'

He said against her lips, 'Come back to my place and I'll tell you.'

'That's another thing—' She broke off, staring at the salon entrance. Where she saw the one person able to tear her from Regan at that moment.

Chapter Seventy-Six

'Katya!' Tatiana ran to where her sister stood regarding the mayhem. 'Of all the days! Where have you been? Where is Harry?'

'At home. As is—' Katya shut down suddenly. 'What is going on here? I came to see the tail end of the launch. I bought a copy of *Ravissante* in Cherbourg when we docked. What has happened to *Ravissante*? Tatiana? Why are you laughing?'

'Because you're home and all you can do is hurl questions. Have you seen Mama?'

Katya shook her head. 'I thought she might be here.'

'No, she's still ashamed to be seen in public with me.'

'Ashamed, why?'

Tatiana groaned. 'It's the longest of long stories. Katya, why did you abandon us?' There were shadows around Katya's eyes and she had lost weight.

'Harry and I went to Russia,' Katya said. 'To find Vera.'

Tatiana gasped. So it hadn't been a delusion of their mother's. 'Did you... find her?'

Tears welled in Katya's eyes, bouncing onto her cheeks as she nodded. 'Yes. Alive, Tatiana. She's at home, being cared for by Madame Roche. We went to Petrograd – St Petersburg – believing she was waiting. But they gave me a box of ashes. A cruel joke, though Vera told me it was because they had released the wrong woman. Another poor soul called Vera, and when they realised their error, it was easier to pretend our sister was dead. It took weeks for the mistake to be put right, but at last they let her go and put her on a train. With no food and no money.'

'How is she?'

'Very frail.'

'Does Mama know she's back?'

Katya shook her head. 'I'm fearful she'll throw herself on Vera's neck. Our sister needs time to adjust. Something else you need to know. Vera is convinced that Mikhail is alive and I don't know how to tell her that he is as lost to her as ever he was.'

'But you can tell her that she has a daughter, a thorough-going sweetie.' That came from Regan who had followed Tatiana across the salon.

'Do I know you?' Katya peered at him.

'In passing, Madame, but I hope you'll come to know me better.'

'Of course, you're the American photographer.' They shook hands, then overcome, Katya reached up and kissed him on both cheeks. Welded by emotion, they failed to see the collection show's crowning event, Constanza Darocca slapping Agnès de Brioude around the face, before punching Gérard de Sainte-Vierge so hard he fell down.

'I haven't asked about you, Tatiana,' Katya said, picking up her sister's left hand. 'You're not wearing your engagement ring. Has anything happened in your life while we've been away?'

Tatiana struggled with the urge to laugh wildly. She contained it, saying, 'Me? Oh, nothing much. Nothing that can't wait.'

Regan watched the sisters leave. Some kind of miracle had taken place, more transformational even than the events that had turned his own life around. He guessed dinner at Maxim's was off. Packing up his things, he slipped away from Maison Javier, relishing the walk to the butte. Work was the cure for what he was feeling right now. He had no special right to be with Tatiana, and that hurt.

Katya and Tatiana took the stairs at the rue Goya apartment, too impatient to wait for the lift.

'Once, we'd have taken these stairs two at a time.' Katya was puffing as they reached her landing. 'I've been unwell, and you are too thin.'

'You should have seen me a month ago.' Tatiana caught her arm. 'Tell me it's true. It isn't a dream from which I'm going to wake, to cry for a whole day.'

'It's no dream. Take a breath.' Katya tapped on the door. Harry let them in. He blinked at Tatiana's sequins.

'Of course, Javier's spring–summer launch. Did it go well?'

'Like a riot in a fish market,' Tatiana said. 'Does she know I'm coming?'

'I told her, but she's very tired and her spirits are delicate. So please, Tatiana, no, um…'

'Antics? Honestly, Harry, give me some credit.'

Harry nodded, though he looked unconvinced as he stepped back to let them in. As they walked towards the drawing room, he let them know that Irina and Anoushka had arrived. 'Vera asked for them. Wanted to know why they weren't already waiting for her.'

'How did Anoushka react, seeing her mother for the first time since she was three months old?'

'The introduction was quaintly formal. Your mother said, "Anoushka, here is your Mama, home from Russia." Vera shook her daughter's hand. She understands that crushing hugs and uncorked emotions will only confuse Anoushka.'

The intense hush in the flat ramped up Tatiana's tension. What human wreckage lay behind the drawing-room door? It opened before they reached it, and Madame Roche came out, carrying a tray of tea things destined for the kitchen.

'Shh,' she said, glancing warily at Tatiana.

What does she imagine I'm going to do, Tatiana thought crossly? Perform an aria? Dance the cancan on the piano?

Katya and Harry's drawing room was two rooms knocked into one with an abundance of furniture. On a massive rattan sofa sat Irina Vytenis. Upright as a marble saint, her crystal-blond hair set in an impeccable chignon, her eyes unblinking pools. One arm was around Anoushka whose flaxen curls were spread over her lap. The child was asleep. Irina's other arm was around a thin woman whose shaven head lolled against her shoulder. A face only just recognisable to Tatiana, features sharply pronounced, youth and softness spent.

'We had to shave her,' Katya whispered. 'The conditions in prison...'

'I know,' Tatiana whispered back. 'I know about vermin. I spent time in Saint-Lazare jail while you were away.'

Katya looked at her irritably, clearly assuming Tatiana was spinning yarns.

Tatiana took off her shoes and went to Vera. Kneeling down, she took one of the thin, calloused hands and gently put it to her lips. The hand twitched. She looked up to find vivid blue eyes staring down at her.

'Tatya.' It came out as a whisper. 'How grown you are and so beautiful. You've got short hair too! Now I shan't feel so odd.'

Tatiana tried to answer, but only sobs emerged. She battled to hold them in, so as not to wake the others but it was no use and, after a moment, she felt a light touch on her cheek. It was her mother.

'Don't cry, darling. This is a happy day.'

'*You've* been weeping, Mama.'

'But not from sorrow. Katya!' Their mother called her middle daughter to her. 'Sit at my feet, let me have all my girls in my arms.' Katya did so, resting her head against Irina's knee. 'I wish my arms were longer,' Irina laughed. 'I would scoop you all up, like a basket of plums.'

'I'm sorry I was rude to you, Mama.' Tatiana plucked at Irina's skirt. 'The other day, wanting to leave you at home. You have every right to be ashamed of me. The way I've conducted my life, I'm ashamed of myself.'

Irina shushed her. 'None of that matters. I have been a bad mother and a neglectful grandmama, but I have vowed never to be unhappy again, and to look upon you all with love and nothing but love. My prayers have been answered. God has been generous, more so than I deserve.'

The tender tableau made Harry Morten's eyes mist over. If only a consignment of malt whisky and a few hundred metres of good cloth could solve all the world's sorrows. He joined Madame Roche in the kitchen, picking up a tea towel to dry the cups she'd washed.

'What's this about Tatiana being in prison?' he asked. 'Another wild story, I suppose.'

'Oh, no, Monsieur. You sister-in-law served time for killing a man. It was a dreadful business. I suppose you didn't read French newspapers while you were away?'

'Killed a man?' Harry put down the cup he was drying. The name Gérard de Sainte-Vierge swam into his head. 'Tatiana isn't wearing her engagement ring, so I presume that "Happily ever after" is not how the story begins?'

Chapter Seventy-Seven

In his darkroom, Pigeon Boccard developed the pictures he'd taken at Maison Javier. The best one showed a well-dressed man ripping the gilded *kokoshnik* off Princess Tatiana's head. *He* looked demonic; *she* looked like an early Byzantine martyr. Pigeon showed it to the man guzzling coffee outside his darkroom door. 'Can you use this?'

Patrice Denois put down his cup and grinned. '*Le Petit Journal* loves a miscarriage of justice. Particularly with a beautiful woman at its centre. Know what I hate about Gérard de Sainte-Vierge? Everything. Yes, I'll use it.'

'I don't work for charity, Denois. How much is it worth? Make it a lot, or I'll take the negative to Sainte-Vierge and see what he's willing to pay.'

After protracted haggling, they struck a deal. Patrice Denois left with the negative, and Pigeon Boccard turned his attention to selling the rest of his day's work.

In the flat on rue Molière, where Gérard had been used to throwing off his collar and tie and using his melting gaze on his latest sexual conquest, 'ice' was the texture of the air.

He had driven around in a taxi with Agnès for an hour after leaving Maison Javier, then brought her back here to wait while Constanza's handprint faded from her cheek. As for him, the bridge of his nose was incredibly swollen. For a while, he'd feared Constanza had broken it. Hell hath no fury.

His cousin had laid into him several times already, and was doing so again, using every aristocratic inflection at her command. How dare he expose her to humiliation? What did he have to say for himself, standing by while a jealous hussy struck her?

For the umpteenth time, he apologised. 'Constanza was born in the gutters of Marseilles. She claims all sorts about her background, but her father made his money canning the parts of cattle nobody else would eat, to feed the troops. You, on the other hand – you know I revere you, Agnès. I always have.'

'Don't drip lies into my ear, Gérard.'

'I speak only the truth when I say I want to marry you.' He touched her polka-dot sleeve, an attempt at an intimate caress. 'We have proof, do we not, that we suit each other rather well.'

'On the contrary, we are thoroughly at odds. You want my money and to take control of my little boy's fortune while I intend to manage it myself. Do you know why I slept with you here that once? To see if I could give my heart to a man other than my darling husband. You taught me that I cannot. Marry your guttersnipe and have done. You treated her predecessor disgracefully.'

'Marry Constanza?' He laughed, until it hurt too much. 'These girls are to make you jealous. I thought if you felt you were running out of time, you'd change your— ah!'

His cousin gave him a ringing slap then ordered him to telephone her household and have her car sent round. When she'd gone, Gérard poured himself a stiff drink. That was when Constanza slipped out of the shadows.

'Faithless dog. I wish I had a gun,' she said. 'But guns wake the neighbours and I won't go to prison for you. I am not sentimental as Tatiana is. You *will* marry me, Gérard.'

'It's over,' he said stiffly, touching his cheek. Agnès's slap had re-awakened the pain of Tatiana's attack with the tiepin. 'You crossed a line this afternoon.'

'And you gave false evidence to the police. That is a serious misdemeanour.'

Gérard went very still. Nothing melting now in the teak-brown eyes. 'You're referring to my statement regarding Tatiana? What makes you say it was false?'

'You talk in your sleep. Oh, and I saw a draft of a letter you wrote to an attorney, which you left lying around.'

'I never leave anything lying around! Did you rifle through my attaché case?'

'Perhaps. I know what you did the night your brother died.'

He told her to get out, and when she did not, he put on a record and made a show of ignoring her. Constanza knew then that Tatiana had been right. This man had never intended to marry her. He had used her. She went straight to a police station where she claimed that Gérard de Sainte-Vierge had tried to kill her. Would have succeeded had she not fought him off. A gouged temple, which she inflicted on herself using the ruby ring, supported her story.

Not that the police cared. Just another lover's tiff. Undeterred, Constanza gave a statement to the effect that her former fiancé had killed his own brother and bullied his passenger into a confession which he had known to be false. 'He is a Svengali and makes women his slaves.' She cried very convincingly.

Afterwards, she went back to her flat and started packing. The obsession to be marquise de Sainte-Vierge and a sixteenth *arrondissement* hostess was dead. Even if Gérard escaped conviction, his career would be finished. In Buenos Aires there were fewer noble titles to marry but more millionaires. The ring, taken to a pawn broker, would buy a first-class liner ticket.

In a different part of Paris, Patrice Denois called his editor and pitched a highly combustible story involving Gérard de Sainte-Vierge, a fatal car accident and a pack of lies. Oh, and a sensational photograph from the lens of Pigeon Boccard.

Chapter Seventy-Eight

Sunday, 20 May 1923

Regan gazed out over the Seine as sunrise turned the sparkling wavelets lobster-pink. The Ièna bridge was to his left and the Eiffel Tower soared on the far bank, veiled by mist at its foot and apex. He never could see a scene like this without hoping that somewhere, an enterprising chemist was inventing colour-receptive film.

'Don't for God's sake fall in,' he shouted. Tatiana was at the wharf edge, staring into the water, testing her nerve.

She turned, her linen skirt and sailor smock rippling around her. 'Or you'd have to choose between me and the camera?'

'I've already made the choice.' He took his shot. Returning the camera to its case, he joined her. On a coal barge upwind of them, someone was frying smoked herring. 'You know how if you borrow money and don't pay it back, the interest mounts up?'

Tatiana threw him a look. 'You have debts?'

'Metaphorically. I had a question for you the night your sister Katya got home and didn't get to ask it. That question has remained on account, and meantime, new ones have added themselves and they're suffocating me. I'm sailing back to New York at the end of the month.'

She gazed down where the water massaged the wharf. Their twin reflection split apart in the ripples.

'So,' he cleared his throat, 'in no particular order. Will you take the job as Maison Javier's New York agent? I know it's been offered.'

She nodded. 'If I turn it down, I'll never hear the end of it from Una. She's invited Artie Shone to Paris to meet me.'

'It means you'll spend time in New York.'

'Inevitably. Though I have to spend time at home, too, with my family.'

''Course. Where will you live in New York?'

She slanted a look at him. 'Hell's Kitchen?'

He gave a gruff laugh. 'How about the Dakota building, Central Park West?'

'Sounds lovely. Sounds expensive.'

'I can stretch to it and I want you to live there with me.' He picked up her hand, her right hand which was bare and smooth. She wasn't wearing the yellow sapphire and he felt hope swing away.

'*Live* with? That's a little too racy for me. Even in Paris, unmarried people don't cohabit.'

'Cohabit sounds like sharing the same raincoat. Tatiana, I want to marry you. And if you don't want to, that's fine. But I don't want to leave without asking.'

'Fine, is it, if I say no?'

'No it's not. Roughnecks like me don't win the hands of princesses. I married a girl higher than me up the social tree first time round, and that didn't work. Maybe it can't work. You've held me at a distance since Vera got home and I understand. She comes first. But now...' At times like this, the adult Regan collided with the homeless scavenger he'd once been. 'I need to know if you've been busy or want shot of me.'

'I've been avoiding you.'

'OK.' He stared at his reflection. 'Your mind's on Gérard? Or someone else or—'

'For heaven's sake, Regan.' She faced him. 'Naturally, I think of Gérard. A month's imprisonment for a man like him will be unendurable.'

'Unlike nine weeks for a woman like you, which he endured without any trouble.'

'My name has been cleared, but I've stayed out of sight so that no journalist can ask me how I feel. And yes, my family preoccupies me. But I've been keeping out of your way because of how you've changed since I first met you. I know you have an interest in *Ravissante*.'

'I own it.'

She nodded. 'So I understand. And I know that your late wife left you very, very rich.'

'How do you know?'

'From Una, who got it from Artie Shone who, by the way she's having a dalliance with, but don't say I told you.'

Regan snorted. 'A divorcé with a wholesale fashion empire and a house near Madison Square Garden? "Dalliance" nowhere near covers it. Brace yourself for Una to come back from New York some day soon as 'Mrs Artie Shone', but hey, I'm not interested in any other woman's heart. Only yours.'

'Why didn't you tell me?' The heart in question was beating wildly. 'About Una?'

'About your money. No, let me answer. You wanted me to come to you thinking you were poor, so you could never say to yourself, "She's after my fortune." So now, if I as much as smile at you, you'll always wonder.'

A silence built. He cut into it, asking, 'Do you have any actual objection to being wealthy?'

'Far less than to being poor! That brought out the worst in me. I suppose it brought out the best in you?' She stepped towards him. 'That's the difference between us. I'm learning to be strong but I haven't mastered being good.'

He kissed her, reading invitation in the curve of her lips. When he raised his head, he asked, 'How bad are you?'

'How bad?' She walked away, turned and held out her hand to him. They linked fingers and walked under Pont d'Iéna. Underfoot were old leaves, drying chestnut blossoms swept off the embankment trees during recent winds. Tatiana put her arms around Regan and enticed him closer.

She shivered as her back touched the wall, as his hands moved down to her hips. When she lifted her left hand to his face, he felt a scratch. She'd put the yellow sapphire ring on the second finger of her left hand, another reminder, if he needed it that Tatiana Vytenis was a woman of secrets. An enigma within a riddle beneath a veil.

'May I take that as a yes to my offer of marriage?'

'OK,' she said, echoing his accent and they laughed. The river rushed between the piers, foaming through the shadows and into the sparkling sweep of a new Parisian day.

A Letter from Natalie

Thank you for reading *The Paris Girl*. If you enjoyed it and want to keep up to date with all my latest releases, just sign up at the following link. Your email address will never be shared and you can unsubscribe at any time.

www.bookouture.com/natalie-meg-evans

I hope you enjoyed following the Vytenis sisters to a happy resolution and that this story answers questions thrown up in the previous novel, *The Secret Vow*. Writing this story was an emotional journey for me, taking me into the heart of troubled times with its themes of betrayal and survival. It's a myth that writers make things up (honest!). What we do is pull out the stuff that is already there, which is why we're always pale and exhausted at the end of the process!

That's not to say we don't love what we do. We most certainly do, and knowing we're connecting with readers all over the world is a big part of the reward. So thank you for choosing *The Paris Girl*, for seeing her through to her own happy ending. Meanwhile, I am taking a short break in my beloved France, to recharge the batteries for the next story. Where will it be set? Watch for news on my website.

If you can, please review my book and let your friends know. Reviews and word of mouth are the most powerful way of creating a buzz about a book you've enjoyed, and writers always appreciate the time you take.

Contact me on Twitter or Facebook, or visit my website.

À bientôt. Till next time.

Natalie Meg Evans
Suffolk, 2019

 @natmegevans

 NatalieMegEvans

 www.nataliemegevans.uk

Acknowledgements

A word of thanks to the team at Bookouture, particularly my editor Kathryn Taussig, Caolinn Douglas and Celine Kelly, for their editing skill and for masterminding the fabulous jacket image. And to Laura Longrigg, my agent and adviser through all six of my novels.

Printed in Great
Britain
by Amazon